Mist across the Pond

Margaret Ann Foster came to writing late in her career, when at the age of 59 she decided to fulfil two of her greatest ambitions. Firstly, she decided to write the novel she had always promised herself she would, and secondly she enrolled at University to read for a BSc in Psychological Studies.

In 2010 she had not only completed her first year at university, but had written and published 'From Pit Boots to Green Wellies'. A novel about growing up in the fifties and sixties, and her life as a pub landlady in the 1980's

In 2011 Margaret was awarded a First Class Honours Degree. Based on her experiences of caring for her father her final year dissertation paved the way for 'Night Time Shadows: Patrick's Story'. A punchy, hard hitting, and very pertinent work that reveals how unprepared the western world is for coping with an ever growing elderly population.

Both books are available on Amazon in Paperback and on Kindle

Mist across the Pond

Margaret Ann Foster

Mist across the Pond

2nd Edition

ISBN-13:9798645268527

I would like to dedicate this book to my friend Claira Newton,

who has been so supportive throughout.

Even to the point of bullying me to finish it.

If not for her I would have given up a long time ago.

Thank you, Claira.

Table of Contents

Chapter 1

Dublin 1941

Bridgett Nugent looked at her watch and made a 'tsk' sound. 'Jaysus, I'll be late fer me own funeral, sure to God I will.' Leaning forward, she tapped the cab driver on the shoulder. 'Can't you drive any faster?'

The taxi driver didn't reply. He was too busy staring out of the window, curious to see why a crowd of people were gathered around the pavement. 'Must have been an accident or something' he said, without the slightest hint of concern in his voice. 'There's a girl at the side of the road.'

'Where . . . stop the car' Bridgett yelled 'she may need help.'

'Well if there's blood, she won't be coming in my car, missus. I had to clean up some vomit only last. . .'

Bridgett was already opening the car door. Thrusting the money into his hand, she climbed out of the car. 'oh, shut up and drive on. Here . . . keep the change.' She pushed her way forcefully through the crowd, who were stood looking, but seemingly doing nothing to help the young girl. A girl who didn't look more than thirteen or fourteen years old was lying on the ground. The wind was bitterly cold and icy rain fell with the occasional fluttering of snow. Bridgett quickly took off her coat to cover the girl, who was wearing a torn cotton dress. Kneeling beside her, oblivious as to how wet and dirty the ground was, Bridgett stroked the young girl's tangled hair from her bloodied face. 'Dear God child, what happened to you? Here darling, wrap this coat around yourself, it'll keep you warm and dry. Jaysus child, you must be frozen.'

'Thank you, I . . .'

'You'll be all right soon love. There's quite a lot of blood coming from your head, but it isn't as bad as it must feel; it doesn't look like a deep cut to me. I don't know about the other injuries, mind, so it's best you lie still for now. Someone has sent for an ambulance and it's on its way from the Mater hospital.'

Marianne tried to force a smile but winced in pain. She was shivering with cold to a point where her lips had felt frozen and was grateful for the warmth and compassion this beautiful stranger was showing towards her. A woman who spoke kind comforting words, whilst wiping Marianne's tear stained face with a clean handkerchief. She tried to sit up but fell back again as the sound of people's voices started to fade away. She felt herself floating above her body . . . looking down on herself. There was noise . . . a siren . . . followed by darkness. Someone was shouting. 'What's your name Miss? You need to stay awake. Open your eyes.' Her eyes flickered open again and she was lifted onto a stretcher. The stranger wrapped the coat tightly around Marianne, reaching into the pocket and whispering in her ear. 'You'll be all right love. Perhaps this is the time to move away and start a new life.'

Bridgett watched with sympathy when the poor girl, obviously in a great deal of pain, was being checked over in the ambulance. The weather was freezing cold without the warmth of her cashmere coat, but she still had a little comfort from the suit she was wearing. Nevertheless, the wind cut right through to her bones, but the child's need was greater than her own. The girl was lucky to be alive, at one-point Bridgett thought she was about to pass over. It was just as well the ambulance arrived. The coat was the girls to keep now, although Bridgett doubted she would know the coat was made of cashmere. Never mind, she smiled inwardly. Johnny, one of her clients would buy her a new coat, especially when she told him what she had done today. Then she made her way quickly to the taxi rank.

Chapter 2

Sitting in the warm taxi, Bridgett lit a cigarette, inhaled deeply and settled back. She had missed the appointment with the estate agent now, but if the house she was after was taken by someone else, then there were plenty more. She couldn't seem to stop thinking about the girl. Bridgett knew the injuries were from a thrashing and not an accident caused by falling down the stairs as the girl had said to the ambulance man. She remembered more than she'd like to about her life as a child. Bridgett still bore the scars from her father, only to marry the same kind of man.

Terry was the boy she fell in love with, and the man who broke her heart. She'd been married just over five years when Terry started to hit her, not for anything, but because he could. During another sleepless night after feeling the weight of his fist, Bridgett realised it was time to think seriously about leaving him. Looking in the mirror she knew it should be sooner rather than later. She picked up her hairbrush and felt like smashing the glass and her reflection. Her bright red curls fell over her face, tears pushing their way through. Terry used to love her hair. He was always saying how beautiful her hair was while running his hand through tenderly. Not anymore. Her hair was tangled where he'd pulled her to the floor with it. Her face was now gaunt. The high cheek bones were still there, but her blue eyes looked lifeless and sad. She gently touched an old bruise which was still sore from the week before, staring at Terry through the mirror's reflection. He was in a deep sleep snoring, which was something else she hated about him now. When they first slept together, she liked to hear his gentle breathing. How could he sleep so soundly after hurting her? Of course, he would be sorry the next day, and cry as usual, saying how much he loved her; how he didn't mean to hit her, blah, blah, blah.

He was the boy she fell in love with at school when she was just thirteen years old. The boy all the girls wanted, the one with the golden hair and brown penetrating eyes, but Terry only had eyes for her. This was the boy she'd hoped to marry one day.

Bridgett was fourteen when she realised, she could be pregnant. She had missed one period, and her following period was overdue by five days when she plucked up the courage to tell her mother. Everything happened so fast. The following day the priest arrived at the house with Terry by his side.

'I'll start the arrangements fer the wedding as soon as possible. Now, get yerselves to confession and pray fer your sins. I'll see you in church.'

'But I'm only fourteen Father.' Bridgett said, wondering if her mother had lied about her age so she could get married.

'You are of legal age with your mother's consent, which I have.'

'I see.' Bridgett replied sullenly. The thought of marriage suddenly frightened her. They were too young. Yes, she did want to marry Terry one day, but not like this.

'I'll be off now. You two have a lot to do, so I suggest you start looking for somewhere to live.'

Shocked, both Bridgett and Terry stared after him in silence. And then the sniffling from her mother grew louder. 'Oh, dear God, the shame, the shame, it's just as well yer da is dead. Jaysus, he'll be turning in his grave now, sure to God he will.'

Terry held Bridgett's hand and whispered. 'This isn't what I had planned, but I love you Bridgett and I'll stand by you and do the right thing.

A week after they married, Bridgett had a period.

*

After staying with her mother for almost four years, they found a place of their own. Terry had been offered a job on a farm just outside of

Dublin, and they welcomed with open arms the little cottage that came with it. Bridgett also found a job working in the local shop, which wasn't too far to travel from their new home. Life couldn't get any better; she was happy and looking forward to eventually getting pregnant, when her life would be complete. However, the periods kept coming, but then, she was still quite young. There wasn't any real rush just yet, and she did have Terry all to herself.

Unfortunately, two years later Terry was asked to leave his job and move out of the cottage. Bridgett was in shock and couldn't get anything out of Terry as to why he was fired. He simply flew into a rage and punched her in the face. This was the first time he had ever hit her. The following morning, she marched across to see Harry, the farmer, and his wife Jane.

'I think you owe me an explanation.'

'I beg your pardon.' Harry yelled back.

'Why are you're finishing Terry. He's a good worker; he works all hours of the day and often works during the night gathering lost sheep. You have already said you could do with more farm hands, so why? I need an explanation.'

'I see, he didn't tell you then.'

'Tell me what?'

'He's been having sex with my daughter, that's what. She's fourteen years old and pregnant.'

Bridgett stood and said nothing . . . she couldn't say anything. 'I don't . . .'

'I thought the world of that lad. I gave him a start in life. He could have gone on to own his own farm one day.' said Harry, staring into Bridgett's eyes, 'she's only a child herself fer Christ sake. Her life is ruined now. He's bloody lucky I didn't shoot him. I was out shooting rabbits when I found out and I was still holding the gun. My wife is heartbroken; she had hopes of Claire going to University.'

Bridgett muttered the word 'sorry' and walked away in tears, just as his wife came out of the house ranting and swearing. 'Get away from here. You must be off your head living with an adulterer . . . a child molester.'

Packing was done in silence at first. Bridgett was wrapping an ornament of a girl holding her mother's hand. She stared down, gently stroking the little girl's head. Standing up, she suddenly threw the ornament across the room where it broke in two. 'You bastard, how could you do such a thing to me Terry? I thought we were happy together.'

'I'm sorry. It was her; she was always coming on to me. All the time Bridgett, I swear to God I tried to stop her.'

'Yeah, I'm sure you did. But it takes a decent man to walk away, should what you say to be true. Now wouldn't it, you bastard. I loved my life, this home . . . I loved *you* Terry.'

'I promise it won't ever happen again. I promise. Please give me another chance.'

*

Bridgett had no choice but to stay with Terry. Where would she go? For she herself would be the centre of her neighbours' gossip had she gone home to her mother. Besides, it was terrible during the four years she lived there. They argued just about every day. She and Terry had no privacy at all with the rest of her siblings hanging around them all the while.

Using all the savings Bridgett had put to one side for when she stopped work to have a baby, they soon found a room in a tenement house. Terry became moody and bad tempered soon after leaving the farm, but he managed to find a job at the docks, working as a casual labourer, making it clear he wasn't going to stay there.

Bridgett had to leave him. She had been very lucky not to be pregnant up to now and was relieved each month her period came. She knew once she was pregnant there would be no escape. *And to think how she so wanted a baby with Terry.*

Sleep wouldn't come to her one night. She lay back staring at the ceiling listening to his snoring as usual, and the plan to get away from him began to emerge in her mind. From then on, Bridgett started to hide the little money she had saved from pawning things Terry wouldn't miss until she had gone. Like his best suit, which was only used for special occasions; of course, if there was a funeral or such, she would have to get it back or run for her life before he found out.

The shop where she worked was too far to travel from the tenements, and the only job she could get was on the fish market for five mornings a week. She ran errands on every opportunity that presented itself, helping anyone out, just to earn a little extra. The money she did manage to save was sewn into the corner of the mattress and undone again each time she put something away. She carefully placed the money in an old glove which was also stitched up to stop the mice from shredding the notes to make a nest.

One cold winter's day in January, Bridgett was asked to go into the City to pick a parcel up from the General Post Office for Mrs McBride, an elderly lady in the next street. The parcel was from her daughter who had moved to Cork, and the old lady had given Bridgett the bus fare and money for herself to collect the parcel. It was late when she had walked into the City; already growing dark by 3:30pm.

Rushing along the pavement beside the River Liffey, Bridgett began to feel afraid, not of the dark, but of the consequence's she would have to face if Terry found her savings. Sewing money in mattresses was common; there were very few places to hide anything in such a small space. The plans to leave Terry didn't include where she would go with the money, she had saved either. She would have just the one chance of getting as far away from him as possible.

Bridgett was so deep in thought she bumped into a woman, knocking her to the ground. 'Oh Jaysus, I'm so sorry, I was miles away. Are you all right?' Bridgett asked, helping the woman to her feet.

'Yes, I'm fine, I was miles away me self, so I was,' she laughed.

The woman was very smartly dressed in a black wool coat, ankle boots with fur trim and a matching woollen hat. Her hair was tied in a tidy knot at the lower part of her head below the rim of her hat. Bridgett's eyes were drawn to her fur gloves. Her own hands had been freezing since she set off from home, as her money was hidden in her only pair of gloves, and she could only imagine the difference a pair of warm gloves would make right now. Although the stranger wasn't a pretty woman, there was something attractive and sophisticated about her which made her look glamorous somehow. She could have been twenty-five to thirty years old or even older. Bridgett had never been good when it came to guessing ages.

They stood talking for quite a while about how suddenly the fog had come down over the city. 'I'm on an errand for an old neighbour of mine. I'm only going to the Post Office. Jaysus, I can't wait to get home for a cup of tea.' Bridgett moaned. Her feet ached from all the walking into the city to save the bus fare Mrs McBride had given her. She wasn't looking forward to the long walk home, especially as it was dark now with the fog closing in all around them. Perhaps she should get the bus instead. She still had the extra money Mrs McBride had given her for the errand.

'Come with me,' said the stranger 'we'll have a hot pot of tea to warm us both up. Sure, I was going there me self. It would be nice to have company.'

'That'll be grand.' Bridgett replied, though reluctant to spend money on a pot of tea.

Once inside the warm, cosy café, the woman insisted she would pay for the tea and sandwiches. She introduced herself as Bernadette and lost no time at all in asking Bridgett where the bruise on her eye came from. Bridgett couldn't believe how words just poured from her mouth. Here she was, telling a stranger just about all that had ever happened in her life. Bernadette listened sympathetically and told her she too had run away from home at the age of fifteen to try and find a better life.

'Did you get yourself a good job?' asked Bridgett, knowing how hard work was to find. 'You must have, from the looks of your clothes . . . sorry I didn't mean to . . . pry.'

'Yes, I got me self a good job all right.' Bernadette took a sip of her tea and said in a very clear and calm voice, 'I'm a prostitute.'

That was thirty years ago. Bridgett never did go home again, and now she ran her own brothel in the red-light district on the North side of the City. She had taken great care to look after her girls, treating them all with respect. Making sure they were clean and smartly dressed. Very few people looked down on prostitutes in Dublin; indeed, they were referred to as the "Unfortunate girls". Some had little choice. Young teenage girls went into prostitution for all kinds of reasons; others, purely to stay out of institutions. Times were very hard. No one could blame a girl for taking the route of selling her body . . . apart from the Church, that is.

Bridgett had a good cliental from all walks of life, but her clients now were mostly professionals such as Politicians, Lawyers, and Doctors. She had extremely rich clients, including Johnny. Bridgett no longer worked as a prostitute, but as a businesswoman. 'Madams', they were called. She lived a very comfortable life with little effort.

Bridgett hoped the poor young girl in the ambulance would find her way in life before it was too late.

Chapter 3

Once Marianne was at the hospital, the questions started. 'Marianne you have internal bleeding, I believe you have ruptured your Spleen. We'll need to operate first thing in the morning. You may have suffered internal damage, I won't know while I look, but we'll get you comfortable first. You have a nasty gash to your head too, which needs sutures, plus other cuts and bruises. Who did this to you? Were you attacked?'

'I fell down the stairs when I tripped over the hem of my skirt', she told the doctor, avoiding eye contact.

Falling down the stairs wasn't a complete lie. True enough, she *had* fallen down the stairs. Her father pushed her through the door, and she had lost her balance. She tripped when a tear in her dress caught on her shoe, causing her to fall down a flight of the stone steps, cutting her head and her arm. Her internal injuries came from her father's boot.

'Okay. We'll leave it at that for now. The nurse will clean you up and I'll be back to see you in the morning. We just need some information about you. Have you ever had surgery before?'

'No. I was never in hospital in me life. Will it hurt?'

'You won't feel a thing. You may be a little sore for a while after, but we'll sort that out for you.'

'Thank you, Doctor.'

Marianne lay back against the pillow. She had never slept on a real pillow before. Her family all slept together in the one room. Marianne and her siblings shared a straw mattress, which was pushed under the bed during the day. Their bedclothes were tatty old coarse blankets and overcoats. The fresh cotton sheets she was laying in now smelt like the stranger's handkerchief . . . clean. She loved the soft touch of the fabric against her skin; it was how she imagined silk to feel like.

The ward was busy, but quiet. Most of the patients were sleeping or reading, but then it was late in the evening. There were three rows of beds in the ward. A row down each side and one in the middle, all very neatly made. A nurse sat behind a desk at the top of the ward where a lamp lit up the papers she was looking at. The nurse wore a different uniform and seemed to oversee all the other nurses, who were busy with patients. At the top of the ward were also two beds with curtains around yet opened enough for the nurse to see them from her desk. Marianne remembered her mother being behind a curtain at the top of the ward, and her brother, Patrick, telling her how they put really ill patients nearest to the door to wheel them out when they die, without having to take the dead past the other patients.

Marianne vomited on the floor. A nurse came rushing towards her with a kidney shaped bowl and passed it to Marianne, who was crying by now.

'Now, don't you be worrying about being sick. It's probably the shock and the freezing weather out there. Jesus, you felt like death warmed up when you came in. Thank goodness, someone wrapped you in a coat; otherwise you could have died of hyperthermia. Really Marianne, it isn't wise to go without a coat in this weather. What were you thinking?'

'I had no choice. I was running away.'

'Who were you running from? You can tell me, you know. You mumbled something about your father when we brought you in. Was it him who did this to you? You may feel better if you let it all out and have a good cry.'

Marianne looked at the pretty nurse, who was dressed in a white apron with frills on the shoulder. She wore a blue dress beneath with long sleeves and frilly cuffs at the end of the sleeves. Her hair was neatly tied back, and she wore a huge hat in white, which also had frills on it. A badge on her uniform read, Nurse Kelly.

'I . . . I don't know where to start and I don't want to make things worse for me ma. She won't have the Gardaí involved; you know. Please don't tell anyone.'

'I won't tell a soul. I promise.' Nurse Kelly had a pang of guilt knowing she had told a lie. If the girl had been physically abused by her father then she would have to report it, especially if other young children were still at home.

Marianne told the nurse how her father had come home in a bad mood and started shouting at her mother. 'He was strangling her Nurse. Mammy's feet were off the floor, even with the baby inside of her.'

'Oh, dear Lord.'

'She seemed all right when I left, nurse. She's only small and I was yelling at me da to stop, but he wouldn't. I grabbed the shovel, the one for raking the ashes, and I . . . hit him over the head. He was so angry. He stopped and glared at me. I was frightened to death, so I ran away and tripped. My little brother was staring in shock. I wanted to hold him and tell him I was all right. I really did fall down the stairs nurse, honest.'

'This is so sad Marianne. You're a brave girl to protect your mammy. Does he harm you in any way, or the rest of the children?'

Marianne couldn't tell the truth. The authorities would be brought in, and Marianne knew they would all be split up into different homes. 'No nurse, never; ma and da fall out a lot of the time, but he doesn't always hit her. I just hope she's all right.'

'Your mother looked all right to me Marianne; I couldn't see any marks on her face or anything. She came to the hospital earlier, but we have strict visiting rules in the late evening. We must think of the other patients. I told her you were doing fine, but I couldn't tell her anything else until after the doctor's visit. She'll be back here tomorrow. Try to sleep now.'

Nurse Kelly had gone back to her chores, and Marianne lay back thinking about her father. The pain in her left side was getting worse, but she had taken some pills so hopefully they would help. She hated the fact that she lied about her father. It was him who had put her here in the hospital . . . it was him who had damaged her insides. Her father was a bully. She had witnessed him beat their mother ever since she could remember, almost killing her on one occasion. Two years earlier, her father had come home drunk and began yelling at her brother, Patrick, for sitting too close to the fire, accusing him of blocking all the heat. Patrick, in his defence, explained he was merely stoking the fire to boil some water. An argument broke out and her mother tried to stop them. Her father pushed her with such force, she was thrown to the other side of the room, causing a massive bleed and killing the unborn child she was carrying.

Of course, her mother wouldn't report him; she never would. The neighbours were always there to dress wounds, give sympathy and listen to the horrific stories, but that was all they could do. No one dare interfere in a marriage. Marianne would never forget the time she had sat with Patrick and Lillian at their mother's bedside; the hospital bed tipped from the bottom, raising her mother's feet and lowering her head, while blood dripped slowly into her mother's arm like the ticking of a clock. It wasn't while the priest arrived, they realised their mother may be dying. After introducing himself, the priest spoke softly to her father to say how sorry he was to hear his wife had taken a bad fall and lost the baby. Her father said nothing apart from a whispered 'thank you Father.' but cried when Father Jackson prepared for the Last Rites, putting on his violet coloured stole. Her mother was barely conscious when the priest anointed her. He blessed her and began the service. They huddled together, including their father who was inconsolable by now, and prayed.

Miraculously, her mother didn't die that night, but wasn't out of danger for a full week. She began to show signs of a full recovery in the second week. The doctor was amazed and remarked about the power of love and prayer.

'Tis the love of God, and the love of her family, that saved Molly's life. Let's all kneel and pray now.'

Her father had wept openly for days, and they all hoped there might be a change in him when their mother was home again. For a while, Marianne believed they were right about their father changing. He did seem a better man. He was very attentive towards his wife and liked to care for her himself. The special treatment was to change once more when her mother found out she was having another baby. Her father didn't like his wife when she was pregnant. She had given birth to five children, besides suffering a miscarriage and of course, the baby who died through her father's temper.

*

Patrick was no longer at home; he had run away a few months earlier. He always did his best to protect his mother. Unfortunately, he was no match for his father, who was tall and heavily built, and Patrick often suffered a beating himself. "But not without a good fight". Patrick used to say to Marianne as she bathed his battered face yet again once her father was out of the way.

'I swear to God I will kill the bastard if I stay here. I've thought many times in my head of ways to kill him. Only last week I was emptying the hot ashes into the bucket and realised how easy it would be to pour them over him while he was sleeping. Right between his legs; that would stop him getting Ma pregnant. But then, what if he survived? I would end up being arrested and sent to Mountjoy prison for nothing, and the beatings would still go on. Jaysus, one day I will kill him if I stay here, I know that. I have to get away Marianne.'

'Patrick you can't leave us,' Marianne cried, 'perhaps if Ma saw a doctor to stop her having more babies. . .'

'A doctor won't do that Marianne' Patrick butted in 'the Church won't allow it. Why do you think women have twelve babies or more? Fer Christ sake Mrs Byrnes had twenty-three kids.'

'But we need you here. What will we do without you?'

'You have our sister, Lillian . . . but I have to go. I can't stand by and do nothing while Da beats the hell out of me ma. I'll write, I promise.'

Patrick's anger died down. Sweeping his dark wavy hair away from his eyes, he spoke more softly, 'I'll be fine Marianne, I have enough money for what I need, and I'll soon get a job somewhere. I've been doing odd jobs for people and working for the auld fellow on the market four days a week. I have managed to save a bit of money, though Da took the rest from me. It's just as well he didn't know about the extra job up at Dolphins barn, pulling cabbages for half a crown, or I would have been left with nothing.

14

I'm just a slave to him Marianne. Here to work and pay for his ale.' Patrick sighed, 'I don't care what sort of job it is, but I'll get one. I can't stay here any longer. I'm leaving, and you should do the same.'

He put his arm around Marianne's shoulder, 'why don't you get a job in the City when you leave school. Perhaps you could go to one of those big houses where they hire young girls. Domestic girls, they call them, and the gentry are always on the lookout for replacements when the older ones leave to start a family of their own. You might be able to ask for a job for Lillian when she leaves school once you've settled in. They say it's hard work, but I know a few of the girls who work in those houses.' Patrick smiled cheekily, 'They have a night off once a week. Perhaps you'll find yourself a good man to marry one day.'

'But what about Mammy, I can't leave her. She needs our help Patrick'

'Listen, you will have to leave one day. You can't stay here and become an old maid. It's no good Marianne; Ma won't hear a word against Da, no matter what he does to her. You can't help her; she doesn't want to be helped. I'll ask around about a job for you when I get out of here and find somewhere to stay, I know some good people.'

Patrick left home a few weeks later without telling anyone. The house wasn't the same without him. Marianne and Lillian fought over the least little thing, probably through the frustration of trying to hide their loss of their brother. Her mother cried all the time because he didn't say goodbye. Her father was angry, calling Patrick all the names under the sun for cheating him out of tipping up his money from work.

Marianne was almost fourteen now and had been planning to run away ever since her conversation with Patrick just before he left home. He was right; her mother wouldn't hear any bad words said against her husband, "He puts the bread and butter on the table. We'd be in a poor state now Marianne without him, wouldn't we? If not fer yer da, you'd have all been taken into care years ago, so mind your tongue."

There was no point in staying. Her mother would have to sort herself out. Marianne fell asleep trying to imagine her future in one of those big houses. Perhaps she would meet a man, like Patrick had said, and fall in love. Yes, she liked the idea of that.

Morning arrived and she was still in a great deal of pain. The nurses had prepared her for surgery earlier and she was very nervous now. She was about to shout for a nurse, when she saw her heavily pregnant mother walk into the ward. 'Mammy are you all right. Did he hurt you again?'

'No Marianne, he hasn't hurt me again and please lower your voice. How are you feeling?'

'I have a lot of pain.'

'I'm so sorry; you should leave things alone Marianne and not get involved. Are you frightened of the operation?'

'Yes, but the doctor said I won't feel anything.'

'You didn't say anything about your father hitting you, did you Marianne? He didn't mean to hurt you.'

'No' Marianne lied, 'but I think it's time you said something though. He's going to kill you one day. You have to leave him.'

'And where would I go. I still have three children at home besides you and I'm eight months pregnant. Father O'Leary would find me wherever I went and drag me back. He would use threats of taking the children, not to mention the baby when it's born, so we'll have no more of that talk now Marianne.' Her mother wiped a tear away with the back of her hand. 'I can't stay long. The nurse let me in to see you to put my mind at rest, but it isn't visiting time, and you're the first in theatre. The doctor reassured me you were going to be all right. We were all so worried about you last night, but they wouldn't let us in to see you. Someone came to the house to tell me she saw you being lifted into an ambulance, or we wouldn't have known you were here.'

'Who's us. I bet Da didn't come to see me.'

'He did, and Lillian too. He didn't mean any harm Marianne, he only . . .'

'You always stick up for him. I'm sick of it. I'm having fecking surgery because of that bastard.'

'Marianne, *please.*'

'Well I am. I'm leaving as soon as I'm fourteen. I'm going to get a job in one of those big houses and I won't be coming back home . . . Never. You might have to live with him, but I don't. I hate him.'

'Marianne . . .'

'I'm sorry Mrs McNamara' the nurse said, pulling the curtain back, 'but we're ready for going down to theatre now, you will have to leave and come back during visiting hours.'

Marianne wept as she saw the look of pain in her mother's eyes, and regretted getting angry with her, it wasn't her fault really. 'Come see me Mammy.'

'I will. I promise.'

*

Three weeks after being admitted, Doctor Morrison was happy with the way Marianne had responded to the operation. The wound was healing well; though he knew it was only the wound healing and unfortunately, not her mind. He had seen many cases of drunken abuse in families, especially in overcrowded houses such as in the Liberties where Marianne lived. In some cases, there could be eight families or more sharing one tenement house, each with as many as twelve children or more in some cases.

Doctor Morrison had been a doctor for fourteen years, and nothing surprised him. Not anymore. Being close to the River Liffey, the Liberties were rife with rats drawn to the smell of yeast from the Breweries, and the nearby warehouses. Infections were rife from bed bugs that lived in the mattresses and that fed off human blood, often the cause of anaemia and asthma in young children. Fleas were a big problem too. The constant scratching opened sores that wouldn't easily heal. Yet, some of the women in the Liberties area were proud people and strived to keep their houses clean. Unfortunately, nothing could keep the vermin away in dwellings that were in such a poor state.

Marianne McNamara had made a grand recovery. He felt quite pleased with himself for the surgery he had performed, which was very complicated to say the least. Up to now, there had been no sign of post-surgery infections, and her temperature was just fine. His joy soon turned to sadness. He knew she'd suffered a direct blow to the stomach. She was a beautiful girl with dark curly hair and blue eyes that sparkled when she smiled. In a few years' time she would probably be married. He hoped she would marry a good kind Irish man, for there were a lot of good men around. The trouble was with some young girls, they were so eager to marry and rush into what they believed would be a fairy-tale wedding. When, the marriage often started off on the wrong path. Most couples were forced to stay with their already overcrowded families. He hoped never to see Marianne in hospital again. Her injuries were so serious, he had wondered whether she would make it or not. He just hoped there would be no lasting damage, but it was too early to tell. He walked towards her bed and her smiling face.

'Good morning Marianne. Everything seems to be going to plan. The operation was a success; we managed to repair the rupture, and it seems to be healing very well, which is good news. At first we were concerned we might have to remove your spleen altogether.' He smiled down at Marianne's young face. 'However, you suffered a haemorrhage and there were serious complications, but you're all right now. In the meantime, it's important you do not lift, or do anything strenuous until your injuries have time to heal, so please be careful with the stairs in future.'

A tear fell from her cheek and the Doctor gently held her hand. Marianne felt touched by his kindness. She was also aware he knew it wasn't the fall downstairs which had ruptured her spleen.

'What is the spleen for, if you can live without it?' asked Marianne.

'The spleen is on the left-hand side under the rib cage near to your stomach and is about the size of my fist.' The doctor clenched his fist in a tight ball, 'it contains white blood cells that help fight infections by destroying bacteria. However, the spleen can rupture when someone receives a blunt blow, as in your case. A rupture is when a capsule like covering of the spleen opens, causing blood into your abdomen . . . internal bleeding.

'I see . . . well, I think I see.' She laughed. 'Thank you doctor for all your help; everyone has been so good to me . . .' she started to cry. Doctor Morrison felt a knot tighten in his stomach. He longed to put his arms around her shoulders and comfort her, but a doctor wasn't allowed to show emotion, or hold a patient. Such behaviour could land him in big trouble. He was concerned for Marianne; she looked young and vulnerable. He could do no more than take her hand and reassure her she would be all right, but he somehow knew she wouldn't.

He composed himself and straightened his shoulders back. 'I would like to keep you here with us for a few more days; just to build you up a little before you go home.'

'That's all right doctor. I don't mind. I'm more than happy to stay a few more days.' She smiled.

In truth, she would be sorry to leave the warmth and friendliness of the ward. Fear swept through her body, thinking of her father. Her mother and Lillian had been to visit her every day since being admitted, but her father had refused to come. Her mother told her he had asked all the time how she was getting on but felt he couldn't face her just now. Marianne didn't believe her mother. She was lying and sticking up for him again. He wouldn't be happy with her being in hospital and having a fuss made of her when she should be out working or forgive her for hitting him with a shovel.

The stay in hospital had seemed like heaven to Marianne, the staff had shown so much care and compassion. A few of the nurses had brought books for her to read, and one of her favourite nurses, Nurse Kelly, had brought some winter clothes, including a pair of boots and shoes she said had been passed down in her family. Marianne would also miss her doctor, who she felt she was falling in love with. When he looked into her eyes, she had butterflies in her stomach. She knew it was just infatuation . . . but she could dream. She supposed there were many more girls who had fallen for him over the years.

*

The morning finally arrived when Marianne was to go home. Try as hard as she could to stop them, tears rolled down her face. A nurse comforted her and placed the clothes she had been admitted with on the bed, all neatly washed and ironed. She asked the nurse the time, dabbing her eyes on a towel. Her mother would be here soon.

When the nurse left her to get dressed, Marianne stood at the side of the bed and looked at the pile of clothes. Suddenly she gasped. 'The coat' she said softly to herself. 'The coat the kind lady had wrapped over me.' Sitting on the bed she stroked the black wool coat, holding a sleeve to her face. When the nurse came back, Marianne asked if she would look to see if anyone had come in to claim it.

'I would like to thank her for covering me with it. It's such a beautiful coat. She must be thinking me bad for not returning it.'

'I'll go and make some inquiries, but it seems strange she hasn't been back for the coat. Sure, she knew where they would be taking you.'

Ten minutes later, the nurse came back into the ward and told her there hadn't been any enquiries regarding a coat. 'You would be better off taking the coat home, it may get lost here. If anyone comes looking for it, I'll give them your address, but after three weeks I very much doubt it', she winked at Marianne, 'Wear it to go home in, it's a lovely warm coat, tis very cold out there.'

'Oh, thank you.' Marianne said holding the coat tight to her body, 'A coat such as this, which she placed over me knowing I was covered in dirt. The coat is made from wool, nurse an must have been very expensive.'

'The coat is made of Cashmere, Marianne and is certainly a very expensive coat. We cleaned the mud off. Sure, it will be very warm for you.'

Marianne had never heard of Cashmere, but she knew it was the nicest coat she had ever seen. She dressed and was ready to go, feeling good in her new clothes. The first dress she'd tried on fitted perfectly and so did the shoes, which surprised Marianne. Second-hand shoes rarely fit; she often wore shoes so small her heels hung over the back of them. She held one of the shoes to get a good look, turning it over.

'The shoes are like new.' Marianne said quite loudly.

All at once, it hit her, the shoes *were* new and so were the clothes. Marianne held them to her chest. She could hardly breathe. The Sister of the ward came over and asked if she was feeling all right. Marianne asked if Nurse Kelly was on duty today.

'She's off work for a while. She's visiting her sister in Liverpool with a view to living there. They're crying out for doctors and nurses in the hospitals with the war and all.' The Sister explained.

Marianne told her about the clothes.

'Well now, all I know is, Nurse Kelly brought the clothes and said they would fit. We were all a bit shocked to be honest; we don't normally do things such as handing out clothes. There are far too many children and young girls, as yer self, to treat them all the same, but there you go. I didn't even know Nurse Kelly had a child, unless the clothes were from a niece of hers. She wasn't old enough to have a daughter as old as you; 'tis very strange. The clothes you were admitted in were very badly stained, so we took the liberty of washing them. We couldn't do anything with one of your shoes which had split from the fall.'

Marianne looked at her own tatty clothes and the only shoes she owned; the split was nothing to do with the fall. She also knew the Sister had already guessed they weren't. Anyone could tell they were worn down at the back through being a size too small. Plus, there was a piece of cardboard cut to fit inside the shoe to cover a hole. Marianne had never had new clothes in all her life. All the clothes Marianne had ever owned were bought from the Iveagh market and were second hand.

She hugged herself tightly and thought of the kindness of the nurses, all of them, and the doctors. She was going to miss them so much.

Her mother arrived and Marianne put the cashmere coat on. It was much too big, but it didn't matter to her, she would eventually grow into it one day. She eagerly told her mother about the clothes and the coat.

'Tis very kind of the nurse' her mother said. 'As for the coat, you need to take care of it; the woman may come back for it. She could have been ill or something.' Molly was shocked to see her daughter's face turn white. 'Marianne, what is it? Are you feeling all right, should I get the Doctor?'

Marianne had put her hands into the pockets of the coat to show her mother how deep they were. She stood looking at her mother in shock, holding a handful of screwed up money.

'Mammy, there's a lot of notes and some silver, what shall I do?'

Once outside the hospital, they found a nearby bench and neither spoke for a while, both deep in thought.

'Fifty-pound Mammy, there's fifty pound in notes and then there's the silver.'

'Marianne, the owner of the coat couldn't have been short of money otherwise she would have come to claim it, whether she was ill or not. She knew they were taking you to the Mater hospital. She must have realised at some point where her coat was. Fifty pound is a lot of money. I have never seen as much money, tis very frightening if you were to ask me.'

'Ma, what am I to do with it, if Da finds out he'll take it from me and spend it on stout, I can't even give it to you. He's not stupid; he would accuse you of all kinds of things. This is a lot of money Ma. I'm not looking forward to him seeing me dressed in these new clothes either. He'll say I stole the clothes from one of the patients, and then he'll pawn them . . . and the coat.'

Chapter 4

The overcast clouds threatened rain; it was a bitterly cold evening. People stood alongside of Molly and Marianne, shivering, rubbing their hands together waiting for the tram. In the distance you could hear the faint sounds of Christmas Carols. Brightly coloured strands of tinsel glistened in shop windows, and the streets sparkled with star like shapes from the frost on the ground. Across the street, a sudden blast of wind caught a woman's hat, sending it flying from her head into the air. The woman chased the hat, running from side to side, until her and her hat was out of view. At another time Molly and Marianne would have found this funny, but not this evening. They had one thing on their mind and everything else was oblivious to them.

Molly wondered if a tram arrived later in freezing cold weather, or if time went slower than it did in the summer. Whichever way, she had spent many times trying to keep warm while waiting for a tram. Her heart felt heavy and it was hard to hold back the tears. At least with the wind and the rain no one would notice.

The tram eventually appeared around the bend making its way towards them, and Marianne hugged her mother so tight she could hardly breathe.

'I love you Mammy' Marianne cried out as she climbed on board, tears falling unashamedly down her face. 'I'll write, and don't forget to tell Da I was gone before you arrived at the hospital.'

'I will. Goodbye Marianne.'

Molly decided to walk home, even though the rain felt like bullets hitting her head. The hailstones now were very icy, but what the hell; she couldn't get much wetter than she already was. She hoped to God her daughter would find happiness. Marianne looked very smart and respectable in her new clothes and had enough money until she got herself a job. Molly believed she would be all right. She stifled a sob. How could she have let a child, not yet fourteen, go out into the world on her own. Molly prayed with all her heart God would forgive her.

Her tears refused to stay inside any longer. Molly sobbed, her face wet with the rain, mingled with the bitterness of tears. She knew it would be a long while before she saw her daughter again, if ever. She had to go home now and face the man who forced her two children to leave home. He was going to be angry. Marianne was three weeks off being fourteen. To Joseph, it would be two workers he had lost.

The wind was blowing, and her steps became laboured. With her head down she walked on, pulling her red woollen coat, which had seen better days, tight around her body. Nearing home, she watched courting couples walking everywhere, holding onto each other lovingly. Her thoughts turned to Joseph and when they first started going out together. With his height and coal dark hair, Joseph was the typical, tall, dark and handsome man many girls' dream of. He was charming and funny, and in every way a gentleman. The first year of courting was like a dream, but the dream was soon to become a nightmare when Joseph started to accuse her of looking at every man who crossed their path.

One cold evening she was waiting outside the Plaza Cinema where they had arranged to meet. Joseph was late. While she was waiting, a man walked over to her asking for a light. She passed her cigarette over to him instead of using her matches, the weather being so windy, and the man politely passed the cigarette back to Molly thanking her, just as Joseph came around the corner. His face was like thunder.

'Joseph, you're late. I was beginning to worry.'

Joseph ignored Molly and carried on walking. Struggling to keep up with his giant strides, she cried 'Joseph, wait. What is it? Why are you angry with me?'

He stopped dead in his tracks 'Why am I angry with you? I'm angry with you because I can't leave you two minutes before you're talking to another man.'

'But I wasn't talking to him. I never spoke a word.'

'Well I saw the way he was looking at you.'

'He only asked for a light and said thank you.'

Joseph suddenly grabbed Molly by the throat. 'You listen to me. You're my woman, do you hear. *Mine.*' He squeezed harder still and finished off by slapping her across the face, walking away and leaving her behind.

Molly knew she couldn't stay with Joseph at that moment. She had grown up in a good home. There were the usual squabbles siblings have, but she couldn't remember a time in her life when there was violence in the house, her parents never fought or argued. She decided to wait until she was safe at home before telling Joseph she wasn't going to see him again. However, the next evening, before she had the chance to tell him, he was already in the doorway begging forgiveness. He told her he was sorry and promised faithfully it wouldn't happen again.

'I love you Molly, forgive me. I'm frightened of losing you. You're so beautiful. I hate it when men look at you. I'm sorry, so very sorry Molly, please forgive me. I can't live without you. I won't ever lay a finger on you again.'

Molly was touched by his gentleness and forgave him. For a while they were very happy together. Unfortunately, the abuse did happen again, but now Molly was pregnant.

Joseph wouldn't look at Molly in the same way once she was pregnant with Patrick. Her body disgusted him, and he never touched her sexually when she reached the six-month stage. However, it didn't stop him punching her. Even on the hottest of days Molly had to wear clothes to cover her bruises. This was something she couldn't let her family see. There was nothing they could do, and Joseph was careful to hit Molly where the bruises couldn't be seen. To others, she and Joseph was a normal happy couple.

Molly hoped Marianne would keep in touch, but she was also wise enough to know once she had a new life, she may want to put the past behind her as Patrick had. The letters from Patrick stopped coming after only a few months, even though Molly had kept on writing for a while. The last letter she wrote was returned by the postman. She hoped in her heart he was alive and well.

Molly felt a kick in her stomach from the baby and was saddened by the thought of Patrick and Marianne never seeing their new brother or sister. She sighed heavily at the thought of having another baby to feed and take care of. Molly dearly hoped this would be the last one. She wasn't young anymore.

The wind almost blew her over as she walked past the demolished houses on the North Strand. 'Spirits wondering around looking for loved ones' she said quietly to herself. It had been only six months since her parents were killed in the bombings, along with her sister, three nephews and a niece.

Saturday the 31st of May 1941 was the worst day in Molly's life. They had all been sleeping when they heard the bombs drop on the City. The whole house had shaken. Glass from the windows shattered. People were screaming and shouting. Four German Luftwaffe bombers screamed down on Dublin in the dead of night. No one knew where to run from the danger; they knew they had no chance of survival staying inside. The houses were so old and dilapidated; it was dangerous to use a hammer without fear of a wall collapsing.

At first, the tenants had gone down to the front parlour on the ground floor, but someone had said they would be buried alive should a bomb drop on the building. They decided they should go out on the street and take a chance. Marianne and Lillian clung to each other screaming hysterically. Molly stood in shock holding on to both James and Shaun. There was a loud whistling noise just before another bomb dropped over the North Strand. She realised the bombs must have been a direct hit on her parent's house. Molly quickly passed James and Shaun over to Marianne and ran barefoot to the bomb site. When she reached what was once her parents' house, she was met by families desperately clawing at the red-hot earth yelling out names. Flames ripped through the streets. She stood in disbelief, staring at the carnage before her. There were sirens blaring and people screaming hysterically.

Molly was dragged away by a fireman when she tried to get to the burning building. She stood and watched in horror. Bodies were brought out and laid on the road. She almost choked on tears when she realised these were the bodies of her family; her mother, father and her sister Delia. Her three nephews were later brought out, one by one, carried on makeshift stretchers. Lastly, they brought out her niece who was two years older than Marianne. Her beloved family had been in the house sleeping when the bomb fell, killing them all instantly.

The following day there were angry crowds demanding to know why the air raid sirens didn't go off. Usually, there were searchlights and flares to warn the German planes they were flying over neutral territory. Air raid sirens were also used to warn people to take cover. Take cover where? There were no air raid shelters she knew of outside of the City centre. Besides, on that night, the sirens didn't go off. Molly was to find out later from the newspapers that thirty-four people were killed and ninety were injured. Two thousand people were made homeless, as three hundred houses were damaged or destroyed. Of the four bombs dropped, the last one, and the biggest, landed on the North Strand.

The Germans quickly apologised and gave compensation for the people who had lost their homes. Molly laughed a bitter laugh. How could they compensate for wiping out families and leaving others homeless? How could it have been an accident when there were so many bombs dropped? Ireland was a neutral country, for God's sake.

All kinds of speculations were going around as to why the bombs were dropped in Dublin; was it accidental or were they offloading bombes on their journey? but it meant nothing to her now. The morning after the bombing, leaving James and Shaun with Mrs O'Conner, Molly, Marianne and Lillian went to the site to try and salvage anything they could of Molly's family home. Marianne had been very close to her cousin. They were the best of friends and had gone to the same school. Both Marianne and Lillian sobbed, their bodies shaking from shock. There was little left of her parent's belongings, apart from burnt out pieces of furniture. All Molly wanted was something as a keepsake, just something of her mothers.

Using a stick to poke about, Marianne found a blackened tin box. Inside were birth certificates, communion and confirmation certificates and other papers. At least it was something. The whole area was eerily quiet with just the sounds of gentle sobs and the sound of people scrapping the earth with their bare hands. The air was filled with smoke for some time, hovering around them like a black shadow . . . *the shadow of death.*

Eventually, Molly and the two girls made their way home. On their return Joseph was very good to Molly and held her tight in his arms while she cried. Joseph had liked Molly's' parents, never having a bad word to say about them. She knew he was feeling very upset, and she remembered he had cried openly at the funeral, a rare sight for Joseph.

She thought of how Joseph was now. How more violent and unsettled he was. Yes, she knew he was sorry for what happened on the day he put his daughter in hospital. He promised as usual not to touch alcohol again and be a better father. The apology came too late. She knew his children, his own flesh and blood, despised him now. Sadly, she had learned over the years, Stout would always win over his family.

Molly had never met Joseph's family. They didn't come to the wedding and when she inquired after them, he would go all moody, changing the subject. She knew he was born and raised somewhere in the West Coast of Ireland and lived on a farm. Molly sometimes wondered if Joseph came from a troubled past. Something she would never know.

Chapter 5

New York 1941

'Hurry up son, the game's about to start.'

'I'll be there in a minute Dad. Just need to put this wheel back on.'

Peter Reiner was fixing an old Buick Sedan car his father had bought for his sixteenth birthday. The day was a Sunday, and Peter wanted to spend as much time as he could on his car today, but he also wanted to listen to the football game on the radio. The match was to be broadcast at 2:00pm and was between the New York Giants, and the Brooklyn Dodgers. He knew it would be a good game, but he was torn between listening to the game, and working on his car. Tomorrow was the day he started work at his father's Real estate Company, Reiner Incorporated, and he wouldn't have much time to work on the car. Still, he wasn't going to miss this match.

Twenty-six minutes into the game, the match was interrupted by a news flash.

'We interrupt this programme to give you a special bulletin. The White House announced the Japanese attacked Pearl harbour by air at 7:55 am Hawaii time. The details are not available, but . . .'

'Jesus Christ. Turn over to CBS son; there'll be better coverage,' shouted his father, Karl.

Tuning in the radio they began to hear the following report

Hello, NBC. Hello, NBC. This is KTU in Honolulu, Hawaii. I am speaking from the roof of the Advertiser Publishing Company Building. We have witnessed this morning the distant view of a brief full battle of Pearl Harbour and the severe bombing of Pearl Harbour by enemy planes, undoubtedly Japanese. The city of Honolulu has also been attacked and considerable damage done. This battle has been going on for nearly three hours. One of the bombs dropped within fifty feet of KTU tower. It is no joke. It is a real war. The public of Honolulu has been advised to keep in their homes and away from the Army and Navy. There has been serious fighting going on in the air and in the sea. We cannot estimate just how much damage has been done, but it has been a very severe attack. The Navy and Army appear now to have the air and the sea under control.

The reports came in waves over much of the day, and both Peter and his father listened in shock as they found out the truth. The Japanese attack on Pearl Harbour had stunned virtually everyone in the U.S. military. American intelligence, with the benefit of intercepted Japanese messages, had known for some time that Japan was planning an assault. But military leaders had no idea precisely when and where.

Hawaii, they assumed, was so far away from Japan that the Japanese Navy could never mount an effective attack. Japan's carrier-launched bombers had found Pearl Harbour totally unprepared.

*

The following morning, along with Peter, Karl Reiner went to the office. The news had come too late to be in most of the newspapers and unless you had listened to the radio there was no way of knowing what had happened. On his way there he purchased a few radios and was surprised when he walked through the building just how many had turned up for work. People were talking to each other, their faces telling the story. Some were crying.

'Good morning, I didn't expect to see so many of my employees here today. For those who prefer to go home, that's fine, anyone else can join us for the latest news throughout the day. We have plenty of radios to listen to and they'll be lots of coffee. This has come as a huge shock. I'm sure we'll know more this morning.'

Karl was astounded to see how many of his staff preferred to stay behind. He set the radios in different areas and they all sat to listen with a sense of dread. With a heavy heart he listened to the following report, as they all did. President Franklin D. Roosevelt was about to speak to the Congress of the United States.

Yesterday, Dec. 7, 1941 - a date which will live in infamy - the United States of America was suddenly and deliberately attacked by naval and air forces of the Empire of Japan.

There was a short pause to let the information sink in, and then the President continued

The United States was at peace with that nation and, at the solicitation of Japan, was still in conversation with the government and its emperor looking toward the maintenance of peace in the Pacific.

Indeed, one hour after Japanese air squadrons had commenced bombing in Oahu, the Japanese ambassador to the United States and his colleagues delivered to the Secretary of State a formal reply to a recent American message. While this reply stated that it seemed useless to continue the existing diplomatic negotiations, it contained no threat or hint of war or armed attack.

It will be recorded that the distance of Hawaii from Japan makes it obvious that the attack was deliberately planned many days or even weeks ago. During the intervening time, the Japanese government has deliberately sought to deceive the United States by false statements and expressions of hope for continued peace.

The attack yesterday on the Hawaiian Islands has caused severe damage to American naval and military forces. Very many American lives have been lost. In addition, American ships have been reported torpedoed on the high seas between San Francisco and Honolulu.

As if to give extra weight to his argument the President added

Yesterday, the Japanese government also launched an attack against Malaya.

Last night, Japanese forces attacked Hong Kong.

Last night, Japanese forces attacked Guam.

Last night, Japanese forces attacked the Philippine Islands.

Last night, the Japanese attacked Wake Island.

This morning, the Japanese attacked Midway Island.

Japan therefore has undertaken a surprise offensive extending throughout the Pacific area. The facts of yesterday speak for themselves.

The people of the United States have already formed their opinions and well understand the implications to the very life and safety of our nation.

As commander in chief of the Army and Navy, I have directed that all measures be taken for our defence.

The speech continued for several minutes, until the President reached his following conclusion

Hostilities exist. There is no blinking at the fact that our people, our territory and our interests are in grave danger.

With confidence in our armed forces - with the unbounding determination of our people - we will gain the inevitable triumph - so help us God.

I ask that the Congress declare that since the unprovoked and dastardly attack by Japan on Sunday, Dec. 7, a state of war has existed between the United States and the Japanese empire.

The United States was now at war with Japan and it was a time for everyone to be with their own families. On their way out, Karl Reiner shook the hands of men and women, knowing there were many changes to come. Good men who would soon join forces to fight the war. He wondered how many would return.

*

The following day, most of the staff was back at work, but there wasn't the usual banter. Instead, the sounds of sobs could be heard from women, who had husbands, brothers, and sons who could soon be going off to war.

Peter waited in reception, waiting to see what he was supposed to be doing. His father had been in his private office a long time, and he wondered if he had forgotten about him.

'I see Dad has added another painting to his collection; an Edward Hopper no less.'

'Yes, different isn't it.' Lisa, his father's secretary, said quietly. 'It's certainly very modern. Not something I would like in my home' she smiled, although her eyes did not.

'Yes, it's unquestionably modern. Dad certainly has an eye for the finer things in life, but, then he deserves it, I suppose. He's worked hard all his life.'

'He's a good man, and greatly admired by his workers. Would you like another coffee Peter?'

'No thanks Lisa, he shouldn't be too long now. It's not like my father to keep anyone waiting; he must be on the telephone.'

'I have to say, he has been a while. Your father told me you're about to join the Company.'

'Yeah, I know I've been coming here since I was a child, but I feel a little nervous. You know what I mean, the boss's son and all that. I hope I don't make enemies when I start work.'

'I doubt it Peter, your father is a very clever man, and knows what he's doing having you start at the bottom, so to speak. You'll probably be the messenger boy for a while,' she smiled 'it's what he does with all the young ones. I think you'll find the employees will think more of you working your way up rather than starting at the top.'

'Yeah, you're right Lisa . . . as usual.'

'Your father is interviewing another young man today; his name is Harry Mitchell. I expect he's a little nervous too. He should be here soon.'

The door opened from the office and Peter stood up.

'Son, I haven't forgotten about you. The phone just keeps on ringing. I couldn't get away. This war will affect every one of us. I have to nip out for a little while, but I won't be long.'

Peter's father, Karl, owned a large Real Estate company. From buying and selling his first property at the age of twenty, his father had worked his way to become a self-made multi-millionaire. His father's older brother, John, had died at the age of twenty-five, and left his house and money to Karl. Not that there was much money, but as far as his father was concerned, enough to start a small business and hopefully expand. Three years later he sold the house, and, with the money, he bought another two houses, and from there, the business grew very quickly. Within twenty years, his father owned properties all over America, from small properties to big tower blocks and offices. He was a multi-millionaire, yet no stranger would know he was a rich man. Working towards his successful business had taught his father, Karl Reiner, never to take anything, or anyone for granted.

Peter was expected to take over the business when his father went into retirement, but he had a lot to learn. His father had insisted he start from the bottom to appreciate the business, and his colleagues, from all angles. Karl employed a great many people and made a point of treating his workers with respect, earning him tremendous loyalty from his employee's. Peter was very proud of his father and hoped one day he too could be as popular with his employees as his dad was. The downside to being an only child, was that Peter had spent many hours on his own while his parents were with clients negotiating deals. One day he hoped to marry and have lots of kids, and promised himself, however successful he was he would always leave quality time to spend with his family. There would be no phone calls or rushing off on business trips on those special days. His father had missed quite a lot of Peter growing up.

Sat nervously in the back of a cab, Harry Mitchell was rehearsing over and over in his head how he would introduce himself. He felt lucky to have been given the chance to get as far as an interview with Karl Reiner. His father had wanted him to carry on the family business, but Harry hated the idea of running a green grocer's shop for the rest of his life. He could understand his father being angry and upset. The business had been in the Mitchell family for generations and being an only child meant the doors would be closed for good when his father retired.

Harry hadn't made his decision overnight. He had dreamed of a career of his own. Working for a Real Estate company would give him a chance to travel and eventual promotion. There was nothing wrong with dreaming of going up in the world, and he was still only sixteen years old. Yep, he couldn't wait to start work . . . if he got the job.

Stepping outside the elevator, he straightened his tie for the fourth time in as many seconds and made his way to Reiner Incorporated, pausing once more to check his tie in a mirror in the hallway. Taking a deep breath, he opened the door and walked into the reception area and introduced himself.

'I'm so sorry Mr Mitchell, but unfortunately Mr Reiner had to go out for a while, he'll be back . . .'

'Bad news about Pearl Harbour' a voice at the back of the room announced. A young man about the same age as Harry, also wearing a suit and tie, and probably here for an interview, stretched out his hand.

'Sure is. Is there any more news of the casualties?'

'Not yet.'

The two of them continued to talk about the news they had just heard, and finally, Harry introduce himself properly and stood up to shake Peter's hand.

'My name is Harry Mitchell by the way. I'm here for an interview for a job. I heard it's a great company to work for. They say Karl Reiner is very fair with all his workers.'

'Yeah, I heard that too, so long as they are fair with him. I start here myself sometime today. I suppose I'll be the messenger and delivery boy for a good while.' Peter joked, waiting to see Harry's reaction.

'Well I suppose I'll be with you on that one if I get the job.' Harry laughed.

Peter was pleased Harry said what he had. He was going to like Harry. Peter had heard from his father how some new employees had refused to go fetch coffee or deliver mail, expecting to go out viewing property on their first day.

'Come on; let's go get something to eat. I need to stretch my legs. What do you say?'

'I don't know Peter, what if Mr Reiner comes back and I'm not here. I really want this job.'

'Ok, I understand, we'll go down to the main reception and grab a coffee. We can sit in the lounge. There's a radio where we can catch up on the news about Pearl Harbour. When Mr Reiner walks through the door, we'll see him.'

'Well if you think that's all right.'

Peter liked Harry, he seemed an honest guy and he knew his father would also like him. They had been sat in the lounge, disturbed by the latest news of Pearl Harbour, when Karl Reiner walked through the door.

'He's just walked in, come on I'll introduce you.'

Harry nervously followed Peter, who in comparison looked pretty confident.

'This is Karl Reiner' he said to Harry, and turning to his father said 'and this is Harry Mitchell, you have an appointment with him.'

Harry gasped hearing Peter speaking to Karl Reiner in this manner. He eagerly held his hand out and hoped to Christ Peter hadn't ruined it for him.

Karl shook Harry's hand enthusiastically. 'Sorry about the delay son, did you hear the news.' He asked Harry.

Harry was surprised he didn't bother to apologise to Peter about the delay, or even look surprised at the way Peter had spoken to him.

'Yes sir . . .'

'Come on up, we'll talk in my office. I take it you've met my son, Peter.'

He felt his heart stop for a second when he looked at Peter. Peter smiled and winked at Harry.

They all made their way to the reception area and Peter sat on the reclining chair while Harry followed his father into his office. Just as Harry was about to close the door behind him, Peter shouted. 'Good luck Harry.'

'Thanks.'

After just thirty minutes Karl and Harry came out again. Harry's big smile told Peter he'd got the job. He shook Harry's hand.

'I don't suppose either of us will ever forget our first meeting or starting to work for Reiner Incorporated.'

'You bet we won't.'

*

News came in constantly about the bombings. Much later, they learned the death toll had risen. Over a thousand civilians had been killed. Honolulu and Manila had also been bombed, and on the other side of the world a British gunboat, the Peterel, had been sunk in Shanghai, China.

Reports were coming in suggesting Japanese warships in the South China Sea, were heading for the Gulf of Siam towards Bangkok. At home, at least two thousand, four hundred people had died. A thousand of those were on the battleship 'the Arizona'.

New York was in a state of shock. They were at war and the people knew the number of casualties was just the beginning, and that many more deaths would follow. Families feared for their loved ones. Within days both the young, and the not so young, queued to join the armed forces and fight for America. A black cloud hung over New York, but New Yorkers were ready to fight for their country.

*

Peter and Harry hit it off instantly and became firm friends. Harry's parents were much older than Peter's parents. His mother was forty-two when she gave birth to Harry and his father was forty-five. They had given up any hope of starting a family and were both thrilled and shocked at the news. When at work, and out of working hours, Peter and Harry were inseparable. Being an only child, made them special to each other, and both Harry and Peter wondered if this was what it would have been like to have a brother. They shared the same interests and spent time listening to music, chasing girls and they were keen baseball players. They very rarely quarrelled, and when they did it was usually to do with baseball.

One day Harry asked Peter if his father had always been a rich man.

'No,' Peter answered, 'he came from a poor family. Mom told me my grandparents suffered great hardship, as most people did in the early part of the century. My ancestors originated from County Cork in Ireland, they fled Ireland during the famine and settled in New York. Dad's father, my grandfather, was born in a wooden shack where they lived until 1912. Dad was brought up in poor conditions, until at the age of seventeen when his brother died. Nobody knew how my Uncle made his money, but he died in suspicious circumstances.'

'Jesus . . . you mean he was murdered.'

'Perhaps, we don't really know. It's said he didn't have a job but bought a house for cash and had some money in the bank. Don't forget by this time it was 1918, the year the Great War in France ended. There was a lot of talk of black-market goods being shipped over to England. Somehow his money came rolling in; whatever it was he was doing, wasn't legal.'

'How old was he when he died?'

'Twenty-five, he was eight years older than my father. My grandfather wouldn't have anything to do with him, and refused to attend the funeral, or so they say. Dad went along, and my grandmother, plus just a handful of people they didn't know.'

'Your father built all this from the sale of just one house.' Harry gesticulated waving his arms around.

'The house left to Dad did help start him up in business, but it's the work he put into it which made him successful. When my uncle died, a lawyer got in touch with Dad to say Uncle John had left the house and all its contents to him, including the money in the bank. The thing is Harry; the house had been ransacked as if someone had been looking for something. The furniture had been slashed with a knife and turned upside down.'

Harry gasped. 'Well I suppose it will always stay a mystery now he's dead.'

'I suppose so. No one ever found out what happened; at least Dad never said anything. He lived in the house for almost three years and as far as I know, nobody ever came to the house looking for Uncle John. Although, Dad did say there were quite a lot of people who wanted to buy the house after my uncle died, which you could say was unusual considering the state it was in at the time.' Peter lit a cigarette and handed the packet to Harry. 'Just after the war and in the early twenties there was an economic boom. Everyone was cashing in on the rapid growth and prosperity the war in France had started off. Funny, how there is always an upside to peoples suffering; I wonder if it will be the same when this war finishes.'

'I hope it doesn't end too soon', Harry butted in; 'I want to get over there and give the enemy a good going over.'

'I know what you mean', agreed Peter, 'Dad says I can't enlist until I'm eighteen. If he had his way, I wouldn't be going at all. He says I must learn the business and leave the fighting to someone else; but as soon as my eighteenth birthday comes, I'm going straight down to the recruitment centre. I want to join the United States Army Air Force. I really want to fly.'

'Yeah, me too; we'll join up together. I hate being sixteen; my father said the same as your father. If everyone thought the same, then Hitler would rule the world. Someone must fight, for Christ sake. But I suppose in some way I can understand my father, he says he saw enough of war in the trenches in 1918. He was in France, and every night since hearing about this war, he prays the conflict will end and everyone will be safe.'

'Yeah, I can understand him not wanting you to go and fight like he did. Dad told me he was lucky because he missed going to Europe and it gave him the chance to start up his business.'

Peter explained to Harry how his father had sold the original house, then using the extra money bought two more.

'Your father's some guy Pete.'

'Sure is. Jesus Harry, look at the time, we'd better go downtown and look at the Wilson property.

Chapter 6

Liverpool 1943

'Bloody hell Kate, its cold,' moaned Helen, her voice barely audible.

'I didn't catch that. What did you say?'

'I said its bloody cold, but I can hardly move my mouth, my lips are frozen. It must have been snowing really heavy while we were in the factory.'

'Yeah, I heard one of the girls say so. This snow is icy. I keep thinking I'm going to end up on me arse. It's madness.'

'What is?'

'Well today we are in winter, and officially, tomorrow March the 21st we're in spring.'

'That's true, Helen. Spring must be the most unpredictable season of them all. You never know what to expect.'

'It's trying to snow again now. Would you believe it, the sun was shining last week, and this week it's freezing?' Kate commented, walking with her head down to stop the cold sleet hitting her in the face.

'There's still a lot more snow to come Kate, the sky is full of it. You can forget the old poem we learned at school. The weather does as it bloody wants.'

'Helen, you always seem to know a song, an old saying, or a rhyme for every event. So what poem is that then Einstein?'

'The famous poem about the months,'

'Never heard of it,'

'You must have heard of it, the one by Sara Coleridge.' Helen sighed and looked at Kate's blank expression. 'Didn't you learn anything at your school?'

'Not really, I wasn't there much. Go on then, tell me the famous poem. If I were to hear it, I might remember it.'

'OK, if my lips don't freeze together first.'

'That'll be the day.' Kate laughed.

'Ha-ha very funny. Well, here goes.

January brings the snow. Makes our feet and fingers glow

February brings the rain. Thaws the frozen lakes again

March brings breezes and shrill. Shakes the dancing daffodil

April brings the primrose sweet. Scatters daises at our feet

May brings flocks of pretty lambs. Skipping by their fleecy dams

June brings tulips, lilies, roses. Fills the children's hands with posies

Hot July brings cooling showers. Apricots and gillyflowers

August brings the sheaves of corn. Then the harvest is borne

Warm September brings the fruit . . . I don't remember the rest'

'I can't say I ever heard that one Helen, you're like a walking library. I'd love to know what October, November and December were.'

'I think I remember November and December. I just can't remember October.'

November brings the blast. Then the leaves are swirling fast

December brings the sleet. Blazing fires and Christmas treats

'Ooh, the last one sounds cosy Helen. I don't think I ever sat in front of a blazing fire. The fires I've ever known have been gently topped up just to keep them going'

'Me too' Helen agreed.

They talked and laughed all the way home, linking arms until they reached the small terraced house, they shared with two more friends, Anna and Brenda. On opening the door, the smell of damp hit them instantly. The nasty odour seemed to disappear once the fire was lit and the house warmed through, but Brenda guessed the smell was still probably there; they just didn't notice it after a while.

'Jesus, it's freezing in here, let's get the bloody fire lit. It's warmer outside than in here for God's sake.'

'We haven't much coal Helen. We'll have to go steady with the last bucket.'

'Bloody hell, it doesn't last two minutes. Where's Anna, she should be home now, she only called at the shop down the road.'

'Oh, you know Anna; she's probably talking to someone. You lay the fire and I'll start on the tea. I'm starving, not that we have much in; my ration book has just about had it. How do you share one egg between four people?'

'Three. Brenda isn't here. Only one egg, you say. Easy, add some flour, milk and water . . . and we have Yorkshire puddings or pancakes. We still have some flour. We haven't much milk, but there should be enough left for our morning cuppa if we add more water to the mixture.'

'Well, that sounds good to me.'

'This bloody war; is there ever an end in sight.' Helen sighed, pulling her skirt above her knees and looking at her legs. 'I'm going out tonight. I don't know whether to tan my legs with gravy browning and draw seams with my eyebrow pencil. Or not to bother at all, I'm out of my last pair of stockings.'

'Tonight, where are you going? It's snowing, not to mention it being freezing cold out there?'

'Oh, only down to the club for a drink with Pat Cummings, I'll only be out a couple of hours. Why? Do you fancy coming with me, he's only a friend . . . but I suspect he would like to be more?' she laughed 'He's not my type really, but he's good for a laugh.'

'No thanks, I fancy an early night with my book and a cup of cocoa.'

'Okay. It seems strange without Brenda, when's she coming back?'

'Wednesday, that's if her mother is strong enough to take care of herself now. That was a pretty bad case of pneumonia she had.'

'Yeah, I'm surprised she pulled through really, she looked more dead than alive when we saw her last week, poor soul.' sighed Kate.

'Poor Brenda, as well as the worry she has with her mother, she's worried about losing her job. This is the second time she's asked for time off.'

'Brenda is a saint. She's the mother hen to us all. You only have to sneeze and she's there with hot water and lemon.'

Helen agreed. 'She'd make a good nurse. I remember her once saying she would like to work in a hospital.'

'True, she certainly would make a good nurse. Borrow my stockings for tonight if you like Helen, you can't go out bare legged.'

'Thanks Kate, I'll rinse them through when I come in.'

'Bloody stockings, they don't last two minutes before they ladder. At least we save a fortune by wearing overalls at work.'

'We'll have to do what all the other girls are doing.' Helen smiled.

'What's that then?'

'Go out with a GI and get some free stockings . . . and some chocolate.'

'I'll give a kiss for a pair of stockings and chocolates any day.'

It took a while to get the fire burning. They had run out of sticks again. Helen rolled some newspaper tightly to make paper sticks and pulled the damper out to draw the flames. However, the flames just wouldn't get a hold. Kate put the small coal shovel in front of the fire and placed a sheet of paper over it, blocking out the air and forcing air upwards from beneath the grate. Eventually, the fire was lit, and heat was beginning to penetrate through their bones. Kate pushed the damper in again to make the coal last.

'I was going to take a bath tonight. I opened the back door to bring the bath inside and it was covered in snow. I'm going to fill the bowl and take an all over wash in front of the fire instead.'

'You'll have to wait while the water heats up first, unless you boil the kettle.'

Helen boiled the kettle and carefully carried the bowl through to the front room, placing it on the table in front of the fire. She stripped down to her underwear just as Anna burst through the door. The cold wind blasted through the house. Helen and Kate shouted, 'Shut the bloody door.'

'Hey, guess what I just heard you two. There's a big dance at the Grafton. There's supposed to be a great band on. Oh. . . I'm so excited; we can't miss this night girls. Think of all those GIs that are going to be there. We won't have to dance with each other anymore; there certainly won't be shortage of men anymore at the Grafton.

'I heard about the dance from one of the girls from work, Kate said 'there are dance competitions for the Jitterbug and the Jive.'

An hour later the three of them sat around the table and talked excitably about the Grafton. Helen suddenly jumped up from the table. 'I'm late. Must dash; sorry I can't stay to help clean the dishes. See you later girls.'

Kate and Anna laughed and started to clear the dishes away, including Helen's bowl of water which she had left on the table, along with the soap and towel. The four girls shared a back to back house with two bedrooms, a small living room and tiny kitchen. They lived in Halewood and worked together at the Rootes aircraft factory, where they'd all met, and became friends from the start. In all the time they had been together, there was never a cross word between them; apart from whose turn it was to wash up. Though the house was cold and damp, it felt good to be independent. The street was dismal, but the neighbours were friendly.

Of course, everyone had their own story of the war to tell; mostly about a relative who was missing in action, or of a loved one who had died. As in all neighbourhoods in Liverpool, the neighbours joined in to help and do what they could. The saddest part was watching someone receive the dreaded telegram. The whole street would stand at their doors when the young telegram boy cycled down the road. The telegram boys were as young as fourteen and often the bearer of bad news. Bad news had 'Priority' written at the top of the telegram, and so the look on the boy's face said it all. When the neighbours were outside chatting, as they usually were on a fine day, silence would fall as they watched and waited to see where the boy was going. Some tried to read his face, while others were too frightened to look at him eye to eye. On one of those days a neighbour had a telegram to say her son's plane had been shot down over Germany. The woman carried on peeling potatoes, still sitting on the step. Ten minutes later there was a howling sound that must have been heard in every nearby household.

*

Once snuggled up in bed, both Kate and Anna reached for their books to read awhile before sleeping. Kate lost concentration, thinking of the dance instead. She loved the Grafton and the Locarno dance hall. The bright warm atmosphere was the only time everyone there could forget about the war for four hours. Friendships were made and a lot of relationships started off at the Grafton. War or no war, Kate had never been happier in some respects, although she longed for the day the war ended. The bombing seemed to have ceased, but you could never be sure if another strike was planned for them. They still had to carry their gas masks everywhere. Kate felt lucky to have such good friends to share a house with. She'd many more friends at the factory, where their jaws ached some days with laughter and singing. Kate also felt proud to be among the thousands of women who helped the war effort in a factory where they made the Halifax bombers.

Helen was the first friend Kate made in the factory. She'd been looking for somewhere to sit amongst the hundreds of workers, when Helen shouted over the noise for Kate to sit beside her. There seemed to be so many people in the canteen, and Kate felt very self-conscious, but the feeling soon passed when a group of girls shuffled round to make room for her. Helen introduced her to everyone around the table, though she knew she would have forgotten their names before the day was out. Remembering names had never been Kate's forte.

'You see him' Helen whispered. 'The one with three chins; he's sitting at the next table.'

'Yes' replied Kate.'

'Watch yourself when you're bending down. He's a bum watcher. We've seen him eyeing girl's bums with salvia drooling down the sides of his mouth.'

All the girls agreed and burst into laughter. Helen's laugh was quite infectious, and Kate saw she had a lovely smile; in fact, she was the prettiest girl Kate had ever seen. Even with her hair tied up in a scarf didn't make a difference to her beauty. Her personality shone through and Kate felt privileged to be her new friend.

Brenda and Anna started at the factory a few weeks after Kate. They all soon became good friends and were lucky to work the same shifts. Just as herself and Helen, they were struggling to find lodgings near enough to the factory. Kate had been living with a family who let her share a room with their daughter, but the girl made it perfectly clear she didn't like Kate from the start. Quarrels were a regular occurrence until Kate was asked to leave one day.

Anna came up with the idea of renting a house to share; a small one, but one not too far away from the Rootes factory. Not many families liked the idea of living somewhere as dangerous as the docks; hence the rent was much cheaper. It also made sense to move near to where you were working, especially in the winter, even though they knew it was high risk. After London, Liverpool had been the worst hit area in the country. The shipping port was very important to the war effort as the Liverpool docks brought in food and materials vital to the country. It was also home to the headquarters of the Western Approaches Command which was a strategic base for the Navy. Unfortunately, that made the docks a prime target.

Each week, ships arrived in the River Mersey bringing in food and other vital necessities. Britain would have lost the war had it not been for these supplies from Canada and the United States. The German Luftwaffe was mainly aiming for the docks, factories and railways. Several Liverpool's docks had been bombed and the surrounding neighbourhoods.

Walking home after a shift was very hard in the winter, mostly down to the enveloping heavy smog. The footpaths and roads were unsafe and extremely dark during the blackouts, making it impossible to see where you were going. The rules were, you had to point the torch in a downwards direction, so the beam lit up your feet and not above for a plane to see. When waiting for a bus, the rule was to switch the light of the torch on and off twice, and never in the bus driver's face. Unfortunately, batteries didn't last very long and were expensive, so the girls walked together each pair sharing one torch.

'When you think about it, we're in no more danger here than we are at work,' Anna stated as they viewed the area they were planning to live.

'Ha-ha, I don't know so much, it's a long walk home on foot, especially if there are no buses. We'll need to find out where the nearest shelters are as well and hope we don't die of any diseases that may be lingering from the last people who lived here.'

'The house just needs a few fires and a little laughter,' Kate said cheerily, and hoped that was true. Unfortunately, this was the only affordable house to rent near enough to where the girls worked, and it really was in an appalling state. Wallpaper peeled from the damp walls, the toilet stood in the yard and was shared with two more families; and was also in need of a good clean. A tatty looking tin bath hung over a nail on the outside wall. The roof let in water when it rained, going by the stains, and the rooms smelt of wet dogs. There were bits of furniture still in the house, and the girls knew at once, when the itching started, that the two beds left behind were a home to fleas.

'Bloody hell, there are hundreds of them . . . not to mention the bed bugs, *and* as we are all aware Ladies, they are well known for sucking the bloody life out of you.'

'We'll have to use some DDT while we can afford new second-hand beds . . . not new but . . .'

'We know what you mean.' Laughed Anna 'The whole house needs a good dousing with DDT before we move in.'

'Well, I suppose it's better than some.' Brenda said softly 'there are some poor souls who have no homes at all now, thanks to the bloody Gerry's. It seems they are hell bent on destroying us and our City altogether. All those lovely buildings are gone or damaged . . . The City Museum, Central Library, and the Cotton Exchange. Not to mention our Churches, factories and hospitals.'

*

Kate put her book down on the bedside table and climbed out of bed to look through the window to see if it was still snowing. All the girls in the factory were saying there was still a lot of snow to come before the end of the month. She couldn't see any let up in the weather. The biting wind was made worse when they walked home, since sometimes it was like a Furness inside the factory.

She pulled back the thick woollen cloth from the window and tugged hard on the sash to lean over and look. A familiar voice shouted out. It was the air raid precaution guard.

'Put that light out'

47

'Oh, shut up, I was just about to.' Kate yelled back.

'Yeah, well next time you might find yourself with a hefty fine, Miss. There's a bloody war on you know.'

'Well, I'm so glad you told me, I didn't know.'

'We'll have less of your bloody cheek. Now block that light out.'

Kate quickly pulled the cloth down, blocking any light from showing, muttering to herself. Of course, he was right. It couldn't be much fun walking around the streets in the cold, looking to see who was showing light through their windows. Even a small pin prick of light could evoke an attack.

Eventually, the once white snow turned black from the chimney smoke, and the streets looked dirty, dismal and depressing. But at least the snow was beginning to melt now the sun decided it was time to come out of hiding.

*

The dance at the Grafton had been fantastic, and as Anna had said, there were hundreds of handsome boys in uniforms eagerly looking for a dance partner. It was hard to believe a place could hold so many people.

'That was what you would call a good night, my feet are killing me.'

'Mine too Anna.' Helen agreed 'I used to love dancing when I was a child. I dreamed of being a dancer in a musical, ever since seeing Cavalcade of Variety at the Plaza with my mother.'

'You must miss your mother, Helen. Sometimes I hear you cry in your sleep and shout out for her.'

'I miss my family so much. My brothers were twins, I don't know if I ever told you.'

'No, I didn't know that Helen. Were they identical twins?'

'Yes' laughed Helen, 'they used to play tricks on my parents all the time. My dad was thrilled when they arrived, but couldn't tell who was who even then. This war has taken so many loved ones from us, and I expect there's more whose lives will be cut short yet.' Helen looked up at the ceiling to try and stop herself from crying.

'I know we tend not to talk of the past, Helen, but did your family die in the Blitz?'

'No, my family was killed on January the 10th 1942 when the Luftwaffe dropped bombs on my home in Upper Stanhope Street. Mam and Dad were with my brothers in the air raid shelter. There was nothing left of the house or the shelter, just a pile of bricks and dust. I was in the air raid shelter near to where I worked nights at the time.' Helen swallowed hard, choking on her tears. 'There were so many killed that night, Anna, some were too shocked to speak or cry. One woman had lost four of her six children.'

'The sheer horror of it all' Anna said gently, holding Helen's hand. 'It isn't only the loss of loved ones; it's also about starting all over again, looking for somewhere to live. My mother died the first night of the Blitz. Dad was in prison for stealing cigarettes and booze. It was his third offence. I don't see him now, and I don't want to see him again. Not after what he put my mother through. It should have been him that died, not her. My sister has moved back to Ireland with her husband, and my brothers are out there fighting. We lived in Ireland when we were young, until Dad wanted to move here to find work. I was happy there in Dublin. I had families on both sides. Things went downhill when we moved here with my parents fighting all the time over money.'

'I'm so sorry Anna. I find it a comfort knowing someone understands how you feel about losing someone you love. They're the only people who do know what you're going through. You're right about starting again. I trailed the streets looking for somewhere to stay, until an old woman took pity on me. Her name was Hilda. I didn't like to ask, but I don't think she had a family of her own. She treated me like a granddaughter. I grew to really love her; she was so kind. I couldn't have coped without her love and comfort. We used to sit for hours talking and drinking cocoa.'

'What happened to her?'

'She had a bad heart. One night she was taken to hospital and never came home. I couldn't stay in the house; the landlord had promised it to a family who had lost their house from the same bombing that killed my parents. I probably knew them but couldn't face them. Hilda left me her belongings, furniture and stuff like that, but I left them for the new tenants and took just the personal things that were . . . not valuable, but very precious to her, as she had no one else. She also left me a little money which helped me a lot. The rest is history.' Helen cried.

Anna reached over and held Helen while she sobbed her heart out.

*

Spring had gone and summer arrived with a passion. The girls started going out more. Both Anna and Brenda had been courting American Airmen since the dance at the Grafton, where they had met. Kate and Helen did have a few nights out with some GIs, but none of them were anything special.

'It's the uniform that does it you know . . . and of course the money.'

'What are you talking about Kate?'

'GI's just look at their uniforms compared to our lads. They look very handsome . . . but would they look as handsome in our lad's uniforms. I think not. *And* they get far better wages than our lads.'

'I think they have charm. We all fell in love with their charm and accents from the start.'

'The women have, yeah. Not the men, Helen. Can you imagine how our men must feel about the GIs? Walking around Liverpool taking other men's women looking like film stars, while they're out fighting the bloody war.'

'They didn't choose what uniform to wear. You can't hold that against them Kate. These men are also fighting the war. They build the planes that kill the Germans and are in danger of being blown off the face of the Earth any day. They're very skilled at what they do and without these men we wouldn't stand a chance.'

Kate carried on, 'There's going to be a lot of GI brides when this war is over. They have women falling at their feet. You won't catch me marrying a GI. They're just show-offs, the lot of them.'

'What's wrong with you today Kate. Did you get out of bed the wrong side?' said Helen.

'I was just thinking about the future. I would imagine more than half the brides just want to marry so they can live in the States. What better than to marry a GI and get away from this war-torn City. Building Liverpool

50

up again is going to take years and years, and there won't be much money to do it. Yeah . . . it makes you wonder.'

'Leave it now Kate. You sound bitter. Live and let live, for God's sake, and show some appreciation for the Americans.'

'Sorry Helen. I'm just having a bad day.'

*

Apart from the war, this was beginning to be a good summer. There was still life at the end of a working day, laughter, good walks and bike rides. The days were long and hot, leaving time to enjoy the outdoor life.

The girls welcomed their full day off from work and decided to have a lazy day in the sunshine, sitting on the pavement outside the front of the house soaking up the sun. Anna hadn't said where she was going, but a familiar figure came into view, dazzled by the sun. They waved enthusiastically when they realised it was Anna, but she didn't acknowledge them back.

'She's crying.' Brenda said quietly, already standing up to see what was wrong with Anna.

Kate and Helen quickly sat upright, as Anna rushed straight passed the girls into the house. She was wearing a dirty old looking coat. They hurried after her to find Anna on the bed. The coat was on the floor and her dress was covered in blood.

'Anna, what is it. Has someone hurt you? Anna . . . speak to us, we're your friends.'

'I've had an abortion.' Anna sobbed. 'He paid for it. He made me do it. I didn't want to do it.'

'Who?' asked Brenda 'and how far into the pregnancy were you?'

'Rob, the GI I was seeing. I was three or four months. Not sure. He was so angry with me when I told him I was pregnant, as if it was my fault. I had to wait a week to see him because he was working away somewhere . . . or so he said.' She sniffed 'I thought he loved me. He talked about us marrying after the war, but yesterday he told me he was already married with two kids.'

'Never mind that for now. How are you? You look terrible. Where did you go? Who did this?'

'Give her time to answer one question at a time Helen.' Brenda snapped 'before we ask any more questions. I'll make tea for us all. Anna needs to catch her breath.'

Kate and Brenda went to make tea and gave Anna time to calm down a little until she was ready to tell them all what had happened.

'He took me to one of those back-street abortionists. Said it was safe and would be done with in no time.' Anna started crying, almost screaming. 'The woman put carbolic soap and disinfectant or something inside of me, then hot water. There was another woman there . . . I think it was her daughter. She had a case with instruments and passed a crotchet hook to the woman, who was forcing my legs open. I bled, but the baby didn't come. The woman said it would come away in a day or two down the toilet.' Anna stopped and had a sip of her tea. 'The pain was awful, I could barely stand, and the woman was so business like . . . you know, packing her bag away like a real doctor.'

'Where was Rob?'

'He was waiting for me outside. He took me to a café for a cup of tea and I could feel the baby coming. He kept saying it wouldn't be ready to come yet because the woman had said a day or two, but I screamed out in pain so loud he took me back to the woman instead of going home.' Anna stopped talking and blew her nose. 'The baby was born on her filthy kitchen floor. I was screaming. She grabbed the baby quickly when it came out and threw it on the fire. The smell was . . .'

'Oh no Anna,' Brenda gasped 'you poor thing.'

The girls gathered round her, but words didn't come easy. They were all in shock.

A week later Anna became ill and the doctor was called for. He took a urine sample and stated she may have a severe kidney infection. Anna was in so much pain that she rolled back and forth in bed clutching her stomach. The truth had to be told.

'For Heaven's sake' the doctor cursed. 'Some of the placenta may still be inside. Leave the room while I look.'

The doctor came out of the bedroom, shaking his head. 'There was no placenta there, but her uterus is very damage. I doubt she will be able to have another baby. She's also traumatised, which is no wonder. Give her plenty to drink and keep an eye on her . . . and don't leave her on her own, God only knows what may be going off in her head. Hopefully the fever will pass. I'll write up some medication and I'll be back tomorrow. And by the way, I have to report this.'

The girls worked different shifts so one of them could be with Anna all the time. Three weeks later she was on the mend, though not mentally. Their supervisor was very understanding. Of course, they had to tell a lie and say she had pneumonia.

'I can't stop thinking of my baby being thrown on the fire; it might still have been alive. Can you imagine the pain? How could I be so stupid to think Rob would marry me? I didn't want to abort my baby. He forced me into it. I should have told him I wasn't going to see that ghastly woman. I should have talked it over with all of you first.'

'Don't beat yourself up Anna.' Kate said bitterly 'he took advantage of you like hundreds of GIs like him. Keep away from them. No one knows whether they're married or not. The woman has been arrested and Rob must be in serious trouble. You won't be seeing him again.'

*

Summer turned to autumn and very quickly winter; the nights started to draw in once more. The smog brought people down with coughs and pneumonia, and there was still no sign of an end to the war.

On New Year's Eve 1943, Kate was to spend the evening at home. Anna and Helen were going out dancing and Brenda had gone to see her mother.

'Oh Kate, you can't stay here on your own. It's New Year's Eve.'

'No Helen, I'm all right, you go and enjoy yourself. I'll be okay on my own, my throat is killing me. Anyway, I want to make some alterations to a dress I bought in time for the big dance next week.'

Helen reached over and gave Kate a kiss on the cheek. 'Happy new year Kate'

'And the same to you Helen, now go!'

Two hours had passed, and Kate picked up the dress she was about to sew, holding it tight against her chest. She did feel lonely and wished now she had gone with Helen and Anna, but her throat was sore, her nose was bright red and her head ached, not to mention the terrible cough. From outside she could hear the sound of people shouting 'Happy New Year' to one another as they walked by the house. The winter winds had arrived with more snow and the house was as cold as ice. The heat from the fire warmed the front of her, but not her back.

Kate decided she would be warmer in bed. She wore a woollen hat and slept with her knees as high as possible to keep warm, not daring to put her feet down to the bottom of the bed until it warmed through. The girls had bought two double beds from a second-hand shop. They were second hand, but clean and cheap. They slept two to a bed for extra warmth. There were no set rules as to who slept with whom. The first one to bed would be the one who warmed the bed up, and so the second one upstairs always made a beeline for that bed. One extremely cold night, when they were without coal, the four of them shared the one bed, two at the top and two at the bottom. They laughed and talked so loudly; the neighbour banged on the wall and told them to be quiet. It was times such as this when they talked about their lives, their past, and the future they would like. There was a great deal of trust between the girls and secrets were told. As usual, there was laughter, but also tears.

In the early hours of the morning, Helen tiptoed upstairs, and climbed into bed next to Kate.

'For the love of God, Helen, you're freezing cold; go over to your side of the bed.'

'I know I'm freezing, but you're so warm. Move over.'

'Yeah, and it took me a bloody hour to get this warm. You're not pinching my heat. Find yer own.'

'Happy New year Kate' Helen smiled sweetly.

'Happy New Year to you too, Helen'

'Yeah, and a Happy New Year from me'

'Anna . . . what a surprise, we thought you were staying out with Joan. I've only just got back myself.'

'She bumped into her sister and I felt a bit left out when you went home. Move over, I'm not sleeping on me own in that bed, its bloody freezing.'

The next morning all three girls ate their breakfast wearing their hats and coats.

'Happy New Year' Brenda shouted as she opened the door.

'Happy New Year to you' they chorused 'shut the door.'

Benda shivered. 'It's colder in here than it is outside.'

'Yeah, it is, and we've heard that saying a few times. Let's have a nice cup of tea, eh. I'll put kettle on.'

'Well, my lovely friends' Brenda called out as she filled the kettle 'it's the first of January 1944. Let's hope this time next year this bloody war will be well and truly over, and things are back to where they were.'

'They keep saying it'll be over soon, they say it over and over again, but the bombs still keep on coming all over the bloody Country.'

'Have you noticed; each time someone mentions the war, they always put 'bloody' before it.'

'Now that's bloody true enough; bloody war, bloody Hitler. Come on girls, altogether now.'

'Hitler has only got one ball.

Goring has two, but so very small

Himmler, has something similar

But poor old Goebbels has no balls at all.'

The girls hugged each other, and Brenda said at the top of her voice. 'We have each other, and always will have. I'd like to make a toast with my cup of tea. To the best friends a girl could ever wish for. Cheers.'

'Aw, cheers Brenda.'

'I think I will remember this morning for the rest of my life.' Helen said, holding her cup of tea high.

Kate and Anna both replied, 'me too!'

'I wonder what will happen when the war is over.' Brenda continued.

'What do you mean, Brenda?' Kate asked.

'Things won't ever be the same really, will they? So many lives have been lost. I mean . . . look at us. We've all lost family in this bloody war. Then there's men out there fighting for a Country they may never see again.'

'True. But they will never be forgotten.'

'What about us. I wonder if we will keep friends after we're married and stuff.'

'Of course, we will, silly.' Anna said, giving Brenda a cuddle.'

'Yes, but what if one of us marries an American.'

'No, that is not going to happen, Brenda' replied Kate. 'They're okay for a laugh, but as soon as the war is over, they'll be off home to their wives and girlfriends.'

'Well, I've had my share of falling for a GI and it nearly bloody killed me,' Anna replied.

'Come on, cheer up. We have each other, and I'd like to make a toast with my cup of tea. To the best friends a girl could ever wish for. Cheers.'

Chapter 7

New York 1944

Karl Reiner was in his office. He was happy with his son; he had made him proud, already selling three properties. The young guy Harry was doing all right too. They worked well together and made a good team. At first, he thought he would keep the boys apart; he didn't want the boy thinking Peter was being treated differently to him, or have the boy feel inferior. He knew they had become good friends and Karl thought being together all the time might cause conflict, but he was proved wrong, Harry was good for Peter. Karl liked him himself and felt like Harry was a second son. Karl hoped to retire when he reached the age of sixty and knew now Peter would keep the business a success, as he himself had. Perhaps Harry could join the corporation.

Karl started to think of himself at their age. Until his uncle left him the house, his future looked glum. Being left a house and a little money gave Karl the chance of starting his own business in property. He was eighteen and doing the renovations himself so he could save money at the start, which was far from easy. Money was tight, but he persevered, working long hours. The hard work paid off and he was able to expand.

People at that time were paying premium prices for good property, and the area he chose for housing was well sort after. There was plenty of work and industrial production was increasing year on year, which meant people were able to get easy credit, but many were living well above their means. Karl was already a shrewd businessman and fed upon everyone's appetite for better accommodation. One house became two, two became six and by March 1926, when Peter was born, he had a portfolio of fourteen properties. His new son gave him the impetus to expand even more. Now he had a good reason to build his property empire and safeguard a future for his family.

By the time Peter was three, Karl had increased his holdings to twenty-three assorted buildings; some of which were individual dwellings on the outskirts of the City, and some were apartment blocks in New York's West Side. Unfortunately, the unthinkable started to happen; the boom years of the 1920s started to unravel. Unemployment began to grow, construction and industrial production dwindled, and people began to panic. Confidence in the United States economy slumped, and the Stock Market began a downward slide. It was on the 29th of October 1929, a Tuesday, that the market collapsed, and between eight and nine billion dollars were wiped off the value of the Dow Jones Industrial Average. In just one day, the market lost twenty-three per cent of its value, and although some of the descriptions of how people reacted to the situation were exaggerated, many thousands lost everything. Some not only lost their livelihoods, but also their lives, as they threw themselves from office windows or quietly committed suicide.

Karl soon realised the main reason for this downturn in the economy was that there was a large disparity between what people had been borrowing and what they earned. So called industrialists had expanded too quickly in order to meet the demands of consumer spending. Then when unemployment grew, and consumers lost their power to buy new consumables, the bubble burst. Indeed, as more businesses failed and unemployment rose, credit became harder to acquire and repossessions and foreclosures became more and more prevalent. As people were forced back into poverty, the marketplace was flooded with repossessed second hand cars, furniture and household goods; making new purchases unattractive.

All this fed the downward spiral of industry and commerce. Like an ever-quickening whirlpool, businesses were sucked into a dark void, and by the time President Herbert Hoover left office in 1932, unemployment had raced passed the twenty per cent mark. Millions of Americans were to find they were homeless as banks and businesses collapsed. Despite searching for work, many were forced out onto the streets and makeshift shanty towns, nicknamed 'Hoovervilles', sprang up everywhere.

Karl was obviously affected by the downturn in the American economy, but he had been wise enough not to borrow heavily. He had used the capital from his property sales to finance his expansion and he owed the banks very little. This put him in a strong position, and an economic downturn can be a good time to start or expand a business. Commercial rents were now cheap, and workers would fight to secure employment for fewer wages. Equipment and premises could be acquired for a fraction of their worth. It was this situation that allowed Karl to expand his empire. As property prices fell, he snapped up whole buildings for a song. Subsequently, he could re-let them to the very businesspeople who had been using them before, as they tried to weather the storm, and survive the depression. He could afford to reduce rents, and allow some to carry on pro bona, knowing that when the turnaround came, he would have tenants who were grateful and loyal to him.

Franklin Delano Roosevelt, the democratic nominee for the Presidency, based his election stance on "The only things we have to fear is fear itself" and Karl Reiner agreed with him. As Roosevelt surged into office on a landslide victory, taking up residence in the White House in March 1933, Karl was one of the many entrepreneurs who expanded their businesses. In fact, it is widely believed more millionaires were created during the great depression than at any other time in America's history, and Karl Reiner was one of them.

Karl Reiner had succeeded when many had failed. He had protected his investment by treating people fairly, and by offering a helping hand when necessary.

When President Roosevelt inherited a United States economy, in which between thirteen and fifteen million workers had no proper jobs, a series of emergency measures were introduced. "The New Deal" for the American people' brought in stock market and banking reforms and created a massive program of public works, to kick start industry. Building hydro eclectic dams and the installation of roads, freeways and a national infrastructure paved the way to economic revival. Roosevelt was reelected for a second term of office in 1936, continuing his re-building of the American economy, so despite a devastating deep recession in 1937, which lasted well into 1938, American industry began to consolidate.

As well as rebuilding the United States economy from 1936, Roosevelt turned his attention to re-establishing the armed forces, which had been side lined since the European conflict ended the Great War. This turned out to be a fortuitous move as, when in September 1939 Hitler invaded Poland, forcing England and France into war with Germany, the need for armaments became a major priority. And so to be ready for the possible inclusion of American forces in the war in Europe, jobless workers were trained in defence jobs, and the draft, which came into effect in 1940 absorbed many jobless workers. When the Japanese did attack Pearl Harbour, the United States was prepared and ready for war.

*

The last two years had flown by and Peter and Harry finally enlisted. They were both going to become soldiers in the United States Army Air Force. Things were hectic at first; they both had to swear allegiance to the United States and to the Army. Then, along with everyone else who had sworn in that day, they were shipped out of New York on buses headed for Florida. It was going to be no holiday in Florida. Initially, they had to complete their basic training at a special camp in Saint Petersburg. At this camp they joined hundreds of recruits who were given basic Army indoctrination, before they would be classified into their military occupations.

The training came as a shock to Peter and Harry. They weren't used to being constantly yelled at when marching back and forth for hours on end.

'This life sucks Pete. The Drill Sergeant made a grown man cry yesterday,' moaned Harry.

'Jesus, I wasn't far off crying myself. He was yelling so close to my face I could see his tonsils. I hate being here in this goddamn place.'

'Me too, but this is it Buddy.'

'Sure is.'

When it came to cross country running and working their way through the obstacle course, they began to feel more eager, but without a doubt the most exciting part of their training was when they were on the firing range. Firing a 30-calibre carbine rifle, and learning how to strip down, clean and reassemble the weapon, felt more like being a soldier. There were trainees from all over the United States and many grew up on farms, or lived in rural parts of the country, and were used to firing guns. To Harry and Peter this was something new and it made them both feel as if they were really a part of the war, and the fight against Hitler.

After completing their basic and technical training the boys were relieved when they found out they had both been given the same posting.

They were going to England.

*

Arriving at USAAF Station 590 Burtonwood, two miles northwest of Warrington, Peter and Harry found themselves on an extremely large base used by the USAAF and a few liaison airmen representing the British Royal Air Force. The Brits were called Airmen, but the American servicemen were referred to as soldiers, as they were in the Army Air Force.

Peter and Harry were immediately despatched to their billet and allowed to unpack. Rows of Nissan huts and temporary cement rendered brick buildings housed most of the service personnel, although some of the lucky ones got to live off camp at Bruce or Canada Hall: being brought backwards and forwards by truck. Peter and Harry were not so lucky and found themselves about to share a huge building, which under its high curved ceiling, boasted twelve beds up either side.

Given little chance to get a good look at their surroundings, they were quickly marched off to an induction meeting to learn all about their posting to Base Air Depot 1, or the BAD ONE as the base was nicknamed.

'You guys will be joining some fifteen hundred fellow soldiers, along with over a thousand American civilians, who have been brought over from San Antonio Air Depot in Texas. You'll be given the job of the assembly, repair and testing of our aircraft and engines.' The engineering officer leading the induction told them.

'Yes Sir.' Everyone chorused loudly.

'This base is the largest airfield in Europe' the Officer continued 'and since we arrived in 1942, over ten thousand aircraft have been assembled . . .'

Peter and Harry were to soon learn just how important a role they were going to play. The production line aircraft mechanics and assembly personnel bolted and riveted together new planes that had been shipped by sea, in boxes. This was the first time in Britain that an American style production line had been seen, and the locals who worked alongside the GI's marvelled at how quickly boxes of aircraft parts could soon be taking off on the adjoining airfield.

*

'Are we out tonight Pete?'

'Sure. Where were you thinking?'

'The Skyline club sounds good. And it's open twenty-four hours to cater for all shifts. I'm told it holds over seven hundred people.'

'I heard that too. I also heard they sell American beer brought in specially, but I'm happy with the local beer, Burtonwood ale, which I hear is brewed in the village.'

'I agree with you on that one. Sure is good beer. There's talk of Glenn Miller coming.' Harry told Peter. 'He's got permission to form a fifty-piece band and come to England to perform for us all. I hear at least eight hundred performances . . . if we can get in.'

'Sounds great, and I expect plenty of girls will be coming from all over Liverpool. You won't be able to move, never mind get to do the Jitterbug.'

'Well, Harry, we can always go to the Grafton or The Locarno, if we can't get in there. They say both dance halls get packed full.'

*

Having been trained in the maintenance and modification of aircraft, Peter and Harry sometimes had to make a journey of twelve miles or so, to the Rootes factory at Speke. Here, they would pick up spare parts and bring them back in the truck. This was something they looked forward to as there were hundreds of pretty girls working there.

On one of those days, they arrived when some of the women were having a break outside, and soon crowded around Harry and Peter asking questions.

'Why do they call you GIs?' asked a girl in an accent that was a little hard to understand. She spoke so fast!

'General Issues.'

'What's that mean then?'

'It's what they call our uniforms.'

The girls giggled 'better than our blooming uniforms.'

Peter was about to ask a beautiful girl her name, when a photographer arrived to take some shots of the factory. The girls stubbed their cigarettes and cushioned up to Peter and Harry and asked for a photograph of them all.

'Sorry I can't do that, ladies, I'm here to take photos of the factories.'

'Ah, go on . . . we could be in the papers.'

'I don't know . . .'

Harry had a word on his own with the photographer while they all looked on, still giggling. 'I'll be great to pin beautiful girls like the ones here on our lockers. Good for cheering us up on a cold morning. They're doing a fantastic job for the war effort. I'll pay you for the prints. Just leave me your name and address and I'll pick them up.'

'Okay, I suppose a few won't hurt.'

The photographer took pictures of the girls on their own stood outside the factory, and some with the GIs, with intentions of using the girls in the papers. As the airman said, the girls are doing a great job. When he was about to walk away to take more photographs of the factory, Harry called out, 'wait, just one more picture.'

He reached for two of the girl's hands, taking them towards Peter. 'Do you mind?' he asked the photographer, 'could you just take one more of me and my friend with these two lovely ladies before they go back inside.'

The four of them stood together with their arms around each other. The rest of the girls were laughing and whistling. The photographer got caught up in the laughter and kept snapping away. He shook hands with

Peter and Harry, giving directions to his office. 'Give me a week or two before you come. I have a lot on just now taking photos of the factories.'

'Sure will. Gee thanks.'

Harry turned to face the girls, but they were rushing back inside the factory. Each time they went after that day, both Harry and Peter had tried to catch hold of the two girls to ask them out, but they never caught sight of them again and presumed they worked shifts, neither did they know their names.

*

The time finally arrived when Peter and Harry had the chance to explore Liverpool and meet some of the people. They walked around the streets talking to the locals, trying their best to fit in.

'Hey, how are you doing with this crazy accent Harry?'

'Not good.'

'They speak pretty fast. Or could it be us Americans that talk slow, which has been said.'

'Yeah, they say we have a drawl. There seems to be a lot of Irish here.'

'At least we're at home with the Irish. There are certainly lots of them in New York.' Harry stated.

'True enough. I think just about everyone I know comes from Irish descendants.'

'Love the accent. The Irish never lose it, no matter how long they have been in New York.'

'True. Liverpool is quite some place, uh. Folk here are pretty friendly.'

'Sure are, and the girls are so pretty too.'

'I can't tell what their saying most of the time, but some of the girls over at the Rootes factory have Irish accents. I understood what they were saying.'

Peter laughed. 'What about this one Harry, I asked a guy where the bathroom was. Jesus, he looked as if I had gone out of my head or something. "A bathroom, did you say . . . bathroom? Why de yis need a bath?" It took a while for me to explain I needed to take a leak. "Ah yea need the toilet". He said.'

Peter and Harry felt proud walking through the streets, yet apprehensive. Most of the locals were friendly, but some were pretty hostile. 'Our guys are handing out stockings and cigarettes.' said Peter quietly. 'I'm not sure I would be pleased to be fighting a war while GIs were after my girl.'

'Me neither. Do you reckon they take off their wedding rings?'

'I'm pretty sure some do. We need to be careful. We don't want to be fighting the English too. The streets are full of our guys in their smart clothes, handing out stockings and chocolates to impress. That must be intimidating to the British soldiers.'

'Yeah, I picked a paper up this morning, reporting how it didn't take long for the Germans to make propaganda about this 'invasion of the Yanks'. They're scattering leaflets over those British soldiers out there fighting, gloating how the American's were at home with their women while they are away.'

'A good few guys have made remarks about the British already being into their third year of fighting before we took up arms.'

Peter and Harry took it all in their stride and said they probably would have felt the same had it been the other way around.

They did date a few girls, usually going out in pairs, nothing serious. One evening they were heading back to base, after walking two land army girls' home. The subject turned to the future and what they wanted to do when the war ended.

'I want to marry and have five kids. I love kids. I don't want one child who's without brothers and sisters like me.' Peter said seriously.

Harry neither laughed nor replied.

'You Okay Harry?

'No. I just don't wanna talk about kids; that's all.'

'Why not'

'Pete. Just leave it, will you.'

'The hell I will. We've been friends a long time. Jesus, you're like a brother Harry. Tell me what's wrong.'

'I can't have kids Pete.'

'Why, fer Christ sake.'

'Whether it was because Mom had me late in life, I don't know, but I used to catch every ailment going. One time I was in hospital with mumps, and there were complications. I was really sick. I wasn't to know while later, but the complications left me sterile.'

'Oh Jeeze, I'm sorry Harry.'

'The thing is Pete . . . at what point do I tell a girl I'm in love with, that I can't have kids. Anyway, let's forget it shall we. There's a war to win. The British have a great sense of spirit, and a good sense of humour too . . . Christ, they make a joke out of every Goddamn thing. They have nothing; they've lost their homes, not to mentions their loved ones. They have their food rationed and only eat as much in a week as we do in a day. Yet, they don't complain, and they laugh and sing. What spirit they must have . . . are we going the right way here?'

'Not sure, it's too dark; I can't see a light anywhere.'

'Yeah, well don't get too far in front Pete, or you might have to send a search party out looking for me.'

'What happens if there's a raid, we're in the middle of nowhere here.'

'We're in the middle of nowhere because those Land Army broads live on a farm, that's why. We've been walking for hours.'

'I can't believe I kissed a gal who milked a cow. I suppose it could be worse. One girl I spoke to said she used to be a rat catcher.'

'The one I kissed drove a tractor and shovelled pig shit. Jeeze'

'Harry'

'Yeah'

What if there's an air raid, I aint seen no shelters.'

'Yeah and we're unlikely to, after all, it was you who suggested we take a short cut. I just hope your Goddamn instincts are right.'

There was a short silence. The two of them looked at each other before starting to run. Out of breath from running and laughing they stopped for a rest. Holding on to a wall, they lit a cigarette and started to walk again. Just as they turned the corner a car pulled up beside them.'

'Put that bloody fag out, there's a war on here you idiots.'

It took some time before they realised he was talking about their cigarettes. They had been warned of this, but being out in the middle of nowhere, they thought it would be okay. The man got out of his car shouting, 'A fighter plane can spot the smallest of lights, including a cigarette. Put the bloody things out.'

Peter and Harry humbly apologised. Then asked the driver where the base camp was.

'You're walking the wrong way. I would say you were good and proper lost, boys. I'd give you a lift, but it's the opposite way to where I'm going, so best of luck.'

The driver gave them directions, warning them not to light another cigarette. 'And stay on the path. Otherwise you'll end up in Yorkshire.' He laughed and drove away.

Feeling like two little schoolboys being caught smoking behind the bike shed. They turned around and started walking back to where they had come from.

'How long do you reckon the fighting will last Pete? I feel sorry for these guys. They've had some pretty bad bombing here. I mean, look at the state of the place, Jesus, Liverpool will take some building back up again. Where do people go when their houses are blown up? I wonder when it's all going to end.'

'Now we're over here. It should be over pretty damn quick.' Peter laughed.

As if on cue they both started to sing at the same time.

'Over there, over there

Send the word; send the word, over there

That the yanks are coming, the yanks are coming

The drum rum tumming everywhere

So prepare, say a prayer.

We'll be over . . .'

'Oh Jesus, what's that? Oh Jesus Christ, Jesus, Harry, what do we do now. Someone's shooting at us.'

They took a dive to the ground as two men with rifles started towards them. 'Who are you? What're doing on my land? This is private property.'

With hands held high, and relieved the men were English and not Germans, Harry explained who they were and how they were lost.'

'We're on our way back to base. We were told to follow the path, but the field looked like a short cut.'

'Well, next time you should do as you're told and follow the path.'

'Sure . . . and we will sir.'

As Harry and Peter walked away, one of the men cursed "Fucking Yankee's" loud enough for them to hear. Harry turned around and Peter pulled him back 'Leave it Harry, their spoiling for a fight and we'll end up with a Court Marshall, as well being hit with the butt of a gun. Keep walking and don't look back.'

Another shot was fired, followed by laughter and Harry and Peter ran for their lives.

*

A month later, Peter, Harry and their friends sat at a table, watching the girls doing the Jive, looking sensational in pretty bright dresses, petticoats and bows in their hair. The atmosphere was terrific. The dance hall was full, and pairs of dancers showed off the latest dance crazes the GIs had brought over to England.

Harry stood at the bar waiting to be served when four beautiful girls walked through the door. He recognised two of them instantly. They were from the Rootes factory. He had the photographs of the girls back at the base. The barman drew his attention away and when he looked again, he couldn't see them. The dance hall, which he was told held thousands of people, swallowed them up. Rushing back to the table with glasses of beer in his hands, he whispered 'Pete, I have just seen the girl I'm going to marry . . .'

Peter laughed and was about to say something when Harry stopped him.

'Quit laughing. I saw her. She was beautiful . . . so were the other three. You remember the two girls we had our picture taken with . . .'

'Where'd they go Harry?'

'I don't know. They disappeared.'

'Probably to the bathroom, isn't that where all gals go when they walk into a dance hall? They might be here with some guys anyway.'

'True, but I'm gonna take a walk. You wanna come?'

'Sure.'

The boys sifted through the crowd from one corner of the room to another.

'Harry, how could we miss four beautiful girls? Are you sure they were together and didn't walk in separately meeting some guy . . .'

'There . . . over there. The four of them are sat around the table near the front.'

Peter saw them at last but couldn't decide which girl Harry had meant. They were all beautiful, but one girl stood out to him too, the one he was next to on the photograph. He hoped she wasn't the one Harry had claimed as his. They stood in the same spot for a while, looking, not really knowing what to do next. The Jives were replaced by a much slower beat and they made a quick step nearer to the girls.

'Harry, which one is the girl you're going to marry. I wouldn't want to step on your toes.' Peter asked, holding his breath. 'Is she the one in the navy dress? Go on Harry, tell me. Are we after the same girl?'

'The girl I'm going to marry is the one in the black and yellow dress.' Harry said confidently.

'That's settled then.'

'Here goes.' Clearing his throat, Harry stood by the table and introduced themselves, 'Hi, I'm Harry and this is Peter or Pete as I call him, would you care to dance?' he asked Helen.

Peter didn't waste any time either; he asked Kate if she too would like to dance. 'Would you care to dance with me?'

'As long as you don't throw me around' she laughed. 'I can't jive . . . well not like the ones on that dance floor.'

'Don't worry, I won't throw you around, I promise.' Peter said, smiling nervously. 'I can't dance at all. I was hoping you would teach *me*.'

Chapter 8

Dublin 1945

Amazingly, Alice was four years old. She had made it against all odds. Unfortunately, she was a sickly child and there were many times Molly thought Alice was going to die. She was a very quiet child, who was late in walking and talking . . . not that she spoke much, pointing to anything she needed instead of asking. At first, Molly thought Alice was deaf and dumb, as she didn't react to her name either. Molly blamed herself. From the second month of missing her period Molly had suffered morning sickness, dizziness, she was tired all the time and suffered terrible back pain. The constant urine infections plagued her for months at a time. She was convinced the baby was too low down and pressing on her bladder. She prayed to God the months would go by quickly. When the baby was born prematurely; her prayers were answered.

Molly had given birth to Alice four weeks early on Christmas day, just a week after Marianne left home. Like all tenement women, she was helped by Peggy O'Hara, who had delivered most of the babies in the Liberties. Peggy was no midwife, but a woman of a good age and experience. For a few shillings she would deliver the baby and take care of the mother and child for a few days after the birth.

On the day of the birth, Peggy had held the baby by her feet and slapped her hard on the bottom, but the baby wouldn't cry. Just as Peggy was about to deliver the sad news to Molly that the child had died, Alice's tiny face screwed up and she screamed loudly.

'Oh, sure to God she took her bloody time. But hear me out now Molly McNamara; I would pray if the child is going to die, then it be sooner rather than later. She was too long without oxygen fer my liking. Sure, yis won't want a mentally ill child to care for.' Peggy said, while swaddling the child in an old tattered blanket. 'Jaysus, the terrible stories I've heard about those institutions. Remember Maureen Sweeny's Baby? Lack of oxygen damaged the bairns head. Institutionalised he was.'

'I remember.' Molly said quietly. 'I wouldn't be letting my child be taken away.'

'You have to face the truth.' Peggy insisted. 'You need to give it some thought; now is there anything else I can do before I go?'

'No. I have Lillian here to see to the kids.' Molly said gratefully.

'In that case I'll be off. Don't forget to set a date for you and the baby to be churched. I'll come with you if you like. What are you calling her?'

'Alison. Alice, after me ma' Molly said softly, choking on her words. 'I wanted to call Marianne after Ma, but since the Irish tradition has it you call the first girl after your grandmother. Marianne it was.'

'That's true enough and the first boy is called after his da. Doesn't have to be; it's just a tradition, so how come yer first was called Patrick and not Joseph.'

'I don't know Peggy, but Joseph was insistent we called him Patrick and I was too tired to argue.'

'Tis very strange . . . but then *he* is very strange. Perhaps he changed his name at some point.'

Molly laughed, but at the same time wondered if it were true.

'I'll be off now Molly, be sure to stay in bed. I'll be back later this afternoon to check up on you. Lillian, make a pot of tea, now there's a good girl.'

When Peggy closed the door, Lillian sat on the bed stroking the baby's head. 'She's so tiny, just like a doll. Mammy, why do we have to be churched?'

'Churching is just another Catholic tradition, Lillian. I suppose the tradition is to introduce your child to the Church and receive a blessing from the Priest to thank God for a safe delivery of the baby.'

'But why do we have to have it, when we are christened as well.'

'Because that is what has been passed down to us. All mothers and babies are blessed by God and the Church. Some say it's like washing the sins away from childbirth. Jaysus, it's been happening fer years.'

'But what sins. A baby cannot have any sins.'

'That's enough now. I won't be going into the laws of the Catholic Church. Now, where's my cup of tea.'

Molly thought about what her daughter had just asked her. How could she explain that at one time childbirth was considered to be unclean and unholy; as it resulted from sexual intercourse?

Lillian obediently made Molly another cup of tea, taking the child from her mother's arms. 'She's beautiful Ma and she looks normal enough to me. Remember the time you told me about Nanny giving birth to a premature baby and strapping him to her chest.'

Molly nodded her head slowly, wiping her eyes with the bed sheet. 'Yes, I remember, and I'll do the same for my baby if necessary.'

Lillian placed the baby back in her mother's arms. Looking down at the tiny figure, Molly did indeed remember her mother strapping her brother to her breast. His name was Michael, and for over three weeks her mother gave the baby the warmth of her body and the smell of her milk. Sadly, the baby died at the age of four. He was a very sickly child and died from breathing problems. Still, if there was a chance, then she had to try and save her baby daughter.

Molly did indeed strap Alice to her chest in a sling. Day and night, she carried the tiny bundle while cooking, cleaning and sleeping, until one day she felt the baby was going to survive. Lillian had asked to take over for a while when she got in from school, but the baby needed the smell of her mother, just as animals do. It was just a matter of time before they would know if there was be any lasting damage, but Molly knew at least there was nothing wrong with her brain in the months she grew. As usual, Joseph had shown no interest in his new-born child and in the early months cursed her for crying all through the night.

*

Down at the wash house, Peggy O'Hara was scrubbing her clothes in a large tub, singing along with the rest of the women. However hard she tried; she couldn't get the blood stain out of her dress. Peggy looked up when she heard a familiar voice behind her.

'Good morning Peggy, you look like you're having a great time hitting that dress with yer knuckles.'

'Ah Jaysus, I delivered a breach baby this morning. Fer the love of God, didn't the woman realise the baby was about to arrive before going to the market. I could hear the poor woman screaming all the way down Francis Street. The child came out arse first. The screams from the mother left me with ringing in me bloody ears.'

'Oh, dear Lord, was the mother and baby all right?'

'The baby was fine, but the mother was torn to pieces. The ambulance came and took them to the Rotunda. Big baby too, poor woman.'

'You're the best Peggy, I wouldn't want anyone else deliver my babies.'

'And how are yis Molly. How's Alice doing these days?'

'She had a bit of bother again with her chest, but the fever has gone now. She gets better every year, and she's coming on grand, apart from her being small for her age.'

'And how're yis doing with the new baby growing inside of yer? You look tired woman, come and sit down. Here, take a chair. The baby looks as if it's about to drop anytime to me Molly, it's about bloody time you tied a knot in the auld fella's banger.'

'Now look who's talking, I've awhile to go before I catch up with yer self.' Molly laughed. 'How many is it that you have now? Eleven it was, when I last counted.' Molly teased. 'You're right Peggy, I am tired, Alice takes a lot out of me, she still hates to be away from her mammy. Me poor aching body is worn out these days, sure, I'm too old fer any more babies, but what can you do. Lillian is a great help. I don't know what I would do without her.'

'Yis have a good girl there Molly. Have you heard from Patrick and Marianne lately? Is Marianne still working in one of those posh houses in Portmarnock?'

'Yes, Molly answered. 'She's very happy there. I haven't heard from either of them Peggy, to be honest, but I suppose they're busy with work.'

'Where does Patrick live now? Sure, he's been gone some time.'

'He's working on a farm in Oath.'

In truth Molly had no idea where Patrick was now. He hadn't written to her since the first year of leaving. The letters were sent to Mrs O'Conner so Molly could keep them away from Joseph. At the time Marianne had written to her as well, but the letters stopped. The last letter was to say she was looking for somewhere else to live, but that was a long time ago, and now Molly had given up hope of hearing from them again.

Peggy looked at Molly's black eye. 'I see the auld fella's been at yis again Molly McNamara. What was it this time? Did yer not wipe his arse?'

'I slipped and banged my head on the step last week.'

'Yeah and I wish I had a penny fer the times I've heard that auld story.'

Molly knew even when saying the words Peggy wouldn't believe her. Peggy O'Hara was frightened of nothing and no one. She was a big hefty woman who took no nonsense, including from her husband. Peggy had been in court a few times for fighting, usually with men, but she had a good heart and was the funniest and most caring woman Molly knew. Peggy brightened up the washroom on the dreariest of days with stories of her life. Her husband was a much smaller man, who looked smaller still when they were together.

Peggy took Molly's face in her hands to look at the bruise and sighed. 'Yis should never have married a man so big, Molly McNamara; yis were asking fer trouble if you were to ask me. My auld fella wouldn't dare lay a finger on me . . . Jaysus let me sit a while, me bloody feet er on fire.'

She sat down and lit a clay pipe, 'I'll tell yis about the other day shall I. After dinner I saw him looking hard at the plates me auld ma gave to me. Didn't think much to it at the time, mind. The next day I was getting the tea fer the kids and saw my best china plates had gone from the shelf. Me ma had given me the plates when I married. They were the only bloody things I had that meant something to me. I never used the fecking plates; I was saving them fer best, sure I was. I bounced down to the pawn shop and asked 'Uncle' if the auld fella had brought in me plates. Of course, Uncle daren't say anything at first, but I think he saw the state of me and feared fer his life. "He'll be picking them up later today Mrs O'Hara." So, he said. Picking them up today? I say. I'll be picking him up, sure to God; I'll be picking him up from the fecking floor.'

Peggy stopped to relight her pipe and went back to her story, 'I gave the kids their tea before the auld fella left Dirty O'Dwyers bar. Calm as a daisy I was. He walked through the door smiling at me. Testing the bloody water, he was. He made a big mistake in thinking I wouldn't notice the missing china and sat at the table waiting for his corn beef and cabbage. I lifted the pan from the fire and scooped the food onto the table without a plate. I tell you now, he was lucky I didn't put it in the piss pot, but then I wouldn't want to waste good food, now would I. He looked up at my face, so he did, "what the. . ." Before he had time to finish the sentence, I pushed his head down into the mash and cabbage. That'll teach yis to pawn me best china, ye drunken auld sod, says I.'

Molly laughed, along with the other women who were listening. 'Did he eat the dinner?'

'Course he bloody ate it. He had to scrape it from his face first, mind.'

The women howled with laughter.

The wash room was busy and it took Molly a while to wash the clothes, making it late when she returned home. She walked wearily up the flights of stairs carrying the tub of clothes, thinking Joseph probably thought she was with another man, pregnant or not, jealousy has no logic. She was no sooner in the door when he started.

'Where the hell have you been woman, I've been waiting fer me tea. A bag of chips I had.'

He picked the greasy paper from the table and rubbed it in Molly's face. Retching, she wiped the grease from her face with the sleeve of her coat.

'Have the kids had anything to eat?'

'No, you stupid bitch, the kids haven't had anything to eat because their mother deserted them. Where the hell have yis been?'

'I'm sorry Joe, the washing took a while today and it was very busy, so I had to wait my turn. I didn't have Lillian's help. Someone has to look after the kids. I couldn't take Alice with all the dampness around, her chest being as it is.'

'Should have let the brat die, you stupid cow, she's going to be sick all her fecking life.'

'How can you say that? 'The child's right there in front of yis,'

Molly turned her back to walk towards the fire to make a cup of tea, and he grabbed her by her hair, dragging her down to the ground. She tried to protect the child with her hands and realised she had fallen face down on a bucket. A panic went through her when she felt a lurch inside her abdomen. A trickle of water ran down her leg and she screamed out in pain.

Mrs O'Conner had known of the beatings, so had the rest of the tenants, but no one interfered between a man and his wife. This time the screams were different. The sound was that of an animal. Mrs O'Conner rushed up the stairs and barged in through the door just as Joseph was walking out. He pushed his way through, knocking her to the ground.

'You bastard, Joe McNamara, you strike me again and sure to God I'll have you murdered in yer bed. Coward you are, beating helpless women and children.'

'Ah Jaysus you old interfering wan, shut yer fecking mouth afore I shove me fecking boot in it.'

'Yeah, you should try . . . Oh, Mother of God. Are you all right Molly? Is the baby coming? I think I need to go and bring Peggy O'Hara. I won't be long. Lillian, get some water from downstairs and bring some to the boil on the fire ready for Peggy.'

Twenty minutes later, Peggy O'Hara hurried quickly up the stairs, almost knocking over Delia O'Brian along with her bucket of slops.

'Jaysus woman, look where yer going Peggy O'Hara. You almost killed me with fright, not to mention sending me head first down the stairs into a bucket of shite.'

'Oh dear God Delia, I didn't see yis there. These bloody stairs are so dark yis wouldn't see a fecking thing.

Peggy came rushing through the door, cursing Joseph in his absence, and threatening to lay him low as soon as she got a hold of him. She could see Molly was in great pain and although she had been there for all of her pregnancies, had never heard her cry so.

'Hush now Molly. Let me take at look.' Peggy O'Hara's face suddenly went white. The baby was obviously dead, but stuck in the uterus, and

Peggy was shocked to feel another baby moving inside the womb trying to make its way out. Realising Molly needed more help than she could give her, she told Lillian to call an ambulance.

Mrs O'Conner offered to go with Molly while Lillian stayed at home with the children. It was by the love of God they arrived just in time to save Molly's life. Three hours later Mrs O'Conner was back to tell Lillian her mother was well. She decided not to go into details of Molly's terrible ordeal.

'Your mammy will have to stay in hospital, but the doctors managed to save the other twin, a boy, and both are doing well.'

Lillian sighed with relief, yet saddened by the death of one of the babies. She held on tightly to James and wished Marianne was here. Marianne had never bothered to write to her, which upset Lillian a great deal. Perhaps, she could visit her sister, if she knew where she was staying. Even in service, surely there'd be time to write a letter. Lillian had heard some of the posh houses in Dublin gave little time off to their workers, but even so, it wouldn't take much to write a few words. *What if she were dead?* How would they know? Then there was Patrick out there somewhere too. Maybe they lived near to each other. Maybe he was dead. It had been a long time now and her mother never spoke of either of them.

Things had gone from bad to worse since Marianne left home. Her father often threatened Lillian time and time again not to think about leaving.

'That sister of yours should be bringing money into the house now. And so should you, you lazy cow.'

'I have an interview next week at three of the factories. I only left school a few days ago Da . . .'

Her father smacked her across the face and she put her hand over the stinging. Tears welled in her eyes.

'What sort of excuse is that?' Her father said piercingly. 'You should have looked fer a fecking job before you left school.'

'I did, in-between school and looking after the kids.' Lillian spat, knowing he would hit her again. His son and daughter had left home, he knew nothing of their whereabouts and all he was bothered about was the money he was losing.

Lillian had her mother's looks, with red hair and a tiny dimple in her elf like chin, but she was the one who often stood up to her father and suffered the most smacks around the head. Now her mother was in hospital once more; beaten by the man who promised to look after her for the rest of his life, in sickness and in health. She rubbed her face where it hurt and carried on giving her young brothers and sister a slice of bread with a little scraping of the butter which was left over.

Lillian desperately wanted to see her mother, but she was needed here. Alice was a frail child and looked much younger than her years, with her thin, fine hair which never seem to grow. She had a sweet and loving nature, but hardly ever spoke. Lillian had tried to coax her to play with the kids in the neighbourhood, but she clung to Lillian's skirt, crying over the slightest of remarks, which made it easier still for the other children to tease and make fun of her.

It was almost midnight when Lillian heard the sound of her father coming up the stairs singing an Irish Rebel song. He had a good singing voice, and at one time the neighbours used to love to hear him sing; sitting on the door step on a summers evening with the rest of the tenants. The song he was singing now was about a father in search of his son during the 1916 uprising, whom he feared dead. The song was called The Dying Rebel. Lillian thought of how ironic was the choice of song. As if he would cry if his son had died. His only thought would be of the money he was going to lose for his stout. The singing stopped and he almost threw the door open.

'Where's me wife, where is she?'

He could see the disgust on Lillian's face and glared right into her eyes. Lillian didn't move an inch.

'I said, where's yer mammy? Are yis deaf?'

'She's in hospital. She lost one of the babies.'

'One of the babies, what the hell is yis talking about?'

'She was carrying twins and one *died*.'

'Twins, Jaysus, don't we have enough kids in this house fer God's sake. When is she coming home?'

'I don't know Da. Is that all you can say.' Lillian screamed loudly. 'You murdered your own child and almost killed me ma.' She jumped out of bed and lunged towards him fisting him in the face. 'You big fat drunken bastard.' He stood still and laughed. Lillian continued thumping him and screamed, 'I hate you . . .'

Before Lillian could say another word he knocked her on the floor with one almighty punch. Immediately, she felt a lump already swelling around her eye from the blow. Looking up at him through her tears, she saw her father with a grin on his face. He started to quickly unbutton his trousers and suddenly he was on top of her.

'Nooo Da, please no.' her cries were stifled by his hand over her mouth.

The pain was excruciating; she gasped for breath, but his arm was pressed on her neck holding her down. The smell of his foul breath made Lillian want to vomit.

When it was over, he stood and fastened his trousers, calling her a dirty cow before climbing onto his bed. Within minutes he was snoring. She looked at Alice, who was now sat in the corner of the room beside the slop bucket; her eyes were wide and unblinking. She was traumatised for the second time in a day. The boys slept tightly as always, used to hearing shouts.

Lillian struggled to pull her dress down over her hips, and felt a trickle of blood run down her legs. She was bruised and battered and frightened for herself and Alice. *What if he was to do that to her?*

'Dear God, Alice, come over here.'

Alice was sobbing and choking on her tears and it was an hour before Lillian settled her down. Full of anger, she filled the kettle to boil water, so she could wash herself, and stood over him, watching his chest move up and down with each snore. It would be so easy to kill the bastard while he slept. The kettle was about to whistle. She took it off the fire, held the boiling kettle over his head, her hand shaking so much she had trouble holding on to it. Across the room, she could see Alice watching her. Putting the kettle down, she whispered; 'another time you bastard.'

Lillian cried silent tears for her mother all night. How could she tell her mother her father had brutally raped her . . . in front of Alice . . . while she lay in hospital, once more fighting for her life? Lillian decided she couldn't tell, it would only cause more problems and her father would only deny it.

*

Molly was home from hospital and looked well, considering the pain she must have gone through. The baby was named Laurence and he was beautiful. His hair was as black as coal and he was the image of Joseph and Shaun. Laurence took to his feeds without any fuss and within a few weeks was sleeping through the night. He hardly ever cried and was a real pleasure to Molly. Surprisingly, Joseph asked to hold him one day, looking down on him with pride, something he had never done since Patrick was born. Molly smiled inwardly as she remembered the day Joseph saw Patrick for the first time. His eyes had filled with tears. Joseph was a proud Dad, eager to hold him and show him off to friends.

Molly sighed and wished her marriage had been like her parents. They were happy all through their married life. She knew there was a much kinder side to Joseph, there were a few times when she saw real love in his eyes for her. Molly blamed the stout, but deep down she knew there was something much deeper. He wasn't normal. Perhaps he had something wrong with his brain; something triggered off by alcohol. How could a person change so much from the charming man she had first met, into the monster he was now. Why wouldn't he ever talk about his childhood?

Chapter 9

Dublin 1946

Four months had passed, and Lillian still hadn't had a period. At first, she was in denial, even when she felt sick a few times in the morning. She couldn't and wouldn't accept the fact she was pregnant. Having never been with a boy, or ever been kissed, she was still a virgin in her mind. She had lain awake night after night, trying to work a plan out in her mind. *Perhaps she could hide her weight; her clothes were usually two sizes to big anyway, but if she could get away with that . . . which she wouldn't, what then? Murder the child? The thought of throwing herself in the Liffey had also crossed her mind.* There was no way out, she had to tell her mother she was pregnant. She decided to wait until they were walking down to the wash house, but the plan was taken out of her hands when this time she couldn't hold the vomit back, and rushed to the bucket to be sick.

'Are you ill Lillian? Or is this morning sickness?' Her mother said with an angry tone to her voice. 'When did you last have a period?'

'Mammy, I'm so sorry . . .'

'I didn't even know you had a boyfriend, you never go out anywhere other than on the street to play with friends. You're only fourteen years old Lillian for God's sake . . . who's the father? You'll have to marry him; you know that, don't you?'

'I . . . can't'

'Who is he? Answer me Lillian. Tell me, for Christ sake.'

Lillian burst into tears. 'I can't tell you Ma, please don't make me.'

Molly smacked Lillian across the face. 'You will tell me . . . and quick, before your da gets home.'

'I can't Ma, I can't. I can't' Lillian cried.

She knew her mother wouldn't believe her now, after all this time, and sure to God her father would never admit to raping his daughter while his wife was fighting for her life in a hospital. Lillian's body racked with sobs, and Molly calmed down a little. She asked Lillian if the father of the baby was a married man. Lillian nodded a yes and Molly hit her again 'You're disgusting. You've brought shame upon this family.'

Lillian fled the room and ran out onto the street.

Molly stood in shock, holding Laurence, who was crying from all the shouting. *Think Molly, think.* She would have to contact Father O'Byrne and see if he had any suggestions of what she should do. Perhaps the priest could find out who made Lillian pregnant. Lillian would surely tell the truth to Father O'Byrne, sure to God he wouldn't give up until she did. *What about Joseph?* How was he going to react to this? *He would do what he does best and beat the truth out of her.* Molly realised she couldn't bear the thought of her daughter being beaten. She needed to get Lillian away as soon as possible before telling Joe. *Where?*

When Lillian returned, her eyes red from crying, Molly cradled her in her arms and wiped her face. 'I'm sorry Mammy, but I can't tell you, please don't be ashamed of me.'

'Lillian, please tell me the truth, did someone force himself on you?'

Lillian didn't reply and Molly's suspicions were right. But who would do such a thing? This was a good neighbourhood. She hoped Lillian would trust her enough to tell her when things had calmed down, but for now, she decided to keep the news of the baby from Joseph while she had a word with Father O'Byrne.

Cover yourself up with this shawl and we'll go to the church. The Father there will know what to do. We have to get you away, Lillian.'

*

Father O'Byrne had only one suggestion, which was more of an order rather than a suggestion, and the same answer Molly would have expected

82

to receive from any Catholic Priest. Lillian would have to go into a home for unmarried mothers and suffer the consequences. There was nothing else Molly could do. Moving Lillian into a home needed to be done immediately.

The priest returned after a phone call he made in the next room holding a piece of paper in his hand. 'Take this address, you can take Lillian there this afternoon' Father O'Byrne ordered Molly. 'They are expecting you both. So be off with you.'

Molly had no choice but to agree with him. She knew she had to get Lillian away before Joseph and the neighbours found out.

Rushing home from the church, Molly dreaded the thought of telling Joseph, but she would think about that later when she got back home. For now, all that mattered was Lillian's safety.

Peggy O'Conner was looking through the window and wondered where Molly and Lillian had been with Laurence in the pram. She had a funny feeling inside of her about this. Something was amiss. Such a strange family, the McNamara's were. A son and daughter disappear, and Molly pretends they're working in Dublin, yet they don't come home to visit. Joseph beats the hell out of his wife and no doubt his kids, and Molly stands up for him. The two boys are always out the way, hardly ever being seen and the girl, Alice, pretends she can't speak. But she *can* speak. She has visions and see's dead people.

'Jaysus, hadn't she kept asking me about Jimmy.'

'Why do they call you Mrs O'Conner when you don't have a Mister O'Conner? It's because he's dead, isn't he?'

'Yes, he is Alice. He died two year after we married. He died from Tuberculosis, t'was a long time ago.'

'I know, he told me. There's a little girl with him, he held her up for me to see her in my dream. She's very pretty.'

Mrs O'Conner gasped, 'Alice . . .'

'He says he's happy Mrs O'Conner, he asked me to tell you he didn't feel anything when he passed over to the other side.'

The other side 'Oh, my dear Lord' Mrs O'Conner sobbed, making the sign of the cross. 'Listen to me carefully Alice. You must never talk to anyone about seeing the dead or mention words like the Other Side.'

'Why?'

'Because people are frightened of things they don't understand, and you could be taken away.'

'It's just a secret between you and me Mrs O'Conner. You always listen to me.'

'Does your mother know?'

'Yes, but she doesn't listen to me.'

'It may be that she's frightened Alice. Please be careful.'

Mrs O'Conner's thoughts were broken when Molly walked through the door with Lawrence in her arms. 'Peggy, would you mind looking after Lawrence as well as Alice for me while I take Lillian into the City. I had a letter from my aunt in Galway. She broke her leg and has no one to look after her and seeing as Lillian has left school now and doesn't have a job, she's going to care for her a while. Who knows . . . she may find a job there, sure, there no work here.'

'I would love to look after Lawrence, sure to God, isn't he my God son.'

Molly laughed 'You're the God mother to the last four of my kids, Peggy O'Conner and heaven knows what I would do without you.'

Peggy O'Conner could swear there was a break in Molly's voice. Something was wrong but she was sure, but she knew in time, Molly would tell her the truth.

*

Molly and Lillian caught the bus to the mother and baby home. They sat silently most of the way there. 'Are you going to tell me who forced himself on you Lillian, it may make things easier for you in the home if you tell the truth.'

'I can't tell you. I wish I could.'

'But you may be treated badly if the Sisters think you had . . . if you . . .'

'If I had sexual intercourse with my consent, you mean.'

84

'Yes. I'm only thinking of you.'

'I know you are, but you can be assured I didn't give my consent.'

The rest of the journey was spent in silence.

*

'Well, here we are. I can't see much of the outside because of the fog. Come on Lillian; let's make a move to the front of the bus before we miss our stop.'

The bus drove off into the distance, leaving Lillian and her mother to walk the rest of the way. Bus stops were few and far between on country roads, but by the look on the rest of the passenger's faces, they knew where Molly and Lillian were bound. There was an eerie quietness around the area. Not a sound from traffic, a human being, a bird, or a tree rustling, nothing. As they approached the home for pregnant girls, Lillian clung to her mother's side looking at the high walls and big iron gates. It was a damp and foggy day to add to the sadness. The large tall building looked dark, grey and dismal as it loomed in front of them. From where they stood, they could just about make out the shape and size of the institution. There was a foreboding heaviness all around.

Molly rang a bell, which was on the outside of the gate, and a few minutes later a Nun came hurrying down a long-gravelled path towards them. Lillian's heart started to race. She felt bile rising in her throat and feared she would be sick. Terrified, she watched the stern looking nun unlock the padlock to let them in, locking it again behind them without a word being spoken. The building loomed nearer, looking much more threatening and sinister. Lillian shivered and pulled her mother's old grey shawl, the one she had given Lillian to hide her pregnancy, tightly around her head and body.

Walking obediently behind the nun in morbid silence, Molly finally spoke. 'When the baby is born and after the adoption, you can come home again Lillian, and perhaps get a job in one of those grand houses in the City as a domestic. The little one will be brought up by a good family who weren't blessed with having a child of their own. The baby will be loved and well cared for.'

'What will people think of me when I go home again Ma?'

'I will tell the neighbours you are staying with an old aunt of mine who needs help while she gets back on her feet again after having broken her leg. I'll tell them she lives over in Galway. I will tell your father the same thing.'

Molly followed Lillian as they walked through the heavy wooden doors carrying the paper bag which contained all the processions Lillian had, which was very little. Trying to fight back the tears, Molly remembered the stories at the Iveagh wash house. Stories of what went off in places such as this, but there was nothing she could do.

Following the nun into a dark dismal, cold corridor, Lillian noticed all the windows had iron bars on them. She was also suddenly aware of an uncanny eeriness in a building of such stature; there were no sounds to be heard. Without speaking, another nun came out of an office to usher them into the room. Behind the large desk, was yet another nun, who Lillian assumed must be the Reverend Mother, and beside her, sat a Priest. Neither of them acknowledged Molly or Lillian as they walked towards the desk, until the priest motioned to them to sit down.

Without any eye contact with Lillian at all, the Priest addressed Molly. 'My name is Father O'Flaherty; we have a few formalities we have to deal with now before you leave, Mrs McNamara.'

He asked a few questions which were directed to Molly, ignoring Lillian, and finally passed some papers to be signed. Molly obediently signed the papers with tears in her eyes. Immediately, the Reverend Mother stood and told Lillian it was time to say goodbye to her mother. The parting was brief, and Lillian was called inside, hardly having the time to wipe her tears as she sobbed and waved goodbye.

Chapter 10

Joseph usually made a big entrance when walking through the door after work, almost throwing himself inside the room. Today was different; he walked through the door and flopped in the chair, and he was early. Something was wrong. Had he already heard about Lillian? Who could have told him? No one knew apart from Father O'Byrne and he wouldn't have told Joseph. Not after she'd begged him to let her be the one to tell Joe. She poured him a cup of tea from the water which was already boiling on the fire, and passed the cup over to him with a slight tremor in her hand.

'Is everything all right Joseph . . .?'

'No, it isn't fecking all right. I'm finished, I lost me fecking job at the docks.'

'Oh Jaysus, what happened?'

'What happened? What happened? Does it matter what happened. It happened, now get out of me way woman, fer fecks sake.'

'Shaun, take Laurence, James and Alice down to Mrs O'Conner. Tell her me and yer da has to talk.'

Molly forced a smile at Alice who looked terrified. Her heart ached for her daughter. She didn't chatter like other children or show any enthusiasm for play. To outsiders she appeared slow and much younger than she was, but her intuition and ability to 'know' certain things, both amazed and frightened Molly.

Molly gently ushered the children towards the door and tried to reassure them she wouldn't be very long. They were good and obedient children, but sadly, their good behaviour came from fear. Alice walked behind Shaun, and shot her father an angry look, staring into his eyes with disdain. Joseph was about to jump from his chair, when Shaun quickly snatched Alice's hand and dragged her out of the room.

'Jaysus, I'll kill that fecking retard one day. Evil she is. Did yis see how she looked at me? Where's Lillian. Why isn't she here to look after the kids? Is the lazy cow out looking fer work?'

'Joseph, I have something to tell you. It may not be the best of days for you. . .'

'Fer Christ's sake Molly, are yis going to fecking tell me or . . .'

'Lillian's pregnant.'

'Pregnant? Are yis telling me she's pregnant? Jesus, she's fecking fourteen years old fer Christ's sakes. Who's the father? I'll break every fecking bone in his body.'

'She won't say who the father is Joe, I begged her to tell me . . .'

'Where is she? Where is the little whore? I'll break every bone in *her* body, sure to God I will. Where is she, woman . . .? Are yis deaf? I said tell me where she is?'

'She's in one of the Magdalena homes.'

'When did the whore go there? How long have you known about this? '

'I only knew me self a week ago and she's not a whore. Someone forced. . . I never noticed how much weight she had put on until then, what with her wearing her coat most of the time, and the only clothes she had from the market were always two sizes too big. I . . .'

'Where is she? Which home?'

'I took to the Sisters of . . .'

Joseph didn't give Molly the chance to finish the sentence before knocking her across the room. She felt a trickle of blood running from her head and was grateful Lillian wasn't here; he would certainly have almost killed her and the baby. The force of his fist caused ringing in her ears. His voice sounded far away.

'She won't be setting foot in this house again; she's no daughter of mine. A whore she is, a fecking whore. Who else knows fer Christ's sake? Are you deaf, I said who else knows?'

'Only Father O'Byrne' Molly replied, raising herself from the floor. 'He made all the arrangements.'

'How far pregnant is she?'

'I'm not sure; I would guess it could be as much as four or five months.'

Suddenly Joseph stopped talking and seemed to be thinking about something. Molly thought perhaps it was just the shock of realising his daughter was pregnant. He had every right to be angry; wasn't she also angry herself? However, that changed when Molly realised she had been forced upon. She wasn't angry with Lillian; she was just an innocent fourteen year old girl. Rape or no rape, this would have caused the whole neighbourhood to look down on the family, and Joseph would have taken his belt to her to find out who the father was. She knew for certain there would be no coming back home for Lillian. Joseph would never let her through the door again. At least she was sure the Sisters would take care of her and hopefully keep her there until they could find her a job with lodgings.

Molly tried to think who the father could possibly be. She had never as much as seen Lillian talk to a married man, other than in a greeting. Lillian was even shy around boys her own age. Her blood boiled with rage as she thought of how the man who did this to her would just carry on with his life as normal, never giving Lillian another thought.

Molly bathed her eye in tepid water and walked towards the window. She wasn't going to give Joseph the satisfaction of seeing tears rolling down her cheeks; tears for Patrick, Marian and Lillian, and poor Alice. The sound of Joseph's voice brought her back from her thoughts.

'Are yis listening to me woman? I asked fer another cup o tea. What's so interesting outside that yis have to be looking through the winda? Expecting someone are yis?'

'No, I'm not expecting anyone Joe, and yes I heard you. I'll pour the tea and then I'll bring the kids up.'

'Does she know?'

'Who'

'Mrs O'Conner. I hate that fecking woman. Why de yis have to go running to her. She knows too much.'

'No, she doesn't know and sure to God I'd be at a loss without her help.'

Joseph lay on the bed and Molly went down to Mrs O'Conner's to face the music about her having another swollen eye. Alice walked over to Molly and slipped her hand in hers. 'Mammy, Da is going to kill you.'

'No Alice. My eye looks worse than what it is.'

'But he is Mammy. He's going to kill you. I saw him kill you in my dream.'

'Now that wouldn't surprise me.' Mrs O'Conner muttered. 'Holy Mother of God,'

'She has a lot of dreams.' Molly explained, 'Alice never sleeps through the night, she's always tossing and turning. Take no mind of her.'

'How was Lillian when you saw her off?'

'She was fine and looking forward to a change.'

'No she isn't mammy, she's . . .'

'Stop it Alison McNamara. Stop it now. Sorry Peggy, I have to be going. Thanks for having the kids.'

'Yer welcome. Did yous have the talk?'

'Talk'

'Shaun said you and Joe wanted to talk.'

'Ah, sure we did. It isn't easy to talk with the noise of four children. I'll be off now.'

Mrs O'Conner watched Molly walk up the stairs, holding the baby. A dark aura hung over her. Something was going on. 'Dear God let those kids be safe and Molly too.' Mrs O' Conner said a prayer for Molly and her children.

'God bless molly dear Lord. All the stress and pain the poor woman has been through. Forty two years old, only two years older than me self and she looks like a fifty year old at times. Please protect her dear Lord and the children too.'

Mrs O'Conner began the Rosary. Tears ran down her face as she prayed with all her heart.

Chapter 11

The Reverend Mother ordered Lillian to follow her, telling her what to expect in the home. 'You will share a dormitory with girls in the same situation as yourself until after the baby is born, you will then be moved across to the mother and baby quarters nearer the birth. After the birth, you will moved again and stay there for three years to feed and look after the baby, until the child is fostered out or placed in an orphanage. That is, unless the baby is adopted of course. However, I must stress that we take great pride in our adoptions, and only allow a perfectly healthy child to go out to the new parents.'

Lillian gasped. 'Three years. Did you say three years?'

'Yes Lillian, three years, maybe even longer than three years. You should have thought of the consequences of the five minutes pleasure you had. You'll be asking yourself if it was worth it, sure enough over the coming years. Now where was I? You will work in the fields or in the laundry before the birth, and carry on doing the same after the birth, besides seeing to the baby's need. You will not visit your baby at any time other than when it is feeding time. There will be early mass each morning as from tomorrow, and we expect prayers throughout the day for your sins.'

'But Sister, I didn't do anything wrong. I was . . .'

'Oh don't give me the old sob story. I've heard it all before. You have brought great shame on the church as well as your family. Your soul is stained and so is the baby's.'

Lillian wanted to cry out, "I did nothing wrong; it wasn't my fault. I'm innocent." But she knew she had committed a mortal sin in the eyes of the church, whether she was innocent or not. Lillian had seen girls in the Liberties rejected by the Church, their parents and society. Was this to be her fate? Her mother didn't tell her she was to stay for three years. Is that what the papers were her mother had signed? She suddenly realised she would not be going home. Her mother didn't have an aunt, at least not one known to her, and her father would have known she hadn't. When her mother tells him about the baby, he will beat her. Lillian fought back tears, unable to swallow for the lump in her throat. She had been rejected by her mother. She had lied to her. If she couldn't go home, then she may be here all her life unless she could find a job and a home to go to, and who's going to just offer her a job.

'You put Da before my life Ma. You imprisoned me for protecting you. I will never forgive you for this as long as I live.'

'Are you listening to me?'

'Yes Sister, I am listening.'

Lillian was passed on to another nun, who led her to the room she was to share with eleven other girls. She introduced herself as Sister Mary Geraldine, and sounded more like a man than a woman, her voice so gruff. She pressed a bundle of clothing into Lillian's arms. She followed the nun out of the office into the dark hallway, heading towards a long wooden staircase. There were big wooden doors to both sides of Lillian and some of them had bolts across, which she thought was strange. The only reason a bolt would be on the outside was to lock someone in.

She was shown her bed and the nun handed her the rules of the house.

'Read the rules. Put these clothes on and bring the ones you're wearing down to my office at the bottom of the stairs.'

The sister left the room and Lillian sat on the bed which was so thin she could feel the springs coming through. She opened the parcel of clothes and was shocked to see a pair of large knickers made of course material. Just the look of them made Lillian's skin start to itch. She opened out what she thought was a brown sack in the same fabric to discover the sack was a dress. Holding it against her body, she saw the dress was far too big. There were other bits of clothing including a white apron and a cap. Lillian started to take off the only clothes she owned, placing them neatly on the bed.

There wasn't a bra in the parcel, and Lillian assumed you wore your own. Ironically, Lillian had only just started to wear a bra the week her father took her virginity, it was one that had been passed down from her mother to Marianne and then to her. She was almost finished dressing when Sister Mary Geraldine walked through the door. Lillian passed her clothes to her.

'Where is your brassiere? Did you have one on when you came here?'

'I have it on Sister; there wasn't one in the parcel of clothes you gave me.'

'That's because you won't be wearing one. Your breasts will be bound. That is what the strap of cloth is for. Now go and take it off and bring it back for fumigation . . . quickly, child.'

With the long corridors and high ceilings, the whole building was freezing cold and Lillian shivered from head to foot. She'd passed a few girls on the way down the stairs and noticed they all kept their eyes down, avoiding eye to eye contact.

Lillian was taken to the laundry; a red brick building which was dark and humid with boiling cauldrons over hot fires. Steaming tubs of water filled the air with dampness. Laundry hung from the ceiling on washing lines. There were baskets of bedding and dirty clothes smelling of vomit and God knows what, making Lillian gag. Looking around the room, she saw girls with red faces and sore hands, slaving away over wet soggy heavy linen. The girls were reciting the Rosary, over and over again. She compared the laundry to the Iveagh; where there was cheerfulness, laughter, and singing. The wash house she saw in front of her now was filled with gloom.

On the way to the Laundry, she had passed heavily pregnant girls scrubbing the wooden floors on their hands and knees, using hot steamy water and carbolic soap; still, no one looked up and smiled. Everyone was quiet and miserable. Lillian didn't really know what to expect, but when they said she was going into an institution, she expected it to be noisy with so many girls being in one place.

Looking around the room for a friendly face, unaware of what was being said to her, the Sister in charge gave Lillian a sharp slap and told her to pay attention. Lillian faced forward while she was given instructions to rub and scrub the dirty clothes with her knuckles using salt to get rid of stubborn blood stains. The nun plunged Lillian's hands into the vat of clothes and Lillian let out a scream; the water was very hot on her freezing cold hands, and unexpected. The nun slapped her across the face again, but this time with such force that Lillian fell to the floor. Although she received a few sympathetic looks from the other girls there, no one said anything.

It wasn't too long in the day before Lillian found out that most of the dirty laundry came from prisons, butchers and institutions across Ireland, and were often badly stained with congealed human and animal blood and faeces. One of the rules was the girls were not allowed to speak to each other at any time. Lillian made her way upstairs to the dormitory and felt uplifted a little when the girls came over and introduced themselves. They warned Lillian not to talk back to the sisters.

'Do what you have to do Lillian, tis hard, but you don't want to be punished all the while or they'll be forever on your back. One of the sisters walks with a stick and is prone to hitting us with the fecking thing so watch yer self with her . . . and avoid looking at her, she doesn't like that unless she's speaking to yis.'

'What about the baby inside' Lillian protested. 'Punishment could kill the child.'

'Jesus Christ Lillian, sure the child is the spawn of the devil. Do you think they care about harming an unborn baby for God's sake?'

'Some of the nuns here started like us and went into the Holy Order when they realised they were here fer good, and as true as God is my word, sure, they are the worst ones.'

The following morning, Lillian was taken to a room to be examined by the midwife, Nurse Carey, who seemed a welcome change to the sisters. Lillian guessed she was in her late twenties. Her face was soft and kind; with high cheek bones and skin so pale she looked ill. The Nurse's hair was scraped back under her cap, with the odd curl that had fallen down. She had a lovely smile which helped Lillian relax for the first time since walking through the gates, apart from being with the girls in the dormitory for a few hours a night.

'You're a bit young to be coming into a place like this. How old are you?

'I'm fourteen.' Lillian said shyly, full of shame.

'Jaysus, you only look about eleven or twelve years old. You don't look the eager type to me, were you taken advantage of?'

Lillian was surprised by this remark. Nodding, she burst into tears.

'I see it all the time.' The Nurse said softly. 'Young girls being lulled into a sense of love and security with a boy, giving her promises of love and marriage, only to disappear once the girl mentions she's pregnant. To be sure, there are girls who have been forced into giving themselves to boy against their will, but it's never the boy who gets the blame. On the other hand, it could be a lodger or a family member, but the girls don't tell, it would only make it worse for them. The sisters here wouldn't believe it; they'd say the girl encouraged them.' She held Lillian's hair in her hand. 'You have beautiful hair; you do realise they will cut it very short, don't you?'

'No,' Lillian shouted, holding the locks of her hair, 'Why? I don't have nits anymore.'

'It's nothing to do with nits. If you did have nits, then your hair will be shaved; beautiful long hair is cut because it's a sign of vanity, the same as having your breasts strapped up tight. It's only because the fecking Nuns have to hide their own tits.'

Lillian stifled a laugh.

'Anyway, after working in the laundry you'll be glad of short hair.'

Lillian thought of the washroom and realised most of the girls did indeed have cropped hair, some had even been shaven. She started to cry.

'Come on now Lillian, I'm sorry if I upset you, but it's better if you know now so it isn't such a shock when it happens, just as all the other girls had to. Life here is tough, Lillian, very tough, and the more you show your emotions, the harder the sisters will come down on you. They do not tolerate tears.'

'I want to go home.' Lillian cried.

Nurse Carey felt sorry for the young girl, wishing she had kept her mouth shut for once. 'Listen, the stronger you are, the easier it will be for you here.' She passed Lillian a cloth to wipe her eyes 'Lillian, I'm only telling you these things to prepare you. You have to be brave. I didn't mean to upset you about your hair, but at least if you know, then you won't be nearly as upset on the day. Just sit and accept it, that way they won't be as rough. It's only hair Lillian, and it will grow back. Now let's take a look at you.'

Lillian shivered as she lay back on the cold aluminium trolley. Whether she was shaking from fear or the sheer coldness of the metal, she didn't know. The nurse examined her and asked questions about her health. Her hands were cold on her abdomen, and though the nurse apologised, the coldness went through her whole body and she shook even more.

'This place is very cold most of the time, but you get used to it eventually. The summer is just as bad in this dismal place.'

'But you don't have to stay here Nurse. Why not leave if you're unhappy?'

'I intend to when the time is right. I never get any sunshine here, hence my pale complexion. Now let me listen to your heart.'

Lillian stared at the ceiling until she put the stethoscope down on the chair beside her. 'Everything seems fine, although it seems to me like a very big baby you have there.'

All of a sudden there were screams coming from downstairs and a lot of commotion. Lillian covered her ears with her hands.

'One of the girls, Mary O'Rourke' said Nurse Carey 'she had to part with her baby today; you'll soon get used to those cries I'm sorry to say. After all this time here, I still hate to hear it. For three years Mary has loved and cared for her son, Kevin, but even though the mothers know one day it will happen, they still try to hang on to their child.'

'Oh dear God, that's terrible. Where will this baby, Kevin, go? Is he going to be adopted?'

'Sadly no, he's going to Foster Parents for a while and then he will go to an orphanage. Only the healthy, good looking babies get to be adopted and they won't allow babies to stay here after the age of three.'

'I don't think it will bother me when I have to leave my baby.'

'Oh, I see. You were raped.'

'I . . .'

'Its fine Lillian, you don't have to tell me, unless you want to. I'm a good listener. However, you will still grow to love your baby, even before it's born, believe me. Anyway, its time you were back at work. Be off with you now.'

Chapter 12

The months dragged by slowly, and Lillian's hands were sore from scrubbing in hot water; the knuckles of her hand were hard where the skin had rubbed away. For ten to twelve hours a day they worked like work horses in the laundry, except for Sunday, when they went to Mass and had the rest of the day off. Occasionally, someone would vomit in the laundry room and the sister in charge would hit the girl on the back with her walking stick, yelling at her to clean the mess away. It was also a regular occurrence for a girl to feel faint from the heat, but they still had to work regardless. 'Pregnancy is not an illness.' They would hear time after time.

In the evening, the girls were forced to knit baby clothes, sitting in a circle without speaking a word. If not knitting, then some girls would be making Rosary beads. Lillian, along with everyone else making Rosary beads, had tiny cuts from the thin wire that blistered and oozed with pus. But no one cared. They were here to be punished and pray for their sins, which was made clear daily. The word 'Penitence' stood boldly in the corridors in big lettering. She soon began to realise that as far as the nuns were concerned, unmarried mothers were the scum of the earth.

Lillian looked forward to her visits with the nurse. They chatted and laughed together, and Lillian could have a little moan now and again. The nurse always had something funny to say, and even mimicked a few of the nuns, leaving Lillian with an aching jaw from laughing. Sometimes she talked about her life on the outside, her days off, her family, and the films she had been to watch at the Plaza.

'Can I just tell you something' Lillian said quietly, 'I'm a little nervous about the delivery now it's getting nearer, and I've heard some terrible tales from the other girls.'

'Everyone else is terrified too, so don't let them fool you. I arrange my days off around the girls who I think are ready to give birth. My room is next door and has a latch that opens to the labour room. I'm near at hand for you. All you have to do is knock on the latch. On the few days I am off duty, the Reverend Mother takes over. She and a few more have experience in midwifery.

'Oh no, I hope I don't get her delivering my baby.'

'They're very experienced midwives Lillian, but you won't get sympathy. You'll be all right. Just remember, it doesn't last forever, and it'll soon be forgotten when the baby is handed over to you. One thing you must not do is give cause to rile the Reverend Mother. Each and every time she'll say, "Is all this pain worth the five minutes of pleasure?" Jaysus, sure, I'm sick of hearing those words. When I was new here a young fiery girl from Sligo screamed back. "Not five minutes Sister, I had an hour of pleasure, you should try it yer fecking self sometime." The girl was slapped across the face, and the delivery of her baby was taken over from me.'

What Nurse Carey didn't tell Lillian was how the Reverend Mother literally tore the child from her. After the birth the girl was locked in a room. Milk was drawn from her breast for the baby to be fed from a bottle. Soon after the birth, the girl vanished, no one knew what happened to her, but the baby stayed for three years before being fostered out. Chances are the girl died from infection to the uterus. She was torn quite badly.

'Is there no one to help Nurse . . .? I mean, couldn't you have reported her or something.'

'Ah no, who the hell is interested in the girl's fer God's sake, they have let the Church and Society down. Nobody cares Lillian. The girls make money for the Church, slaving away twelve hours a day and more without a penny to their name. The only thing that would happen is, I would lose my job and good jobs are hard to find.'

100

Like everyone else, Lillian had her hair cropped short and was beaten with the walking stick a few times, usually for speaking without realising one of the sisters was present. As her pregnancy progressed, her breasts were enlarged and sore from the rough material used to bind them tightly. She was suffering from back pains and had itchy skin all over her body. Her hands and feet were swollen and she was so tired.

As it neared the final stage of her pregnancy she was still working, but had been put on lighter work, which meant working all day in the kitchen. Unlike the rest of the building, the kitchen had windows, which unfortunately, were covered with bars and opening them for fresh air was impossible. The sun burned through the glass and the steam from the cooking made the kitchen unbearably hot. There were many times when Lillian almost collapsed from the heat, only being allowed to sit down with a glass of water for five minutes before being told to get on with her work. The meals were cooked for the Sisters, while the girl's meals were little more than bread and margarine, or bread and dripping, with a handful of watery mashed potatoes. Once a week they were allowed an egg. Breakfast was watery porridge and a slice of bread.

Nurse Carey was beginning to feel concerned about Lillian's pregnancy. She had been complaining of blurred vision, headaches, itchy skin and feeling tired. Her face, hands and feet were swollen, and she had raised blood pressure. Being a midwife for eight years, she had witnessed women who had died from a condition called Preeclampsia Toxaemia, and was certain Lillian was suffering from this. Plucking up courage, she asked the Reverend Mother if she could have a doctor to do some tests, but she refused. Indeed, of all the years she had worked at the home, she'd only seen a doctor on two occasions. There had been many deliveries where the baby had died unnecessarily from complications, simply through not having a doctor on standby. Nurse Carey wasn't even allowed to give stitches to the poor mothers who were badly torn during childbirth, or even hand out a simple aspirin to ease the pain and soreness. It was almost as if the Reverend Mother enjoyed seeing these poor girls suffer.

There was nothing she could do other than be there for them and bring the aspirin in herself to give them sometimes if she thought the girl needed pain relief. Nurse Carey was merely classed as a worker and nothing more and had learned years ago not to question the Sister's actions. She knew Lillian should really be resting, but there wasn't the slightest chance of that happening.

*

Lillian started having severe pains at the bottom of her back, and the Sister in charge sent her to the Nurse to see if she was in labour. Holding on tightly to the wooden banister, she almost crawled her way there. Nurse Carey immediately ran to her aide and asked how long she had been having pain.

'Since 3.00 clock this morning, but I thought it was backache . . . I mean, don't you have a belly ache when you're in labour? I saw Mammy holding her belly when she was about to give birth . . . oh! Nurse, I've peed myself, the Sister will kill me.'

'Your waters have broken.'

'What's that mean?'

'Oh Lillian, don't you know anything about giving birth.'

'No,' she sniffed, 'I was always sent out once I'd put the water on to boil and prepared the bed with newspapers and old sheets.'

The Nurse explained to Lillian what the procedure was and asked her to lie on the trolley to be examined. Lillian moaned when she felt the coldness of the trolley next to her skin. 'Is the baby ready to be born now?'

'You have a long way to go yet, the baby is not ready for being born, I'm afraid, but the labour has started. You have to be brave now Lillian; it may be a long time before the baby is ready for coming into the world. The length of Labour pains differs from one person to another.'

Lillian started to think what she had said to the Nurse when she first arrived, about not caring for her baby; but since living with the innocent child inside of her, feeling her growing and kicking; she realised she'd loved her. Lillian was convinced it was a girl and had chosen a name for her, which only Nurse Carey knew of. How was she going to part with her now? Lillian felt she had already bonded with her child before she was born and talked to her when she was alone. She had seen friends have their babies literally ripped from their arms for adoption, and then there were the ones

102

who nurtured and loved their babies for three years, before they were taken away. The mothers often doing without the measly rations of food themselves to give to their children, who cried constantly from hunger pains.

For hours Lillian had sat with the girls, knitting little baby clothes, reciting the Rosary until the sister left the room. Once she was out of hearing, they would all talk and make plans of escaping with their child. Of course, it was all fantasy. Where would a mother and child go once they fled the building? The Gardaí would soon bring them back and the girl would be severely punished or sent away to another institution. Lillian had wondered why the girls would want to try and do such a thing in the early days. Now she knew why and wanted to keep her child. The healthy bonny babies were adopted almost straight away. Her father was a good-looking man, but she hoped her baby wasn't going to look like him.

The pains became stronger causing Lillian to cry out, and Sister Assumpta charged through the door. She was the worst of all the sisters, and Lillian had heard many stories of how brutal she was in the delivery room. Nurse Carey was the only midwife at the home and when she had a day off; it was down to the sisters who were trained in childbirth, including the Reverend Mother. The girls prayed their baby wouldn't be born on the day when the nurse was off duty.

Sister Assumpta stormed over to Lillian, slapped her hard across the face. 'Stop that wailing, I could hear you down the hall. I won't have this kind of behaviour. Do you hear?'

Tears ran down Lillian's face and she wished her mother was here, even though she could never forgive her. When Sister Assumpta left the room, the nurse gave her a rag to put between her teeth to muffle the sound. Fifteen hours passed and Lillian still wasn't anywhere near ready to deliver the baby. Nurse Carey was worried. After another three hours, there was an almighty cry from Lillian, and the nurse ran down to the office to ask Sister Assumpta if she would consider bringing in a doctor.

'There's complications Sister, her blood pressure is very high and I'm concerned she may have a seizure . . .'

'Knock before you enter this office in future, don't come barging in here like that ever again Nurse Carey. I heard you running on the corridor. We do not allow running in this house. Now leave and I'll be there in a few minutes.'

'But Sister, she's started to hallucinate. I've read books on this condition when I was studying midwifery, and it can cause the mother to go into a coma. If she has a seizure, she may suffer brain damage or die. We need to get a doctor to take a look at her. The baby will be in distress and is greatly at risk of dying too.'

'How dare you tell me what I should do, I've been delivery babies for thirty five years. I'll be there shortly, now get out of my office.'

There was nothing more Nurse Carey could do other than hold Lillian's hand and reassure her she was doing well, but the young girl was becoming more delirious as the night wore on.

'Nurse, there are people in the room, can't you see them? Little people and they are all talking at once; please ask then to go away.' She cried. 'I have to tell you nurse, come here, I have to tell you.'

Nurse Carey bent down beside her, Lillian said in a whisper. 'It was me da . . . it was me da who raped me . . .'

Lillian began to drift in and out of consciousness, seeing people in front of her, lots of people. Little people, not from this world, all dressed in white.

'No, no, Nurse, he's coming for me . . . he's here.'

'Lillian, listen to me, you're hallucinating. You have a very high temperature and . . . well it won't be long now before the baby is born.' She examined Lillian and could see the baby's head was showing. 'It'll be over soon; on the next big pain I want you to push real hard.'

Lillian screamed and pushed with the little strength she had, just as Sister Assumpta walked through the door.

'All this fuss Nurse Carey. If you can't manage the job, I'll get someone to take your place.'

'But Sister, she isn't out of danger yet . . .'

All of a sudden there was another scream and the baby arrived. Sister Assumpta held the baby by her legs and slapped hard, but there was no sound coming from the tiny girl.

Nurse Carey tried to stop Lillian falling into a coma. 'It's a girl Lillian; she looks like you. She's so beautiful Lillian.'

Sister Assumpta shot the nurse a look and said. 'Well, let's hope the child doesn't turn out like her. She will have to carry the sins of her mother all her life as it is.'

The nurse ignored the remark and gently took the child from the nun's arms, placing the baby on the trolley, next to Lillian. 'Here's your little girl, Lillian.'

'Hello, my little sweet, you are so beautiful, and I will always love you, wherever you are. I have a name for you; I'm going to call you . . .' A fierce pain ravished her body. She heard someone calling her name. "Lillian".

'Mammy, she screamed loudly. Oh Mammy, I knew you would come to take me home . . .'

The room was noisy again and Lillian was aware of panic around her. Then silence. She knew she was dying, she felt a numbness creeping up her body. A bright light appeared to be floating around the room until it hovered above her and grew brighter still. Soft, warm images of lovely people began to form. Lillian turned towards Nurse Carey . . . her friend, the only one who she could talk to, and smiled sweetly.

'Sister' the nurse shouted. 'She's slipping into a coma . . . I can barely feel her pulse.'

'There's nothing we can do now. That child isn't looking too good either. She hasn't cried or made a sound. Too much birth trauma, she's probably brain damaged. Put her on the table next door and don't try to revive her. Better she dies for her own sake. *Nurse Carey*, are you listening to me, put that child in the next room this instant.'

Nurse Carey was used to delivering dead babies; she was also used to babies dying within a short time after birth and beyond. This time however, she held the child in her arms and looked down on her with an ache in her heart. The poor mother of the child was dying, a victim of her own father's lust; a young girl who might have been saved with the right treatment. For the first time in her career, Nurse Carey cried.

Chapter 13

Dublin 1950

Five years had passed and life without Lillian was lonely. Molly missed Marianne and Patrick, but she and Lillian had grown so close since they had left home. Alice tried hard to do the jobs Lillian had done, but she was weak and sickly compared to all her other children. Her dreams were becoming more regular and they frightened Molly. Only a few days earlier, Alice was staring into space when she suddenly whispered: 'I saw Lillian last night, she comes to see me sometimes.'

'Lillian didn't come to see you. Sometimes your imagination runs away with you Alice. Lillian is living with an aunt of mine and has found a job in Galway. You know that.'

'No she isn't in Galway. I saw her in my dream last night. She's not here . . .'

'That's all it was Alice, a dream. She's happy.'

'She wasn't happy, but she is now, Mammy. She said I have to tell you she forgives you.'

'Alice. That's enough now. Go and play, and don't be talking like this in front of anyone else.'

'Mammy, Lillian said it was Da . . .'

'Alice, that's enough. You do not talk to anyone about these dreams; including Mrs O'Conner. Do you hear me?'

'Yes, but Lillian told me I was going to be hurt, Mammy, and it was .
. .'

'Alice, Stop!' Molly screamed loudly, setting Laurence off crying and Alice too. 'You never listen to me' cried Alice through her sobs.

'I'm sorry Alice, but I worry about hearing you speak of dreams as if they were real.' Alice didn't reply to her mother, there was no point. She would tell Mrs O'Conner later.

Molly raked the ashes, thinking of what Alice had said. She was too frightened to hear the rest of the dream. Was Alice going mad? Had the lack of oxygen at birth caught up with her? *Dear God, please help my child.* Perhaps Mrs O'Conner was right saying Alice had the gift, but Molly wasn't going to encourage her. She was just a child who was having a hard time at school as it was without everyone calling her a freak.

*

Molly was cutting cardboard to fit into Shaun's shoes to cover the holes, when suddenly she thought of Marianne. She'd made cardboard cut-outs for her the day before she went into hospital. Molly smiled when she remembered Marianne admiring the shoes the nurse had given her, and how thrilled she was when they fit. Marianne was right; if she had come home from the hospital with those new clothes, especially the woollen coat, they would have been pawned the following day.

Having Joseph home during the day was hard for all the family. He had a job, but was fired again, this time for swearing at the foreman. Shaun and James were hardly ever indoors. Laurence was constantly up to mischief and a real danger to himself, while Alice followed her around everywhere. Then there was the struggle of trying to feed everyone. With Joseph being out of work they were living off bread, potatoes and whatever scraps of meat Molly could get from the butchers with the money from the Vincent de Paul charity. Joseph took most of the cash in the excuse of looking for work, which was usually in a bar hoping to meet up with someone who knew where there were jobs going. All the jobs he'd ever had were from someone who he'd met in a bar.

'I need to go into the City Alice. I won't be long.' said Molly, reaching for her coat.

'I'm coming with you, mammy.'

'Alice, I won't be very long, I need to try and find a little job so we can eat.'

'But Mammy, I'm frightened. Please take me with you. I can help you.'

'I can't take you. Da will be home soon, and you have those picture books from Mrs Braun to look at.'

'But Daddy *will* hurt me. He *will*. He hurt Lillian, she told me.'

'He won't hurt you Alice. He has never raised a finger to you, or Lillian, so don't talk that way . . . and don't be such a baby.'

'Why can't Shaun stay with me?'

'He's potato picking for a few hours and he's taken James with him. You didn't want to go, remember. I'm only going for an hour or so, fer the love of God. Please don't make it hard for me. Mrs O'Conner is watching Laurence and if you need anything, she's only downstairs.'

'Can I stay with her?'

'No, she's enough on with Laurence. You're old enough to look after yourself now, you're almost ten years old. I won't be long, I promise.'

Thankfully, one of the stall holders took pity on Molly. He let her take over the selling while he stocked the empty baskets with fresh fruit and vegetables for a few hours. She was exhausted, even though it *was* only a couple of hours, but she had made enough money for food for a while. She had been feeling really tired and hoped to dear God she wasn't pregnant. The bus home was just pulling away, which meant she had to walk. The bags were heavy with the vegetables the stall holder had given her, and she almost fell through the door when she arrived home.

'Oh my God Alice, what's happened? What is it?'

Alice stared into space, her face was white and she was sucking her thumb, something she had grown out of years ago. Molly bent down to lift her into her arms and cried out when she saw blood on her dress. Was she having her first period? She lifted her dress to see where the blood had come from and gasped in horror when she saw Alice had red marks on her inner thighs. Gently taking Alice's dress off, she could see bruising coming through, in the shape of what seemed like fingerprints. Someone must have held her down. Her daughter had been brutally raped, or at least sexually abused.

'Alice, who did this to you, Alice, please. You won't be in trouble, you have done nothing wrong, please tell me.'

But Alice was in shock, and Molly didn't know what to do. Where was Joseph? He should be home now. 'Oh dear Lord, what do I do, will someone please help me.'

She'd started filling a bowl with water to clean Alice, when Joseph walked through the door.

'Oh Joseph, something awful has happened.' Molly yelled frantically. 'Alice has been raped or abused and she's in terrible shock. Who would do such a thing to a child? Look at her. She's traumatised Joe, she can't speak. She's only nine years old, fer heaven's sake. She's just a child.'

'Raped? Let me get my hands on the bastard. Has she told you who did this to her?'

'No. I told you. She won't speak. She's in shock Joe, and I'm not sure if she will ever be the same again. Whoever did this to her, hurt her. She has bruises all over her body.'

Joseph bent down beside Alice. She neither moved nor flinched but stared into empty space. *Molly was right,* Joseph thought; *she wouldn't be able to say who had raped her. He'd also threatened her not to tell. If she stayed this way, then he might be able to make a bit of money from this. Although he would insist they are gentle with her, not like him. She is so fecking fragile, you only have to look at her and she gets nervous.*

'Who did this to yea Alice? Tell yer da and he'll sort him out.' He said, stroking her hair.

When she didn't respond, Joseph stood to turn and walk away, going on about getting the person who did this to her and how he was going to sort him out.

Molly suddenly felt a rush of vomit rising inside of her. Joseph had blood on his trousers near to his crotch. Her mind raced, *'Oh Jesus. Lillian! Is that the reason his face changed colour when she told him Lillian was four or five months pregnant? Is that why Lillian wouldn't tell her who the father was?'* Molly's breathing was rapid. She had to think. Her legs suddenly felt weak and she could feel herself falling.

'Jaysus, sit down woman before you fall down fer Christ's sake. What the hell is wrong with you? She'll get over it, give her a wash and I'll be back in an hour. I have to see a man about a job.'

The door slammed and Molly was left shaking. Alice. She had to think of Alice. She started to clean her down and wept at the size of the bruises where she had been gripped. Alice said nothing and was oblivious to what was happening. Her body limp, her face pale, she made no attempt to make eye contact with her mother. How could Joseph say she would get over it, after he'd raped his own child? *What was wrong with him*?

Putting a clean dress over her head, Molly noticed a bruise around her lips, where he had obviously bit her. 'Alice, listen to me. I'm going to take you downstairs to Mrs O'Conner's. Now, I'm going to have to tell a few lies. If anyone asks, you tripped over something on the stairs and fell head first. They won't see the bruises on your body with your dress covering your arms. We wouldn't want something like this to get around the neighbourhood . . . at least not yet. I know what happened, Alice, and I will do something about it, I promise. This will never happen again. I'm going to make sure your da is locked away in Mountjoy prison for this, but I have to see Lillian first.' She held her daughter tight 'I'm so sorry I left you. I'm sorry for not listening to you. Don't give in Alice; we need to get through this once and for all.'

Molly needed proof, and she wasn't going to put her already traumatised daughter through an interview with the Gardaí. Raping your own daughter was unforgivable in the community, but she knew the Gardaí would believe Joseph if Alice couldn't tell them what had happened. He would lie, saying he'd only just arrived home. She could see him now.

'No sir, I was at Flannigan's bar, there'd be plenty down there who would vouch fer that now sir. Raping your own child? Jaysus, I would never do such a thing sir. I love my kids.'

'Lillian. I have to speak to Lillian.' She said out loud, 'If I tell her about what happened to her little sister, she'll speak up. He'll go to prison and

Lillian and the baby can come home. I won't protect his reputation either. People will know the truth.'

Molly half walked and half carried her child down to Mrs O'Conner's. She had thrown a change of clothes in a paper bag in case Alice started bleeding again. She knew she would have to tell Mrs O'Conner the truth when she got back home.

'I'm sorry Peggy, but could you watch Alice and Laurence for a couple of hours. I have to go somewhere, but I promise I will tell you why when I get back. Alice is suffering from shock. That's all I can say for now. Something terrible has happened.'

Mrs O'Conner agreed and took the child's hand. Go off widcha Molly, I'll take care of her.'

When Molly left the house, she asked Alice if she would like a drink of water. She didn't reply and seemed strange, but she was used to Alice and her strange ways. She had the gift all right. There was something special about Alice. Peggy O'Conner never mentioned to Molly all the other things Alice had told her. Alice was a natural, and when she spoke of the dead, or told her of the premonitions she'd had when sleeping, her voice was that of a much older child, and not the child who couldn't communicate very well. A shiver went through Mrs O'Conner. Something very bad had happened. She suddenly felt Molly was in danger.

*

In a dreamlike state Molly boarded the bus for the Magdalena home, giving her time to think. Passengers looked at her as she cried almost all the way there. When the bus drove away leaving her stood by the bus stop, she walked up the country lane until the large gloomy building came into view. The last time she was here it had been foggy, but without the fog there was still an eeriness and coldness to it. As Molly pressed the buzzer on the gate, she thought back to the day she brought her daughter here and the fear on her innocent face. *'Poor Lillian, I wasn't there for you. Oh, why didn't you tell me? I'm so sorry. I'm a terrible mother.'*

'What do you want at this hour of the day and why are you crying.' The nun shouted, unlocking the gate.'

'I need to see my daughter; I have to see her. Something dreadful has happened.'

'Stop babbling and walk this way. We do not tolerate emotions here, so clean your face with this cloth before the Reverent Mother sees you.' The Nun snarled, passing her a handkerchief.

The Reverend Mother sat behind the desk and Molly recognised her from the day she brought Lillian here.

'Sister, I have to see my daughter, something has happened. I believed she was raped . . .'

'Oh, fer pity's sake isn't that what they all say. It's never the fault of the girl is it? They're the ones who entice men in the first place, flaunting their bodies. What's her name?'

'Lillian. Lillian McNamara.'

The look the Reverend Mother gave the nun who had opened the gate, didn't go unnoticed by Molly.

'I'm sorry Mrs McNamara, but Lillian isn't here anymore. She's moved on. This happens after the baby is born.'

'Moved to where? Where is she, where's my daughter.'

'I'm afraid I can't tell you.'

'Why? Why can't you tell me? I have to see her, I want her home.'

'You signed a contract when she was admitted here, pity you didn't read it; I have a copy if you'd like to be reminded of what it was you signed for. She can't just go home because you've changed your mind.'

'But she can come home now and so can the baby, I'll take care of them. I didn't know what I was doing. I brought her here for her sake.'

'You did it to protect yourself from scandal, like all parents do. You should have thought hard about it before we made the agreement. Now it's time you were on your way. We have Mass in ten minutes. Goodbye Mrs McNamara.'

'But, but, did she have a girl or a boy? Has the baby been adopted, or does she still have it? Will Lillian be home soon? The baby is welcome; I'll take care of the two of them.'

'Good bye Mrs McNamara. Now leave before I call the Gardaí.'

Molly was shown to the door and as she left the building, she heard the piercing sound of a scream. It sounded like someone shouting for their mammy. Molly thought the scream may be Lillian calling her. Perhaps she had seen her from a window. Molly ran back to the house and into the Reverend Mothers office without knocking 'I heard her shout out to me. She's here, isn't she?'

'For goodness sake this is where they give birth, of course there's screaming. It wasn't your daughter. She had her baby almost three years ago, now go away.'

The Reverend Mother shut the door behind her, and Molly followed the nun who led her back to the gates, keys jangling as she walked. She had noticed the time she brought Lillian here, that all the nuns seemed to have a bunch of keys hanging from their Habit and wondered at the time why they needed so many. A shiver ran through her body. She could hear the sound of a girl calling out again. *'Mammy.'* but she was too far away from the building for it to be coming from there. Was Lillian working outdoors? The shout came from the grounds at the back of the house. Molly needed to see the priest. He will know how to get Lillian home, especially when she told him the truth.

The Reverend Mother watched Molly walk down the gravelled path towards the gate and hoped that would be the last of her. Lillian McNamara was buried in an unmarked grave in the grounds, alongside the other girls and babies who had died in the home.

The day after Lillian's death, the Reverend Mother had spoken to Nurse Carey. 'You just keep quiet about this. The girl wouldn't have been saved with or without a doctor. Preeclampsia is the biggest killer in childbirth, very few mothers survive, and you know that.'

'Yes I do, Reverend mother.'

'I will deny any allegations Nurse. I will not take the blame. You were meant to be looking after the girl; after all, you are a midwife. I could say it was neglect on your part, now who will they believe, a Nurse or someone of the Holy Cloth?' the Reverend Mother said facing the window with her back to Nurse Carey 'You will be gone from here without a reference and as you know jobs are very hard to find these days.'

'Yes, I do. Please may I leave now, I have a girl who is about to give birth.'

'You may go.'

'Thank you, Reverend Mother.'

Chapter 14

Molly decided to leave Alice and Laurence a little longer with Mrs O'Conner, she was sure she wouldn't mind.

Joseph was already home when she walked through the door. 'Where the hell have you been? I'm waiting fer the milk fer me tea and where is that mute of a daughter, still in outa space. I told you she would end up a retard. Who's to say she was raped. She might have done something to herself for all we know, she's fecking stupid.'

Molly picked up the bread knife, which was lying on the table and stabbed Joseph in the back, screaming with rage. 'You raped your own kids, you bastard; how could a man do something like that? But then, you're not a man, are you Joe? What is it with you? Were you raped and beaten? Did someone mess your head up . . . you coward? Isn't that what cowards do . . . beat up women and kids and think they have a *right* to rape their own daughters. Who abused you, Joe? Was it your mother or your father? Did you enjoy it?' Molly screamed, still sticking the knife in his back.

She stood back, still holding the knife, ready to strike again if he came anywhere near her. Joseph recovered from the shock, stared at Molly in disbelieve and snatched the knife from her hand. Molly realised at this point she hadn't had the strength to push the knife deep enough inside his body. She had only given him a flesh wound. Joseph stood and smacked her hard across the face and she fell to the floor.

'You fecking stupid bitch, think you can hurt me do yis. Yes, if you must know, I raped me own kids, asking fer it they were. Whores, just like their mother.'

Molly scrambled to her feet and started belting him with her fists. He lifted her up into the air by her throat. The last image of her husband was not the tall handsome man with the beautiful blue eyes she had fallen in love with, but an ugly, unshaven monster who had a sickening look on his face. 'Alice.' She whimpered. Joseph let go, her limp body falling to the floor.

Sheer panic rose in his throat. He was crying and frightened. He didn't mean to kill her. 'Oh Jaysus, I'll go to jail for this. Molly, Molly, I love you. I'm sorry Molly, wake up, I didn't mean it Molly. Please wake up, I'll be better, I'll give up drinking, I promise, please wake up Molly.'

Molly was dead and Joseph paced up and down the room crying. This was the first time since running away from home, he was frightened. How was he to get away with this? He knew Alice wouldn't talk and he didn't mean to hurt her, she just wouldn't be still; she was like a wild cat, just like her sister. He hardly touched Molly since Laurence was born; he was too frightened of her getting pregnant again after the last time. What was he supposed to do? He hated fat woman. They reminded him of his mother. He had to think about how to get rid of the body; any idiot could see this was no accident.

What if he told the Gardaí he saw a man running down the stairs as he walked up? He could say it must have been the same man who raped Alice. 'He must have come back Sir. Perhaps he was trying to silence Molly before she told the Gardaí who raped Alice. Not that she could tell sir. My daughter's a mute most of the time, she doesn't speak.'

No, that wouldn't work, what if they were to question Alice and use an expert to get the truth. She can speak, but chooses not to, not when he's there. She knew things; he could see how she looked at him with disgust. He sometimes heard her talking in her sleep to someone. Her voice was different. Then there's the other one, what if they go and see Lillian. He had to get rid of Molly's body.

Joseph had an idea; he could get his auld mate, Mike, to lend him his brother's horse and cart and take the body to the peat bog. He owed him a few favours; it was because of him he had lost his job at the docks. Stopped a fight, he did, when Mike was getting the worst of it, but not before pinning the man to the ground while Mike stuck his boot in. The man had to be carried off to hospital and the Gardaí were involved. Instant dismissal the two of them were given.

He wrapped Molly's body in a blanket from the bed; at least there was no blood. Shaun and James would be back soon. Alice and Lawrence were probably with Mrs O'Conner. He had to act fast, but how could he carry a body down all those stairs without being noticed. There was always someone going up and down, and how was he going to explain where Molly was to the kids.

He put Molly's body in bed and covered her with blankets only minutes before Shaun walked through the door with James.

'Yer mammy is asleep; she isn't feeling too good so leave her be. Go downstairs and bring Alice and Lawrence back from Mrs O'Conner's; Alice had a fall and is still a bit sore. Get straight to bed when you get back. If you disturb yer mammy, I'll take me belt to you, do you hear? I'm going out but only fer an hour.'

Shaun and James knew they had to do as they were told, but couldn't understand why their mother was asleep before they were, and assumed she was ill again. They were greeted with a smile when they knocked on the door of Mrs O'Conner's, but Shaun sensed something was wrong when he looked across the room to his sister. 'What's the matter with Alice? Is she all right? She looks funny.'

'She had a fall down the stairs.' Answered Mrs O'Conner, and Shaun knew she had been crying, something he had never witnessed before from their loving neighbour. 'The child hasn't spoken a word, she's just sat there sucking her thumb and staring at the wall. The poor child is in shock. Where's yer mammy.'

'She's asleep and da said not to wake her.'

Mrs O'Conner paced around her the room. *Should she take a risk and call the Gardaí. What if Molly really was asleep, she had shown signs of tiredness lately. The Gardaí would think she was sticking her nose in other people's affairs and Joseph would take it out on Molly.*

Meanwhile, Joseph had gone to Flannigan's bar to see if he could get hold of Mike, while there was still time to get the horse and cart from his brother, who delivered coal and turf. Luckily, Mike was there, and this saved Joseph from going into one bar after another. 'Mike, I need a favour. An auld mate of mine is giving me a mattress fer the kids. I need a horse and cart to pick it up before he lets it go to someone else. Can you get Shamus to lend me his horse and cart tonight, to give me an early start in the morning; I'll have it back in time fer his rounds sure enough.'

'Yeah, I owe you Joe, sorry you lost yer job. I hear the bloke had a shattered jaw; he was in a bad state. I shouldn't have stuck the boot in like that Joe, it wasn't a fair fight. Shouldn't have done it, he has nine kids.'

'Yeah, well it's done now. I need the horse and cart Mike. I have to get back home to me kids, I don't know where Molly is; she went out this afternoon and hasn't come back yet. Molly isn't herself. She's gone all weird on me and hasn't the patience with the kids anymore. She lost her temper with Alice and buggered off.'

'Sometimes they go like that Joe, something to do with hormones or something every month. She'll be back. Where else could she go?'

They walked over towards the Strands to see Shamus. When Mike explained what Joseph needed the cart for, he gave his brother a gentle nudge, 'He'll have it back before eight, ready for your rounds.'

Shamus rubbed the bristles on his chin, undecided. He didn't like Joseph McNamara and wondered if he'd be okay with the horse, but then he knew he had lost his job a while ago, though he didn't know why; other than he had stood by Mike for some reason or another. Mattresses were hard to come by and he didn't want Joseph's kids to be without just because he didn't like the man.

'You'll have to pick the horse and cart up from here; I can't leave the horse on the street all night. Jaysus it won't be there when yis wake up.'

'No problem,' Joseph said, I'll come and pick it up in the early hours and the horse will be back in its stable before you wake up. Thanks Shamus.'

Returning home, Joseph wasn't going to wait while morning. The kids were fast asleep huddled together on the mattress. The kids very rarely woke up during the night, apart from the retard. He gently lifted Molly's body from the bed to carry her downstairs and was surprised how light she was.

A thought suddenly crossed his mind. Sometimes tramps slept at the bottom of the stairs. Doors were never locked in the tenements, and the tramps would wait while everyone slept before curling up for the night. Occasionally, a tenant would leave bread and a bottle of cold tea out for them. Joseph just hoped there were no tramps on the stairs tonight, if so, he would have to sort them out at the same time. Nobody would miss a tramp.

With Molly over his shoulder he struggled down the stairs. The stairs were so dark he was frightened of dropping her and waking up Mrs McNiff, who missed nothing day or night. Joseph dropped Molly's body behind the privy building, covered her with lumps of stone and went to get the horse and cart. The streets were quiet and he soon returned home and managed, without being seen, to put the body in the cart, along with a spade, and set off to the peat bog.

'Why did it have to fecking rain? And why is this stupid mare so slow fer God's sake?'

Joseph unfastened the belt from his trousers and whipped the horse on the back end. The horse neighed loudly, obviously not used to being hit and moved more quickly as if trying to run free from the cracks of the belt. Eventually, Joseph reached a good spot on the peat bogs. Of course, he would have to clean the horses legs before taking it back; even though it rained there wasn't a good reason to explain why the wheels of the cart and the horse's hooves were full of mud. Joseph smiled at his clever thinking.

He could hear the sound of the waves crashing in the distance and wondered if it would be easier just to dump her body in the sea, but then wouldn't the tide just carry her body back again. Better if the tide was going out, but he couldn't wait.

'Jaysus, why the hell did yis have to strangle her? How would you explain to the Gardaí why she had bruises around her neck?' He shouted to himself, 'any idiot would know someone depressed was likely to commit suicide by throwing themselves off a cliff, and *that* could explain the injuries.' He decided it would be safer just to bury her.

The rain lashed down and the cold wind bit hard into his skin. He found a good spot to bury the body close to a wall where it was unlikely anyone would walk. He was as wet from sweat as he was from the rain. A clash of thunder made him shiver, followed by a bolt of lightning which lit up the sky for a few seconds. His torch was playing up and he cursed, banging it in the palm of his hand. Joseph stood for a while, looking down on the hole he had dug out.

'Holy Mother of God, I must have another three feet to dig. Just as well the ground is soft from the rain.'

Wiping his face on his wet sleeve, he wished he had a dry piece of cloth to wipe the rain and sweat from his brow. Rain fell from his eye lashes and he could hardly see. A feeling of sadness came over him. Molly used to tell him he had beautiful eyes, and how long his eye lashes were . . . and now he was burying her. He started to cry, and the tears suddenly turned to anger towards his own mother. Looking up at the sky, he shouted, 'you bastard. I hope you rot in hell. You ruined my life, you fat ugly cow.'

He was just about to start digging again when sheet lightening lit up the sky, and he saw a young girl standing under an oak tree. She was dressed in a long white dress, her hair blowing in the wind, and there was a mist around her. Strangely, she didn't appear wet from the rain.

'Who's there, what do you want?'

He strode over towards the girl, another flash of lightening lit up the sky but she was nowhere to be seen. He ran all around the area, his feet sticking in the bog, holding his spade, ready to strike. 'Must have been a trick of the light from the sheet lightening, what the hell is wrong with you Joe McNamara?'

He placed Molly's body in the grave very gently, for he owed her that much, and shovelled the earth over her. He stood pondering whether to say a prayer but decided not to. He wasn't into this religious rubbish even though he went to mass on Sunday. His confessions were all lies, just for the sake of confessing before communion, and to stop the priest knocking at his door, asking why he wasn't going to mass; the interfering old bastard.

All finished, Joseph started to walk back to the horse and cart exhausted. He swore at the horse for neighing. 'What's the matter, you lump o shite, frightened by the thunder. . . '

His eye caught sight of the same girl, sitting on the wall where he had buried Molly. He took the spade from the cart and ran towards her, but the rain blurred his vision and the girl vanished again. Joseph felt very frightened. Who was she? Was it his imagination? What would a girl be doing out on a night like this in the middle of nowhere, dressed in an old-fashioned communion robe?

Joseph jumped onto the cart, but the wheels were stuck in the mud. He unfastened his belt and started to strike the horse. A piercing scream filled the air and he looked back to see the girl pointing a finger towards him, her mouth resembling a big round black hole, letting out an unearthly sound. Joseph got off the cart and started to quickly dig out the cart with his spade. He pulled hard on the reins to guide the horse towards the road. He was about to turn right towards the City, turning to catch one last look at the girl. She was gone, but he could still hear the piercing scream in his head.

Chapter 15

'Tis a sad time for you Joseph, I know that, but the police have looked everywhere for Molly, including the Liffy, and there's no sign of her. No one seems to have seen her.' explained Father O'Byrne. 'Now I know it must be upsetting, but the children should be taken into homes Joseph. The Christian Brothers will see to the boys, and young Alice will go into a special home where they will take care of her. You can't look after the children and look for a job, now can you?'

'No Father.' Joseph sniffed, 'I know Molly wasn't herself. And Alice took a lot out of her, you know, being the way she is, but I'll be prepared to look after the child me self. She needs her da now.'

'How is Alice by the way? I heard she had a bad fall. Has she spoken yet?' The Priest asked.

'She won't speak at all now Father, she just sits rocking to and fro with her thumb in her mouth. I have to force her to eat or she'd starve.'

'Oh, but its hard Joseph, let me take the children before you make yourself ill.'

'Bless you Father. But I will take care of Alice. . .'

Before he had time to finish his sentence, Alice screamed and ran down the stairs to Mrs O'Conner's. The Priest held his hands together and threw them in the air as if he had made his point that Alice needed to go into an institution.

'Ah, ye wouldn't want to care for a child with mental problems and work at the same time. No Joseph, we'll be taking her to a place where others are just like her.' The Priest insisted.

'I'll manage okay with the neighbours help.' Joseph argued 'Alice will be better off with her da,'

'She'd be better off in a home Father Ryan.' Mrs O'Conner said loudly, standing at the door with Alice by her side. 'Tis a shame, but it'll be too much fer you Joseph McNamara.'

Joseph stared eye to eye with Peggy O'Conner. He could have sliced her in two. Why can't she mind her own fecking business? Alice had that look in her eyes again and stared at him with hatred. There was more to the girl than people knew . . . more than he himself knew.

Later that day, the neighbours stood and watched the children being dragged out of the house by official looking men and a Nun. Laurence was screaming, not exactly sure what was happening, Shaun was kicking and fighting, and James looked terrified. Alice just walked silently behind them. Turning around to face her father, she stared straight into his eyes. Joseph was taken aback by this and quickly walked away. She had frightened him this time. The neighbours thought he was upset of his family being taken from him, but Mrs O'Conner knew differently. Who in God's name would believe she was told by a child that her mother was going to be murdered? The day before the 'accident' Alice had drawn her mother on paper with a brown mark around her neck.

Joseph appeared again as the car drove away, just in time to hear the neighbours crying. 'How could a woman leave her children like that? May God forgive you Molly McNamara for the terrible deed you have done.'

Mrs O'Conner stared straight into the eyes of Joseph. 'Tis a strange thing fer a loving mother to do, now isn't it, Joseph.'

Chapter 16

Keene O'Neil sat at the back of the pub. He had heard the story of Joe McNamara and the disappearance of his wife. He also knew his kids had been taken into institutions. Joseph was a strong looking man and . . . yeah, he'd heard he was quick with his fists, but Keene was busy now and could do with extra help on the farm. He walked towards Joseph, who was standing at the bar, a bit worse for wear, but then, perhaps he was probably drowning his sorrows.

'Good day to yis, my name is Keene O'Neil and I have the farm up near Portmarnock, on the way to Malahide; I hear you're looking for work. I could do with extra help if you're interested. To be sure, I'll have to see how you go on for a month first before setting you on permanently.'

'Oh Jaysus, that'll be grand. When can I start?'

'Let's say Monday. They'll be a bit of potato picking, besides milking the cows and cleaning the sheds to begin with. There's plenty more to do and it's all hard on the back, but I'm sure you're up to it.'

Joseph thanked the man and made arrangements for the following Monday. The job had come just at the right time. He was about to be evicted for not paying the rent and wondered where he would stay. He didn't want to end up like those tramps that slept in doorways, but it was beginning to look that way. Still, he was pissed off with what the farmer had said. "I'm sure you're up to it" Joseph mimicked, when he left the bar, "I'm sure you're up to it." Of course, he was up to it. He was working on a farm from the age of four; his parent's farm. A slave he was, working before school and after school. No time for play. During harvesting, he worked fourteen hours a day. He was beaten constantly by his father and uncle while his mother stood by and watched.

'Well what do yis expect Patrick' for that was Joseph's real name; 'you weren't pulling your weight.' She'd spit.

'Ma, I'm tired, I only slept four hours last night; we were out looking for the sheep which escaped.'

'Yer Da has to look out fer them and yer Uncle Mathew, and they don't complain.'

'No because they stand and talk while I do the running. I'm twelve years old Ma and I've been working since I was four. I'm sick of this bloody farm.'

His mother grabbed him by the ear and dragged him into the kitchen, throwing him on a chair. She forced his mouth open and shoved in a bar of carbolic soap, almost choking him, clasping her hand over his lips while holding his hair with the other hand, one knee holding his body down. He struggled, but his mother was a strong woman with plenty of weight behind her and a temper worse than anyone he'd ever met; even the men were frightened of her.

'That'll teach you not to swear' she spit, showing her rotting teeth, 'they'll be no tea fer you tonight, now get back to the fields.'

Gagging and pushing a hand full of grass into his mouth, he wished his mother was dead. He wished she was rotten with disease and died slowly. He hated his mother. Patrick was an only child and swore he was conceived for one purpose, and that was to work the farm. He was never given any money; he was expected to work for as long as there was daylight in the summer months, and during the winter he worked without appropriate clothing, cold and hungry. His father might have beaten him black and blue, but his mother used mental cruelty. Anytime he dared to complain, she would make him stand with his back to the wall with his knees bent; striking him with a stick each time he tried to stand straight. She was the coldest woman Patrick had ever known. He wasn't allowed friends, and only went to school because his mother was told by officials, they would take him away. He wished they had.

Patrick's mother was built like a man. She wore trousers tied up with a rope, her stomach hanging loosely as if being held in place by the rope to stop it falling. And, when she walked, the back of her looked like a rhino:

the cheeks of her arse moving up and down. Her jowls shook as she spoke, with spit sitting on her bottom lip.

The years went by and the abuse continued. He was sixteen now and found it hard not to hit back. He could handle his father and uncle, seeing as he was bigger than them, but he was still frightened of his mother. Joseph shuddered when he though back to that time he saw his mother naked; she was the ugliest thing he had ever seen. Layers of flesh hung from her stomach almost to her knees. Her large breasts were almost to her waist. This was the only time in his life he had ever seen a woman naked and it sickened him. She was about to step in the tin bath when Patrick accidently walked into the room, looking for matches. He quickly ran out into the snow before she had chance to grab him. When he went back later that night, all the doors were bolted, and a lock had been put onto the cow shed. He slept in the privy all night with the smell of sewage and a leaky roof. The next morning his bones were so stiff he couldn't move his fingers.

Making his way into the farmhouse kitchen, he was tired and found it hard to wake up properly. His mother yelled at him to hurry up, swiping him hard across the head. Patrick swore at her. She snatched the hot iron off the fire, and she lashed out at him. He put his arm up in defence, but not before she held it on his arm and burnt him. Patrick screamed and grabbed the iron from her hand. Oblivious to her screams, he hit her with it time and time again. Once he started, he couldn't stop. It took a while for him to realise he had killed her. Pacing the floor with his hands over his head, he screamed. 'Jaysus, Jaysus. What have I done?'

He had to act fast. Through tears, pain and fear, he dragged her body through the door, using a rope around her feet. By the time he reached the top of the cliff, his hands were bleeding. The wind was bitterly cold and the ice on the ground made the walk harder still. From where he was, he could see for miles and there was no one around. With the rope, he secured some loose heavy stones, by pushing them inside her clothes and knotting the rope into place.

'Jaysus, I hope it fecking rains hard today. There's blood everywhere.'

Patrick realised when looking down at his hands and seeing the burst blisters, he couldn't lift the body to throw it off the edge, so he lay on his back and with an almighty kick, her body rolled down the rocks and into the sea. She would surely sink to the bottom of the ocean with the weight of the stones. The tide rushed in, banging on the rocks with an almighty crash and out again. The icy wind ripped through his body and he was shaking. The sea was rough today, rough enough for a ship to turn over. He sat on the cliff for what seemed like hours, waiting for the body to disappear, while gathering bits of grass and mud to clean off the blood as best he could.

Walking back through the open door of the farmhouse, he heard a sound and crouched on the floor with his head under his arms. The fecking cat! Patrick swiped her with an almighty kick.

'Yis scared the fecking shite out o me. Gerrout' he shouted.

Luckily the old teapot, which lay on the shelf for years, was almost full to the brim with money.

'Yeah, she thought I wouldn't know where she kept the pot of gold the fat bastard made out of me.'

Grabbing a freshly cooked joint of ham and some bread, he threw the food into an old sack, along with the few items of clothing he possessed and a blanket.

It was weeks before he reached Dublin, stealing food on the way and sleeping in any old shelter he could find. Finally, he was able to get a job as a potato picker, saving as much money as possible to buy second hand clothes from the market. Giving a false name of Joseph McNamara and putting his past behind him, he managed to get a job at the docks and started to live in lodgings. This was about the time he met Molly. She was the most beautiful girl he had ever seen in his life. He wanted her badly. She was so gentle and delicate; he longed to protect her and love her forever.

*

Joseph felt sad and sobbed real hard tears that night. 'Oh Molly, where did I go wrong, we were so happy before we had kids. You were the only girl I ever loved. Molly, oh Molly, I'm so sorry.'

Sleep took over his sobs, but he woke in the early hours to see light shining in the usually dark room. The light seemed to be moving until it formed the shape of a young girl, dressed in a long white dress. She was pointing her finger. A glow emitted from her body and as suddenly as she came, she disappeared. Joseph tried to get up, but he couldn't move. He couldn't open his mouth to shout. He was paralysed, as if being held by some unseen force. He wanted to scream for help. After what seemed like hours, the feelings returned to his body. Forcing himself out of bed he turned on the light switch and the bulb blew, making Joseph jump and cover his head with his hands, just as he did when he was cowering from his mother. Groping about in the dark he found some matches and lit a few candles. Shaking, he made a cup of tea, too frightened to go back to sleep.

*

The following night, in O'Brian's bar, Joseph told his friends what happened during the night.

'You're drinking too much Joe. I've heard of these so-called hallucinations from drinking too much ale. Me auld mate, Mick, saw spiders and snakes. It's all in the mind but seems real.' Remarked John Keenan, propping himself up on the bar discussing Joseph's ordeal.

'Spiders, fer the love of God, I would rather see fecking spiders than a bloody ghost of a girl.'

'Sounds like the banshee to me.' Billy Sheridan laughed. 'Jesus. I hope you're not going to die Joe. The banshee is the messenger of death. She makes a sound no man would want to hear. Points a finger, so she does . . . just like the girl in your dream. She sure fits the description Joseph.' Billy Sheridan demonstrated how the banshee pointed her finger 'Like dis.'

'Go way wid yer' replied John Keenan 'I never heard of the banshee being young. Sure, the Banshee's an old hag with scraggly hair. And it's a comb she throws at the person who's going to die. She doesn't point a finger, not that I know of, but den, no-one comes back to say what she did.'

'Oh, thanks yous two, I came in here for a drink and someone to talk to. I didn't need someone to tell me *dat*, yis fecking eejits. I know what the fecking banshee is. Christ . . . who doesn't. I'm not dying, it's in my head. The drink does it.'

'To be sure, Joseph, it's a ghost.'

''Tis the bloody drink Billy Sheridan.' Joseph snapped back.

'Why would anyone haunt you?'

'I don't know, do I?'

'Is it yer auld granny?'

'I told you, she's only a young girl. I'd know me own fecking granny now, wouldn't I. I tell you, tis the drink' Joseph said, downing the last dregs of his stout and banging on the table for the barman.

'Young girl, you say. Then send her to me. I wouldn't mind being haunted by a young girl'

'It isn't fecking funny.'

'All ghosts are young, aren't they? Don't they get younger when they die?'

'How would I know? Will yous shut up fer Christ's sake? I haven't seen a fecking ghost before. Let's forget it shall we. I wished to God I'd never told you eejits.'

Joseph was still working on the farm and grateful for the money. At the same time, he was making extra cash by stealing vegetables and selling them to the market traders at a lower price. Things were looking up; for some time now Molly's disappearance had been forgotten, although he had moved to a new address to avoid the neighbours. On the other hand, he was sure Mrs O'Conner knew something. Still, she couldn't prove anything, or she would have gone to the Gardaí long ago.

He wondered how the boys were getting on with the Christian Brothers. He'd heard many horror stories about those places; some of the people in the neighbouring village often heard screaming in the night. The Gardaí was sometimes informed, but obviously, the institution knew in advance when officials were due to visit. Joseph suspected none of the boys would dare to tell the truth. After all, weren't the Brother's doing God's work by caring for them? 'A load of Shite' still, there was nothing he could do. His sons would be older now and Shaun may have left the institution. Alice? She would probably be in a mental institution for life. Molly should have let her die at birth. Joseph knew from farming that less than perfect animals were rejected at birth. Nature didn't take kindly to a disabled animal on a farm. Strange somehow, Alice being the way she was, made Molly love her more.

It felt good to be free; he could take a woman whenever he wanted, preferring young girls. He was told often enough he was still a good looker. Joseph smiled to himself at the number of girls he had slept with. They were falling at his feet. He complimented himself on still having his charming ways. There were just a few who had to be awkward. One was Sarah. He cursed under his breath, thinking about her. Coming into the pub of all places to tell him she needed to speak in private.

'Joseph, we have to talk.'

'About what, can't it wait?'

'No Joseph, it can't wait. I'm pregnant.'

'Jaysus what the hell do yis want me to do. How do you know it's mine?'

'I have never slept with another man. You were the first and you know that. I thought you loved me.'

'Did I tell yis this?'

'No but . . .'

'Well then, what do yis want from me?'

'I don't know what to do, my parents will throw me out and I'll be sent away. We already have twelve living in our house. Can I stay with you?'

'Oh yeah, and have an anchor round me bloody neck, and a screaming bastard. The answer is no. I'll just say the baby isn't mine. Who's going to believe different, yis can't prove it. Go away and leave me alone.'

A week later a body was pulled out from the River Liffy. It was Sarah's. Joseph was sick to the stomach; he hadn't wanted this. He did love her in a way, and she loved him; she was very sweet, pure and innocent, just like Molly had been.

Joseph knew before he went to bed the ghost girl would come to him that night. He tried to drink as much stout and whisky as possible to knock himself out, but he still woke up from the light which shone from her. She stood at the bottom of the bed, pointing her finger.

'Go away. Do you hear me? Leave me alone. I've done nothing to you.'

The girl looked straight into his eyes, and he thought for a moment she was about to speak.

'No, no, don't speak. Leave me alone, please, don't speak. I promise I'll be better. I'll do anything, just leave me alone. I didn't know she was going to kill herself, or I would have stood by her. Please.'

The girl pointed her finger again and opened her mouth to form a round black hole. Joseph thought for a second she was going to say something and quickly hid under the blanket. When he looked up again, she had disappeared.

The morning after, Joseph's boss asked if he would make a delivery in Howth, not far from the peat bog where Molly was buried. He had recently learned to drive and passed his test the first time, courtesy of Keene O'Neil. He loaded the van with fruit and vegetables and set off on his journey. When he reached the spot where he thought he had buried her. He wasn't quite sure where she was.

'Where the feck is she?'

Joseph decided he was in the wrong place and went a little further looking out for a wall, and an old oak tree, which stood out from the other trees. He remembered the tree distinctively from when the lightening lit up the sky and *she* was there. The branches looked like two long arms with fingers on the ends, but now, the trees were in full bloom.

Eventually, he found the place where Molly was buried and was horrified to see yellow flowers had grown in the exact spot. He looked around but there were no other flowers anywhere in sight. Had someone planted them? Is it because he had dug so deep? Luckily, this particular bog was untouched and would be for years before they reached the area where he had buried Molly. He would probably be dead from old age by the time they found her remains. He plucked all the flowers out and looked towards the tree where he had seen the girl.

'Fecking imagination, there was no girl.'

He jumped back in the van and fled the area. Unaware he was being watched.

Chapter 17

Dublin 1963

Angela Murray was so excited; she couldn't keep still. At the age of fifteen this was to be her first ever grown up party, her cousin's eighteenth. Jeannette's parents had hired a room for the night in Branigans bar. There was going to be a good band playing and Jeanette told Angela they sang songs from the Beatles, Gerry and the Pacemakers and all the Mersey sounds.

Angela couldn't wait; she'd been looking forward to the party for weeks. In fact, the party was all she could think of. Her mother had bought Angela a dress which was the latest look in Dublin and what all the girls were wearing. The mini dress was brightly coloured in a flowery pattern and was very short, but not nearly as short as her friend Karen's dress, who was also invited to the party. Karen was much taller and a mini dress on her was a *true* mini dress, whereas Angela's dress stopped at her knees. In fact most of her friends had been even more daring and gone for the even shorter version; a micro mini. Her mother also bought Angela new shoes and a matching handbag, *and,* after much persuasion, let her have the bright green psychedelic earrings, which Angela had pleaded for. The earrings looked like two green dice dangling from her earlobes.

Two hours before catching the bus into the City, her friend Karen arrived. 'Here, look at these; false eye lashes, I bought us a pair each, you stick them on with this little tube of glue. Everybody will be wearing them.'

'Jaysus, I've seen these worn by girls in magazines, not sure if Da will let me wear them, he's a bit old fashioned. He wasn't too keen when I tried my dress on, said it was too short can you believe.'

'Too short, you must be joking. It's to your knees.'

'I know. I wish it was a few inches shorter Karen, I feel a bit like a schoolgirl compared to you and the others.'

'Take it up a couple of inches.'

'I can't do that. Da won't be happy.'

'He'll hardly notice, especially when he sees how all the other girls dress; come on, get me a needle and thread and I'll take it up for you.'

Karen finished sewing and Angela stood on the bed to see the length of the dress through the dressing table mirror.'

'Wow, it certainly looks better now, thanks.'

'No problem. Now let's take a look at these eye lashes.'

Angela couldn't believe the transformation. The girls were really in the Party mood.

'Why don't I go home and get ready now. From my house we can call for Marie and go straight to the party from there.'

'Yeah, that'll be fun. I'll leave a note for Ma and tell her I'll see them at the party.'

They arrived at the party in time to have a good chat with the other girls there, mostly Angela's cousins, before the music began. When the band began to play, the atmosphere was electric and the music was so good, you could hardly tell the difference from the real artists. As well as being good musicians, they were all handsome lads and all the girls tried hard to dance as near to the stage as possible. Angela joined a group of girls, just feet away from the band, and couldn't help but notice one of the guitarists looking at her. He was singing 'Just One Look' by the Hollies and seemed to be singing the song to her and her alone. When the band had a break, everyone sat at their tables. Angela sat next to her friend Karan, who looked very grown up and pretty. Her hair was blond and backcombed enough to add four inches to her height. She looked like Dusty Springfield

135

in her short flowery mini dress and the dark eyes, made darker by using her false eye lashes and eye liner.

'Karen' Angela whispered with her hand over one side of her face to stop others hearing. 'You know the guitarist next to the end on the left-hand side.'

'I know which one you mean. What about him.'

'He sang the last song to me Karen. He was looking at me all the while.'

'Don't be silly. Bands are like that Angela; they flirt everywhere they go. It's what they do. On the next song he will be doing the same to another girl. Don't be taken in you idiot, he may have been looking at every girl on the dance floor, and you just *thought* he was looking at you. He probably has a girlfriend at home in England.' Karan sighed heavily 'honestly Angela, you're so naïve.'

Angela was disappointed by her friend's reaction and assumed she was just jealous. She was about to say so, when she saw her parents arriving. She left the table, giving her best friend a glare and rushed across the room to greet them.

'Ma, the band is really grand and . . .'

'What the hell have you got on your eyes?' Her father said angrily, 'and as for you Doreen,' he said, turning to face her mother, 'how dare you shorten that dress behind my back. Look at the state of her, she looks like a trollop. Go get our coats Doreen, right now, we're going home.'

'Oh please Da no, please let me stay . . .'

'Get your coat.'

'Oh, fer the love of God Roger, don't make a scene. Everyone here will wonder why we left the party. Angela has so looked forward to this evening . . . look!' pleaded his wife. 'All the girls are wearing short dresses. Please don't spoil her first night out with her friends.'

Angela waited patiently for her father's reply. 'I'll let her stay . . . but only because I don't want to spoil my niece's birthday party, but when we get home that dress is going on the fire, and I won't hear a word said about it. Go and take those stupid eyelashes of your face right now before I change my mind.'

Angela ran to the rest room, trying hard not to cry and be left with red swollen eyes. She gently peeled the eye lashes from her eyes and put them in her bag. Leaving the ladies toilets, she bumped into the boy from the band who had been looking at her earlier.

'Hi.' He said, looking deep into her eyes, 'I noticed you earlier, are you all right? You look like you've been crying.'

'No. I have a cold. That's a strange accent yis have there, where are you from?' She said quickly, changing the subject.

'Yorkshire, we're touring Dublin right now, playing at weddings and so on. Lovely place you have here, it's a fantastic City, and we love the Irish accent, and of course the pretty Colleens such as yourself.'

Angela blushed and there was a little silence as they looked at one another. She began to wonder if he was also shy and was just about to leave when he spoke. 'I was just going out for some air before the next session, fancy coming with me.'

This boy was the one all her cousins liked the best, and she was flattered he had given her a compliment. In all her life Angela had never been paid a compliment before, not by a boy, she'd never even been kissed. Some of her friends had been kissed and one even had a boyfriend. She walked towards the exit with him, her face still blushing.

'Where are yis going Angela, sure it's very dark out there?' a voice rang out. She turned to see her uncle.

'Nowhere Uncle Jamie, I was just going out for some air.' Angela replied, hoping to God he wouldn't tell her father. They watched him walk away and the musician looked at Angela.

'Angela, now that's a pretty name' he smiled, showing beautiful white teeth, 'a pretty name to match a pretty face. My name is David by the way.'

She liked the way he held her eyes, almost looking through her very soul when he spoke. This gave her a strange fluttering in her stomach. The passageway was narrow, and Angela let him lead the way to a fire escape door, standing at the back of him while he pushed the door open, giving her a chance to look at his fine physique. *Oh, she couldn't wait to tell Karen about this, she will be so jealous.* The air smelled fresh and sweet, and although there was no moon, the night was warm. She was feeling grown up at long last.

Leaning against the wall, David lit a cigarette. She watched him deeply inhale the smoke and turn his head to exhale away from her face. He passed the cigarette to Angela. 'Oh, I don't smoke.'

'Well now, there's a first time for everything. Here, take a draw.'

'No, I don't want one.'

'Here, try it. You might relax a little.' He insisted, handing her the cigarette.

'No, honestly, if me da smells smoke on me, he'll take me home.'

'I see. I have to be going back in soon for another number.' He said, this time blowing the smoke into her face.

'How long have you been playing in a band?' she asked nervously, wafting the smoke away from her. 'You're very good.'

'Oh, about five years, I was only fourteen when we put this band together.' He laughed 'we've come a long way since then, I might add.'

It didn't take Angela much to work out he was nineteen years old. Realising she shouldn't be standing outside with a boy as old as he was, she blushed and said. 'I must get back to my friends now David, it was nice t . . .'

Without warning he threw the cigarette to the floor and grabbed hold of her, forcing his lips on hers. She tried to push him away and was terrified when she felt him opening the zip to his trousers, pushing her up against the wall at the same time.

'No please, let me go . . .'

He pushed his hand under her skirt just as her father unexpectedly appeared, who pushed David with such force, that he fell to the floor. Then, grabbing hold of Angela, he shoved her towards the room where her mother was sat chatting to relatives. 'Get your coat and don't say a word, we're going home.'

Her mother looked at Angela's face and saw a red mark on her cheek bone. She knew her daughter had been slapped and was surprised; her husband had always been a controlling man who demanded respect, but he never once resorted to violence. Something had happened for him to hit Angela. Without a goodbye to anyone, she followed her husband outside, fully aware of all the onlookers.

*

The next day, Angela stood facing Father Flannigan. 'I've been speaking to your father, and we agree you need to go away to repent. You'll be going to the Magdalena laundries. The Sisters there are very good, sure I've met them me self.'

'Please don't send me there Father, I didn't do anything wrong.'

'Tis fer the best Angela,' Father Flannigan replied, 'you don't want to be giving the wrong impression out to young men now de yis? You're far too pretty for your own good and from what yer da tells me, you're also very vain.'

'But Father Flannigan, I'm innocent, and I'm not vein. I tried to fight him off, but he was too strong, I didn't know he was going to kiss me. I was just about to leave when . . .'

'Well now' Father Flannigan cut her off 'yis shouldn't have led the man on in the first place. Now should you?' The priest said angrily. 'Going outside in the dark with a stranger, don't be telling me you're that naïve Angela, you were brought up in a good catholic family. He had the zip to his trousers down. Had it not been for your father God knows what would have happened? Losing your virginity before marriage is a sin Angela. The boy was married too, did you know that?'

'No Father, I didn't get the chance to speak to him before he tried . . .'

'Married with a baby, how does it feel to know he almost committed adultery with you when he has a wife and child at home? Do you realise you could have ruined the boy's life if you were to become pregnant, leading him on so?'

'I'm so sorry, please don't send me away. I didn't lead him on, honest.'

'Angela is a good girl Father Flannigan; she would never have let him have his way with her. He tried to force himself on her. Why don't you have a go at the boy? Sure to God, he was married and trying to seduce my child. She's the innocent one here, not the boy.' Angela's mother yelled.

'You keep out of this Doreen. My own brother saw her happily go outside with the boy. She should have known what he wanted. I won't have this kind of behaviour in my house.'

The next morning, Angela was whisked away in a black car by a driver and two straight face nuns who never spoke a word. Her heartbroken mother chased down the road after the car crying out for her daughter and cursing her husband. The neighbours stood and watched Doreen Sweeny before going indoors without speaking. The word had already got out.

*

'Jesus, Mary and Joseph I hate this fecking job.' Fiona muttered to herself.

'What was that you said Fiona?' She looked up to see Sister Mary Bernadette looking down on her.

'Oh, I was moaning to a stubborn stain that I can't seem to rub off the floor, Sister.' Fiona lied.

She was used to lying. It was just a case of going to confession, having her sins forgiven and starting all over again. She would say *"Pray Father for I have sinned. It has been a week since my last confession."* Fiona admitted to the same sins every week, which were lying, talking, whispering and laughing. She was given absolution and the same penance, which was to say three Our Fathers and three Hail Mary's. The prayers had to be said out loud to the sound of everyone else saying their own act of contrition; all at the same time, but on different levels.

'Well, just make sure you clean the floor properly and stop the mumbling.'

'Yes Sister. Sorry Sister.'

When the Sister carried on down the hall, Fiona stuck her tongue out before continuing to wash the floor. Then she heard a commotion.

'But I haven't done anything wrong. I shouldn't be here.' A girl was shouting. The girl was dragged into the Reverend Mother's office and the door was closed. Fiona knew something must have happened on the journey for the Sister's to be so angry with her; usually punishment started after the first day. Fiona carried on scrubbing the floors and knew how the new girl would look when leaving the room.

Twenty minutes went by and Fiona was right. The terrified girl came out of the office with all her beautiful hair hacked off. Blood poured down her face from the cuts to her scalp. She watched the girl walk slowly and quietly in shock, carrying a bundle of grey clothes.

'Get back to cleaning the floor, before you find yerself in front of the Reverend Mother.' Sister O'Brian shouted.

'Yes Sister. Sorry Sister.' As the nun and the girl walked past, Fiona stuck two fingers in the air this time.

For as long as she could remember Fiona had seen sights like this. She had known nothing else in her life, other than the orphanage she was brought up in. The girls were here literally for one purpose, and that was to work. Institutions had been her life since she was born, and she was seventeen now. The sisters told her she had no known relatives, so no one was ever going to come and take her out of here. She was found outside the gates of the orphanage in a dirty shopping bag, they said. No note, they said. She didn't even have a surname. She hoped her mother would rot in hell. 'Sure to God, your mother was a prostitute.' The nuns would remind her when she was in trouble for anything. 'And you child, have the devils blood in yer veins. You should be grateful you were taken in by people who care for your welfare.'

Like everyone else in this place, there were moments when she'd thought of running away, but so many times she'd seen girls being dragged back by the Gardaí only to be cruelly punished. Sometimes they could be locked in a dark damp room for up to a week.

Fiona's life was the same day in day out. The only time she ever left the home was to go on a daytrip to the seaside once a year. The nuns were much kinder and allowed them to bathe in the sea, even if it rained or was very cold. She and the girls soon learned to be very careful not to upset the nuns a month or so before the big day, otherwise the punishment was staying behind on the day of the trip.

Fiona really loved to see new girls arrive. She could hear what life was like outside the gates. Quite often she was punished, along with whoever

141

she was talking to in the dormitory, for asking one question after another. Talking wasn't encouraged when the lights were switched off at night. The punishment was harsh at times, but it didn't stop Fiona, who had a great thirst for knowledge. Occasionally, someone would sneak a magazine under their garment that a visitor had brought in with them, giving Fiona a chance to learn about life on the outside. Reading magazines was seen as corrupt, but certain books were allowed on Sunday afternoon from the small library, and Fiona loved to read.

They were also allowed to listen to the radio, if one of the nicer nuns was on duty, and Fiona was taught to dance by the new girls. Some of the nuns liked to sit and watch, laughing and clapping along. Her favourite song was Summer Holiday by Cliff Richards. She loved the words to the song and lay back at night dreaming of going where the sun shines brightly and where the sea is blue. Some songs made the girls homesick and they would cry, especially the sad songs. One was 'You'll never walk alone' by Gerry and the Pacemakers. That song did it every time and Fiona felt sorry for them. They had known another life, a life of freedom. They'd had a life where they could talk as much as they wanted without looking over their shoulder. They'd had a life without being beaten or held under cold water, just for simply laughing. They also knew what it was like to have a family, good or bad.

When Fiona had finished scrubbing the corridor floor, she could go back to the dormitory. She worked out she should be finished for six thirty. When she finally emptied the bucket of dirty water and put everything away she climbed the stairs. She was surprised to see the new girl was in a bed next to hers. There was blood all over her pillow from the cuts on her head.

'Hello, my name is Fiona, what's yours?'

The girl ignored Fiona.

'Hey listen. I didn't put you in this place so don't start being funny with me. I asked your name to make friends with you, but if that's the . . . '

'Angela, my name is Angela', she sobbed 'I didn't do anything wrong and no one believes me.'

'I believe you, I see it all the time, so don't worry about that because everyone else will believe you in here, apart from the nuns of course . . . oh and the lay nuns.'

'What are lay nuns?'

'They are the ones who didn't have the money to become a nun, and so they have to work. Some say they are skivvies for the nuns, but to be honest, they take their anger out on us because they get treated like slaves themselves.'

'Why don't they leave?'

'What for, they have nowhere to go, like the rest of us who have been here all our lives.'

'Oh, Mother of God, you've been here all your life. Where are your parents?'

'I never had any. Apparently, my mother was a sinner who slept with men and dumped me outside the gates of the orphanage. I don't even have a surname. I was brought up to believe the nuns saved my soul and I should be grateful to them.'

'And are you?'

'No. I wish they would have left me to die.'

'That's so sad Fiona.'

Angela explained to Fiona what had happened to her, and how her mother had begged her father not to inform the priest.

'Now that's a story I've heard many times before.'

'But it's true.'

'I believe you, just as I believed the other girls Angela. Don't be so defensive.'

'I'm sorry. How long will I be here?'

'I don't know the answer to that. If your parents agree to have you back home, and you're no longer a threat to young men.'

'A threat? In what way was I a threat?'

'You said the priest believed you led the man on.'

'But it wasn't my fault.' shouted Angela.

'Don't yell at me, I'm telling you what I see here.'

'Jesus, and how will they know I'm no longer a threat.'

143

'When they have broken your spirit; to be honest, they will keep you here as long as they want, unless your parents ask for your return, but it's still down to the Reverend Mother whether they release you or not. They make money out of the girls here, doing other people's dirty laundry. They get good money, so they try to hang on to the girls.'

'I'm not staying here, I'll run away.'

'Don't you think that hasn't been tried, the girls almost always get picked up by the Gardaí. Did you try to escape when you were on your way here?'

'Yes, how did you know?'

'Because that's why they shaved your hair. Without a hat you won't get far, everyone knows you're from an institution.'

Angela felt at her head and cried. She had lovely hair; her friends told her all the time. She did try to escape on the way here. She jumped out of the car when the driver stopped to use a toilet, but the nuns grabbed her by the hair and forced her to the ground. Angela was placed in between the nuns for the rest of the journey. But she would escape. She wasn't staying in this hell hole.

Fiona saw the sad look on Angela's face and her heart went out to her. 'Come on, let's get you cleaned up. I know where they keep the fresh bedding; I'll get you a clean pillow slip. You must have put up quite a fight to save your hair.'

'I did. How did you know? You know everything.'

'Experience' laughed Fiona 'I never had the opportunity to have long hair, but I know if you make a fuss you end up with cuts and bruises. Better to let them get on with cutting it.'

'What are these rags for, the Sister gave me?'

'Your monthly periods; you wash them and reuse them. Using washable rags saves them money.'

'But . . . oh never mind.'

When they returned from the bathroom, the other girls were back from making Rosary beads. 'Who's this then, a new girl? And what have you been up to?' said Bridie McCarthy, while patting Angela on the head, 'is this the latest fashion out there these days?'

144

'Leave her alone, will yea, she's been through enough. Take no mind of her Angela; she's like that with all new girls.'

Fiona introduced everyone to Angela, and they all gathered around the bed, asking questions. She was honest with them and told the girls the whole story with tears in her eyes, waiting to see their reaction.

'Jaysus Angela, this bloody place is full of girls that were abused so don't take on now, we know you were taken advantage of, it's a man's world out there. The girls are always the ones to blame.'

Most of the girls had their own sad story to tell, some similar to hers, but some so much worse, it was hard to imagine they had managed to live through it all. Everyone scattered towards their beds as they heard the familiar sounds of footsteps.

'It's 10.00 clock and time you were in bed now girls. Goodnight.'

'Goodnight Sister.' They chorused

The lights were switched off and silence fell amid a few whispers and the sound of someone crying.

*

Angela had been at the Magdalena's three months now, and her hair had grown back a little. She accepted she couldn't have her hair long again, but all the girls had short hair and it was better than having none. Thanks to Fiona, she felt she had someone to help her through the horror of being held against her will. She'd seen a lot of bullying in the home from older and tougher girls. She knew if it hadn't been for Fiona, she would have been at the receiving end of those who considered her posh. Telling the girls about her life at home had been a huge mistake. Her father was a manager at the Guinness brewery and earned quite a good wage compared to most people, and she was lucky to live in a nice house with a garden in Malahide. This did not go down well, especially as a lot of the girls came from very poor families and had only known poverty and neglect. From now on, she would keep her mouth shut and only speak to a few of the girls she could trust.

The days dragged by and Angela was shattered with all the hard labour. She didn't so much as wash a cup at home. Not being able to speak was harder still. She had already been hit with a stick by one of the nuns, who threatened to take her to the Reverent Mother if she was caught talking again, and she knew only too well from Fiona the kind of punishment she dealt out.

'They're sick, Angela.' Fiona told her, after Angela had seen someone being hit with a stick across her buttocks. 'They get pleasure from dealing out pain, you can see it in their eyes, and I've heard some strange tales about some of them.'

'What do you mean strange tales?'

'I'll tell you one day but not now, there are too many ears,' she whispered 'of course there are some of the sisters who are really nice. Unfortunately, they get into trouble themselves because they're considered soft. The heavier the footsteps outside the dormitory after lights out, the nicer they are.'

'What do you mean?'

'It's warning to get into bed, so they don't catch us out of it.' Fiona laughed. 'I'll let you know in time who to trust and who to be very careful with, including the girls here and the lay nuns.'

Depending on who was on duty in the laundry made all the difference; some of the sisters insisted on the girls praying out loud at certain times of the day until the sound seemed to send you into some kind of trance where voices became one, while others turned a blind eye to whispers and giggles.

Angela thought how a bit of music, or gossip would have made the days go so much quicker, but they weren't here to enjoy themselves, they were here to work. Then Angela thought of Fiona and the girls who came from an orphanage. They had no sins to pray for. They were innocent children who never had seen the outside world. She felt sorry for Fiona; left in dirty rags outside the door. What if no one had heard her cries? Fiona could have died from the cold or been eaten by wildlife.

*

A few months later, Fiona asked Angela if she believed in ghosts and the afterlife.

'Oh yes, I do. My nanny, on my mother's side, was a fortune teller and she read palms and had a crystal ball. I used to sit for hours with her

146

listening to her talk about spirits, and how people came back from the dead to watch over us. I'm a little psychic me self, not like nanny though, she's very popular. People queue up to see her.'

'Oh, dear God Angela, don't let anyone hear you say that, the nuns will have you put in a mental institution, declaring you are possessed by the devil, I've seen that happen as well. Once a girl only pretended to read someone's palm, it was just a little bit of fun, *she couldn't see people's future Angela*. She did it for a laugh, but the Sister on duty that night walked into the room and wasted no time in having her taken away. She screamed and shouted that she was only joking, when she was dragged through the corridors by two men in white coats the next day. We will never know what happened to the poor girl. She's probably in an asylum.'

'My God, thanks for that, I'll be careful in front of the Sisters . . .'

'Angela are you listening to me. 'Fiona whispered angrily. It isn't only the sisters you have to be careful with. How do you think some girls get much lighter work than the rest of us? Because they're the ones who listen and tell tales . . . spies they are. And the strange tales I told you about earlier. Some of the girls have been seen to kiss a nun.'

'Oh no, my God, Fiona that is so sick.'

'You have so much to learn about this place, Angela, it isn't just the nuns; it's the priests and laymen. Believe me; you don't want to be reporting anyone. If anyone touches you in anyway, then you keep it to yourself. You'll get over it. Girls who report abuse always end up in an asylum, no one will believe you. Who would take a sinner's side of a story against a Priest?'

'I hate the word sinner. We've done nothing wrong. But I suppose that's what happened to me. If my uncle hadn't seen me, I might not be in here. I could have kept it to myself.'

'You could have ended up pregnant more like, with your word against his that he was the father of the child. That was different anyway. What I'm saying is, if a Priest ask you to do disgusting things to them, then you just have to do it and forget it.'

'What things.'

Fiona told Angela the tales she had heard from some of the girls. 'Be careful Angela, I've lost a few friends who have just disappeared because they told the truth. From now on, you speak to me and no one else about anything you wouldn't want to get back to the Sisters office, especially being able to read palms and the like.'

'Thank you for being my friend Fiona.'

'That's okay' Fiona said looking around to see if anyone was there. 'I also have some kind of psychic power, I think. I sometimes know when things are going to happen, for instance, I know things about people before they tell me. I dream all the time about life outside of these walls, and then a new girl will come, and I already know what she is going to say. Not all the time, but the dreams can be as real as reading a book.'

'Nanny started like that. You know, dreaming, she used to dream of people dying before they were sick. She said it was a gift. At first, I hoped I would never have the gift because I didn't want to know when someone was going to die. The strange thing was, although I was really looking forward to the party, I had a strange feeling something bad was going to happen. I know things like fortune telling and stuff are frowned upon by the Church, but since I was a child, I have had what I know now as premonitions. Nanny has been reading the cards and using a crystal ball ever since I can remember. I used to love staying at her house and listening to her talk. You know, it's amazing how many devout catholic people are regular clients of hers.'

'Did you pick anything up with me?'

'You know the first day when I was rude to you, and turned to tell you my name, well, I saw spirits around you, in fact, I feel one of the spirits is with you a lot of the time. The others come and go. It takes a lot out of them to stay very long.'

'I can't see where I would get visits from dead people, I don't know anyone dead, apart from a few who died in here. Will you read my palm, I don't mean just now, but when we know no one will be coming in at any minute?'

'Yes of course, but listen, if we get caught with me holding your palm, let's get this straight, you have a thorn in your hand, and I was trying to get it out.'

'That's grand; I'll tell you about my dreams . . .'

'What are you two whispering about?' one of the girls shouted as she walked through the door, throwing herself on her bed making a squeaking sound.

'We weren't whispering. We were talking quiet Lauren, so keep yer nose out will yea.'

'Jaysus, I was only asking, Fiona, no need to yell at me fer fecks sake.'

'You made me jump and frightened the shite out of me.'

'If I did that to you, then you're up to no good' she laughed 'so *what* were yis talking about.'

'We were just talking about what it was like to wear a mini dress and listen to a pop band. Angela was telling me about the party and how excited she was. Come and sit with us, we have an hour before that auld wan can find something to have a go at us for.'

When the rest of the dormitory was sleeping, Fiona climbed into Angela's bed. It would be a good hour before the next visit from the night Sister, *and* she was known for nodding off in her office.

'I had another dream last night, the same dream I've been having since I was a young child' Fiona whispered, 'in my dreams, I'm able to fly and travel across the sky and see the whole of Dublin and even further, although I have no names for these places.'

'Could it be wishful thinking Fiona, after all, you have spent your whole life in here.'

'Angela, how could I describe a place I have never been to?'

'Because you like to listen to the girls who have had a life out there, and you do tend to read those magazines you somehow manage to get a hold of. . . I don't know how, and you listen to the radio sometimes.'

'How the hell can listening to a radio make me see places I have never been to. It's you that's not listening Angela.'

'I'm sorry Fiona; I was trying to think of a logical explanation first.' Angela said sympathetically, 'if you have a dream over and over again, it's called a recurrent dream and there is usually a logical explanation for it, but then flying through the sky and travelling is different.'

'I remember being punished for screaming out in the night when I was in the orphanage, but I can't remember those dreams now. All I remember is wetting the bed and being punished time after time. Jaysus, I had to carry the fecking mattress over my head across to the boiler room with everyone mocking me. It reached a point where I tried to stay awake by holding my eyelids open with my fingers, which doesn't work by the way. If I wasn't being punished for wetting the bed, I was put in a freezing cold bath for screaming out in my sleep. I do remember one of the Sisters there who used to comfort me, she was so nice Angela, and on the days when she was on duty, I never wet the bed. Her name was Sister Rose, but I think she was a lay nun, because the other sisters used to shout at her all the time for being too soft. She used to tell me stories and made me a doll once. The doll was made from a wooden clothes peg. She dressed the peg in a bit of cloth and drew a face on it. She told me to hold the little peg doll close to my heart, and I wouldn't dream. One day I looked everywhere for my doll but one of the sisters had taken it; I screamed the place down and kicked a nun. I was put inside a dark cupboard for what seemed forever Angela; I was bitten all over by things that were in there. I didn't see Sister Rose again after that.'

'Oh Fiona, that's so terrible. Did the dreams go on?'

'Yes, and I started to remember them clearly. In my dreams a woman was smiling down on me, but I can't really describe her, my mind goes blank when I try to think of her. She kisses me on my forehead and says something, but I don't know *what* she is saying. One night I opened my eyes and she was standing there at the side of me smiling.'

'A spirit; that's a spirit you have described Fiona. Who is she? Is this the recurring dream?'

'No, it was, but not anymore. I still dream of flying, but I can't remember much the morning after now. I vaguely remember seeing a man once though, who looked right through me as if I was the ghost and he was real. Shit. How do we know whose who anyway, fer Christ sake?'

'I have dreams where I feel I'm in another time, perhaps . . '

'Shush, someone's coming.'

The same night Angela had a dream herself; she was at home with her mother and they were baking. The house was clean and tidy, and a roast was cooking in the oven giving out a wonderful aroma which made her stomach rumble with hunger. They were sitting down at the table in all eagerness of this lovely Sunday meal as her mother stood up to get the carving knife. Instead of passing the knife to her father, she stabbed him in the back, and he slumped to the floor bleeding. Angela screamed and screamed as her mother's face changed into someone else's face. The girls in the dormitory woke and Sister Mary Stanley came rushing into the room. Fiona and the girls looked on in horror as she was dragged out of the room by the Sister and a lay nun. An hour later Angela returned, wet through. Fiona waited until the nuns had left the room and immediately asked if she was all right.

'The bastards tried to drown me in freezing water, I thought I was dying Fiona, I couldn't breathe.'

'Oh, there'd be no chance of you dying; they worked out how long you could hold someone under water years ago. Come on, get those clothes off and we'll put them to dry, I have another gown in my locker, it has a few holes in it, but I keep it just in case.'

'Thanks Fiona, I had a nightmare . . .'

'Will yis shut yer fecking mouths?' a voice bellowed 'we're trying to sleep.'

'Shut yer gob' Fiona yelled back, 'it was different when you had it done to you, now wasn't it. Crying like a baby yis were, all bloody night.'

Silence followed and when everyone was asleep Angela told Fiona about the dream. 'The dream you had was very similar to the one I told you about. Only the surroundings were different and there wasn't a meal on the table.'

'Oh Jaysus Fiona, I must have dreamed your dream.' She laughed. 'Did you know these people in your dream, you know, like my dream was about Mammy and Da?' I can understand the logic. I'm angry with my father and feel sadness for my mother. I will never forgive him for thinking I was girl who would give my virginity away to the first boy who looked at me.'

151

'Perhaps she killed him.'

'I hope not. I wouldn't want Mammy to suffer in prison because of me.'

'No, I suppose you wouldn't. She tried to save you from coming here. I never had a Mother or Father. I hate my mother for leaving me outside of the orphanage. And I hate my father, whoever he is. I had a nightmare once when he was chasing me with something in his hand.'

'What *like* something in his hand, fer God's sake?'

'I don't know, but it was scary.'

'Can a person be murdered in dream?'

'Who knows; only last year one of the Sisters died in her sleep. Natural causes they said.'

'Perhaps someone from here had a dream she was murdering her.'

They ducked under the covers to stifle their laughter, shushing each other at the same time.

'I suppose the anger in me provokes these nightmares.' Angela sighed.

'That could be true. Like you said Angela, flying in my dreams could be wishful thinking. It could be a way of getting out of this place.

'I wonder if you're astral travelling Fiona.'

'Astral travelling . . .'

'Yeah, that's what it's called; Nanny told me all about it.'

'It's too spooky; what if I'm chased on one of my journeys by a man who wants to murder me.'

'Oh, sweet Jesus, if yis don't wake up tomorrow I'll know he caught you.'

They ducked beneath the bed clothes to stifle their laughter once more, trying to laugh in silence. When they had calmed down again, Fiona explained more of the dream.

'The thing is, it's the same dream each time, as if I'm reliving it, and it's been happening for ages. Angela, what the feck *is* astral travelling?'

'It's sort of an out of body experience, you know, when someone feels as if they're floating outside of their body, and they can see themselves laying there. Nan told me all about it. This happens quite a lot when a person has 'died' and is brought back to life. For instance, they can see doctors trying to save their lives, and have given proof by telling the doctors and nurses what they had seen when they were supposed to be dead. Some say they see a light at the end of a dark tunnel and people waiting for them who have been dead a while.'

'How do you know that? Do they come back and tell everyone?'

'Yes, because they were sent back, but in some cases the person does not want to come back to this world, because they feel happiness and immense love. They see wonderful colours and hear music. But if it wasn't their time to go, loved ones will send them back to this world.'

'But I was never dead, Angela.'

'Keep your voice down fer God's sake Fiona, I know you're not dead, I'm talking to yis aren't I, and I'm getting to that part. Apparently, a person can leave their physical body behind, and travel in their sleep, though it's said there's a silver cord that keeps us attached, but if the cord snaps, then the person cannot return to his body. Astral Travelling, that's what they call it.'

'Jaysus, I wouldn't want that to happen, left floating about in another world, where I see what people do and cannot communicate fer Christ's sake. How can I stop it?'

'You can't, there must be some sort of connection as to why you keep seeing the same thing, it usually happens when a person is asleep. You can travel anywhere, and according to Nanny, people put it down to dreaming. Although in a sense, you are dreaming. You're not actually flying out of your body all over the place. I always think it strange that a baby's life starts by cutting the cord. The baby can no longer return to the warm of and comfort of the womb, maybe it's . . .'

'I'm so fecking confused Angela, stop now. Sure, to God, I'll be dreaming tonight. I'll be going into my freezing bed now before we get caught and they think we're queer.'

'See you in my dreams.'

'Not if I can help it.'

They laughed and settled down to sleep.

Pauline McGuiness smiled to herself as she listened to the conversation, she would certainly be in favour when she told the Reverend

Mother what she had just heard. It will serve that Fiona right. Just because she has been here the longest, she thinks she is the leader. Well not anymore, same goes for that posh friend of hers. When they're gone, she can take over and rule the roost, especially when the Reverend Mother knows the conversation was about stupid things like time travel.

Angela knew something was wrong. Pauline was smirking and staring at her all morning in the laundry. A shiver went through her body. She prayed to God she hadn't heard anything from the night before. She couldn't wait to talk to Fiona for reassurance, but she hadn't seen her all morning which wasn't unusual really, she supposed. Fiona sometimes worked the gardens and didn't see her until the sun set. Angela's heart dropped. *Fiona would have known the day before that she was working outside.*

The moment she was dreading came. Her name was called, and she was summoned to the Reverend Mother's room. This was it. She was sure it had something to do with Pauline. She started shaking, even while she was still sweating from the heat in the laundry. When she knocked and opened the door, she saw Fiona; her face was all swollen from being slapped. She had obviously tried to keep her out of trouble, she knew Fiona too well. She will have told the Reverend Mother it was her who had been talking. Pauline would have told the truth and added more to it, but Angela wasn't going to let Fiona take the blame. The two of them were told to stand while the Reverend Mother wrote out some papers; the hot sun burnt down on them through the window, making Angela feel faint. They were ordered to stand in the same spot for over an hour, until two men dressed in white walked into the room and dragged Angela outside to the waiting car.

Fiona awaited her fate.

Chapter 18

Things were never the same for Fiona after Angela was taken away. Fiona missed her far more than anyone else in her whole life. There were other friends she had over the years, but when they left to move on . . . either back home or to a family member, she was happy for them and wished them well. Angela was different; she could really talk to Angela, laugh with her and trust her. She didn't deserve any of this in the first place, but to be taken away was so unfair. They were both to blame, and she hoped with all her heart that Angela didn't think she had betrayed her to protect herself. The Reverend Mother had beaten Fiona until she almost passed out, but she refused to put the blame on Angela. She knew Pauline had told on them, probably adding extra bits to be on the safe side, but there was no point saying anything. She knew from experience that once the sister's minds were made up, "that is the end of the matter".

'We're going to let things be with you Fiona.' The Reverent Mother had said the following day. 'You've been with us some time now and before that girl came here, we had no trouble from you . . . well, most of the time. She's possessed by the devil, so she is. Think yourself lucky we saved you from her evil clutches' the reverend Mother stood up from the chair 'It's important that you forget about her and everything she put into your head. Time travel. . . Fer the love of God, what sort of family was *she* from. Goodness knows what could have happened had she stayed. You're not to mention that girls name ever again, do you hear me?'

'But sister, we were talking about dreams and nightmares. Angela didn't do anything wrong. We were just talking. It was all said in fun. None of it was real. Please bring her back.'

'Fiona, she was overheard saying her grandmother was a witch . . .'

'No . . . *please*, her grandmother was just . . .'

'You were talking about murder, the afterlife and flying. You need to catch up on praying for your sins Fiona. You won't go unpunished. I haven't finished with you yet.'

'But she was innocent; she should never have been here in the first place. She was telling the truth. The boy tried to rape her.'

'How *dare* you use words like that in front of me? Don't push it Fiona. She will not be coming back, and that is the end of the matter. Any more talk of this and you *will* be joining her young lady.'

Fiona cried herself to sleep for a second night. Angela would not be coming back. She knew the Reverend Mother wouldn't change her mind. Poor Angela; she didn't deserve any of this.

Pauline McGuiness was keeping out of the way. She expected Fiona being carted off with Angela and was shocked to hear she was staying. Everyone liked Fiona. Her bed had the biggest group around it every evening, while she only had the odd friend or two. Now, hardly anyone spoke to her. Some spiteful person had put beetles in her bed last night, and she had screamed the place down. The sister in charge took her to the bathroom and forced her to eat soap for cursing and swearing at the girls. She knew there was more to come. The girls had their own way of punishing tell-tale tits.

She also knew it wouldn't be Fiona. She wasn't like that. She liked Fiona and hated her at the same time. The stuff they'd been talking about was interesting, and it would have been nice to have had the opportunity to take part in the conversation herself, for she had many tales to tell about ghosts, especially in this place. There were tales of hearing crying, and screaming coming from the graveyard, and then there was the mist floating eerily around the lower grounds at night. Pauline believed the whole building had spirits wondering around. Sometimes there could be a sinister atmosphere, a feeling of heavy sadness; everyone could feel it. A few girls claimed to have heard a sighing or a sobbing coming from empty rooms. There had to be ghosts. How many girls had died in this place through disease, heartache, or severe depression simply because they gave up the will to live? Then there were girls who disappeared . . . they may have been moved to an asylum, another home, or perhaps they escaped. Or perhaps they were buried in the grounds. Pauline believed the latter. A lot of the girls in the home, think there were girls murdered and that's why there were no names on the graves, but Pauline knew they all like to speculate through being kept in the dark when someone left. Yes. She would have loved to have been part of the conversations between Fiona and Angela. She was so envious of the two of them laughing and giggling all the while after lights out. Discussing ghosts and spirits had made her blood boil. She so wanted to be a part of their closeness.

She didn't gain any favours from the Mother Superior after all.

*

Angela sat in the back of the van looking out the window and listening to the two men talking.

'Do you know where Ballinasloe is?' 'I'm new here; in fact, this is only my second day on the job.'

'Yeah, I know them all. I remember *my* first week on the job. The bloody place scared the hell out of me, but I'm used to all the screams now. Jaysus, you should hear the sound of the electric shocks. I couldn't get out quick enough the first time I walked past the room where they were doing it. Ran fer me life I did.'

'What's this one going there for; she looks sane enough to me'. The man nodded his head towards Angela. 'She's only a young kid.'

'Not sure, they never told me. If they're violent, they usually tell us to strap them up in a jacket, but they didn't say anything about her . . .'

'Excuse me' Angela interrupted. 'I'm here you know, and I can hear what you're saying, and if you're trying to scare me then you've succeeded so shut the fuck up will yeah.'

'Jaysus, she's a fiery one.'

157

The men stopped talking and the co-driver fell asleep. Angela stared out of the window with tears blurring her vision. She had to get away, she had to, there was never going to be another chance once she was in that place. She looked at the lovely scenery, but it meant nothing to her now. Fields of barley and a few clusters of trees were on her right and she knew she could outrun the men if she could only get out of the car. The driver had been warned to keep an eye on her, after her attempt to run away before, so she was stuck. The men looked fit enough to catch up with her even if she had the opportunity to run. Thoughts were going through her head all the way there. *She had to do, she had to do it. Think Angela, think.*

Ten minutes later, her body started shaking violently and she was making chocking noises. Her eyes rolled to the top of her head. 'Stop the car' the co-driver yelled. 'She's having a fit. She needs help. Have you any knowledge of First Aid.'

'No. Have you?'

'No, I haven't, but there may be a First Aid kid somewhere in the van. For the love of god, they could have mentioned she had epilepsy.'

The driver pulled to the side of the road and gently lifted Angela out of the car and laid her on the ground while the co-driver ran to find a phone to call for an ambulance. He climbed into the van looking for a first Aid kit. Not that he would know what to do with it, if he found one. Angela waited until he was inside and quickly jumped to her feet towards the field. The driver spotted her through the window sprinted after her. Angel was surprised and disappointed of the speed he was running. The Barley crops slowed her down being so high; she just hoped he too was struggling.

'You little bastard,' he yelled 'you'll be in a jacket as soon as I get you back in the van.' But he was finding it hard to run any faster. He stopped to catch his breath, bending over, gasping for breath, cursing all the time. When he straightened up again, the girl had disappeared into thin air. He could see for miles, yet there was no sign of her. The crops weren't flattened anywhere as far as he could see, unless she managed somehow to straighten them up again . . . but that would take time. 'Where the fuck is she?' He was going to be in real trouble for this. The little cow.

Angela watched the men look for her, swearing and yelling at each other, arguing who was to blame. She was as high as she dared climb, hidden in an oak tree. She was always good at running and jumping and had been able to climb trees since she was very young. Something she had learned to do on her aunt's farm. The men sat down too near for comfort and lit up a cigarette. Angela hardly dare breathe and hoped to God they didn't stay long. Branches do sway and sometimes break. A squirrel appeared before her, looked at her and jumped to the ground startling the men, who decided it was time to go and face the consequences. Angela waited for some time before she climbed back down, but she didn't know where to go from there. She contemplated dying of cold and hunger *or* being locked away in an asylum where they attached wires to the head and gave electric shocks. *'Fer the love of God, I did nothing wrong.'* She didn't want either.

The sound of crows flying overhead woke her. She knew it must be morning but had no idea of the time. She was thirsty and her arms were sore from the spikes on the branches. She started to cry. She couldn't stay here. Somewhere in the distance was a stream, she heard the sound of water running during the night and could hear it now but couldn't see it. Following the sound, she thought of how her mother will feel when she finds out she is missing. Would they have informed her mother she was being locked away in an asylum? Her father would be fuming with her for causing trouble. She will never forgive him as long as she lived for shortening her life, all because of his bullying dirty mind. Her mother was beautiful, and Angela often wondered what she saw in him, but then, as her Nanny had said, aggressive behaviour makes people ugly, not just on the inside, but on the outside too. Angela had to hand herself in for her mother's sake; it was unfair to have worry.

She thought of her dear friend Fiona. She was right. The girls always ended up back in institutions again, as they had nowhere to go. Alas, this was different, she wouldn't be going back. She would be going to a mad house. She carried on walking towards the sound of the stream. In the distance she could see a few houses dotted here and there and wondered if . . .'

'Hello, are you all right. Your dress is torn . . . dear God, you have scratches everywhere' the woman said sympathetically, while touching a cut on Angela's face.

Angela fell to her knees and sobbed; she was about to tell the lady what had happened when she offered her a hand to stand up. 'Come on, don't talk now, let me bathe your wounds and make you a warm drink.'

*

Whether it was because Fiona was thinking of Angela all the time and feeling upset that brought the dreams back, she didn't know, but every night since Angela was taken away, she was in another time. She was floating in her dream, looking down on the girls sleeping, and feeling her being sucked out of the building, the cool fresh air on her face. Down below, the intricate patterns and colours of the ocean made her skin tingle. She watched how the waves crashed on the rocks and out again. People were walking and talking. Houses were everywhere. Lights glistened and shone. She wasn't close enough to hear conversations but could see across a huge span. Was this how it felt to be dead? If so, then that's where she wanted to be. Dead. Free to travel and see wonderful colours.

There were no colours in the Maggi laundries; everything was black and grey, apart from the white sheets and shirts they washed daily. What did Angela say? If the silver cord broke, you couldn't go back. 'I want the cord cut. Please cut the cord . . . I don't want to go back, please cut the cord. please let me go . . .'

'Fiona, shush, they'll hear you.'

'Pauline.' Fiona whispered, wiping the tears away with the back of her hands. What's happened? Why are you sat on my bed at this time?'

'You were dreaming, something about cutting a cord. I didn't want you getting into trouble and I was awake anyway.'

'Thank you. I must have been dreaming about the sewing room.'

'Yes, I thought that too Fiona,' but Pauline knew different, 'I am so sorry for what I did to you and Angela. I've had time to think about it, and deeply regret it. I can't sleep for thinking about Angela and what sort of life she will have now, all because of me. I will never be worthy of your friendship, but I was so jealous. I wish I was like you Fiona. You're very popular, and . . . and, I'm just horrible.'

'I suppose this place gets to us all Pauline. 'Tis sad about Angela, she was here for the wrong reasons. But I don't blame you. You didn't send her away, not really. Life is so unfair. I miss her so much. But things can't be changed and she won't be coming back.'

'Oh Fiona, I wish I could turn the clock back. I'm so sorry.'

'I know you are Pauline. We have to move on now, and we should all stick together until . . .'

'We die,' Pauline said quietly.

'Yes . . . 'til we die. How did you come to be here? I know you were here a while before you were moved into this dormitory. What did you do?' Fiona whispered.

'I had a boyfriend, Luke, his name was. He was older than me. Jaysus, me ma would have killed me there and then if she knew about him. We used to meet in Saint Stevens Green and spent the first few weeks sitting on the grass just talking. I could tell he wanted to kiss me, and to be honest, I wanted him to. He was so grown up at the side of the boys at school, and I didn't know what he saw in me really. I was young and naïve, and I suppose I was flattered. Once the kissing started, his hands were all over me and I used to push him away, giggling at the same time.'

Pauline started crying and Fiona put her arm around her. She felt sorry for the poor girl, who had probably bottled everything inside all this time.

'I'm sorry Fiona. I haven't told anyone else why I'm here, but one day he said I didn't love him. I told him I did love him, more than anything in the world. "No, you don't" says he. I was confused and asked why he would think I didn't love him. He said if I loved him, I would let him touch me . . . you know, down there. I adored him . . . and so . . . I let him touch me and things sort of got out of hand. It was all over within a few minutes. He said he loved me more than anything in the world now and wanted to marry me when I was sixteen. I was fourteen at the time.' Pauline broke down again. 'That was the last I saw of him. He didn't turn up in the park where we used to meet the next night. I went there for weeks. I didn't

161

know I was pregnant; I only ever had the one period before and didn't know when the next one was meant to be. I was very fat when Ma realised, I must be having a baby. She'd thought at first, I was just putting weight on. I was still a child at fourteen years old.'

Fiona held her again, she felt so sorry for this girl. She had no idea what she had been through. 'What happened then?'

'Of course, the Priest was sent for and I ended up in an institution for pregnant girls. I had a little boy, Antony; he was the most beautiful baby I ever saw. I begged my parents to let me keep him when they came to visit me, but they looked at the baby in disgust. I never saw them again after that day. Antony was adopted. They had to tear him from my arms. I'm not allowed to know where he lives, or if he has good parents. The thing is, I try to remember his little face and sometimes I can't . . . I can't see him.'

Pauline was sobbing by now, and Fiona held her tight. 'My family will never have me home again. They have disowned me, and it was my own fault.'

'Oh Pauline, you poor girl, it wasn't your fault. The boy got what he wanted, your virginity, through lies and false promises. If it's any consolation, I was dumped on the doorstep of an orphanage. My mother was a prostitute. I have no one coming for me either. I don't even know my birthday or the year I was born. I've never had a surname.'

They held each other and cried.

*

A few months later, Fiona plucked up courage to speak to Sister Theresa about Angela. Sister Theresa had spent time sitting and talking with Fiona and a few of the girls in the summer evenings. It was Sister Theresa who persuaded the Reverend Mother to allow the girls a transistor radio. She often joined in singing along to the songs, especially at Christmas and even joined in to do the twist. The dormitory was in uproar when she fell on the floor when the song sang out "round and round and up and down you go again." The girls had helped her up and she did see the funny side. The fall didn't stop her doing the Locomotion either. Sister Theresa was very well liked amongst the girls.

'Sister, please may I ask you something.'

162

'What is it Fiona?'

'Well, you know how close Angela and I were. She was my friend. I was wondering what happened to her. I know you can't tell me where she is, but, well . . .'

'No, I can't tell you where she is Fiona, but she isn't where she was supposed to go. That's all I'll be saying.'

'But where is she. Is she in a lunatic asylum?'

'No, she isn't. No one knows where she is. I must get on dear.'

As the nun made her way inside, she turned to wink at Fiona. Fiona gasped. Could she be right? 'She escaped, didn't she? Oh. Sister please tell me she escaped.'

The nun simply smiled and walked away.

Fiona kept going over the conversation in her mind. "No one knows where she is, but she isn't where she was meant to be going". 'She escaped. Oh thank you dear Lord.' Fiona worked out that by now she must be safe. When one of the girls escaped, they were usually brought back within a few days. Angela always said she would escape one day.

"I'm going to run away from here Fiona. I can't be locked away for something I didn't do. I know I can do it. I have an aunt, mammy's sister, just outside of Dublin, in Howth. She'll take care of me. I trust her. Perhaps I will get to see me ma. Mammy didn't want me locked away Fiona; she begged da not to do it. Aunt Sissy lives on a farm in the middle of nowhere. I can help on the farm.'

'Oh Angela, if only it was so easy. You'll be caught and be dragged back. The least is, your head being shaven, but worse, you could be sent away. Please don't try. What would I do without you? You've brightened up my life Angela'

'You come with me Fiona, there's plenty of room at the farm.'

'I've been here all my life and I have tried to run away, both from here and the last place I was in. I got caught straight away and I had to face the consequences. Angela, girls have tried to run away. This home has security all over. The fence is too high for anyone to climb and the gates are always locked. Don't do it.'

'If I could just get out, I can run really fast Fiona. I was always winning school races and I can jump, although not as high as the fence here. There has to be a way. Fiona, listen, if I ever do escape, I promise I will come for you. If you have a home to go to, and you have a job, they can't stop you from leaving."

Fiona wished she could travel out of her body and see the place where Angela was now. She felt in her heart her friend had made it. Sadly, she would never know if she was right.

Chapter 19

Dublin 1966

Joseph downed his last glass of stout of the day and made his way outside. He wiped his brow with the sleeve of his jacket, 'Jesus, it's still fecking hot and the sun has gone in. Still, I suppose this weather saves money buying coal.'

'Who're talking to now Joe, another ghost? Give her a kiss from me.' Paddy O'Brian laughed.'

'Fuck off will yea. I was talking to me self.'

'It's the first sign of madness if you ask me.'

'Yeah, well I wasn't asking you, was I?'

'Yer getting a right fecking miserable auld sod.'

'Yeah, well it's the fecking company I've spent too much time with.'

'Well, feck off then Joe.'

'And you feck off.'

When he was alone again, he fiddled with his loose change, checking if he had enough for his ale the next day. Money was tight these days. He needed to cut down on drink and buy some light bulbs instead of using candles. His eyes were drawn to a girl walking towards him. 'Jacqueline, I was thinking about you, I . . .'

'*What* were you thinking Joseph? Were you thinking about . . . taking care of me and the baby? I don't think so. You made that pretty clear yesterday. I only came to tell you I will be seeing the priest tonight.

Something has to be done. I need support, even if it means me going into the Maggie home. Ma and Da will kick me out, especially when I tell them how old the father to my baby is. You're a dirty old man Joe; who goes after innocent girls. I've heard all about you. Daphnia O'Rourke told me last week, how you use your good looks and charm to take girls virginity and then dump them. I don't know what I ever saw in you.'

'Ah yes, well you shouldn't listen to gossip. It's all lies. Yis didn't think like that when yer were in me bed, now, did yis.'

'I was stupid to think we had something between us. Young, naïve and flattered that an older man could be attracted to someone plain like me. I know I'm not the best looking girl in Dublin. You took advantage of me; then rejected me with a flick of your hand when I told you I was pregnant. Told me to go and sort the mess out me self, so yis did. The news will be all over the place soon Joseph McNamara, I'll make sure of that. What are your so-called friends going to think then, eh? They all know you took me back to your place.'

'Calm down, lets discuss this shall we. How do I know it's my fecking bastard anyway?'

'You know full well the baby is yours, but then, whether you know or not doesn't matter Joe, because you and I know I'm telling the truth. You took advantage of my insecurity and lack of self esteem. You led me to believe you loved me. I have proof you took me to your place; people saw you trying to sneak me upstairs to your hovel.'

'Are yis going to tell yer ma and da who the father is.'

'No, I'm too ashamed. I'll tell them I was raped.' Jacqueline started to cry at this point and Joseph put his arm around her . . . though his thoughts were purely on himself.

'Let's not stand here discussing something as private as this. There are people about. Let's go to my place for a cup of tea . . . nothing else, I promise; just to talk things through.'

'All right' she said through her tears.

Joseph unexpectedly felt a pang of guilt. The girl was just a kid at eighteen. She was right about not being the best looker in Dublin. He never

166

did choose a girl for their looks. He had no intention of getting serious at his age.

The room was bitterly cold and had an awful strange smell. Jacqueline covered her nose and assumed it must have been left over stale food, or rat droppings. The stench could have been Joseph farting all the time too, not caring where or who he was with. The fire wasn't lit, and the damp air made her shiver. A far cry from her first coming to the flat; when the fire was big and bright, and he had candles lit to give the place a romantic feel. She was a virgin, and believed he loved her. No one had ever said that to her before. What a bloody fool she had been. Looking around the room, Jacqueline realised she couldn't live with Joseph and his disgusting habits. The place was a pig sty; even the bedding had dirty coal marks everywhere and urine stains. The slop bucket at the side of the bed also stunk to high heaven. For Christ sake, he had a toilet opposite the bedroom, unlike in the tenement houses. There was no need for a slop bucket.

Jacqueline had a short glimpse of how her life would be if she were to live with Joseph. A baby sat on her knee, huddled as near to the fire as possible . . . if there was a fire. Joseph would be out drinking stout every night as he does now, while she and the child would go hungry. How blind she had been. Life at the Maggie's had to be better than this. The only thing being, she wouldn't be able to keep her baby. She decided there and then to go home and beg her mother to let her stay there and keep her child. If her mother said no, she would try her grandparents; surely, they would want to help.

Jacqueline was about to tell Joseph she didn't want to see him again, and to promise him that she wouldn't tell anyone he was the father, when she felt his hands around her neck.

'Oh Joseph, I did love you so, but . . .'

Joseph started to caress her neck and Jacqueline allowed herself to relax into his large warm hands. She laid her head back and raised her eyes to look at the handsome man who had swept her off her feet with mixed emotions. Could he change? She did love him. This was the Joseph she fell for. His touch was sensual and brought back memories of the wonderful time when they first met. Suddenly, his hands began to tighten. She tried to pull away, but he was holding her tight by the neck. He was strangling her!

She started gasping for breath, her hands on his as she tried to fight him off, gasping and choking. The blood vessels in her head began to burst and she heard a loud ringing in her ears. Her eyes fluttered open and shut and she was aware of shadowy shapes all around her, arms reaching out to her. A voice in her head was saying 'I don't want to die.'

The next thing Jacqueline heard was the loud crack of her head as she fell to the floor. Silence came, followed by calmness, and then came the darkness.

'Blackmail me would yer, well that's what happens to bastards who blackmail me.' Joseph roared, looking into her bulging eyes.

He sat down and lit a cigarette. 'Now, fecking what next; I have to get the body out of here and into the truck without being seen. Not as easy as last time. There are too many fecking nosy cows around here.'

He found a hessian coal sack and put the body inside. It was strange how different he'd felt when it was Molly's body he was going to bury. He'd really loved his beautiful wife, who'd always stood by him. To say Jacqueline was pregnant, this sack was light enough to throw over his shoulder with ease. Slowly he gently lowered the sack to the floor.

'Jesus Christ, a baby. I murdered another unborn child. My own child; what the hell is wrong with me? I need help.'

Sitting down with his head in his hands, Joseph cried.

The alarm went off at 1:00 am. Joseph reckoned it would be quiet outside at this time. He didn't see anyone on his way to the truck, and he was blessed by a dull, dreary night, with no moon.

'What a fecking difference. Just a bloody horse and cart I had last time. It's taken no time at all in the truck.'

He parked the truck on the roadside to avoid getting stuck in the mud again, and half carried; half dragged the body towards the wall. It was pitch black, but he had his torch, spare batteries and a cloth to wipe his brow in case it rained. He laid the body of the girl by the wall and went back to the truck for his spade. On his way, he thought he'd seen something out of the corner of his eye. Joseph fell to his knees cowering in fright just as a bird cried out and flew over his head. 'Eejit, it's a fecking bird.'

Halfway through the digging, Joseph stopped for a rest and mopped his brow. This time he was more aware of the girl dressed in white, rather than seeing her. He ran towards the tree with his spade, using the torch to find her.

'I'll fecking kill yea? Who are yea? Come here and show yer self, you coward.'

When he reached the tree, he saw a scrap of material caught on a branch which must have come from inside the sack. The cloth he was going to place over Jacqueline's face. There was no one there. 'They'll be fecking locking me in an asylum one of these days; dreams, hallucinations and now I'm fecking talking to me self.'

He walked slowly back to the wall, looking over his shoulder all the while, listening for sounds. He stood over Molly's body and cried again. 'Oh Molly, I wish I could turn back the clock. I would be different and look after you and the kids. Molly, please forgive me. I love you.'

He gently placed Jacqueline on top of Molly, who, thank the Lord, was still wrapped in the sack. He wouldn't have wanted to see her remains. No, he preferred to see his beautiful wife as he had in real life.

Joseph felt shattered and needed a rest before filling the hole up again. While resting on the wall and admiring his handy work, he wished he had brought a drink of some sort. A loud scream startled him. Half expecting to see a crow of some sort, he relaxed and turned his torch to the off position to stop anyone from the road seeing the light. That was when he saw the golden glow ahead of him. A noise like no other emitted from her mouth. The nearer she came towards him, the larger the hole was where her mouth should have been. He quickly jumped of the wall intending to face her and hit her with the spade which was still sticking out of the ground. However, the girl somehow floated towards him with such speed, he fell into the grave backwards. He heard another screech, and he knew.

'Lillian.'

Chapter 20

New York 1973

'This is so perfect' Mary squealed in excitement. 'The apartment is like a dream. I couldn't have imagined how beautiful it was going to be. There's so much space, yet still looks cosy. Oh, thank you Mom.'

'It's your father you should thank; he's the one who found the apartment for you.'

'Yes, and I'm so grateful to him, but you helped me fix the place up. It's just wonderful. How did you know what I liked? I mean, I know I left you to choose the décor, but it's perfect, I couldn't have chosen better myself.'

'Mary, you were always leaving magazines on the table and showing me pictures of interior designing, so it didn't take much working out. I enjoyed it. I wouldn't mind starting a new career in interior design.' Kate smiled.

'Really, that would be great Mom, but what about your photography. You love taking pictures.'

'I do, but it would be nice to try something different before I get too old. I really enjoyed designing the apartment. I've been a photographer for a long time now, maybe I need a change.'

'How did you get into being a professional photographer in the first place, I never did ask you?'

'When your father brought me to this wonderful city from Liverpool, I was completely in awe. I had never seen anything as beautiful in my life. I wanted to capture everything in my mind, but it wasn't enough, so your father bought me a Kodak camera. I was in Central Park on my own one day taking photographs of the autumn colours. We had only lived here three months when I wanted to explore this new world I was about to spend the rest of my life in. Your father was so impressed with the pictures, a year later he arranged for a developing lab to be built in our apartment while I was in England visiting a friend I lived with in Liverpool. You've heard me mention Brenda before, haven't you?'

'Yes, it was her wedding wasn't it. I don't remember you going to England; I must have only been a baby.'

'Yes', said Kate. I had no idea about the lab, but then, your father was always full of surprises.' Kate stopped for a few seconds and swallowed a lump in her throat.

'Are you all right Mom?'

'Yes. Where was I . . . oh yes? I was thrilled at the idea of being able to develop my films, but at the time, going professional was something I never dreamed of.'

'I vaguely remember seeing a large photograph of a woman sitting on a bench.' Mary said.

'That's right. I started to develop some of the prints I had taken in the park once. I noticed a woman sitting on a bench beside a pond where children were feeding the ducks. Nothing unusual, I knew I would be able to take her out of the picture. When I was looking at the prints, I noticed something in the woman's face; a kind of sadness, loneliness or loss. The lady was around sixty years old and she was looking at another couple walking by, around the same age, laughing together. I decided to focus on the woman rather than the autumn colours and scenery. Your father entered it in a competition without telling me and I won first prize. The rest you already know.'

'Oh, the poor woman Mom, did she ever get to see the print?'

'She did. I was back in the park one day when I saw her sitting on the same bench. I sat beside her and told her about the photograph, asking if she would mind if I used it. Of course, I knew nothing of the competition at the time, which was lucky really. Can you imagine the shock of seeing an enlarged photograph of yourself in a public gallery? I explained to her how her being in the picture was unintended. The following week we arranged to meet for lunch when I could let her see the print. She was quite pleased when she saw the photograph of herself. I mentioned the sadness I'd seen in her face. She told me she'd lost her husband the year before in a work-related accident, and she still hadn't recovered from the shock of losing her son, who had died in the Pearl Harbour bombing.'

Mary saw her mother's eyes fill with tears, touched by the sadness. 'Did you ever see her again?'

'Oh yes. I did see her again and we became very good friends. To be honest Mary, she was like a mother figure, I guess. I could talk to her and tell her anything. I trusted her. I found myself telling her things I hadn't even told your father. You were only very young the last time I saw her. She adored you and always insisted on holding your hand when we were out walking. You used to call her Aunty Jane. but you wouldn't remember her. She used to write you stories.'

'I remember the stories, you used to read them to me over and over again for years; in fact, I still have the stories somewhere. I can't believe the picture was of her, although, I can't remember her really. How come you stopped seeing Jane, especially as you had grown so close?'

'She seemed to suddenly disappear. I went to her apartment and a neighbour told me she had moved without a forwarding address. Jane had given me lots of help and motherly advice when you were very young. Sometimes I don't know how I would have coped without her help at the time. Becoming a mother is not something you are trained to do; you have to learn the hard way.' Mary watched as her mother stared into space, her mind lost in time, 'I don't know where she is now.'

'That's very strange.'

'Yes, it is. It was very sad not knowing what happened to her.'

'Did you fall out with her? It's unusual for someone to be so close to a person and suddenly leave without telling them.' Mary asked suspiciously.

'I did upset her one day when I told her . . . never mind, it was a long time ago and I really don't want to talk about it Mary.'

'Did she have a family?'

'As far as I knew she had another son and two grandchildren in England. Her eldest son had been stationed there during the war and married an English girl.'

'Perhaps she moved there.'

'Yes . . . yes, perhaps she did. Can we please close this chapter in my life?' Kate said, half smiling but serious too.

Mary knew her mother was holding something back but decided to leave it and change the subject. 'We'll have to work out for a moving date. Would you mind if Amy helped? I'll understand if you would prefer her not to.'

'That's perfectly fine. What's gone is gone. I have good memories and would like to keep it so. We can't change the past. I'm happy, and your father and Amy are happy.'

'Thank you, Mom, I love you.'

*

Mary's apartment was in Astoria Park South overlooking the end of Central Park, near to the East River. Her father had come across it in one of his business deals. The apartment was a substantial brick built; double fronted, semi-detached building, with huge rounded bay windows overlooking the park. The front door was framed by a canopy and Palladian pillars which gave it a superior appearance and made it stand out from the surrounding residences. Mary had chosen the apartment, along with her father, opting for the first floor as it had a good view of the park, giving her the feeling of living in the country while still being close to the hustle and bustle of her hectic city life.

Mary never underestimated how lucky she'd been in her life, being blessed in having a father who was part owner to one of the largest real estate companies in New York, Reiner Incorporated. She'd been given support and encouragement from her parents to achieve a Law degree. Within a short time of graduating, Mary had been offered a job in a reputable family firm in Franklin, near to her parent's house. Her grandfather, Jack Reiner, wanted Mary to go into business with him and her father, but Mary wanted to be successful in her own right and chose the law.

Sadly, her parents divorced six years ago. Her father had left her mother for another woman who was pregnant by him. Her name was Amy, and surprisingly, her mother took the breakup considerably well, taking into account they were happy together, or seemed to be. There was no bitterness or fighting over the divorce like some of her friend's parents. Mary eventually came to like Amy in time, and thankfully with her mother's blessing, strangely enough. Her father and Amy had three children now, giving Mary two sisters and a little brother that she adored.

*

Kate couldn't ignore the lump any longer. Six months had passed since she first felt a tiny pea sized lump in her right breast. Small or not, she knew she had to face the truth.

A trip to her doctor confirmed what she herself had thought. 'We have to act fast here Kate, if you found the lump six months ago.'

'I believed the lump was getting smaller, but I was fooling myself. Is it cancer?'

'Now let's not jump to conclusions. There are other possibilities. Quite often a lump could just be a simple cyst . . . and to be honest, most of the time that's what they are. I'll make an appointment with a very good friend of mine, John Richardson, who is one of the best in this area.'

'I don't know what to say.'

'I understand Kate. Breast cancer is one of a woman's greatest fears. I'll ring you as soon as I have spoken to John.'

Mary walked out of the building in a daze. *A lump isn't always cancer, it could be a cyst.*

Two days later the consultant rang Kate and a date was set for the following Friday. *The day Mary moved into her apartment.*

'But Mom you were looking forward to helping me move. I need you Mom; I can't visualise moving into my first home without you.' Mary sobbed down the phone to her mother.

'But this exhibition is really important to me Mary. You have to understand, I can't turn it down. I'm so sorry the date coincided with you moving into your new apartment but . . .'

'Is it because Amy will be there?'

'No, it has nothing to do with Amy. You should know that.'

'But . . . I won't be living at home anymore, only to visit.'

'I'm sorry Mary.'

The line went dead.

*

Kate sat in the plush waiting room pretending to flick through the glossy magazine. Her name was called, and she almost jumped out of her skin. She opened the door to see a very distinguished looking man around fifty years old dressed in a pinstripe suit. Both the doctor and the room showed no sign of anything clinical.

'Pleased to meet you Kate, I'm John Richardson, I'm sure my secretary asked if you wanted any refreshments.'

'Yes, she did thank you, but I'm all right.'

The doctor informed Kate of the procedure. Breast biopsy, scan, x-rays, but it flew over her head. She wanted to scream *get the goddamn thing out of me. Just do it.*

'Kate. Are you all right?'

'Sorry, yes I am.'

'Would you like to come this way?'

The doctor opened the door to another room, which *was* clinical looking, with complicated looking machinery, a couch and a tray of instruments.

'Don't look so worried' the consultant reassured her 'I just need to examine you and take a biopsy. If you'd like to pop behind the curtain and take the top half of your clothes off and put the gown on, while I ask my assistant to come in.'

Kate nodded and walked slowly towards the changing area. She wondered why people say *'Would you like to . . .'* no, I wouldn't *like* to take my clothes off and lie on a couch. I wouldn't *like* to be in this situation. But here I am, waiting to know if I'm going to die.

175

All the while the doctor was examining Kate; he talked about how most of the time lumps were benign. 'Often, a lump in the breast is a cyst, but we have to be certain it isn't cancer and that's the reason we do a lot of tests. We'll do the biopsy first and get a . . .'

She didn't want to hear the rest.

The doctor's voice came back again. 'Are you taking all of this in Kate?'

'I'm sorry. Yes I am.'

'Okay. I'll send the biopsy to the lab, but I have to say at this point, the biopsy only provides general information about any abnormalities. You may need further tests and perhaps surgery. I will ring you as soon as the results come back, which won't be more than a day or two.'

'Thank you, Doctor. If my daughter should answer the phone, please don't say you're a Doctor. I need to know the results before I worry her.'

'No, I wouldn't do that.'

*

Kate was expecting Mary to ring and tell her how the house move went, but she hadn't heard anything from her. She knew Mary was inclined to sulk when things didn't go her way, so Kate decided to leave things as they were. Two days later the phone rang. Kate raced to answer guessing it was Mary.

'Hello, is that Mrs Reiner?'

'It is, yes.'

'John Richardson here, I have the biopsy report back and I'm afraid we need a more accurate diagnosis of the lump. You're on the list for an open surgical biopsy to produce enough tissue for a pathologist to fully examine. We can fit you in next week if that's all right with you . . .Mrs Reiner, are you all right.'

'Yes, yes, just send me the details and I'll be there.'

The following week Kate lay on the trolley on her way to the theatre. She had told Mary she was going on a short break with a friend.

'Mom, a break is just what you need right now. How long are you going for?'

176

'I'm not sure yet, we're leaving it open. Mary, I'm so sorry I wasn't there for the move. I couldn't . . . I . . .'

Mom, don't be worrying over that. You know how selfish I can be sometimes.' Mary laughed. Let me know when you're back and we can meet for lunch.'

'I will. Mary, I love you.'

'And I love you too. Bye Mom.'

Kate still held on to phone and cried after Mary had gone. She was sick of lying.

One week later, Kate attended her appointment at the clinic.

'Mrs Reiner, can you hear me.'

Kate nodded her head; her mouth was too dry to speak.

'I'm just going to add an intravenous drip into your arm.'

'Is it . . . is it cancer? Kate croaked.'

'The doctor will be coming to see you shortly.'

Kate must have dropped off to sleep again and was woken by the doctor. 'You've had a good sleep Mrs Reiner. You've slept most of the day.'

She could tell by the doctor's face it was cancer.

'I'm sorry to be the one that has to tell you this Mrs Reiner, but the lump in your breast is cancer, and quite advanced. We removed the breast which as we discussed with you earlier, was a possibility. . .'

'Am I going to die Doctor?' Kate interrupted, knowing she had put him in a predicament. He couldn't give her any false hope; neither could he say outright, "Yes Mrs Reiner, you are going to die."

'We're going to do everything we can to make you more comfortable. . .'

'So . . . I am going to die. How long do I have?'

'We have drugs, chemotherapy and there's always hope. Hundreds of people have been helped by this.'

'If I'd come to see you sooner, would you have been able to cure the cancer? I ignored it for so long, just hoping it would go away.' A sob caught in her throat. 'I wasted time. I was in denial I suppose.'

'Whether or not we would have been able to beat the cancer in the early stages is a difficult question to answer. Some cancers are very aggressive and spread faster than others, while some are hard to detect. Don't blame yourself; no one knows how they would have reacted, and no one wants to believe the lump could be cancer.'

When the doctor left, Kate felt her stomach tighten, thinking of how she was going to give Mary the news about the cancer; and how it had spread. She'd be heartbroken enough knowing that Kate had kept the doctors' visits from her.

*

'Kate's handheld the receiver tightly, 'Hi Mary is it all right to talk or are you busy.'

'Never too be busy to speak to my mom. Did you and Stephanie have a good time?'

'Can you come over after work? I need to speak to you Mary.'

'Why, what's wrong?'

'I'll tell you when you get here.'

'I'm coming right now. Something is wrong, I can tell by your voice.'

Mary arrived an hour later. Her face was white, as if she already knew. Kate didn't know which the worst was, the tears or the long silences. Mary was the first to speak.

'This is 1973; they have come a long way with cancer. New drugs are coming all the time, and people live normal lives now.'

'Yes, so they told me. Mary, I'm not afraid of dying. I just want you to know.'

'Oh no, please Mom, don't talk of death.'

'I'm only telling you in case I don't get the chance. I've seen people dying and I know from the drugs they take for the pain; they never get the chance to talk. Mary, I'm sorry.'

'Sorry for what? For giving me the best childhood anyone could wish for. We'll have no more talk of dying. We need to be positive.'

*

Gruelling hours of Chemotherapy had not stopped the cancer spreading. Be it now, the day after or next week, the smell of death was here. Kate was back in hospital and knew this would be the last time. She

178

wouldn't be leaving alive. Mary was inconsolable when the doctor broke the news.

'I'm sorry, but it's only a matter of weeks. We did everything we could. The only thing now is to control the pain the best we can and make you comfortable. I'm so sorry.'

Mary threw herself into her mother's arms and sobbed. 'You can't die, you can't.'

'Don't be upset Mary.' I've had a good life. Some people die never knowing happiness. You and your father have given me so much. Meeting him in Liverpool was the best thing that ever happened to me. It was love at first sight.'

'You have always been more than a Mom to me.' Mary cried 'you're my best friend. I can't imagine a life without you.'

'You still have your father; he adores you Mary. How is he? I know he will be hurting too. I didn't hold it against him for leaving me. I want you to know that too, and I'm happy for them. Amy is a very nice person and I feel much better knowing she will be there for you when I'm . . .'

'Oh Mom, don't say it.'

'I prefer not to see anyone Mary . . . not even my closest friends. I want them to remember me as I was. And that includes your father.'

*

That was just four days ago, and now Kate was waiting for the Angel of death to pay her a visit. She was ready to die now. The pain was unbearable, and her body couldn't take anymore. It was hard at times to open her eyes, but she knew Mary was there beside her. Sleeping didn't allow her to escape; she was having such frightening dreams.

'Mary' Kate screamed out. 'Mary, I have to tell you something . . .'

'It's okay Mom, you're dreaming again. Do you want me to go get the nurse? Are you in more pain, I can . . .'

'No, I'm fine; I should have told you Mary . . .'

'Mom, try to rest now.'

Kate settled back down again and drifted in and out of sleep and dreams, not quite knowing which was real anymore. A song unexpectedly came into her head. One she had taught Mary as a child.

Bless my daddy, my dear, dear Daddy.
He's the nicest Daddy in the world.
When we have good weather, we go out in the sun.
We play together and we have lots of fun.
He buys me popcorn and ice cream sodas.
Then I fall asleep upon his knee.
I love my daddy.
And he loves me.

Mary only four years old at the time, she looked up at Kate, her eyes big and bright. *'Momma, did you sing the song to your daddy when you were a little girl?'*

'No, sweetheart, I didn't. This song is for you and your daddy. It's very special.'

'Will you teach me a song to sing to you like this one, Mommy?' Mary asked eagerly.

'Yes, I promise.'

Suddenly, Kate felt herself being propelled into a dark tunnel. She could see a light shining and for a split second wondered if the end had come. The sound of a child crying was coming from somewhere.

'I want my mommy, I want my mommy.' The child sobbed. *Kate followed the cries. Treading very lightly, she slowly opened the door to a bedroom, already knowing what she was about to see. In the bright coloured room, a young child, about the age of three is sobbing, holding a baby's knitted jacket to her face. The heartbroken child looked up to see Kate standing before her and cries. 'Mommy, I want my mommy.' Pushing Kate away, 'and I want Emmy. Where's my Emmy?'*

Kate held on to the child tightly as she struggled in her arms, and gently rocked her to sleep as little sobs filled the quietness of the night. She gently tucked the child in her cot, kissing her forehead. As she was about to tiptoe out of the room a life sized doll walked towards her, holding a pair of scissors in her hand. The doll grabbed Kate's hair and started to cut ferociously. Blood trickled down her face and she screamed hysterically.

'Mom . . . Mom.' Mary cried anxiously, 'are you all right? I'm going to get the nurse.'

Mary came back into the room with Nurse White who gave Kate a shot in the arm and gently consoled Mary, reassuring her it was a dream.

'It's the medication Mary that can cause nightmares and hallucinations sometimes; I see it all the time with patients. She'll be all right soon.'

'Oh, Nurse, it was awful, she was screaming. Her eyes were wide open in terror and she was staring at something or someone in the room, crying out she was sorry . . . something about a doll and blood.'

'The mind plays terrible tricks when you're on as much medication as your mother, but then, medicine is the only way to help with the pain. Would you like a cup of coffee? I'll go and bring us both one, shall I? And sit awhile with you.'

'Thank you.' Mary sobbed.

The nurse came back with two coffees in her hand and sat opposite Mary. 'All we can do now Mary is pray for a peaceful death. Sometimes things that have been locked away in the mind come back from the past. It may be something trivial, but dreams can soon turn into terrible nightmares, as in your mother's case.'

*

Mary sat alongside of her mother's bed all night and welcomed the daybreak, watching the sun rise. At any other time, this would have been a lovely sight to see on a beautiful June morning. The blue sky and the sun's warmth penetrating through the window seemed to shout; 'good morning New Yorkers. Have a nice day.' Mary always loved this time of year; the early morning sunrise, the late balmy nights, barbeques and laughter with friends. Sitting on the porch swing with her mother; both talking and laughing together.

Her thoughts were broken when she heard a sob from her mother while she was sleeping. She sighed and wished those happy days were back again. Her mother let out another groan and Mary wondered if she was in pain, or if she was dreaming. She had been given strong medicine, but the effects of the drug weren't as lasting now. The woman who lay in the hospital bed bore little resemblance to her mother. Her frail body had shrunk into skin and bone, her cheeks were hollow, and her eyes were closed from the medication which dripped, drop by drop, into the veins of her neck through a tube. Although her mother had her eyes closed most of the time, Mary was certain she was aware of her presence. For three long days and nights now, she had sat holding her delicate hand watching her drift in and out of an unsettled sleep.

The nurses had provided a recliner chair for Mary to at least lie back and rest awhile and Nurse White came into the room every thirty minutes to check on Kate's condition. She sometimes stayed when she wasn't busy and chatted to Mary about her life as a nurse. She told her how she had been nursing for over thirty years and had given up her one chance of being married.

'I was seeing a young man, Richard, for three years when he asked me to marry him, but unfortunately in those days you couldn't have both, not like today. I loved my job and knew I wasn't the 'stay at home' type Richard wanted me to be, so I turned down his offer and carried on nursing.'

'Have you ever regretted that decision?'

'Oh yes, many times. I will never know what it's like to have a family, my parents passed away long ago, so I'm on my own really. But I love my job.'

Nurse White looked over to Mary and noticed a tear running down the corner of the young girl's eye. The last few weeks of a cancer patient's life were much harder to bare for the relatives than the patient themselves in some ways. The terminally ill were often so full of drugs they were unaware of time. She wished the end would come sooner than later, for Mary's sake. Nothing could bring back her mother.

The nurse left the room when she heard a patient cry out and Mary couldn't help but feel sadness for her. The day would come when she would retire with no-one to love or care for her. Death or dying was something Mary had never thought of much in her life. The most serious illness in her family was when her mother had caught a severe chest infection, which she seemed to be prone to all her life, often turning to Pneumonia. Mary's grandparents from her father's side were still living, and though she saw little of them, they were pretty fit and active as far as she knew. Deaths never occurred in Mary's life. Death happened to old people.

As for her maternal grandparents, she knew very little of her mother's younger years and Mary wished now she had asked her mother about the life she had as a child. The only thing she did know was her parents met in Liverpool and married very young when her father was stationed there during the war. She supposed very few people liked to be reminded of the war, especially if they had lost loved ones.

She gently let go of her mother's hand and tenderly kissed her on the forehead as she walked across the room and opened the window slightly. The birds were chirping away to each other as they woke from their sleep. Strange, how just one bird would chirp, another would chirp back and before long it appeared the whole population of birds had joined in the morning chorus.

Mary closed her eyes and took a deep breath into her lungs before closing the window again. She tiptoed slowly to her mother's bed and lightly touched her cheek, quietly closing the door behind her. She looked at her watch. 6.05 AM. She needed to get some air, away from the clinical smells of the hospital for a while. She made her way to a vending machine, her mouth felt dry again from all the coffee she had consumed to keep her strength up all through the night. It seemed the more coffee she drank, the more she needed.

Walking along the brightly lit corridor, Mary passed the hospital rooms, glancing at the patients sleeping peacefully, though most of them slept through heavy medication. Sometimes the doors were closed when patients cried out in pain, so as to give them dignity.

*

Kate drifted in and out of sleep. She was awake when Mary left the room, but had kept her eyes closed. Tears ran down her face, but she was too weak to reach for a tissue and dabbed them with the bedclothes. There was so much she wanted to tell Mary, but it was too late now, she didn't have the strength to speak. Kate wished to God Jane was still in her life. She was such a good friend and would have been support for Mary, and if she had enough strength, she would give Mary the phone number to call Jane. *'You're a fool Kate.'* She thought to herself, *'if only you hadn't been so stubborn.'* Kate remembered the last time she saw Jane. They had a huge argument, all because of a stupid doll.

'Give her the damn doll, Kate.' Jane had said, 'What harm can it do, for Christ's sake.'

'No Jane, not this one, I'll buy her a doll myself.'

'Kate, you have bought her a doll and she didn't want it, she wants *her* doll. She's heartbroken poor child, look at her. Give her the doll.'

'No, I won't. I'll keep it and give it to her one day, but not now.'

Of course, Jane was right. Kate could see that now. There had been many more disagreements over Mary's upbringing and one day Kate had told Jane to mind her own business, and to stay away from her and her child. That was the very last time she saw her closest friend.

'Oh, dear, dear Jane, I'm so sorry, I ruined everything.' Kate cried. The one person she would have told on that fateful day she found the lump. Jane would have insisted on taking her to be examined there and then. She was also the one she would have asked to accompany her to see the specialist for the results.

Nurse White walked into the room. 'How are you feeling Kate, the doctor will be around this morning. Would you like a drink of water?'

Kate nodded her head and the nurse left the room to get fresh water, her footsteps becoming fainter as she walked along the corridor until it fell silent again. Looking towards the window, Kate realised she would never again feel the sun on her head, or the wind on her face. No more snowball fights and Christmas shopping with Mary. She thought about the end. Would death come suddenly, or would she feel a warning of some sort. Would anyone be waiting for her? Kate was pleased her daughter had respected her wishes and kept visitors away. She didn't want pity or comments about how ill she looked, or their own embarrassment of seeing a person dying from cancer.

*

Sitting on a bench overlooking a garden, Mary shed a few more tears. Looking up towards the blue sky, she wondered how long it would be now before she lost her mother forever.

'You would love this garden Mom.' Mary said softly.

The garden had been planned with a lot of thought, with flowers and shrubs intertwined on a pathway broad enough for wheelchair access. Tall tree's acted as windbreaks, allowing the sun to glisten through the leaves, a small water fountain trickled slowly into a fishpond which was filled with brightly coloured fish and water lilies. Bees flew from one flower to the next as if on a mission and the sound of birds twittering to each other finished the whole tranquil scene. 'Yes,' Mary thought, 'very well planned, this hospital's own little Garden of Eden.'

She tried hard to keep the image in her mind of how her mother used to look, and not as she looked now. People on many occasions commented on how alike they were, though her mother had mousy coloured hair which she'd dyed blond for as long as she could remember in contrast to her own dark hair, but they both had the good fortune of having natural curls which framed an oval shaped face. Her friends had envied Marys curls, and laughed how they had to spend sleepless nights with curlers in their hair to get the same look. As for her father, Mary looked nothing like him really, apart from inheriting his dark hair. She was tall like her mother, whereas her father was slightly shorter. She laughed to herself how her mother had complained about not be able to wear high heeled shoes since meeting her father.

Mary wondered if her father would come to the funeral. *Funeral*, how could she use the word funeral when her mother was not even dead? How could she. Opening her bag Mary brought out a tissue to dab her eyes. She knew all along her mother would never find love again when her father left home, as pretty as she was. She had plenty of admirers and offers of love from men, but she wasn't interested and seemed happy on her own.

As far as Mary was concerned, her parents had the perfect marriage, until a few months before he broke the devastating news. The once loving and attentive husband began to distance himself, becoming easily irritated and angry over the slightest thing. Her father once looked adoringly into her mother's eyes before things changed.

Her home was everything to her mother. Mary often caught her gently stroking a piece of furniture with pride in her eyes; everything had a place and was carefully put away, which sometimes angered her father.

"It's like living in a damn show house. Fer Christ's sake Kate" he would moan. "The place looks like a museum or an advertisement for selling homes. I put something down and the goddamn thing is gone when I turn around."

Privacy was something else her mother was insistent on, refusing hired help as suggested by her father, or even a nanny when Mary was young. Once in a while a cleaning company would come and pull the furniture out, clean everything in the house from top to bottom, giving the house a good overall. Catering staff would also be employed with the large amount of entertaining her father liked to do, otherwise her mother insisted on cooking meals herself the rest of the time.

Mary remembered clearly when the change in her father began. He always preferred to work from home if possible, but all of a sudden, he started to spend more time at the office. Thinking back now, she realised the nights he had gone to the office, and the long weekends away from home, were probably spent with the woman he had previously engaged as his secretary. Her father had invited Amy and his colleagues for dinner the year before leaving, and Mary noticed the two of them had gone into the garden together. When they returned, Mary could have sworn her father had a red mark on his face near to his lips and noticed too how he went straight to the bathroom. Amy was a petite woman compared to her mother. She was also extremely attractive, with long thick blond hair that hung to her shoulders.

Mary stood up from the garden seat. The morning sun was already hot, and she guessed it was going to be a scorcher today. Making her way back to the ward to be with her mother; her shoulders drooped slightly forward, showing the signs of a woman of great sorrow.

Chapter 21

Peter pushed the swing higher and higher and his four-year-old daughter Beth squealed in delight; 'More Daddy, faster.' He gave her an almighty push and looked down on his sleeping son holding his little blue baby cover to his cheek; the cover he preferred to hold rather than cuddly toys. Tom was almost a year old now. He and Amy had been trying for another baby for three years before she phoned him at his office to tell him the news. He was thrilled and so was Amy. Peter had watched all three of his children to Amy come into the world. The first being Lauren, almost ten years ago, he remembered tears falling from his eyes when the nurse placed his daughter into his arms. He was proud of his children and at one time wondered if he was too old to try for another baby, but Amy had said that three children were enough.

Since the age of eighteen, Peter had dreamed of having lots of kids with Kate, and would picture the children running around the house. That was not to be. However, falling in love with another woman was never his plan either. He had loved Kate from the first time he set eyes on her, but his life changed the day Amy walked into his office. It wasn't her looks . . . yeah, she was beautiful, but it was the warmth of her personality. He loved the mischievousness about her and her outlook on life, and the way she always made him laugh. Amy had something very special about her which made him feel complete when he was with her and extremely lonely without her.

She had worked for him for three months when, after a stressful day, he asked if she wanted to grab a bite to eat. He had already planned to eat at the Mexican restaurant, where he usually took his clients, as Kate was out with friends on that particular evening. The circumstances couldn't have been better planned.

That was it; he was hooked. He loved her. Peter had felt tremendous guilt, he'd never looked at another woman since meeting Kate, but he couldn't see enough of Amy. She had opened up something inside of him that he never knew he had. She was full of life. They had so much to share and talked for hours into the night when they managed to get a few weekends together. A few months after the affair began he had taken Amy away for a week, which turned out to be the best holiday of his life. She liked adventure and didn't care to lounge about on a beach all day as Kate had. He'd forgotten how much he loved sports, and was bursting with energy and happiness. Amy had so much enthusiasm and each and every day with her was new to him.

Exhausted after another day of activity, they sat by the pool, getting to know one another's past and what their dreams had been. Peter told Amy how his life in real estate had already been mapped out for him by his father. 'I guess I never gave a thought to anything else, other than having kids and saw myself being a great Dad.'

'Yet you had just the one child, how come?'

'Kate had problems and . . . enough of me. What about your dreams?'

'I hope to teach and maybe travel to countries where I can really help. You know, teach kids in poor countries; I don't see myself working in an office for the rest of my life.'

His heart sank at the thought of not seeing Amy at the office every day. He was terrified of losing her. She was young and beautiful, and it wouldn't be long before another man came along; someone without any commitments to slow him down. The day came when Amy walked into his office and told Peter, without a greeting or a smile, she needed to speak to him in private, away from the office. She looked as if she had been crying. *She was about to break their relationship.* He was going to lose her.

*

Peter sat on the bench, which was their regular meeting place in Central park, along the side of Turtle pond, far enough away from the office. The sun shone brightly down from the sky, and the pond glistened with the iridescent colours of autumn. He looked around the park and watched children laugh and play and remembered how much Kate loved

188

this time of year. Thinking of her almost made him want to cry. He had suffered sleepless nights of guilt when his relationship with Amy began. He was grumpy on a morning and irritable in the evening. Peter never wanted to hurt Kate. He knew if she was ever to find out about his affair with Amy, it would break her heart. And here he was now, waiting for Amy to finish the relationship. He knew from the look on her face and the urgency to see him she was going to end it all.

Would things return to normal with Kate? Could he love her as he had? He wasn't sure. The day he brought his wife to the Park for the first time, he felt so happy and proud. He smiled inwardly when he remembered how much in awe Kate was of the park's beauty. How he laughed when she insisted, they went there once a week until she had seen everything. Different times of the year, the Park had given Kate the inspiration to photograph the amazing colour of the ponds, the trees, children playing, children feeding the ducks.

Kate's photographs surprised Peter. The preciseness and her ability to see things in a different way to other people deeply impressed him. He remembered the day he hired someone to create a developing room of her own. Kate had gone to Liverpool to attend her friend's wedding. She screamed with delight when he opened the door to her studio complete with a lab.

Although Peter had gone to the Park many times over the years, he had never appreciated its true beauty until he went there with Kate. It was the little things he never really noticed before. His eyes were opened to the park's loveliness for the first time. Who would have thought she would be a successful photographer a few years later? Kate had led such a simple life before he met her, and she had very little in the way of education, yet, over the years her eagerness to learn became a passion.

Peter watched the ducks run to one side of the pond chasing after a piece of bread someone had thrown in, and suddenly caught sight of Amy's figure walking towards him. He jumped up from the bench and almost ran to meet her. She started to cry on seeing him. They kissed and sat on the wooden bench, Peter dreading the words that were about to come.

'Peter, I don't know how to say this . . .'

'Oh Amy, please don't tell me you're leaving . . .'

'I'm pregnant Peter.'

'Pregnant?'

'Yes. Believe me when I tell you, it wasn't planned; I took my contraceptive pills every day. I suppose it could have happened when I had the flu, perhaps the pills lose their effect . . . I don't know how it happened, I . . .'

'Oh Amy my darling, Pregnant, why, that's wonderful . . .' he stopped mid-sentence to embrace her. 'I thought you were going to tell me you had found another job and didn't want to see me anymore and you.'

'Peter, stop it. What about Kate? I'm pregnant. Don't you get it? I can't keep the baby, Peter, not on my own, and I never expected you to leave Kate. I don't know really what I expected from you; I tried not to think about our relationship in future terms, I always put it to the back of my mind. I just knew I loved you, and I was willing to put up with sharing you with your family, but I have to work Peter, I need a life too. And before you say anything, let me get this straight. I don't want you to rush out and buy an apartment for me and the child. I don't want money from you, I want my own independence. I have no choice but to terminate this baby, and very soon.'

Making the decision to leave Kate and start a new life with Amy was much harder than Peter had thought, but he wasn't prepared to abort his child. Amy was right; she'd not once put pressure on him to leave Kate, and had literally put her own life on hold, choosing to stay at home while he spent time with his wife. Christmas time being the hardest for Amy, as Peter had no reason to leave the family home without raising suspicions.

*

His thoughts were suddenly broken into when he heard a scream. Beth had fallen from the swing with a bump. He dried her face gently and rubbed her elbow. 'It's time to go now sweetheart.'

'Please Daddy, can we stay just a little longer, please, please, please.'

'No, not today, I have some work to attend to, maybe later.'

Peter often worked from home and had never taken his success for granted. He now employed hundreds of workers, the business was very

190

good, and the money kept pouring in. Being the boss gave him the opportunity to spend time with his family, and he chose to work from home as much as possible rather than spending time in his office.

Walking away from the play area, his mind went back to his other family, his daughter Mary and his wife Kate, who was now lying on a bed with death hovering over her. His heart felt heavy.

Amy was looking out of the window, watching Peter and the children walk up the driveway. She noticed Peter looked as if he was about to cry. She knew how he must be feeling about Kate; there was always going to be a part of him that still loved her, Amy knew right from the start he would always have feelings for Kate, and she understood. She was lucky enough to have a good relationship with Mary. It had taken a while, but Mary had been very understanding once the initial shock of her father leaving home was over. She had come to visit when Lauren was born, bringing her a big bunch of roses and a card.

There, Mary stood at the bottom of the crib looking at her half-sister's tiny frame.

'Oh, she's so beautiful, I have never a seen a baby as cute in my life Amy. What's her name?'

'Lauren, your father chose the name, would you like to hold her Mary?'

From that moment a bond grew between the two of them and Mary adored her baby sister, often coming to bathe and feed her.

The poor girl was going to be lost without her mother. Amy had to wait now for Mary to get in touch. Kate had shown no bitterness to either her or Peter, which in some ways made it harder for Peter rather than easier. Amy was always afraid of him going back to Kate in the beginning.

They had all been there together for Mary's graduation day and had gone back to Kate's house afterwards for a meal with friends. Kate had been kind involving Amy at Mary's special day, there was no bad atmosphere between them; which had surprised everyone. Amy had tried to keep in the background as much as possible, but the glares from Kate's friends didn't go unnoticed.

Amy wasn't proud at what she'd done; she hated herself for breaking up a happy home. The divorce was very hard for both Peter and her to live with the guilt, and Amy wondered, in those early, years if Peter would have eventually tired of his adultery, had it not been for the pregnancy. It wasn't easy for him, and after the divorce, Peter made sure Kate lived the life she was used to. He gave enough for her and Mary to be financially secure.

She recalled the day she'd helped Kate move into her apartment in Astoria Park. Kate told Mary she had to go to an Art exhibition in Long Island and how important it was for her to go.

'How could she Amy,' Mary sobbed 'she knew how I wanted her to help me move. It's so unlike Mom, she never put work before me. Today is such a big day.'

'I'm sure there is a good reason Mary, and who knows; she might just suddenly turn up.'

'She won't. I know she won't. I can't help but think I've done something to upset her, she hardly spoke to me this morning when she left the house.'

It was obvious now where Kate had been. She was probably in the breast clinic, waiting to be told if she had cancer or not. She would never have put an Exhibition before Mary's move to her new home. Kate was looking forward to it. The move had been planned for weeks. How courageous Kate had been, keeping the worry to herself so as not to spoil Mary's big day. Amy dabbed her eyes; the poor woman must have suspected for some time it was cancer.

*

Back at the hospital Nurse White stood and watched Mary through the window. Poor child, why does life have to be so cruel? She had seen hundreds of patients die from cancer. Relatives gather around the bed, praying and willing a loved one to suddenly make a recovery; never giving up hope. Nurse White had lost count of the number of times she'd heard a person cry out; 'Why?'

Of course, every cancer patient is special to a relative, however old they are, but to see parents holding a young child who has barely lived long enough to even understand death; now that must be the saddest of

192

all. She had seen babies and young children suffer more than any adult could ever take, and still manage to laugh and play games. Perhaps it was because they have no understanding of pain or death. They simply accept it. On the other hand, older children would often take on a parental role, comforting and reassuring the dying parent, in some cases even hiding the fact they are going to die.

Mary was on her way back to the ward and Nurse White knew it wouldn't be long now. Kate was going into the final stage of the dying process. Working in a hospital for terminally ill patients, she had learned to know when the time was near. On some occasions, she had seen a white mist hovering above a patient waiting to take them to the other side. Not that she would tell anyone. They would think she was imagining it and may even suggest she left the job. But no, it wasn't her imagination. She had seen the mist, and she had witnessed enough people on the verge of dying who saw it too.

So many times she had stood beside the bed of a patient, who hadn't been able to move for weeks, suddenly sit up straight and call out a name while holding out their arms, reaching to someone in the room not visible to anyone else. In some cases, the room would suddenly go cold and once she had even heard soft music. Music she had never heard in this world, and too hard to describe. She had even seen colours around a patient, just for a few seconds.

Patients, who had been dying for a longer period of time, had told Nurse White about seeing angels, or a dead relative. The sudden relief on their face knowing they wouldn't be on their own when leaving this life obviously gave them tremendous courage and made it easier for them to pass over.

During her training, she was offered a placement in a children's cancer unit. Eighteen years old at the time; she was devastated and constantly broke down in tears whenever a child died. She knew she shouldn't get emotionally involved, but nonetheless spent endless time on and off duty, comforting the parents the best she could. She was present when a child spoke casually to an unseen person in the room a few hours before death. Interestingly, she discovered how children often spoke of seeing Angel's without wings. The first time, she and another nurse, witnessed a child describe an angel in this way, they put it down to the child's imagination. A few of the nursing staff thought it was the medication they were taking, after all, certain drugs are known to cause hallucinations.

'If that were true,' Nurse White said one day during a break, 'then why wouldn't the child see Angels with wings as depicted in art and literature. Most children like angels and fairies, and in all children's books they show angels with wings.'

'Well, that's a very good point Joan. One young girl I was in charge of, told me she had seen an angel and described a black man. Now, there's nothing in children's books I've seen to show a black Angel. Angels are seen as pretty white females.'

'To be honest, I always think of them as being beautiful fairy like human beings with huge wings, but I never recall seeing an angel without wings. Even the Archangel Gabriel had wings *and* he was a man by the way Betty.'

'Yes, because we were brought up to believe that sort of thing. Just like we were brought up to believe all angels and fairies have wings.'

'My point is a child wouldn't describe an angel without wings. Anyway, Gabriel wasn't an Archangel; he was an angel of God.'

'What's the difference?'

'Oh come on now; let's not be going into all that.'

The discussions about angels were often spoken of during break periods and Nurse White kept the other strange happenings to herself. She was once in a room with a four-year-old boy called Michael and his mother. Suddenly he reached out and shouted, 'Uncle James, you came to see me, I knew you would,' then turned to his mother and asked who the old lady was, holding his uncle's hand.

'What old lady, sweetheart? I don't see anyone, and Uncle James isn't very well. Perhaps you had a dream . . .'

'Uncle James is here Momma, and so is the old lady. She came to see me last night and was holding a baby . . . she told me her name is Katherine. Who is she Momma?'

The distraught mother ran out of the room and Nurse White followed her. 'Are you all right? Perhaps he's hallucinating. It's very common with the drugs they take.'

'No, he's not Dreaming or Hallucinating.' Composing herself, the mother spoke through tears 'His uncle James died the first week Michael was admitted here, three weeks ago. We didn't tell him because we didn't want to upset him; Michael was very close to my brother. Katherine was my mother. Michael never knew her; she died two years before he was born. The year she died, I lost a baby, probably with the shock of losing my mother. The strange thing is, I rarely mentioned my mother to Michael, and if I did mention her to anyone else, I always referred to her as Mom. No one ever called her Katherine when she was living either. She was referred to as Kathy, or as I said . . . Mom.' The woman wiped away the tears which were now running down her chin. 'Michael kept asking me when Uncle James was coming to see him and I told him he had a tummy bug.'

Joan White had always kept an open mind, but too many things had happened for it all to be nonsense. Whether the visions were in the mind or not, knowing a loved one had come to take them to the other side made passing much more bearable for the ones who were dying. She had seen a calm serenity wash over a patient when they knew they were not leaving this life alone. Be it a friend, relative or an angel. Years ago, Nurse White would have laughed at the possibility of being told angels were real, or there was such a thing as life after death. Not anymore, and that applied to quite a few of the other nurses who had worked with terminally ill patients.

Kate passed away early that evening. Mary had just left the room to have a coffee in the visitor's room, leaving the nurse to check her mother's intravenous drip. On her way back Nurse White was waiting by the bed.

'She's gone Mary. She's at peace now.'

'Mom, why didn't you wait for me?' Mary cried, throwing herself across her mother's body. The nurse watched and gently helped Mary from the bed onto a chair.

195

'Sometimes they prefer for a loved one to leave the room before they pass away. I see it all the time Mary, otherwise, they're just holding on for their sake. Sit with her for a while if you wish to say goodbye, I'll be in the corridor.'

Mary held her hand and kissed her forehead. 'Goodnight, God bless Mom. I love you.'

Chapter 22

New York 1973

Holding her father's hand, Mary stood by her mother's grave. She looked at the small crowd . . . handkerchiefs at hand. Just a few family members and four close friends had attended. Not many mourners, but then, that was her mother's wish. Mary had hoped Amy would attend the funeral but understood her decision not to come. But she so wished she was here. Only Amy knew the right words to say. How strange to think Amy was the one she needed the most now. She felt lucky to have found a true friend in her; things could have been so different.

The priest began the dreaded words. 'Dearly beloved, we are here today in the sight of God . . .'

She wondered if her mom was here now, looking down on everyone. Floating in the sky like an angel, hovering over the crowd who stood around the freshly dug grave. Mary knew her mother wasn't a religious woman, but she did know how much she believed in the afterlife. Drops of rain fell from the sky and the mourners quickly opened umbrellas before the drops became a big downpour. A typical funeral; people dressed in black, standing in the pouring rain, holding an umbrella in one hand and a handkerchief in the other. She looked towards the sky and smiled inwardly to herself, wondering if the old saying her mother once told her was true. "If it rains at a funeral, it's a sign the deceased person is happy."

The rain stopped just as the service finished and the mourners closed their umbrellas and headed towards the cars. There was just Mary and her father left behind.

'I'm so sorry Mary', her father said sadly, 'I never meant things to work out as they did, you know. I loved your mother, only Amy and I . . .'

'Dad you don't have to say anything, this is not your fault. Mom would still have died, and she never hated you for what you did, she wasn't that kind of person.'

Her father held her tight. 'I'll always be here for you. I love you Mary.'

'I love you too Dad.'

She linked her arm through his and started to walk back to the car. He tried to convince Mary to go back to his house, but she insisted she needed to be alone. Instead, she hailed a cab and went straight to her mother's house. As she opened the door, she paused awhile, waiting to hear her mother's voice. She felt as if she was in a dreamlike state; her body was slowly moving through the house without any effort from her at all. She finally sat down staring into empty space until darkness fell.

The morning light flooded through the lounge window and at first Mary felt disoriented. She had fallen asleep in the chair holding a photograph of herself and her mother with Misty the Labrador. Mary remembered the photograph being taken; she was about six years old when her father had taken the picture. It was the week before Christmas. She'd just got home from shopping with her mother, and both of them had flopped on the sofa exhausted. Her father had wanted to capture the moment he surprised them with a puppy, and as the day was damp and misty, Mary had chosen Misty as the name for the pup. There were so many happy memories of her life with her beloved Labrador. She was fifteen years old when Misty died, and that was the first time in her life she had known real sorrow.

*

The first few months passed in a daze after the funeral, and Mary was convinced on more than a few occasions she had seen her mother in stores, across the road, driving in her car or sitting in a coffee shop. Amy had been sympathetic and told Mary it was very common for bereaved people to think they had seen a loved one who had recently passed away.

'Time does heal eventually Mary, but you never really get over the death of someone you loved, I know from my own experience of losing my mom. It's been nine years now and I still have days when I cry. I miss her so much. I really do know what you're going through sweetheart, and I'm here if you need me.'

Amy had been so kind. She couldn't have coped without her love and friendship. It was a year after her mother's passing when Amy asked her about the house. 'Have you decided what you want to do with your mother's house Mary? Are you going to move back in there?'

'No, it's too big for one person, and anyway, there's so much of Mom in the house it would be too upsetting. I feel her presence in every room. I don't think it's a good idea really; the house was always too big. I can't understand Mom wanting to live there after Dad left. I tried to persuade her to move, knowing I was going to be leaving, but she was adamant she was staying put. She stopped having overnight guest's years ago, and only ever used a few rooms, of course her studio being one of them.' Mary dabbed her eyes with a tissue. 'Sometimes she would sit in there for hours staring into space, and I once found her crying uncontrollably, holding a letter in her hand. She told me she had the blues. When I think about it now, I guess it was the letter from her hospital appointment, she must have known all along it was cancer.'

'They wouldn't have told her it was cancer by letter Mary, did she have any relatives who could have died that you know of.'

'I don't know; she wouldn't talk about her life in England other than her few friends. According to Dad, Mom's family died during the Blitz. I don't remember her ever having talked about living relatives, but whatever was in the letter had upset her.'

Amy put her arms around Mary and held her tightly. They drank coffee and Amy mentioned the house again, not that it made a difference to her and Peter; it was Mary's house if she wanted to keep it. Her and Peter had enough money of their own.

'Do you want to rent the house or sell it? It's entirely up to you, but it's been empty a while now Mary.'

'I know, I suppose I should sell it and give my father his share. Would you mind coming with me to sort her things out. I'm really dreading that part of it all Amy. I know I've been putting it off. The thought of giving her clothes and personal belongings away, haunts me.'

'I know how you feel, but the sooner it's done the better, and of course I'll give you a hand.'

A month passed by and Mary contacted Amy to meet her at the house. She was determined not to cry. This was something that needed doing, and she would cry later, in private. Together they boxed the clothes and shoes. Mary insisted they shared the jewellery between them at first, but Amy said it didn't feel right, her being the one who took Kate's husband away.

'But I don't wear much in the way of jewellery Amy, and I really don't want to sell it, or give it away to a stranger. Would it be all right to give it to the girls, they are, after all my sisters.'

'Okay, but what I'll do is keep hold of it until they're older, and if you have children yourself, then it should be shared.'

'Funny, but I can't visualise me having kids' Mary laughed 'I haven't even found a man I like yet and sometimes wonder if I ever will. But yes, that's a good idea; I like the sound of that.'

A week later the furniture was put up for auction, and her father started with the sale of the house. There was just the paperwork to sort through and Mary decided to take it all home, along with the family photos and her mother's pictures from her studio. While packing away the things she was taking home, she stood leaning against the door looking at the framed pictures in her mother's special place. Her mother had been very clever at photography.

Sighing, she walked into what had been her own bedroom as a child to check nothing was left behind. Looking around the room, Mary thought back to one of her earliest memories. She must have been five or six years old, and loved the story of Cinderella, asking for it to be read to her night after night. On her birthday, her mother surprised her by having an interior designer decorate her room. Mary was led with her father's hands over her eyes. When opened them, she was amazed to find a fantasy Cinderella bed. The bed was built as a coach, made to look like a pumpkin, with big wooden wheels and two pink rocking horses on reins. Mary had screamed in delight, and immediately climbed inside while her father stood proudly with his arms around her mother, who was both laughing and crying at the same time. Everything in the room had been designed around Cinderella going to the ball, including glittering pink shoes, a ball gown, including a tiara set with sparkling stones which looked like real diamonds.

Her parents had been over generous with Mary, but there was always strict discipline and Mary soon learned when to draw the line. She had a few tantrums as she grew older, and was sent to her room until she was ready to apologise for her behaviour. Mary would stay there for hours pretending she didn't care, all the time believing her mother would come to comfort her. But she never did. Around the age of ten, Mary asked her parents if she could have friends stay over for the night. Her father firmly said no. He was having two important clients around for dinner, and knew from the last 'stay over' how much noise the girls could make, screaming and shouting.

'Another time darling, but not tonight'

'Why not tonight, I've already told them they could stay, Daddy'

'I have people coming and don't want children shouting and screaming like they did the last time I had guests. And anyway Mary, you should ask Mummy or I before you make arrangements for sleepovers. Now go and phone your friends and tell them another time.'

'I hate you and I hate Mommy.' Mary screamed, stropping off to her room and slamming the door hard. Her father immediately went after her and forced her to sit on the bed while he told her how selfish she was. 'Your mother and I are fortunate to be able to give you what you need or wish for, but I will not tolerate you being a spoilt little brat, young lady. I too was an only child, and just like you, I had everything I ever needed from my folks, but I'll tell you now, I also had respect. Slam that door again, and all the things in this room you treasure the most will be gone to kids who have nothing. You'll be given presents at Christmas and birthdays once a year like everyone else. Do you understand?'

Mary had a good childhood and was grateful. She went with her mother, on many occasions to her charity events, and saw for herself how a child's face could light up from the simplest of gifts.

She sighed heavily; sighing had seemed to become a habit now. She had been to see a doctor when her mother died. For weeks she had been suffering from bad headaches and sleepless nights. The doctor told Mary she was suffering from depression brought on by grief, explaining constant sighing was a classic sign of depression. She sighed all the time she was with the doctor, in-between crying. He told Mary to let nature take its course, rather than take medication, at least for the time being.

Sunlight lit the room, just as she remembered when she was a child. Each morning, intricate colours and patterns danced around the walls; the sun catching anything in its path that glittered. There were so many cupboards and drawers filled with items Mary hadn't seen for years, and some she hadn't seen at all. She never realised her mother was a bit of a sentimental hoarder. *I'm going to be packing for weeks here Mom. I would never have put you down as a secret little hoarder.'*

Each time Mary thought she had packed everything, she would find another box, filled with childhood possessions her mother had held onto for all those years. Not toys or games, but pictures Mary had drawn at school, swimming certificates and birthday cards she had sent her mom when she could hardly write. She rummaged through everything, taking one last look before putting them in a plastic sack.

Behind the box of drawings and cards, was another box tucked away right at the very back, in fact, she didn't see it at first. The box somehow caught her attention as she was about to close the cupboard door. *'Another container of drawings and cards,'* Mary thought. She gently opened the lid and pulled away layers of tissue paper to find a beautiful Victorian doll. The doll wore a pretty blue satin dress trimmed with lace and a white apron. Her hair was dark with ringlets falling over her shoulders. In her hand was a parasol also in satin and lace.

Mary held the doll. 'Oh, aren't you just gorgeous, I . . .' As she held the doll, Mary wanted to cry, there was a sadness linked to the porcelain doll, with her big blue eyes and long dark lashes; she could feel it. She tried to think back to the time when she was first given the doll as a child, but nothing came to mind. The doll must have been really special to be wrapped so well.

'Perhaps it was Moms doll when she was a little girl. How could she not show me something so beautiful?' Mary said to herself, looking at the doll's face. All the other toys had been given to the charities her mother did voluntary work for. The doll must have been stored away all those years, but why? She held the doll to her chest but couldn't remember ever playing with it as a child. There was something strange about the doll, but she . . . suddenly, an image flashed through her head. Mary saw herself sitting on a woman's lap, cradling the doll in her arms like a baby. She couldn't put an image to the face of the woman, but assumed it was her mother.

She carefully placed the doll on the bed and sighed once more. The bedroom had been a place of sadness for the last few years. This was the room where she came to secretly cry when her mother's cancer had been diagnosed, and later when she stayed with her mother through chemotherapy. Choosing this room . . . a room where pain was once nothing more than a scraped knee.

She took the boxes into the hallway, closing the door of the nursery very quietly, as though she was leaving her childhood behind for good. A sudden breeze passed through the house and Mary shivered, she was certain she had closed all the windows. If her mother had been here, she would have said 'It's only a spirit passing through,' and Mary and her father would laugh.

Amy walked into the dining room and asked if Mary was all right. Then she saw the doll lying on the table. 'What a cute little doll. I haven't seen one as beautiful as this before, it looks really old.'

'Yes, it does. I don't remember the doll much either, other than a flash of holding the doll and crying.'

'Perhaps it was your mothers' or even her mothers. It certainly looks original.'

'Perhaps, but I feel a sadness around it. I suppose the doll could have been Moms . . . although it can't have been, everything went up in smoke the day of the bombings when all her family was killed.'

'Did you ever meet your maternal grandparents?'

'No, I didn't. Mom said they had died years before. She wasn't one for the past. Everything with Mom was the here and now. We'll never know where the doll came from; it could easily have been bought for me. Perhaps I didn't like it. I was never one for dolls to be honest, but I'll keep this doll.'

Mary thanked Amy for her help and headed home with her car overloaded with the stuff she wanted to hold on to. The rest was either dumped or made ready to give to charity. She opened a bottle of Claret as soon as she arrived home. She made herself comfortable in front of the log fire and started taking the doll out of its wrapping. As soon as she held the doll, a vision swept through Mary's mind of a lady with brown eyes and very short hair. The vision lasted for a split second and that was all.

'Who are you, little baby girl. What's your name?' she cooed, holding the doll at arm's length to get a better look. 'You have certainly been very well cared for, and you must be extremely old. What a pretty dress you have on.'

Exhausted, she headed for the bedroom, the doll in one arm and the bottle of wine in the other. At least the wine would help her sleep a good few hours before she woke again.

Mary found herself in dimly lit room dressed in a white robe; the robes dead people wear in coffins. Three girls were with her and a baby wrapped in a knitted shawl. The girls were smiling and handing the baby to each other in turn. Without warning, the girl's faces suddenly turned grotesque. There was blood everywhere in the room. The girls and the baby were splashed in blood. In a corner was the doll, and she was laughing. Mary wanted to run, but her feet felt glued to the spot. A black figure was approaching with large scissors that were also soaked in blood. The dark figure pointed a finger at Mary and she screamed.

Mary woke up from her nightmare, breathless. Her clothes were wet through with sweat, and tears streamed down her face. She climbed out of bed and made herself a coffee. She was never frightened of being on her own, but she felt scared and very lonely now. Apart from her father and Amy, she wasn't particularly close enough to anyone to call at two in the morning. She had gradually lost contact with her friends from University, and although she'd lots of colleagues, she had no close friends. Her mother had tried to warn her not to let her work stop her from having a social life. She wished at this very moment she had taken her advice.

Making her way back to the bedroom, she could see the doll. Out of the blue, something flashed through Mary's mind. 'Jesus Christ, Emily, your name is Emily. I gave you that name and called you Emmy.'

Every night since bringing her home Mary slept with the doll at her side; there was a bond between them. There must have been a bond when the doll was given to her. Yet, there was something about the doll that troubled Mary. Why did her mother hide it for all those years? Was it haunted? She knew how superstitious her mother was.

*

The box with the personal files stood in Mary's bedroom for six weeks before she finally made the effort to look through the papers. She was surprised to see there were loose photographs in the box mixed up with paperwork. Usually her mother ensured all photos were put away in an album of the appropriate year. There were quite a lot of her father's files too. Files he never bothered to take with him for some reason, although he was probably in a hurry to leave. Perhaps he intended coming back for them later and forgot they were still there. She sifted through, placing the documents in three separate files, hers, her mother's and her father's, smiling when she saw a photograph of him in his uniform, feeling a rush of pride. Standing beside him was another man who she hadn't seen before; they were both laughing at the person taking the picture. Mary guessed the one taking the picture must have said something funny to make them laugh so much. She turned the photo over to see if it had writing on the back as some of the old photos did.

The words read . . . *Harry Mitchell and Peter Reiner Liverpool 1944.*

She decided the man standing with her father was probably a friend he met in the forces, and assumed they didn't stay in touch after the war. She would have known. She knew all her father's friends.

There were more photographs of the man; one with a baby in his arms. She came across another photograph of the man . . . Harry. A woman stood by him, who was almost certainly Harry's wife and the baby's mother. Mary thought Harry's wife looked vaguely familiar but couldn't think where from. She picked her way through the photographs of the proud parents, which was obviously at the baby's christening; the child being dressed in a christening gown. It appeared her own mother and father was the baby's godparents. Mary held a photograph of her mother stood at the church font, holding the baby and smiling down on her tiny face.

'Mom, look at you holding the baby in your arms, the very privilege of being a godmother clearly showing in your face.'

Mary looked again at the photo of the couple with the baby and wondered why her parents had never mentioned being godparents . . . and where were the couple and the child now.

'That's the trouble with being a Lawyer. Everything has to have a mystery to it, for Pete's sake.' Mary shouted out loud, 'They probably moved away and lost touch, the photo was taken years ago. People often move to other States.'

She put the photos to one side and started on the paper work. There was a big brown envelope with certificates inside and Mary put it in her father's pile. Another envelope contained papers for Harry and Helen Mitchell. Mary put the envelope to one side to add to her father's papers so he would see it first. Her mother's papers were already neatly in order according to date.

'This is so like you Mom, everything in order, right down to the last detail.'

As Mary put her mother's papers to one side, a photograph fell out. It was a photograph of a British soldier. The soldier was a young man who looked around eighteen years old. He was a very handsome man, who stood tall with dark hair and beamed a beautiful smile. Holding on to the picture, Mary stared into the face of the handsome young soldier. Was this an old flame? Did Mom have an affair with a British soldier? As far as she was aware, her mother had only ever loved her father, she said so. Should she mention this to her father? Why not, hadn't he himself had an affair? If her mother did have a secret lover, then she must have been with her father at the time. Why had she kept his photograph? Why had this photograph been hidden among her papers and not with the other photos?

'He must have meant a great deal to you, Mom, whoever he is.'

Mary decided to put the rest of the boxes away for another time, it was late, and she had to be away early the next morning. She was going to meet a private detective someone had recommended to her. The one she'd used before was retiring and she needed someone to take his place very quickly. She wanted some information regarding a case she was working on. Her client's ex-husband had snatched the couple's three year old daughter, and there was reason to suggest he would take her out of the Country.

A colleague of Mary's told her about a detective named Jack Langley, who was exceptionally good at tracing missing people. Mary was told the child's mother had to be sedated by her physician on the morning of her daughter's abduction. She had recently suffered a heart attack and the doctor was concerned about her health. Of course, the mother didn't realise at the time it was the child's father who had taken the little girl, and naturally, feared the worst. The child was playing in a sand pit, and the mother had taken the clean bed linen upstairs, insisting she was gone no more than a few minutes.

'It was the silence that hit me.' She cried 'Rosa is always singing or chatting away to herself. The latch on the gate is too high for her to reach, and besides, she wouldn't have wondered away without her fluffy bunny. She carries fluffy everywhere. Someone has taken her. You have to find her . . . Please.'

It wasn't while the police spoke to a neighbour who recognised the child's father, the woman calmed down a little. At least her daughter was safe, so she believed, but then anger and fear quickly took hold. Her husband had threatened once before to take the child to his family in India.

There was no time to waste.

Chapter 23

Jack Langley sat at his desk eating candy, flicking the wrappers with his ruler. He was bored. He was supposed to be running a Private Eye Agency and all the work of late, was spying on people's wives or husband. 'Jesus,' he thought, 'what's the point of staying with a person when you have to go to all the trouble of getting a private dick to prove their infidelity for Christ's sake.' Then of course there was the money aspect to divorce. On one occasion, when his client was disenchanted to hear her suspicions were unfounded, and unable to get her hands on her husband's money, she asked Jack if he knew any 'hit men'. The woman laughed at Jack's shocked reaction and turned it into a joke. When she left the office, he wondered what his client would have said if he had told her, yes, he did know a hit man . . . not that he did. He threw a candy wrapper across the room and missed the trash can. 'Jeeze, I need to cut down on candy' he said to himself, putting his hand to the side of his face. 'And I must get this Goddamn tooth sorted out.'

Jack tapped his pencil on his desk and looked around the dimly lit office. 'This place needs a brightening up; it's like an old-fashioned school class room in here.'

Money wasn't really a problem, he just didn't have a clue how to make a room look modern, not that he would say no to a little extra money if it came his way. Yeah, business had been on the quiet side for a while, but at least it gave him time to catch up on paperwork. He poured himself a coffee and sighed, his job was okay, and he liked being his own boss, though he thought how good it would be to be asked to investigate a murder. *Yeah, that would be real good.* He went to the bathroom to freshen up. Washing his face, he caught his reflection in the mirror. 'Jesus, look at the state of you, Jack. You look like shit.'

He stood six foot two, with light brown hair and brown eyes. He hadn't shaved in two days, and his hair desperately needed a cut. He squeezed the muscles of his biceps and smiled. 'At least you still have the body, Jack Langley, though there's not much to say about the rest of your looks, least not today.'

On his way back from the bathroom, he emptied all the candy from his desk, put the candy in a paper bag and placed them in the rubbish bin. He decided to turn over a new leaf, have his hair cut, buy new clothes and take up sport again.

He flicked through his diary. There were three appointments for tomorrow, 9.00am John Kaminski, 11.00am Emily Wilkinson and the last one, 2.00pm Miss Reiner, a lawyer. He thought about the telephone conversation he'd had with Miss Reiner and tried to picture her in his mind. This was a game he played with all his lady clients and was usually wrong. A young sounding name means nothing; neither does a sexy voice on the other end of the line. Jack had been shocked to find how an obese middle-aged woman could sound just like a twenty-five-year-old babe. Lucy had a gruff voice yet was a stunning red head. 'The bitch', he yelled, visualising her beautiful face.

Lucy was Jack's ex-wife. She was a traitor and an adulterer. On this particular day the client he was supposed to be meeting couldn't make it, so he decided to surprise his wife, rather than go back to the office. He planned a trip out somewhere. They very rarely went places these days. He couldn't wait to see her face when he told her they were heading out for the day.

Unlocking the door, he was quite startled to find his wife running towards him in her underwear. 'Hi honey, you're home early. Do me a favour sweetheart and drive down to the store, I have a terrible headache and I need aspirin. I had to go to bed and lie down awhile.'

There was something in her eyes that told Jack she was lying. Something wasn't right. He kissed her on the lips, making his way to the bathroom. Opening the bathroom cabinet, there, staring him in the face was a box of aspirin. He took the box out and threw it over to Lucy, whose face was now white. He was about to leave the room when he noticed the toilet seat was up. He knew for sure a man was the last person to use the toilet, Christ, Lucy had yelled at him often enough to put the lid down when he took a leak. Jack went into the bedroom and the bed was unmade. He opened the closet doors, slamming them shut again. Grabbing hold of the mattress, he threw it across the room. There was Richard, under the bed clutching his clothes dressed only in bright coloured boxer shorts.

'Jack, I can explain . . .'

Jack said nothing; he flung open an overnight bag and put a few clothes in, while Richard almost fell down the stairs in fright. His wife sat crying, crouching on the floor. Jack didn't say a word. He closed the door behind him and drove away. That was the last time he saw anything of Richard. He had, of course seen Lucy. He had to manhandle her out of his office each time she came pleading with him to forgive her. She refused to leave the office on more than one occasion. He had to call the cops once, when she started to trash the room and throw his clients records through the window.

Yes, he was upset. Very upset. He loved Lucy. There were warning signs, but he'd ignored them at first. She had changed over the last few months before they broke up. Little things she said made Jack's suspicions grow, especially when her routine suddenly changed. The line was always busy when he tried to phone her from the office. Yeah, he knew then there was another guy, and his gut feeling told him it was his best friend, Richard. It's usually the eye contact which catches them out. They either avoid eye contact altogether when their partners are in the same room, or they hold each other's gaze a little longer than needed.

Lucy was Jacks first love, and they had been lovers since they were young kids, marrying as soon as Jack graduated. For months Lucy begged for forgiveness, but Jack didn't believe in infidelity, he was a one woman guy and expected his wife to be as faithful as he was. There was no going back. Trust was lost.

He searched the drawer of his desk until he found one last candy. He popped it in his mouth and threw the wrapper towards the trash can. This time the wrapper hit the can instead of landing on the floor.

'Damn you to hell Richard.' Jack yelled.

Jack missed his best friend. It was hard enough losing your wife to another man, but to lose her to the one person you would have needed at a time like this, makes him a bigger bastard still. He had put his trust in Richard in the beginning; even confided in him. They had been friends since High school days. The two of them had shared a room when they were at University for Christ sake.

Jack felt his heart beat fiercely as he recalled telling Richard he suspected Lucy was seeing another guy.

"Jack, you look too deeply onto things", Richard said, patting Jack on the shoulder, "This job's getting to you . . . you suspect everything and everybody. Chill out man."

Richard never wanted to be found out; he was married to one of the wealthiest women in town. Wealth she had inherited from her father, as well as her share in the family business. Richard stood to lose everything, including his job. To him, Lucy was just another trophy to add to his collection. He was constantly boasting about the girls he had slept with from the tennis club.

'Keep away from single girls.' He boasted. 'They want more than sex. They want commitment.'

Too right, Richard did not want commitment, he wanted fun. Always the popular one down at the club with the other guys; who thought Richard was great to be around, when in fact he was sleeping with their wives.

His heart sank when he though back to how he and Lucy had been planning to start a family. How could she talk about wanting a baby, when all the time she was seeing another man? Jack tapped his pen so hard on the desk, it snapped in two. How long would it have continued if he hadn't gone back home in the afternoon? Was the child she miscarried a year ago, his or Richards? He grabbed his jacket and headed off for home. He didn't need this negative thinking in his life. His marriage was over.

*

The following morning, Jack felt good. He'd done as he said he would, had a haircut, bought new clothes and cleaned himself up. He was pleased with the results, and the first two of the three clients booked in that morning, decided to hire him. He was just making a coffee when there was a knock on the door.

'Come in.'

He was stunned for a few seconds and just stared at the woman. Jeeze, he was right about this one. She had the face that matched the voice. She looked as he had imagined, pretty, slim, a brunette with sparkling blue eyes and a touch of mystique about her.

'Mr Langley? My name is Mary Reiner. I spoke to you yesterday.'

'Yes, yes, come in, sit down.' He watched her walk towards the desk, feeling ashamed of himself for such thoughts. 'I was about to pour a coffee would you like one?'

'I'd love one; I haven't had the chance of a break since early this morning.'

They spoke idle chat for a while, drinking coffee. When silence fell, Mary took the folder out of her briefcase and gave him the lowdown on the missing girl. Several coffees later, Mary said she had to go. 'I didn't realise it was so late. I'm very sorry Mr Langley for taking your time.'

'No, no it's been a pleasure.'

Jack just knew he had to see this girl again. She was good in her line of work, Jack could see this, but he felt something he had never experienced before with a woman. He took all the details he needed for the case and Mary handed him her private phone number, apologising for taking so much of his time once more.

'Thank you, Mr Langley for your help, if you need me please ring me on this number. Unfortunately, I'm out of my office most of the time so I'll give you my home number too.'

Jack walked to the door and held it open. They paused and held each other's gaze before parting company. Mary was on her way down the flight of stairs when Jack shouted after her. 'Jack, my name is Jack.'

'Yes, I know' she laughed, 'my name is Mary.'

Jack walked back to the office. 'You idiot Jack, of course she knew your damn name; it's printed on the Goddamn door.'

Chapter 24

The telephone rang and Mary rushed to answer it. Normally, if she wasn't within reach of the phone, she would leave it until a message went onto the answering machine. Since meeting Jack Langley, she had answered every single phone call. Four days had passed, and he still hadn't phoned her. Was she imagining the chemistry she had felt between them that day? For all she knew he could be married. She was beginning to feel a fool. She let go of the receiver. The answering machine started up. 'Hi, I'm unable to answer the phone just now. Please leave a message'.

Jacks voice came on the line. 'Hi, it's Jack Langley here, I . . .'

Mary quickly grabbed the phone. 'Hello Jack.'

'Erm, I was wondering if we could meet, I've a few things to discuss with you regarding the case, I . . . Oh shit, to be honest, I rang to ask if you care to go for lunch sometime, that's if you're not in a relationship, or even if you would want to go with me . . .'

'That would be lovely Jack; yes, I would like to have lunch with you.'

They talked a full hour on the telephone and made plans to meet the following day at Nadir's Italian restaurant in Brooklyn. Both Mary and Jack had met clients there and knew the place.

Jack was the first to arrive and rushed from his seat to greet her. He looked even more attractive than she remembered him. He stood tall and was very athletic looking, with brown eyes and light brown hair. She imagined his hair was blond in his younger years and pictured him being a real cute kid. Jack escorted Mary to a table in a corner of the room and in gentlemanly fashion, pulled the chair out for her to sit down. The waiter handed them a menu each and Jack ordered the wine. While waiting for the meal to arrive Jack mentioned he had some leads on the abduction and discussed the case for a short while to break the ice.

'How long have you been a private detective Jack? It must be very interesting work.'

'It is, well most of the time. I get to do a lot of spying on cheats.' He laughed 'I've been in business a few years now. I was a Lecturer before then.'

'You were a Lecturer?'

'Yeah, I was a lecturer in history, Irish history, in fact.'

'Why did you choose Irish history? You don't sound Irish.'

'I have Irish blood from Dad's side. When my father died, I discovered his father, my grandfather, was Irish. I never got to meet him, unfortunately. He died before I was born. When I grew older, I decided to do some research on my Irish ancestor's background, which in turn led me to become a private detective. I enjoyed the research and the travelling. I'm also interested in Criminology. I have a degree in Forensic Psychology.

'A Forensic Psychologist, wow.'

'Perhaps that's something to look at in the future. For now, I'm happy in my work. I like the freedom.'

'Did you enjoy your visits to Ireland? They say it's a beautiful place. I'd loved to go there myself one day. My mother's side was Irish. She had a slight Irish accent she says she picked up from her parents. Her parents didn't live in Ireland it seems, they lived in Liverpool, but her ancestors lived in Tipperary. Of course, my grandparents were Irish, but I never got to meet them. Mom shared a house with three girls in Liverpool who had Irish parents, not far from where she grew up.'

'Your mother is from Liverpool?'

'Yes, she met dad when he was stationed there during the war. He laughed about how just about everyone he met in Liverpool had an Irish accent. . . Sorry, I do tend to babble on sometimes.'

Jack laughed. 'That's okay, I do that myself. I've been to Ireland a few times now and it really is a beautiful place. County Cork was the place my great grandparents were from. It's also true what your father said about a lot of Irish living in Liverpool. Liverpool is known as having the strongest Irish heritage of any British City. Apparently, a very large percentage of

216

Liverpool natives have Irish blood in their veins. Now, here's an interesting fact; did you know three of the Beatles had Irish ancestors.'

'No, I didn't, but I suppose there isn't much distance between the two countries really.'

'No, I suppose not. Thousands of desperate people flooded to Liverpool with the intentions of moving to the States during the famine in 1847. Some of them came over already half dead. From Liverpool, many crossed the Sea to Montreal on vessels called 'coffin ships.' A large percentage of the passengers died of starvation and disease.'

'Coffin ships? It must have been awful Jack, all those families leaving Ireland in the hope of a better life only to die on the journey there; those poor people.' Mary said quietly 'I suppose a lot of Irish families moved to Liverpool to work in the mills too, especially if they had daughters. I also remember being taught in school about the cotton from the slave plantations being shipped to Liverpool.'

'That's true, along with thousands of slaves. Liverpool was called the 'Capital of the slave trade' and well documented for the town's development and prosperity. I still remember a poem from years ago about slavery in Liverpool. Do you want to hear it?'

'Yes, of course.'

'This is an excerpt from 'Slavepool' by Mohammed Khalil.

"Branded like beasts who feel no pain
And all for Merry England's gain
But England's changing and rearranging
Only we can clear our name
Growing, knowing, trade winds are blowing
Things will never be the same again.'

'Oh Jack, that's given me goose bumps, how sad.'

'I'm beginning to think I'm talking too much history.'

'Not. Absolutely not, I find it all very interesting. I can imagine you being a very good lecturer.'

'Thank you, I did my best. I hope to go to Ireland again sometime soon. There are so many places I would like to visit there. I haven't found the right person to travel with yet and it isn't much fun on your own.'

Jack looked into Mary's eyes and was about to say something when the waitress arrived to collect the plates and the moment was gone. Mary offered to pay half of the bill, but Jack held up his hand. 'No, my treat, you can pay next time.' he teased.

Mary blushed. She knew he had assumed they were going to meet again.

'Where do you live, perhaps we could share a cab.'

'Jackson Heights'

'Oh, I live in Long Island City so you could drop me off first.'

They hired a cab and snow started to fall. When Mary thanked Jack for a wonderful evening, he gently reached over and kissed her on the cheek.

*

Pouring herself a glass of wine, she wondered if she should have asked Jack in for a nightcap. She would have liked to have spent more time with him, but then, in hindsight believed she did the right thing. After all, she hardly knew him, and anyway, what would he have thought of her if she had . . . that she did this sort of thing all the time. Still, she wished he was here now.

It was too early to go to sleep, and too late to do any work, so Mary decided to go to bed with a hot chocolate and a book. She fell asleep within a few minutes of opening the book but woke up crying. Mary had the same nightmare again. Ever since finding the doll, Mary had trouble sleeping all through the night without wakening from a dream. They were usually dreams of women without faces. Two of them were covered in blood, one with outstretched arms holding a baby's jacket, and another one was holding a baby in arms. Much as she didn't want to, Mary put the doll back in its box.

She was still suffering from grief; and wondered perhaps if this kind of behaviour is normal at times like these. Mary decided to talk to Amy; she would be going to see her next week for Tom's birthday party, which reminded her she had yet to buy him a present. 'I'll call at a toy department store on the way home; though what to buy him, I have no idea.'

The telephone snapped her from her thoughts. She looked at her watch; 12:30am.

'Who the hell is it at this hour?'

'Hi, Mary, is it too late to have a chat, only I . . .?'

'No Jack, it's lovely to hear from you.'

They talked into the night. He told her about Lucy, leaving Mary relieved. Asking Jack if he was married had crossed her mind when they went for the meal but had decided against it. He might have thought she was presuming they were about to start an affair. She had hoped with all her heart he wasn't a married man. Mary didn't see herself as being the 'Other Woman.' In her line of work Mary had seen the outcome of situations where affairs had turned very ugly. Her father and Amy had been lucky her mother had taken the affair with a sense of dignity. Which is very rare in most cases.

Mary told Jack about her mother's death, he was very sympathetic, and it was good to talk to someone other than Amy. They arranged to meet the next night and almost every night for two weeks. Mary finally plucked up courage to ask him if he would like a meal at her apartment. Jack was delighted and they arranged a date.

She bought cookery books and instead of working on her paperwork, she began to write down recipes. Cooking had never been her forte; being on her own meant calling somewhere for a quick dinner after work, and many times she didn't bother with dinner at all, eating snacks instead. Her mother wasn't a good cook either, but she liked to try new recipes. Her father said there wasn't much food during in the war to cook fancy meals, and how cooking was all new to her mother, who was young anyway when she arrived in New York. Mary loved how her father always jumped to her defence. He was very protective towards her mother.

Mary surprised herself with the three-course meal she had meal made. The table looked as good as the meal, a candlelit dinner with soft background music and low lighting. 'Perfect', she said out loud, looking around the apartment; 'now, what should I wear?'

Opening her wardrobe, she stared at the new sexy little black silk Prada dress. She had bought the dress the previous year on impulse, and it still had the price tag on. Holding the dress in front of her, she wondered if perhaps she was going over the top. The last thing she wanted was to frighten Jack away by being too extravagant . . . or posh. Instead, she chose to wear a less revealing black dress instead, which was more fashionable. Dinner was almost ready, leaving a little time for a drink or two first. She stepped back to admire the table, checking everything was in order. The glasses sparkled; the glow from the candles left a delicate aura around the silver and crystal centre piece her mother had bought her as a housewarming gift. She straightened a table napkin slightly and felt pleased with herself. Very much like her mother would have set a table . . .

'Oh no, what am I doing.' She snuffed the candles, grabbed hold of the centre piece, putting it back in its box, turned the lights up full and reset the table, just as Jack arrived. She ran her fingers through her hair to plump it up a little, took a deep breath and opened the door.

'Hope I'm not too early, but . . . Mary you look beautiful, and something sure does smell great. I bought these; I hope you don't think me old fashioned. I mean, do guys still give their women flowers.'

Mary blushed and motioned Jack into a room with an open log fire and a large sheepskin rug, which lay on the floor surrounded by brightly coloured cushions. The furniture was a mixture of modern and olde worlde and he like that. Jack cracked open the champagne and Mary noticed how smartly dressed he was and wondered if she should have worn the Prada dress. This was the first time they had been completely on their own since they met, and Mary felt nervous; her heart fluttered every time he looked into her eyes.

Jack was blown away by Mary's cooking and told her so; in fact, Jack loved everything about her. Her bright chatty personality, her laughter, the little dimples in her cheeks when she smiled. A certain shyness she let creep through when he complimented her. He found it hard to believe he had found someone as wonderful as Mary. He wanted to be with her all the time, he couldn't think straight anymore.

*

A week later, while Jack was away on business, Mary took the opportunity to shift through the rest of the paperwork. Amazingly, since meeting Jack, her depression had lifted. Just the mere image of him in her mind made her smile. She lifted the boxes of papers down from the shelf and started to sift through the first one, which was a mixture of photos, brochures and papers. Putting them in order as to what needed to go where, Mary came across more photos of the baby and the mystery couple. The baby looked about six months old, dressed in summer clothing and a cute little cotton bonnet. Mary put them to one side to take to her father's house with all the other papers.

She had all the papers in order now, placing the papers belonging to her mother with hers, to keep, if her father didn't mind. Reaching to put the files back on the shelf, she took the photo albums down to take a look at the ones she hadn't seen before. Opening the very first album marked 1940s to 1950s, she laughed when she saw her mother in overalls. Her hair was hidden beneath a scarf which was tied with a knot at the top of her head. The photo was taken in 1944 with three other girls standing outside a factory, and they sure looked happy.

There were photos of her father in his uniform stood with her mother outside a dance hall. Her mother wore a spotted dress with big shoulder pads and high heeled shoes, towering above him. Mary laughed. 'I bet those were the last pair of high heeled shoes you ever bought Mom; you must have been three inches taller than poor Dad.'

There were also a few wedding photos of her mother and Father, and also wedding photos of the couple from the christening shots. 'Mmm, she mused, they must have married the same day.' Mary opened the next page and saw the baby again; she must have been a year old. She turned the photograph over to find the inscription *Lauren Mitchell 1947.*

There were a few more photos of the baby with her parents taken about the same time and then they suddenly stopped. Mary's photos came on the scene, taken in 1950. She looked through each page filled with loving memories of herself and her mom and dad. She caught a sob as she turned the page and saw a photo of herself sat on a rocking horse in front of the Cinderella bed, and on the back of the photo read; 'Mary's sixth birthday.' There were more photos of each of Mary's growing years, school photo's, holiday snaps, photos of friends all the way to 1959 when the album was full.

*

Jack had managed to find the missing child; the child's father was at the airport about to board a flight when he was arrested. He had dressed the girl in boy's clothes and her hair was cut short. The child's mother was hysterical with emotion. The father was arrested and charged.

Jack and Mary celebrated solving the case with a three-course meal cooked by Mary. After the meal, they sat on a pile of cushions by the log fire sipping brandy. The photo albums were still on the floor and Jack asked. 'Do you mind if I look through these?'

Mary jumped up, playfully snatching the one he had in his hand from him. 'Give that back to me.' He put the album behind his back as she struggled with him until they fell on the floor and embraced each other.

'I love you Mary, I fell in love with you the day you walked into my life. I've never felt this way before, not even with Lucy.'

'And I love you Jack. It was love at first sight for me too. I thought I would never fall in love.'

Mary reached across to retrieve the album and passed it to Jack,' Okay, you can see the photos, providing I get to see photos of you the next time I'm over at your place.'

'It's a deal.'

Jack looked at the photographs of 1940 to 1950 right up to the last page. Smiling, he flicked through the album again. 'You sure were a cute kid. How come there are no photos of you as a baby?'

'There is silly, there's lots photos of me.' She laughed, taking the album from him to show him. She flicked through the album, twice, and couldn't see a photo of herself as a baby.

'This is so weird, there's a photo of just about every part of my life, yet not one photograph of me as a baby. Strange, but then I suppose people didn't take photographs like they do now, back then in the forties and fifties.'

'That's true, I don't have many me in my younger years. In fact, could put all my life's worth of photos into one album.'

'Well I suppose that's true of most people born in the forties and early fifties Jack. It's just that Mom had a passion for photography. In fact, there's probably another album somewhere full of me as a baby. I haven't got round to sorting through everything yet.'

Jack looked through the first album again. 'Who's this?' Jack said, pointing to the couple with the baby.'

'I don't know. It's someone Dad was in the forces with. That's his wife next to him. There are wedding photos of them in there too. Can you believe they all married on the same day? They called the baby, Lauren. It's a pretty name. I think Dad and Amy must have named my sister after her.'

'That's odd.' Jack said, more to himself than Mary.'

'What is odd? That they called my sister after her.'

'No, not that, but how the baby looks like you.'

Mary took the album from his hand and looked at the last picture taken of the child aged ten months.

'She's nothing like me. Anyway, isn't it true that all babies look the same?'

'Mary, she's your double. She might be a cousin of yours, yet there are no photographs of you and her together. You would have thought you would have been at the christening.'

'Hey, she could be a cousin, that's possible . . . or my dad could have fathered the child. Oh, my sweet lord.' laughed Mary pretending to look shocked.

'Mary, listen to me. It's odd there are no photos of you under the age of three, and none of the baby over the age of one. Something isn't right here.'

'What are you saying, I don't understand.'

'I don't understand either.'

Mary jumped up from the floor and dragged out all the photos of her childhood. After nearly an hour of sifting through every album, there were no photographs of Mary until the first one when she was about three years old.

'Perhaps Dad took some of the photographs of me with him when he went to live with Amy.'

'Possibly, but Mary sweetheart, there's something else. From the dates on the back of the photo, she was born the same year as you. She even has dimples in her cheeks. Look.'

He passed a photo to Mary; one she hadn't come across before. The baby was sat on its mother's knee holding a doll. Mary could hardly breathe.

'Oh my God, the doll is on the photo. Are you suggesting . . .? I may be adopted. Is that what you're saying Jack.' Mary yelled.

'I don't know. Mary it would have been better if I hadn't said anything. There has to be an explanation. What has a doll got to do with it?'

Mary rushed into the bedroom and brought out the doll. Jack looked at the picture and back at the doll. They were the same.

'Maybe she's a cousin as I said,'

'What about the doll?'

'It's possible you were both bought identical dolls. Folk do things like that. Or all of the photos taken of you at that age were taken by your mother in a relative's arms, and it was your christening. That happens . . .'

'Jack, I don't have any cousins and if I had, don't you think there would have been a mention of her, or more photographs. Her name is Lauren, it says so at the back of the photo . . . and why is she holding my doll? On the back of the christening photo it's made perfectly clear the child is the Mitchell's. I need to know Jack and I need to know now.'

Mary put her jacket on, tears flowing from her eyes.

'Mary, where are you going?' Jack shouted.

'To my father's house, you stay here, Jack, I need to do this on my own.'

'No way Mary, I'm coming with you. I'll call a cab. This is all my doing.'

Mary bundled the contents into her bag and waited for the cab to arrive.

'Mary, do you think this is the right thing to do at this hour? They have kids. You can't just barge in there at two in the morning.'

'I can't wait Jack; I have to know my whole life wasn't a lie.'

Chapter 25

They travelled to her father's house in silence. Mary had the code for the electric gates and a key for the front door. She let herself in and tiptoed into her father's bedroom while Jack waited nervously downstairs. She didn't want to disturb the children, and gently shook her sleeping father's shoulder which startled both him and Amy.

'What the hell . . . Mary, what . . .'

'I have to talk to you, it can't wait.'

Her father said he would see her downstairs when he was dressed. Amy was the first one to come downstairs in her robe. 'Mary, honey, whatever is the matter, are you all right?'

'No, but I have to wait for father before I say anything.'

Her father walked in the room and somehow Mary guessed he knew why she was there.

'Am I adopted father?'

Amy drew her breath, shocked. Mary repeated the question.

'Am I adopted?'

Her father's face drained and suddenly he looked older. 'Yes Mary, you are adopted. Let me speak before you say anything. We adopted you at three years old. Our best friend died in an automobile accident. A car on the opposite side of the road skidded on the ice and ploughed into Harry and Helen. Helen died instantly; Harry died a week later. You were in hospital at the time of the accident suffering from a chest infection; they were on their way to see you.'

'Jesus Christ, Dad. Why did you never tell me? It can't be true; people have always told me I look like Mom and I have your dark hair.'

'I know. As for looking like your Mom, it was pure coincidence. Sometimes in adoptions, the child starts to grow to look like one of their adoptive parents. The child often picks up their parents' mannerisms.'

'But we were the same, we had the same personalities. I can't believe this is happening to me.'

'The reason you both had the same personalities was probably because you were so close to her, Mary.'

Mary started to cry, and Amy put her arms around her.

'Did you know I was adopted Amy?'

'No Mary, it's come as a shock to me too.'

Peter tried to hold Mary's hand, but she snatched it away.

'No one knows Mary. Your mother and I brought you up as our child, and everyone assumed you were ours. My father knew of course and my mother. Kate had a miscarriage and soon became pregnant again, but when she was seven months pregnant, she lost the baby, a girl, and it almost killed her. They had to perform an emergency hysterectomy. She was just twenty years old.'

Mary was struggling with her emotions, only an hour or so ago, she had a mother and father she loved and adored. Now she had a feeling of resentfulness and hatred. This was too confusing to take it all in; she had so many questions, but worse was yet to come. 'Why couldn't you just have told me, I could have taken it when I was younger? I would have still loved you both.'

'It wasn't so easy Mary. You would have asked questions I couldn't answer.'

'What do you mean you couldn't answer? Where are they buried? Do I have any grandparents or family on my parent's side?'

To hear his daughter say those words broke Peter's heart. 'These are the questions I knew you would ask.' Peter covered his face with his hands and paused. Looking at her again, he said quietly, 'Mary, you were adopted.'

'Yes, I think we all know that now.'

'No Mary. You were adopted by Harry and Helen . . . '

'*What*, who the hell am I for Christ sake?'

'I'm not sure; the home you were adopted from wouldn't give Harry any information about the child's mother.'

'What home? It can take years to adopt a child, and you're telling me I had three mothers before the age of three for Christ sake. It isn't that easy to adopt a baby, I know that, I'm an attorney for crying out loud.'

'You were born just after the war; things were going off like that all the time Mary.' Peter lit another cigarette and took a deep breath. 'Harry was infertile; I'd known for years, something to do with a childhood illness. They had tried to adopt through the normal procedures when we were back in the States, but there were big demands for babies, about one baby to one hundred couples. Adoption could have taken years, like you said, if ever at all. Kate was four months pregnant and I think Helen, more than Harry, was feeling 'broody' I believe the word is.'

Peter paused and Mary knew there was even worse to come.

'There were rumours going around the camp over in England before we left for home, about being able to adopt a child from a mother and baby homes where they were desperate to find adoptive patents. There were quite a lot of Americans adopting Irish babies at the time. Harry soon learned he couldn't adopt a baby in the States easily. He had to put his name down on a long waiting list with hundreds of other would be parents. Helen was naïve enough to think they could adopt a baby immediately, so the child would be the same age as Kate's baby. She was extremely upset by the fact it could be years before they were even considered to adopt a baby, being as young as they were.'

'Will you please tell me where I came from?'

'Dublin.'

'How . . .'

'Mary, please let me finish. The catholic run homes for unmarried mothers just wanted good Catholic families who were willing to bring the child up in the catholic faith. It was so easy.'

'Jesus Christ, so you're saying anyone could adopt a baby without legal documents as long as they were *Catholic's*, including paedophiles, child abusers, not to mention child slavery.'

Peter stood with his head down. 'Some of these young mothers had nowhere to go Mary; they could never take the child home with them . . .'

'So, my *real* mother could possibly be a prostitute, is that why she was put into a place like that? And who the hell is my father. She must have been a tramp for her parents to put her in an institution.' Jack put his arm around Mary's shoulder, and she shrugged it off again and stood up. 'My God, my life will never be the same, do you realise what you have done to me.'

Mary headed towards the door; Peter knew there was no point trying to stop her. Her last words felt like a knife in the heart.

'I hate you. You're not my father. I never want to see you again.'

The door slammed and Peter slumped on the sofa, holding his head in his hands. 'Oh Amy, what have I done?'

'I don't know Peter, why didn't you tell me?'

'I never thought there would ever be a need to tell you. She was as good as our child. Mary also had a good life with Harry and Helen too, they adored her. We were her godparents, so she knew us; it wasn't like she was going to live with strangers.'

'How come you adopted her?'

'With his attorney present Harry managed to write a will while he was in hospital. He knew he was going to die. He begged Kate and me to take care of the baby.'

'Why didn't Mary go to live with her grandparents, surely, they would have wanted her, ever given a chance?'

'There was no one left in Helen's family. As far as I know, her family died in an air raid. She lost her younger brothers in the bombing as well. Harry's parents were too old to take care of a baby. They had Harry late in life. Kate adored Mary from the first time Helen let her hold her in her arms, but I could see there was a little resentment from Kate.'

'Did Kate know Mary had been adopted?'

'Yes, the four of us were friends; we met at the same time, and we married the same day. Things took a bit of sorting out to bring our new brides to live here, but we were eventually given permission.'

'So, Harry and Helen went back to Liverpool?'

'My father flew over to Ireland with Harry, Helen and his Attorney, to go take a look at the mother and baby home. They were shown a baby girl. My father arranged everything for the baby to travel to the States. A birth certificate was sorted out with Harry and Helen as the parents, and father paid a substantial amount to the Mother Superior, more than she requested, just to get the baby away from there. Harry didn't have that kind of money they were asking for and I...'

'You paid for the baby? You bought a baby? Jesus Christ, Peter.'

'Yes. My father bought a baby, Amy.' Peter said more loudly than intended. 'Will you listen for Christ sakes?' He poured himself a large scotch. 'Falling pregnant in Ireland was the biggest sin of all, be it through incest, rape or being dumped by a loved one. They were abandoned by their families, hidden away for years . . . sometimes for life, by the Catholic Church. To make things worse, even if a parent decided to let the child home again, the church had the power to forbid it.'

'How do you know all this Peter?' Amy said with a little suspicion in her voice.

'I found out from my father. When he came to England to sort things out for Harry, he broke down crying when we were on our own. Kate had gone to bed and we were drinking into the early hours. I was shocked to say the least; I had never seen my father cry. When he was younger, he had to go on a business trip to Ireland. I was still a young boy, and my mother couldn't go with him as she had always done in the past. While he was there, he met a pretty Irish girl, Rose Marie. He poured the whole story out to me.

"I need to tell you this Peter. "I never intended to be unfaithful to your mother; I never believed in that kind of behaviour; I was in love with my wife. But it happened. I was about twenty-eight at the time and Rose Marie, that was her name, was seventeen. She was so sweet and pretty with long dark hair and striking blue eyes, a real Irish colleen. I was her first. She was a virgin. We wrote to each other, though I sent her mail to her grandmother's house and she passed the letters on believing I was her boyfriend. I made every excuse possible to travel to Ireland on my own. The last letter I had from Rose Marie was to tell me she was carrying my child. Of course, I immediately told your mother I had to go away on business urgently. I had never been to Rose Marie's parent's house, but I knew where she lived, and I went there. Her father was angry to say the least and if I hadn't been twice the size of him and three times stronger, I believe he would have killed me. Eventually, after much persuasion and a few dollars, they told me where she was taken. It was a mother and baby institution; one of the Magdalena Laundries.

Peter, they treated these girls like slaves. I saw young heavily pregnant girls working in fields, clothes drenched to the skin, weak and frail, bent over and working without proper tools. I went to the Mother Superior so many times, pleading with her to let me see Rose Marie, and each time I was ordered to leave. On my visits there I saw girls no more than children being beaten and dragged across the floor. They were all so painfully thin and malnourished, with pale complexions, scabs on their faces, cropped or shaven heads and the saddest eyes I ever saw.

One time, I saw a girl being held down by three nuns. The poor girl was kicking and screaming for her baby, her chest wet from milk which seeped through her clothes. The baby had been given to a couple and was about to leave the convent as I arrived. I don't know what I would have done if I'd found Rose Marie, it wasn't as if I had any rights to her, and on my last visit the Gardaí was called for. I was told not to come back or I would be sent to prison. I couldn't leave you and your mother, but given the chance, at least I would have made sure Rose Marie and the baby was looked after, Peter."

Amy cried when Peter told her the story, and he put his arms around her. 'My father went to Ireland for years Amy, desperate to help Rose Marie. He couldn't go to the home anymore, but it didn't stop him waiting outside of the gates, desperately trying to see her. Let's face it Amy, they were making money from these girls. Slaves they were, doing dirty bloodied laundry, working twelve or more hours a day, working the fields until the sun went down. It's no wonder they didn't want them to leave, plus the horror of it all coming out in the open. Years later my father made a visit to her parents. They told me the Mother Superior claimed she didn't know what happened to Rose Marie after she left the home. Her parents weren't even aware she had left. They had tried to get in touch with Rose themselves three years after the baby would have been born; thinking she could come home again, but the nuns told her she had been moved.'

'Why didn't your father go to the police?'

'He did, the police, or Gardaí as they call them, were powerless to help. They wouldn't dare go against the Catholic Church. God knows what happens to the children who were not lucky enough to get good adoptive parents. I suppose they send them to orphanages. Chances are a lot of babies would have died without proper care.'

'How soon was Harry able to bring such a young baby home to New York?'

'Three weeks.'

'Where did the Mother come in all this? Did she agree to give her child up for adoption?'

'Amy, these mothers were just kids themselves. They weren't even old enough to sign an adoption paper. The choice wasn't theirs. Perhaps it still goes on. The nuns also made the decision when or where the child should go. Not all adoptive couples wanted a baby so young, and waited until the baby was out of diapers, and sleeping through the night. My father told me some girls were lucky to keep their babies two to three years, or even older before they were dragged away from them. It was taken out of the mother's hands Amy.'

Amy felt a chill down her spine. The very thought of parting with a child. 'Oh Jesus Christ, the children could easily have got into the wrong hands. Mary was right; they could have been victims of paedophiles or taken for slave labour. Harry, this is awful. Does all this still go on?'

'Unfortunately, yes, though it's only the word of the ones who managed to escape the homes, and who's going to believe a girl placed in institutions like that. Daring to say she was beaten by a nun or raped by a priest or a layman. They would have been dragged to a mental asylum . . . which they often were, never to come out again.'

231

'Raped? Peter what are you saying? They were raped by the priest.'

'Yes Amy, girls were raped in these places, how else would they have been made pregnant in an orphanage or convent. They were soon whisked away because the day Harry went to pick the baby up from the home, there was a commotion going on. He could hear a girl crying. The Mother Superior stared at Harry with cold steel eyes.' "If you want to take your baby home Mr Mitchell, I suggest you come this way. We have another couple who are interested in this child."

'Where do the babies go from there? The ones who aren't adopted' Amy asked, dabbing her eyes.

'Sometimes they are fostered out, but that's not always a good thing. Some see it as a way of earning easy money. When we were in Liverpool, we were told by a young man how he had been beaten and deprived of food by his foster parents and treated like a slave. He ran away the first chance he got. He still bears the scars from his beatings and that's just the visible ones. He also told me of a child being put in a bath of hot water. The child died, but the Foster mother said he fell into the bath himself and they got away with it. There were no witnesses to say otherwise.'

'Oh, my Lord; what those poor children must have suffered.' Amy sobbed.

'At least some of them were saved . . . at their mother's expense in a way, but like Mary, she was blessed in having two sets of parents who loved her. God knows what life she might have had.'

'Life is so unfair Peter, after going through all the trauma of trying to adopt a baby, Harry and Helen both die when Mary was just three years old.'

'It was a terrible shock to me and Kate when the police arrived to tell us the news of the accident. Harry had asked if they could contact me, and I went straight to see him. Kate was distraught. She had known Helen for years; they had been through a lot together, what with the Blitz and the hardship. I was the same with Harry. He was a brother to me.'

Amy threw her arms around Peter's neck and held him tight, 'I'm so sorry Peter.'

'Losing Harry was hard. I loved the guy but being given the chance to look after his baby I felt closer to him, if you know what I mean. I still had a part of Harry, even though the child wasn't his blood. But Kate changed. She soon became very possessive once we took Mary home. I suppose Kate losing our baby didn't help matters. It didn't take much persuasion for Kate to accept Helens baby, but after the papers were drawn up and Kate realised that she was now Mary's mother, she threw all the clothes and possessions away which were from Mary's life with Harry and Helen. I had never seen that side of Kate. She also changed the baby's name from Lauren to Mary. That must have been so confusing for a three-year-old, but there was no reasoning with Kate. As far as she was concerned the child was hers now.

'This gets worse and worse Peter. Mary now has nothing left of Helen and Harry, after all they went through to adopt her.'

'She kept just a few photographs of her with Helen and Harry, because they were the only ones we had of Mary as a baby, plus an old doll that belonged to Helen. Mary loved the doll; she carried it everywhere with her, crying for her mother all the while. But Kate took the doll away from her. Lauren . . . Mary, I should say, searched for the doll everywhere, calling out 'Emmy,' it was so sad to see a child suffer this way, and me and Kate had the biggest argument, in fact, I didn't like what I was seeing. This was not the Kate I married. In her mind, she decided the doll was a memory of Helen and she didn't want that. She wrapped the doll in tissue paper and placed it in a box promising to give Mary it when she was older. But I knew she never would. Mary cried so much, Amy. She was looking for her mother coming through the door, and now her doll was missing from her life and her name was now Mary. I thought she would never be a normal child again with all the confusion, but Kate refused help for her.'

Peter lit another cigarette and had a swig of whiskey. 'I was too soft with Kate; I regretted not making a stand all those years ago. She was downright cruel. It would have been much kinder to at least let her keep the goddamn doll, but she wouldn't give in, "She'll get over the doll Peter, I'll buy her a new one", she said, but Mary didn't want another doll, in fact throughout her childhood years she never wanted a doll.'

'Oh Peter, that is the saddest thing. What about friends and family, didn't they wonder how you came to suddenly have a three-year-old child?'

'No, we moved soon after, far enough away from people we knew and started a new life. No one knew at the office. We never talked about our personal life.'

'Why didn't you just tell Mary the truth about Harry and Helen dying? At least she would know she was adopted without going into her first adoption.'

'Goddamn it Amy, I told you, it would have led to questions about her family, her grandparents, aunts and uncles, she would have wanted to know where she originated from. Damn Kate to hell for keeping those photo's, I told her to get rid of them. No one knew of the adoption, only my mother and father.'

'How come you and Kate didn't adopt a child in the same way as Harry and Helen had after her surgery?'

'Kate wouldn't hear of it and was against Helen adopting this way. At first, she didn't want to adopt Mary. She wanted a child of her own, which obviously she couldn't, or none at all. She was like that Amy. It always had to be all or nothing with Kate. When we picked the child up from the hospital and Kate saw how ill she looked, she wouldn't let her out of her arms. Kate stayed up all night comforting her. She couldn't part with her after that night. She threw all of the baby's identity out, when she got rid of the doll, her name and her clothes. Helen's name was not to be mentioned again. She was Kate's baby. She even tried to push me out, but I wasn't going to let her take Harry's daughter away from me.'

'I hoped to God Mary will forgive you Peter. I think she will, but you have to give her time now. What about Mary's birth mother, you must know something?'

'No. I could have a word with my father; he was there with Harry the day Mary was offered. I don't have a clue which home they went to. There are some papers of Harry's in my file, but I think Kate got rid of all evidence of the adoption when we sorted the paperwork out at his house.'

*

Eight weeks had passed, and Mary wondered if she should get in touch with her father and Amy. She missed both of them and the kids too. Out of the blue Amy phoned to ask if Mary would meet up with her. Mary started to cry on hearing Amy's voice and after a lengthy and emotional chat they arranged to meet the following day.

'Mary, I know it's been a real shock to you. Please don't be hard on your folks. While it may not be their blood that runs through your veins, they couldn't have loved you more. Your father told me they loved you even before they adopted you, when you were just a baby.'

'You're right Amy. It was such a shock. A double shock actually. I've had three mothers and lost them all. I can't stop thinking about it. I'm finding myself grieving over two mothers I never knew and hating my natural mother. I had a dream you know. I was going to tell you about it before this happened.'

Mary described the dream about the faceless mothers and the doll. 'I can see where the three people came from and the doll, but I can't understand why two of them were covered in blood, and why was one holding a knitted baby jacket; although I suppose Helen might have knitted one. All Mothers used to knit in those days.'

'It could have been your natural Mother who knitted the jacket Mary. We don't know the circumstances of why she was in the home. Try not to judge her.'

'She could have knitted the jacket, I suppose. I just don't know any more Amy. I wish I knew why my birth mother had given me away. In my dream, the woman who knitted the jacket held it with pride. She might have loved me. How old was she, I wonder? Was she a young teenager? Had she had an affair with a married man? Was she a prostitute? Do I look like her?'

'I don't know Mary, but please phone your father. He's heartbroken.'

'I will Amy. In fact, I'll come by this evening with Jack.'

'He's seems a nice guy, Jack, it was sad that we met him in those circumstances.'

'We're in love, Amy; I've never loved anyone like I love him. I couldn't have coped with all this if it hadn't been for him. When I went through hating Mom and Dad, he got angry with me one day and said. *"Aren't you forgetting something here Mary, your parents adored you. Yeah, you lost the parents who adopted you, but you were lucky to have been loved so much by two sets of parents. God knows what would have happened to you if you were to spend the rest of your life in one of those places for Christ's sake; I've heard what goes on in those institutions Mary. I think you came out very lucky."*

I am lucky, Amy. Like Jack said, lucky to have two sets of parents that loved me. Perhaps the doll brought back memories of wondering where my first Mom and Dad were; after all I was only three years old. I probably thought they had left me for being naughty or something. A lot goes through a child's mind in those early years. I hated dolls when I was growing up and cut off their hair when I was given one as a present.'

'Your father told me the doll belonged to an old lady that Helen lived with when her family died; she was very close to her. Helen gave it to you on your first Christmas.'

A tear fell from Mary's face on hearing those words. 'I realised something else when I had left your house that night Amy. Your daughter, Lauren; was it my father who chose the name for her you say?'

'Yes, he did, and I thought the name was perfect for her, so you could say she was named after you. It was your name for almost three years. I wanted to name her Beth, but liked the name Lauren. Anyway, I named the next one Beth.' She laughed. 'Mary your father didn't want your mother to change your name, he was against it, but I suppose it had been hard for her knowing she would never have a chance to name a baby of her own. She was very young to have had a hysterectomy.'

'I know, I've thought about it a lot since finding out I was adopted, I'm going to the cemetery this afternoon and I would love you to come with me. My mother never had a bad word to say about you Amy, she kind of blamed herself. She was grateful I had you to help me come to terms with her illness and encouraged me to see you.'

'I would be honoured to come with you Amy.'

Chapter 26

The shrill of the telephone gave Mary a start. Sighing, she reluctantly answered. Today was the day she had hoped to work on a case that needed her full attention. She had taken the work home with her to gain some peace and quiet without interruptions. There was no point leaving the caller to the answer machine, she already had a list of calls waiting for her to reply. She knew it wasn't Jack. They had spoken earlier in the evening and he appreciated how busy she was.

'Hi, can I speak to Miss Reiner please.'

'Yes, I am she, how can I help you.'

'Hi there, I'm Jerry Grant, I bought the house from your father and you left me a card with your phone number should I need to get in touch.'

'Is there a problem,' Mary sounded more abrupt than intended.

'Oh no Miss Reiner, quite the opposite, my wife and I absolutely love the house and the garden is . . .'

'I'm sorry Mr Grant, but I really need to get on with my work.'

'Oh, my apologies, only it's just that I found an envelope right at the back of our dressing room. I would never have found it, but my son's kitten got stuck, and we had to climb up there to get him down. The envelope was wedged right on the very top of a shelf.'

'Whom is it addressed to.'

'No one, it's sealed up. There's no address, only the name Helen written on the envelope, so we thought it must belong to you. Of course, we haven't opened it.'

'That's all right. Sorry to have been so irritable when I answered the phone and thank you for letting me know. Will it be all right if I pick them up tomorrow?'

'Of course, you can. No problem.'

The next day, Mary opened the brown envelope and spread the contents onto the floor. There were photographs of her mother, Helen and friends outside of a factory. Mary held one of the photographs to her chest. Her mother couldn't have been more than sixteen years old. There were quite a few photos taken at other times of Helen and an older looking woman, and a few taken outside an old derelict house with tatty looking windows covered in tape of some kind, obviously to prevent the glass from splintering during an air raid.

How could they all look so happy, knowing they could be bombed at any time? From the photos, anyone could sense a special bond between the girls, yet her mother hardly ever spoke about her friends. Mary knew she had kept in touch with one of them who still lived in England, but as far as she was aware, only ever went to visit England a few times; once to a wedding and once to a funeral.

She felt her heart miss a beat, and a lump in her throat on finding photographs of Helen holding her new baby wrapped in a white shawl. Harry had his arm around Helen, and Mary could really feel the love in these photos.

'Jesus. I'm just a tiny baby. These must be the very first photographs taken of me.'

She held the photos to her chest and a tear fell from her cheeks and down her chin. Mary composed herself and was about to put the photographs to one side, when she realised, she had missed one. It was the same photograph of the good looking young man she had seen earlier. On the back of the photograph, was written 'all my love x'. The very same photograph she had seen in her mother's album. She wondered if the man had been a previous lover of Helens, and not her mother's as she'd thought. As well as the photographs, there was a bundle of letters tied with string.

Mary poured herself a coffee and sat awhile pondering whether to open them or not. She decided to see what Jack thought about them. He answered the phone after the first ring as usual and Mary explained about the envelope and its contents.

'I haven't opened them in case they're love letters. I can't understand why they were hidden away; Mom clearly didn't want them found.'

'I can't see your problem.'

'But they might not be Dad's letters, Jack. They could be from the man in the photo, either to Helen *or* Mom.

'Mary, they were divorced . . . and anyway, I can't see any reason now why your father would be upset even if it was your mother's old boyfriend. And anyway, I doubt very much they were your mother's letters if everything in the envelope were personal items of Helens, anyway.'

'You're right.'

'How are you feeling, it must have been quite upsetting to see the photos of you and Helen?'

'Yeah, it was upsetting. I'm okay now. I'll phone Dad and make arrangements to go see him.'

That afternoon Mary met up with her Dad in his office. When she handed him the envelope containing the letters and photos Peter stared at the photograph.

'Whoever it was, must have fought in the war and lived in Liverpool the same time as Helen and Kate', he said quietly. 'Why would Kate hide these from me?'

'The man in the photo may have been killed Dad; she had a life before you, remember.'

'Yeah, but why didn't she mention him if it was an old boyfriend of Helens.'

'I don't know. Mom could have promised Helen she wouldn't tell anyone. Do you recognise the other girl in the picture?'

'Yeah, sure, that's Anna. The four of them were great friends.'

'Mom never spoke much about her past, did she?'

'Perhaps she didn't like to think of the bad memories of living in Liverpool. Yeah, I know there were fun times, people made the best they could of life. But there were very few families in Liverpool who were lucky enough not to lose a loved one during the war. They had it real bad. Liverpool was almost obliterated. Half of the docks were out of action, power lines were down, and although the main targets were the docks and the city centre, sadly, most of the residential houses were also bombed. Bootle, where Kate's and Helen's family lived, was the worst hit. There were barely any houses left. Not everyone liked to be reminded of those times.'

'That's terrible. Poor Mom, it must have been awful for her. Could the man in the photo be Helen's brother?'

'Could be, but I don't think so. She would have said if she had a brother fighting in the war and I'm sure Helen only had the two brothers who died in the air raid. I'm certain Kate would have told me, I was a serving soldier myself. We would have been like comrades in arms. She had no reason not to tell me. I guess we'll never know Mary.'

'Are you going to read the letters?'

'Yeah, I suppose so. Did you read them?'

'No, I haven't read them. I wanted to wait until you were here in case they were personal to you and Mom.'

'I never had the need to write letters, I was stationed to where she lived.'

Peter quickly scanned through the letters first before reading out loud. They were about the young man's time in Normandy who talked of the fighting.

'These letters are not Helen's . . . or Kate's. They're to someone called Marianne.'

'Did Mom know someone called Marianne?' asked Mary.

'I never heard her mention a girl by that name, but she did have a lot of friends when working in the factory. I remember when we first started seeing each other how she mentioned losing a few close friends during the bombings, though she found it hard to talk about them. Kate didn't like to show her feelings, you know that Mary. She was a very private person.'

'How sad, perhaps her friend, Marianne, died before you came along.'

'I guess so.'

Peter passed the letters to Mary so she might read them for herself.

Dear Marianne.

Hope you are ok. I hear Liverpool has been hit badly. I hate the fact that you are there amidst it all. I dread hearing the news. Did you do as I asked about passing my address on to your friends? How else would I know if you were lying in a hospital somewhere, or God forbid, worse? How are your friends? I love to hear the funny stories you send me about them. It's amazing anyone could still have a sense of humour with all that bombing going off around you. It isn't very good where we are right now, but I'm not allowed to say where that is. I have lost some friends to this bloody war and seen some horrible sights, but we have to fight on. Only yesterday, I had to help take two dead soldiers off the field where we were fighting. Not a sight I hope to see again. It's hard to believe one minute you're sharing a joke and next, they're dead. X

Dear Marianne.

If you don't hear from me, don't worry. It's getting harder to write these days, we're up to our knees in sludge and the weather has taken a bad turn. My fingers are frozen most of the time, and I think I may have frost bite. I think about you over in Liverpool all the time and pray to God you won't be killed. One of my friend's wives died along with all his family while they were in a shelter, not far from where you live. When I hear news like that, it's the not knowing if you're dead or alive that gets to me, and I feel relieved when I receive letters from you. War or no war, you seem very happy. Keep the stories coming in. x

Dear Marianne

This is a very short letter. My fingers are so cold, I cannot write. The sky is full of dark clouds that seem to add to the misery of this bloody war. We sleep in pup tents, but there are no beds in them, and I suppose after a while you get used to sleeping on the floor. The cold is an awful thing for making my bones ache. We can hear the wind and rain lashing at our tents, and then there's the sound of gun fire in the distance. Keep safe X

'The rest of the letters are all pretty much the same. They don't give much away.' said Mary, clearly disappointed. 'But there has to be a reason why there is no forwarding address or surname.'

'There was probably a name and address on the back of the envelope. People used to do that sort of thing in case the letters got lost. Or maybe the house was bombed. Guess we'll never know who the letters belonged to.'

'Mom must have kept these letters and photos as a reminder of Helen and Harry. Most of the pictures were of those two. Then there's Helen with Mom, in a group, outside the factory. People we don't know. These are a collection of photos of Helen from different times. They're obviously Helen's photos.'

Peter looked at the photographs. 'I was there when these were taken outside the factory. I didn't realise Kate had kept them. The girls were Kate's work friends, and Helen of course, who Harry fell for there and then. He never stopped talking about her.'

'They seem a lovely couple.' Mary added sadly. She kissed her father goodbye and asked the cab driver to take her straight to Jack's office.

*

'What a wonderful surprise darling. I thought you were busy.'

'I am, but I can't get this thing out my head about Mom and Helen. It seems they have taken a lot of secrets to the grave when they died.'

Mary poured herself a coffee and noticed how bright the office looked now Jack had changed the décor. The walls were adorned with framed pictures of famous detectives from old movies. A chaise lounge stood opposite the desk, which was also new, and a beautiful marbled coffee table with easy chairs.

'Do you still believe your mother had a lover?'

'Not since reading the letters. I don't know what to think Jack, but something is eating at me. Anyway, how do you feel about finding more about my birth mother . . .not that I have any sudden feelings of love for her, but I would like to know where I was originally from'

'I know I'm a detective Mary, but I'm not a miracle worker. The only real people who would know are dead. We don't have any leads.'

'What about my grandfather. He was there.'

'Well I suppose that's a start. Make arrangements for us to go see him, it would be a pleasure to meet such a famous man.'

Mary was about to speak when Jack jumped up from his chair and held her tightly in his arms. 'You look beautiful in that dress.'

*

An hour later Mary picked up the telephone.

'Hi Grandpa'

'Mary, how lovely to hear from you'

'Sorry I haven't been in touch. I've been rushed off my feet. Will it be all right to come over and see you tomorrow evening, and bring Jack to meet you?'

'Of course, darling, will you be coming for dinner?'

'That would be great. I have to go now, but I'll see you about six tomorrow.'

Mary made her way home, her mind spinning. She poured herself a wine and sat crossed legged in front of the fire. Beside her was the envelope. As she reached across, all the contents fell onto the floor. Cursing, she put the letters into the bag, and what seemed to have come out of nowhere, was a Christmas card addressed to *Mrs Margaret O'Conner 41, Moore Street, Meade, Dublin Ireland,* Nothing was written inside the card, but there must be a connection somewhere.

'Oh wow. I have an address. I have a lead.' thought Mary excitedly.

*

Mary's grandparents had decided to move to a smaller house six months ago, and Mary was surprised to see how *big* the smaller house was. She imagined a small house with just a few bedrooms. But then, after the last home they had, Mary supposed the house could be seen as smaller. The large heavily carpeted staircase swept down to the entrance hall; a beautiful crystal chandelier hung from the ceiling. Her grandfather came out of a room downstairs and hugged her so tight; she almost came off the ground.

'You look absolutely stunning young lady. And this is Jack the detective, is it?' He offered his hand to Jack, and Jack noticed the warm firm handshake, which said a lot about a person. He liked a good handshake. 'Come through and I'll pour you a drink' gestured Karl.

Jack stood looking at the room for a minute, speechless. The fireplace was in the centre of the room and gave out bright coloured flames from artificial logs. There were sofas and cushions everywhere. On one side of the wall, was a gigantic portrait of Karl Reiner seated like a King on his throne. The picture windows on both sides overlooked large gardens with trees, shrubs, and fountains. At the back of the house was a swimming pool with the finest sun loungers and parasols. Jack knew Karl was a man of great wealth, but he was more surprised by the décor which would be more fitting of a younger couple. He also knew Mary was used to this sort of life with grand houses but had hoped when he asked her to marry him, which he had been thinking about for some time, she would prefer something less elaborate.

An hour into the evening, Mary plucked up the courage to question her grandfather.

'Grandpa, I'm going to ask you something now, but please, if you don't want to talk about it, say so, I won't be offended.'

'Just ask, you know me, if I don't want to do anything, then I won't. What is it?'

'I know about my adoption.'

'I knew it would come out sooner or later. I did tell Peter. You should have been told . . .'

'No. I mean my first adoption.'

244

'Oh, you know about that as well' said Karl, opening a cigar box and removing a corona cigar. He began to light the cigar with a very expensive looking lighter in the shape of cruiser. 'Does your father know you're here to ask questions?'

'No, but I'm sure it's all right. We have spoken at great length about my adoption, obviously he wasn't there . . . but you were.'

'Where do I start . . .?'

'At the very beginning please Grandpa. There won't be any tears, or emotion, I can assure you of that.'

'Okay. Well now, it was just after the war. I had a phone call from Peter saying he wanted to see me. Kate was pregnant at the time, and I thought perhaps something had happened. "No" Peter said when I asked him, "it's about Harry." Peter told me Harry couldn't have children and had tried to adopt a child but were told it would be years before they could adopt in the States. He said Helen was beside herself. God only knows why they wanted kids so young; they had all the time in the world to adopt a kid. But I suppose it was because Harry was an only child who was born late in his parents' life. I don't know the rush for sure.' Karl sighed, wishing he didn't have to do this. 'Through a friend of his, Peter had heard about the homes for unmarried mothers in Ireland. His friend told him they were actually selling babies to Catholic families, as they had more babies than they could handle.'

'Selling babies? That can't be true Grandpa. Surely it can't be legal.'

'It was true Mary. Let me finish now I've started, and then you can ask your questions. Anyway, I asked Peter what he wanted me to do and he told me.'

"He doesn't have the money Dad, and he may need an attorney. Dad, please, he needs your help. Helen was born in Dublin, which will help quite a bit, but Harry doesn't know how to sort it out on his own like this."

'I was on the plane the following week with George my attorney and Harry and Helen, to see what I could do. We went to a few institutions for pregnant girls while we were there, just kinda making enquires before finishing up in a place just outside Dublin, I can't remember the name now, but it'll come to me. The building was a dismal looking place. Grey and eerie, even though it'd probably only been built in the 1930's. But then, all the buildings of these so call homes were as dismal outside as they were inside.'

Mary wondered how her grandfather knew so much but didn't want to interrupt him. He suddenly stopped talking for a few seconds and seemed to be lost in own thoughts. Then Karl continued 'You could say they weren't built to look like hotels, they were purposely built for the babies of unmarried mothers. The Reverend Mother sat opposite us in an office with sickly green coloured paint on the walls. The desk was huge, and I felt sure she had deliberately piled cushions on her chair to make anyone sitting opposite look small and inferior. I felt like a child waiting to be slapped, such was the look on her face. I sat as tall as I could and handed over my business card, introducing myself and my attorney. The transformation was incredible. She was listening now.' Karl smiled. 'We explained the circumstances . . . well, Harry did, telling her how he had a childhood illness which left him sterile, and how he and Helen didn't want to wait too long before they adopted a baby.

"Are you Catholic Mr Mitchell? We have strict policies which only allow a child to be adopted by a good Catholic family." The nun said, staring into Harry's eyes. He told her he was, and she ask what age or sex Harry would prefer . . .'

'Asking him what age or sex sounds like they had a good selection. It's so ridiculous. They are human beings, not puppies.' Mary said with contempt.

'Yes, well, it wasn't as if you were allowed in the nursery, or wherever they keep the babies, to choose. The Reverend Mother told Harry they had a good range of babies from one month to three years.'

'But surely the mothers would still be nursing the babies.' Mary gasped.

'Not necessarily. If the mother's parents were willing to take the girl home again, then you could pay a fee for the child to be adopted or fostered after ten days. Harry asked if all the babies were healthy as he couldn't believe how easy it was. He began to wonder if the reason was because they were rejected in some way, but the Reverend Mother insisted they only allowed perfect babies up for adoption.

Mary felt a lump tighten in her throat. 'So, I was considered perfect. How could the mothers allow letting their babies be sold?'

'When you went into an institution, it was usually to hide the fact you were having a baby in the first place. Sometimes the father of the pregnant girl wouldn't even know, never mind family and friends. It was quite a sin to be an unmarried mother, an outcast that brought shame to her family, you have to remember this. The girls had no choice.'

'They must have been heartbroken to give up a baby they'd loved.' said Jack. 'What about the father to the child? Did they just leave the girls to go through this life of shame on their own?'

Karl Reiner wanted to say how hard he fought to save the girl he loved, and their child, but instead, he continued. 'They had no say in the matter. They weren't allowed near the girls . . .'

'Would you like more coffee?' Joan, Mary's grandmother asked, and if Karl didn't know better, he would have thought his wife had a suspicion about his affair and was trying to change the subject. He suddenly had a rush of blood to his head.

'Yeah, why not' let's have a break.' He answered, trying hard to sound natural.

Jack stood up and walked towards the garden. 'I think I'm just gonna stretch my legs, if you don't mind' he explained as he moved towards the French windows. Once outside, he lit a cigarette and mulled over what was said. There was more than meets the eye with Karl Reiner. He seemed very passionate about the girls in these homes. Joan, his wife, sensed it too. He was sure of it. Mary joined him and linked her arm through his. He suddenly felt her pain.

'You sure you want to carry on with this Mary. It can't be easy for you.'

'I'm okay. My birth mother may have been forced to leave me behind. I know that now. I wonder how old she was. I could even have Grandparents in Ireland somewhere. Not that I would want to see them.'

'Why's that?'

'They didn't help my mother, or I would still be with her.'

'And I would never have met you.'

'That's true. I can't think of a life without you now Jack. I love you so much.'

Jack embraced her in his arms as Joan called out to say coffee was ready. When they finished chatting about the garden and how good the new gardener was at growing vegetables, Mary asked her grandfather about the adoption.

So, did Harry and Helen choose me?'

'Not really. They didn't mind the sex of the child but preferred a younger baby if at all possible. We waited about an hour before a nurse came into the room with a bundle, stating quite coldly it was a girl. The Reverend Mother said the baby . . . you, were four weeks old. Of course, Harry and Helen, who hadn't spoken much up to then, were completely blown away by you. We never asked your name. Isn't that odd? I think we were just in awe of you. Harry was in for another surprise to learn he could take you home in a few weeks when all the papers were drawn up.'

'I can't believe it. He bought a baby, just like buying a new car.'

'Suppose so. Harry and Helen went straight to the stores to buy food and clothing for the child. As it happens, Helen helped her mother bring up her younger brothers, so she was quite capable of looking after a baby; but the Reverend Mother didn't know that. She allowed a child to be taken away without any background information, apart from the address of where they lived.'

'I wonder how my mother felt at the time. Would she have cried or was she just glad to get rid of me?'

'Mary, the girls had no choice' Karl shouted. 'Their babies were taken from them without their permission. These girls didn't know the babies were going to be adopted of fostered out until the day it happened. Who could they possible talk to anyway, the poor young girls . . .?'

'Karl.' Joan said softly 'you're starting to sound angry. Calm down darling.'

'I'm sorry. I didn't realise. I would like to stop now Mary. The rest is history anyway.'

'Thank you, Grandpa' replied Mary throwing her arms around her grandfather.

Karl watched the couple walk hand in hand towards their car. A tear fell down his cheek.

Chapter 27

Just as Mary and Jack stepped off the plane in Dublin airport, a sudden gust of wind almost knocked them off their feet. Looking up toward the sky and pulling her collar a little higher, Mary shuddered. She hoped the weather would at least brighten up. It wasn't the cold wind, rather the dull grey skies. When they left New York, it was snowing. At least frost and snow were bright and cheerful looking. She wished now she had listened to Jack and come in the spring when it would be warmer, but she couldn't wait until then. Yet, throughout the flight she was beginning to regret her decision about coming to Ireland at all. There were so many questions in her mind. Why didn't her birth mother try and find the daughter she had given up at birth? Was it true she had no choice other than to have her baby adopted, as her Grandfather had suspected? Or did she simply want to put it all behind her and start afresh. Would she be happy to tell her new family she had borne a child and given her away?

'Mary, try not to worry.' said Jack softly. 'I can feel the tenseness coming from you. We have nothing to lose by trying, but that doesn't mean we will find her. I can't promise anything. Besides, not everyone who are lucky enough to actually find their mother, come away happy. I can imagine a lot of girls who lived in these so-called Magdalena homes just wanted to get on with their lives and put the trauma behind them. But it doesn't mean to say they don't think about the babies who were given up for adoption. They must have known at the time they would never see them again.'

Tears were beginning to fill Mary's eyes and Jack put his arms around her shoulder. He had a bad feeling about this and wished he hadn't agreed to it. He couldn't see anything in front of him other than disappointment.

'I understand that, Jack. I promise I won't be upset if we don't find anything.' She whispered sadly. 'Remember when we had our first date, and you said you would like to go to Ireland again with the right person?'

'Yes, I do remember, and I am here with the right person.'

'I don't suppose you reckoned on coming for something like this.'

Jack laughed. 'No.'

'Oh Jack, if it wasn't for you, I would have gone all my life without knowing I was adopted.'

'Maybe that might have been a good thing.'

'No Jack. I might have found out in other ways, for instance, if I ever needed a medical history of my family, or if I have a child who had an inherited illness.'

'Mary, you may never know anyway. Stop it.'

Jack hired a car and suggested they spent a week as tourists before going straight into any research. Hopefully, this would relax Mary a little as well as give himself time to think, something he hadn't had much time for. Trying to find Mary's mother would not be an easy task, especially if she didn't want to be found, which, in his job, had usually been the case. He'd seen very few happy reunions in his years as a private detective. This was harder still. There were so many babies adopted by Americans just after the war and Jack suspected most of the records were 'lost.' But he'd promised Mary he would do his best and so he would.

Right from the start Jack was surprised to see how much Mary loved Dublin, and true enough, she was beginning to relax and enjoy the change.

'It's so strange, I feel at home somehow. I wasn't expecting that to happen.'

'It could be in the genes.' Jack pointed out. 'Or you may have subconsciously believed you would suddenly feel at home. It would have been interesting to have come earlier, before you knew you were born here.'

'Ha-ha, the psychologist is coming out now, but you're right. Dublin is a beautiful place. Your ancestors were from Ireland as well. Do you feel something too?'

'Yes, in a way I do, and although my family originated from Cork, I have always been drawn to Dublin. I'm looking forward to going to Cork with you when this is over. I can show you where my grandfather was born. Hey, perhaps we can kiss the Blarney Stone while we're there.'

'Oh wow, that would be something.'

'It sure would. Now, would you like me to be your tour guide here in Dublin city, where the girls are so pretty, and my lovely lady?'

'I sure would, kind sir.'

'Then follow me.'

They held hands and laughed as they set out to see the sights of Dublin, staying out until it was dark. The city lights were amazing. Enthusiastically, in the coming days, Jack pointed out various historical facts about Dublin.

'The River Liffey starts high in the mountains of Wicklow, working its way towards the Irish sea until it reaches Dublin, where it is spanned by thirteen bridges. The bridge over there' said Jack pointing 'is known as the Ha'penny Bridge. It was originally a toll bridge, hence the name Half Penny or as the Irish say, Ha'penny, which is what it cost to cross it. Come on, I'll show you the Post Office.'

'The Post Office, why would I want to visit a Post Office, we don't need any stamps. We haven't written home yet.'

'This is no ordinary Post Office Mary. This is where the 1916 uprising began between the English and the Irish. There is still shrapnel damage on the stone pillars that form the entrance. British gunboats sailed up the Liffey and fired their cannons at the Irish Republican Army, who were occupying the building. And, it was outside the General Post Office where the proclamation of Irish Independence was read out. This Post Office is a magnificent building.'

'I wouldn't mind going to Trinity College to see the book of Kells tomorrow Jack. I read an article about it a while ago.'

'I can tell you a little of the history of the Book of Kells if you're so interested. I did a thesis about it when I was in Uni.'

'Let's go for a coffee after the Post Office, and you can tell me then. I don't want to miss anything. Sure is good touring with an Irish Historian.'

After checking out the site of the old Post Office, where Jack explained about the Irish fight for independence from the British, Mary chose a quaint little cafe where they could stop for a coffee.

'The book of Kells is eleven hundred years old and is kept in a glass case to stop the daylight spoiling the lettering. The pages are turned every day so that people can marvel at the beautifully illustrated manuscript' Jack explained enthusiastically.

'What is the book made from for it to survive so long? Mary asked, intrigued by the history of the famous book.

'It's written on calfskin. Different colours were used in the illustrations, some of them very rare and expensive dyes which were imported from the continent. I won't tell you anymore as we're going tomorrow. Now this is an interesting fact; the Viking settlement in the year 841 was known as Dyflin, from the Irish Duiblinn, or Black Pool. This was referred to as a dark tidal pool where the river Poddle entered the Liffy.'

'So, the Vikings were in Dublin,' asked Mary.

'Oh, yeah, they certainly were. They ruled Dublin for three centuries; they were expelled in the year 902 but came back again in 917. It wasn't until 1171 when Viking Rule completely came to an end.'

'I can understand why you were interested in history. I could listen to you all day.'

Jack laughed 'I could go on and on. There's the Norsemen, the Anglo-Norman Conquerors etc, but we're going to see a lot more of Dublin in the next few days, so I won't tell you anymore.'

Mary found the museums in Dublin fascinating, and she was overwhelmed to see Ireland's most historic treasures, the Tara Broach, the Ardagh Chalice, and the Cross of Cong. But now it was time to trace Mrs O'Conner and somehow find the connection with her first adoptive mother.

*

'Well, this is the place.' Jack said stopping the car and bending his head low to look through the windscreen.

'Yes, but most of the windows are boarded up, it seems the building is about to be demolished. Now what do we do? Give up looking for the woman who knew Helen, my first adoptive mother, or start looking for my birth mother? It's just a Christmas card to someone for Christ's sake. Helen must have bought the card just before she died and never got the chance to send it. None of this has anything to do with my birth mother, Jack.'

'True. I admit she may not have anything to do with her, but there is a link somewhere and it's the only bit of information we have Mary. We didn't get anywhere when phoning the Magdalena home, and I'm almost sure we won't get a response by going there. Come on, let's try the local bar.'

'Jack are you mad. Try them for what. They look so old.'

'They are old. Wait 'til you see inside. The old pubs in Dublin have real character and the Guinness is good too. . .'

'Jack. . .'

'Mary, the reason I want to go into a local bar is because the people who lived in the tenement houses formed close communities. Someone must know where the tenants were re-housed.'

'Okay, but I say we start making our way to the orphanage . . . or whatever they're called here, first thing in the morning. Please Jack.'

'Sure, that's fine with me. Come on. Try a glass of Guinness. You'll never taste one as good anywhere in the world.'

'I think I'll stick to orange juice.' Mary smiled.

Inside the pub, very little sunlight came through the windows and the low ceiling and dark wooden furniture only added to the dark smoky atmosphere as you walked in from the outside. There was also a strong smell of beer and pipe tobacco. The large number of men who were gathered around the bar suddenly stopped talking, turning towards Jack and Mary for a few seconds before carrying on with their conversations. Jack wondered if it was a good idea after all, bringing Mary into what was obviously a man's pub. There were no women in the bar anywhere, and Jack guessed he and Mary were obviously over dressed for such a place.

'Now sir, what can I get you and yer missus?'

'A pint of Guinness and an orange juice please.'

The barman looked puzzled. 'Ah, so yous are Americans. Welcome to Dublin. Are yis here on business?' the barman assumed, noticing how well dressed they were. Most American tourists he'd encountered always carried a camera around their necks and a rug sack on their backs; walking around as if they were visiting another planet rather than another country. The Japanese were the same, only they talked constantly to one another. But these two looked professional.

'No, we're on vacation, but while we are here, we promised a friend of mine we would try and find a female relative of his. The address he gave me isn't there now though. The houses are boarded up.'

'From these parts, was she? Most of the old houses are derelict, waiting to be knocked down fer those so-called corporation flats. They've already built some further up the road. Would yis want something to eat before the kitchen staff goes home?'

'Oh no thanks, we have to be. . .'

'Yeah, that would be great.'

When the barman went to get a menu, Mary was furious. 'How can you expect me to eat here? The place smells of beer and stale smoke and look how small the tables are.' She whispered.

'Mary don't be such a snob. They've welcomed us into their lives. Every one of those men spoke or acknowledged us. I'm the detective and I know what I'm doing, just trust me.'

She had to admit when the meal arrived, which was meat and potato pie and mash and cabbage, it was well presented and piping hot, and although she didn't finish it all, she enjoyed the food. Jack ate every bit of his and was looking at the pudding and custard dessert on the menu.

The barman came to collect the plates and Jack asked how long he had worked behind the bar.

'I'm the landlord. I own this place like me da before me.'

'So, you'll probably know Mrs Margaret O'Conner.'

'No, not many women drink here, but the name rings a bell. How old is she?'

'I'm not sure of her age to be honest. I just have her name and what was her old address. But I said I would look her up.'

'I'll ask around fer yis. This place gets busy in the evening and a lot of the auld tenement dwellers still come here fer the stout.'

'That's fantastic. And now, I would like to try some of your treacle pudding and custard, and a coffee for me missus.' Jack laughed.

*

Jack and Mary went back to the old pub three times before finally getting an address for Mrs O'Conner. Mary had taken Jack's advice and tried her best to join in the conversations. She eventually began to relax and even had a few glasses of Guinness.

'Jack, why are all the locals sat squashed around the bar, when all the tables are empty, no one sits down.'

'You can't mix with everyone whilst sat around a table. They stand at the bar so they can join in the craic. I noticed almost every one of them offered their bar stool for you to sit on.'

'Craic, what's the Craic? Mary asked looking puzzled.

'Craic means the talk, the banter, you know everyone getting together and enjoying themselves; just like the Irish bars in New York' Jack explained.

'I know what you mean now; I'm getting to feel right at home here.' She laughed, throwing her head back, flicking her hair, her eyes bright and shining. Jack adored Mary and when this search was over; his intentions were to propose to her, here in Ireland.

A rough looking man with a red nose and puffed up eyes, clearly from years of heavy drinking, walked over towards them, squeezing his way between the crowds.

'I hear you're from America. Hope yis are enjoying yer holiday. I also hear yer looking fer Peggy O'Conner?'

'Yeah, we are enjoying our stay, thanks. But the name is Margaret O'Conner we're looking for, and not Peggy.'

'Ah, to be sure, Peggy is short fer Margaret. She lives up in Summer Hill. I can't give you the exact address, but you can be sure to find her, someone up there will know her. Most of them are from the tenement houses.'

The man gave directions and Jack wrote them down and thanked him, buying him a Guinness just before they left.

'I didn't think much to him. He gave me the creeps.'

'He's an alcoholic. Still, he was very helpful. We got the address, didn't we?'

'Yea, we did. I'm sorry for the lack of enthusiasm Jack, but this is only going to tell me things about someone who adopted me and died when I was three years old.'

'We don't have to do this Mary if that's how you feel. We can ignore Helen and go straight to looking for your birth mother.'

'No. You're right. I ought to know more about the woman . . . Helen, who loved me for three years. I'm sorry Jack, I should be grateful. I'm just all mixed up right now.'

Once Jack and Mary arrived in Summer Hill they soon found a local who knew Mrs O'Conner; in fact it appeared that almost everyone knew, or had heard of her.

Peggy O'Conner stood on the little balcony of what she considered her new accommodation, or 'flat' as the corporation called them. She hated the new buildings, rows and tiers of modern-day housing. She missed the old tenement houses where every door was open to visitors. The long summer days and nights, when all the tenants would congregate on the street; enjoying the craic, the singing and the laughter. Peggy O'Conner also missed those cosy winter nights around the turf fires sharing tales of Irish folklore, while the wind howled and rattled the windowpanes. No, they didn't have hot water and an inside toilet, but they had each other. They had humour, trust, and they shared all they had when times were hard.

'Jaysus, why couldn't they leave us where we were? We were one big family. . . Jesus, Mary and Joseph, aren't I talking to me self these days er what?'

She was about to refill her cup of tea when there was a knock on the door. 'Holy Mother of God, who the hell is this'

'Mrs O'Conner.'

'Tis I, what do yis want? Has someone died?'

'No, we're so sorry to bother you, but . . .'

'I won't need anything from yis then, thanks.'

Mary looked at Jack as the door closed with a thud. 'She thought we were selling something. Now what do we do?'

'I have an idea. Come on' said Jack, grabbing Mary's hand 'let's go for a coffee.'

They drove towards Parnell square, and walked on O'Connell Street and into the first café they came across. Jack opened his folder, containing all the papers and commented on why Mrs O'Conner assumed they were door to door salesmen.

'She obviously saw the folder in my hand. No wonder she shut the door on us, two strangers speaking what would seem a foreign language to her, and holding a folder full of papers, for Pete's sake.'

'What have you in mind Jack?'

'Well, she's never going to let us through the door to talk, is she?'

'No, neither will she talk to us if we phone her. She'll just put the phone down.'

'She won't have a phone, but they still use the old-fashioned way of communication.' Jack beamed, holding a pen and piece of paper in his hand. 'We'll write to her, telling her we'll be back in two days if she will talk to us.'

'That's great Jack. It gives her time to think too.'

The letter wasn't easy to write. 'How can a person explain a situation such as this?' Mary sighed, after screwing up yet another sheet of paper.

'Let me have a go.'

Jack gave a brief description of why they were there, explaining how Mary found a card with her old address on the envelope. He also apologised for just turning up out of the blue and commended her on not allowing strangers into her home.

He ended the letter by saying they would call again in two days' time, during the morning.

Chapter 28

An unexpected blast of wind caught Mary of guard and she wrapped her coat tightly across her chest. Not that she was cold, but it stemmed from an old habit of her mother's whenever she felt nervous. The sun shone in the sky and a strong smell of fruit from a nearby wheelbarrow filled her nostrils. She looked up towards the block of flats and wondered if her birth mother lived in something similar. The windows were very small, giving the impression that it must be dark and dismal inside. Outside, a tower of spiral steps climbed to the foot bridges that separated the flats and a few people peered over the tops of their balconies. Jack held Mary's hand as they began to climb the stairs once more.

Mary gagged, covering her mouth, gasping. 'What's that smell? It smells like rotting vegetables.'

'Rubbish.'

'Sorry.'

'It's the smell of rubbish.'

'There is no rubbish.'

'In the centre of the tower block are hatches, to allow the tenants to send their rubbish down a chute. It's emptied weekly. What you can smell is vegetable waste. Most of the household rubbish people burn on their fire.'

As they reached Mrs O'Conner's door Jack knocked and called out, 'Mrs O' Conner, I really am sorry to trouble you again but . . .'

'Jaysus, come in. Yous wouldn't want the neighbours to hear your story now would ye.' Mrs O'Conner spoke, while looking with suspicion at a woman shaking her table linen over the edge of the balcony. She closed the door and escorted them to a table and four chairs. 'Now, would yis like a cup of tea?'

'Oh no thanks . . .'

'Yeah, we sure would love a cup of tea, wouldn't we darling.' agreed Jack nodding.

Mary understood the message Jack was sending to her. 'That would be great, yes.'

Mrs O'Conner opened a curtain to a kitchen which couldn't hold more than one person at a time. The small kitchen's only appliances comprised of a stove, sink and a kettle. A tall cupboard stood at one end of the room and the only other storage was a cupboard beneath the sink. Letting in some sunlight was a small window above the sink, which looked out onto the front balcony.

Mrs O'Conner appeared old at first, but Mary reckoned she wasn't as old as she had first thought. Her skin showed very few signs of wrinkles, and her movements were swift. She was very small and slim. Her bone structure was perfect, and Mary believed she must have been a beautiful woman once, and in some ways she still was. Her hair was pure white and still had a healthy fullness. Mary looked around the small room. On the shelf above the open fire were a few photographs of a young man, but none of any children. In the corner of the room stood a small television, which was switched on but without any sound. The reception was so poor to a point where the picture was barely visible, probably because it wasn't tuned in properly. At the other side of the room was a picture of Jesus placed over a shelf where candles were burning. There was Holy Water by the door and a faint smell of incense lingered. The flat was furnished with just the bare necessities and little else. There was, however, plenty of light, much more than Mary had expected, and the back door led to a small terrace where a chair stood in the corner, allowing Mrs. O'Conner somewhere to sit outside.

To Mary's surprise, Mrs O'Conner walked backed into the room and placed a plate of bread and butter on the table. When she was out of earshot, pouring the hot water into the teapot, Jack leaned over to Mary. 'Soda bread is always offered with tea, it's an Irish tradition, just as the English offer tea and cookies.'

'Oh.' Mary smiled and looked towards the tiny kitchen. 'Would you like a hand in there Mrs O'Conner?'

'That'll be grand. Take the cups and saucers while I mash the tea.'

Mary jumped up and walked toward the kitchen and mouthed 'mash the tea' to Jack with a puzzled. Jack laughed. When they were all seated, Mrs O'Conner began pouring the tea. 'Help yerselves to bread now, while I pour.'

'Thanks,' said Jack cheerfully, already tucking into the thickly cut bread. 'Sure is good. I haven't had soda bread for some years. Nice little place you have here Mrs. O'Conner, just the right size for one.'

'Holy mother of God, sure I hate the place. In my auld home we didn't have a posh kitchen or separate bedroom like we have here, but we had company, laughter, and friends. We were one big family. We helped each other out and shared what we had. Life was good in the tenement houses. The Corporation has split us all up. I was never lonely . . . and I never locked the bloody door.' Mrs O'Conner sighed and composed herself. 'Now, how can I help? You say you found a card addressed to me.'

Mary explained about the card. 'I guess Helen never got around to posting it. There were some letters from a soldier too.'

'Well now, sure that's to be expected seeing as there was a war on.'

Mary was taken aback by the comment but carried on. 'I believe Mom kept the letters after Helen died, but unfortunately, I've forgotten to bring the photos I intended showing you, although I have a photo of Helen and Mom in my wallet. The picture was taken outside the factory where they worked together. We believe Helen's name was Marianne at some time.'

'Fer God's sake, will you slow down. This mother, that mother . . .What the hell. Start from the beginning will yis and give me time to think . . . Holy mother of God.'

262

Stunned by Mrs O'Conner's sudden outburst, Mary started at the beginning. Right back to her parents meeting in Liverpool that is.

'Mom was born here in Dublin, but her family moved to Liverpool when she was a young child, though she still had an Irish accent. Helen was also born in Dublin, but Dad said they didn't know each other until they met at the factory in Liverpool. He said most Liverpudlians had some Irish links.'

'Yes, tis true. Many families went to England looking fer work, but they weren't welcomed much by the English, you know. The Irish were renowned for being drunk and always fighting. Ah, sure to God that might have been true in some cases, but they were good workers. A lot of me very own family went to live over there. Birmingham it was. An Irish accent is fer life and that's fer sure, no matter how young yis were when you left dear old Ireland.' She looked closely at the photograph Mary handed to her. 'I knew a Marianne all right . . . Marianne McNamara. Yes, that's her on the photo. Tell me again, who she is to you.'

'She adopted me, but of course her name was Helen Mitchell at the time.'

'Adopted you, Jaysus, Mary and Joseph, couldn't she have babies of her own? Sure to God her mother had no trouble getting herself pregnant.'

Mary didn't know whether to laugh at the remark. How could a woman possibly get *herself* pregnant?

'Apparently, it was Harry, her husband, who had a problem. Helen knew from the very start. He told her so', replied Jack, 'he gave her the chance to find someone else before they became involved with each other, but she obviously loved him.'

'You say in your letter they both died. Holy mother of God, May God have mercy on their souls.' Mrs O'Conner made the sign of the cross. 'Jaysus, the poor girl, and what a terrible life she had. Terrible, and then there's her mother running away leaving her young ones behind . . . or so they say.'

'What do you mean, 'or so they say' Mrs O'Conner?'

'I won't be saying anymore on that matter now. Would yis like another cup of tea?'

This time Mary answered. 'Yes please Mrs O'Conner, but I'll skip the bread, thank you.'

The three of them sat around the table, talking about the old tenement blocks. Suddenly, and out of the blue, Mrs O'Conner said.' 'He was a fecking bully. He bullied his wife and those poor bairns, so he did. Cruel he was.'

'Who was a bully? Sorry I don't follow.' Gulped Jack, almost choking on the slice of bread he was eating.

'Joseph McNamara. That's who. Ah Jesus, the times I had to bathe the cuts and bruises on his poor wife's frail body. He killed a baby once you know.'

Mary wondered what they were getting into. Mrs O'Conner was, after all a stranger. The talk of killing a child made her feel frightened and she whispered 'I think maybe we should go now' to Jack.

But Jack wanted to hear more and gave Mary a reassuring pat on the knee. 'Was he charged for the murder?' he asked Mrs O'Conner gently, trying to find out more without sounding too eager.

'No, Molly wouldn't tell the Gardaí. And really there was no proof. He kicked her, you see . . . in the stomach. She lost the baby and nearly lost her own life. That poor woman went through hell.'

Mary felt relief in knowing it wasn't murder as in *murdering* a child, but the relief soon turned to sympathy for the mother.

Mrs O'Conner was quiet for a while, poking the fire and staring into the flames as if seeing the past come to life. 'Marianne was also beaten by the fecking excuse of a man. Put her in hospital, so he did. She never came home again. Christmas 1941 it was. Of course, it was a while before I knew she had fled to Liverpool. Liverpool, of all places! They were being bombed off the face of the earth fer God's sake. I don't know how or why she went to live there. She was only thirteen years old, although, it was her birthday in January which was just a month away. She used to write, and I would pass the letters to Molly, but they soon stopped coming. I used to get Christmas cards at one time too, but there were no more letters for Molly. Whether Molly had them sent straight to the Post Office, I don't know. There was always a risk of Joseph finding out; us all being in the same building. Molly didn't talk much about her, and everyone assumed she was working in one of those big houses as a skivvy.'

'What's a skivvy?' Jack asked puzzled.

'Have yous never heard of a skivvy? They work as a cleaner or scullery maid fer the rich people. They do everything for the gentry but wipe their bloody arses.'

Mary's head was spinning. 'So, her family weren't bombed in the Blitz, as we were led to believe.'

'Yes, but not her immediate family so to speak, but all the family from her mother's side. A bomb dropped on their house, killing them all.'

'I'm sorry Mrs O'Conner but I thought you said . . .'

'Here . . . not there. They were bombed over *here*. All of Molly's family, God rest their souls. The bombings that weren't supposed to bloody happen . . . fecking eejits.'

'Oh, of course' said Jack. 'That must have been the Strand bombings.'

'That's right. Molly was heartbroken and so was Marianne, who was such good friends with Molly's niece. They were at the same school you know, and Marianne often stayed the night with the poor girl. Could have been her that was bombed had it been the night before. Took it bad, so she did, I mean, why she would go a City like Liverpool where people were getting killed all the time. Now that's something I will never understand.'

'There *was* a war on Mrs O'Conner, but there was also plenty of work, for men and women alike. Without these people working in the munitions factories and working on the land, we would have lost the war. Marianne would have got a job straight away when she went there. There were hundreds of young Irish girls who went to work in Liverpool.'

'Ah well, each to his own I say.' muttered Mrs O'Conner.

Mary realised at this point Mrs O'Conner didn't know anything about her birth mother and her heart sank. She also felt a strange longing to hold her first adoptive mother, Helen . . . Marianne in her arms.

Jack was intrigued by the story being told and wanted to know more. 'Can I just ask you, what happened to the children when their mother ran away?'

'Well now. They said Molly was depressed and an unfit Mother . . . God strike me dead if I tell a lie now, but Molly was a good Mother. Not at all the kind of woman *he* wanted everyone to believe she was. She wouldn't walk out on her kids. I have my own ideas of what happened to that poor woman, but I wouldn't be opening me mouth about that now. I knew her better than anyone. His idea was to have the kid's taken away into institutions. If she had run away as he said, wouldn't he be waiting to see if she came home first? No, he couldn't get the kids out quick enough.'

Mrs O'Conner dabbed her eyes with a tea towel that was on the table. 'I don't know where the three boys went; probably to the Christian brothers.'

'What about the father. Where is he now?'

'He moved to a corporation flat like me self, up on Dominick Street. I've never seen him since. Never want to. He was there on that day, taking all the sympathy bestowed on a broken-hearted husband. I watched helplessly with all the neighbours when the car came and took the kids. Terrible it was. They were screaming for their mother, you know, wondering where she was. Of course, Alice just stared into space. She was a bit, you know, not all there. . . or so people thought. She was 'there' alright. I would imagine she's in a mental institution now. She was better before she was raped though.'

'Raped?'

'I shouldn't be telling yous this but, I suppose you won't be telling anyone yerselves, seeing as you're leaving soon. The day Molly disappeared; she carried Laurence downstairs and Alice was holding her hand. Molly asked if I would mind looking after them while she did some errands. She told me Alice had fallen down the stairs . . . kids were always falling down the bloody stairs so I took no mind and said, of course I would take care of the kids. Shaun and James were always out playing after school. They hated to be in house more than they had to. Jaysus; how old

266

would they have been then? I don't remember, and then there was . . . now, where was I?'

'Mrs O'Conner, you said a child was raped.'

'That's right. Well, I noticed the child seemed a little strange, as if she was here, but she wasn't, if you know what I mean. I thought perhaps she had seen her mammy taking a hiding and was in some sort of shock. Anyway, she wet herself, which was unusual for a child of her age. Now how old was she . . . nine or ten. Anyway, I changed her clothes. Oh, dear Lord! I can't tell you how shocked I was to see blood stains between her thighs and the bruising coming through. On her shoulder was a bite mark. It doesn't take much imagination to know when a child has been raped.'

Mary felt sick, excused herself and rushed to the bathroom. Jack was shocked too. 'Who would do such a thing to a child in what sounds like a good community for Christ sake? Did they catch the person who raped her?'

'No. the doors were always left open in the tenement blocks so anyone could have gone into the room. Molly came back later in the evening, popped her head through the door and said she'd be back down again in five minutes. She rushed upstairs before I could speak. And that . . . was the last I saw of her. Shaun came down for Laurence and said he would be back to help Alice up the stairs. When he saw the state of her, he asked what had happened; he had obviously been told she'd fallen downstairs. Shaun told me his mammy was sleeping when I asked why she didn't come down for the kids.'

Mrs. O'Conner was very agitated, and her voice began to rise. 'Sleeping?' Says I shocked to hear this. I offered to carry Alison up the stairs, but the child wouldn't let me near her, and walked by herself. Sleeping, how could Molly sleep, with Alice in the state she was in fer God's sake?'

'Perhaps the mother was ill. You know . . . in shock. Although that doesn't explain why she disappeared in the night, leaving Alice when she needed her mother the most. I feel there's more to this Mrs O'Conner' Jack said, walking round the small room in a circle. 'Being a detective sets your mind wondering a bit.'

'A Detective, Holy Mother of God. A detective so you are. And Jesus, you're on the right track there and that's fer sure. Molly would never leave the kids, but *he* got all the sympathy from the Priest and the Gardaí. He fecking lapped it up. Another thing here, now, this is between you and me. He was overheard asking the priest if he could keep Alice at home.' Mrs O'Conner straightened her shoulders back all high and mighty. 'Now that's a new one. He hated the sight of the child, who he always referred to as a retard.'

Mary came out of the bathroom, her face white and her eyes red. 'We must go now Mrs O'Conner. Thank you so much for the information you have given me. At least I know more of my first adoptive mother.'

'To be sure tis a pleasure, she was a lovely child. Marianne was a very pretty girl.'

'She was pretty. Of course, I don't remember her, but I have photos, and Mom told me she was very pretty.'

'I'm sorry I couldn't tell you anything about your birth mother, God bless her. There's so much secrecy goes on behind those Maggie laundries, and that's fer sure.' Mrs O'Conner apologised, 'Tis always the girl who gets the blame. They never blame the sins of the man.'

'It appears so . . . oh, by the way. I was in such a hurry to see you; I forgot the rest of the pictures I was going to bring of my mother Helen . . . of Marianne. But before we leave, we'll call and see you again if that's okay.'

'Of course, yis can. It has been a pleasure. God bless.'

'Just before we go Mrs O'Conner, I'll tune your television in for you.' Jack said, already moving towards the set.

'Now, that's very kind. The bloody thing drives me up the wall.'

While Jack was tuning the television, Mary asked who the photograph of the soldier was.

'That's my husband Jimmy. He's been gone some time now, bless him. He was much older than me, but my parents gave me permission to marry him when I was sixteen. He was such a lovely man. Tuberculosis killed him when he was twenty five years old.' Mrs O'Conner's eyes misted when she held the photo in her hands. 'We met when I was fourteen years

268

old, so we were sweethearts for two years before we married. He was the only man in my life, and sure to God, I never had a man since. He was the only one for me.'

'What about children? Do you have any?'

'I had a little girl; her name was Mary, named after me Nan. She died from tuberculosis when she was three months old. Jimmy nursed her all the hours God sent when she became chesty. The poor child couldn't catch her breath. Terrible it was. Three months later Jimmy died himself from the disease.'

'I'm so sorry Mrs O'Conner.'

'Ah, sure, it was a long time ago now, but I say a prayer every night for me husband and daughter. Tuberculosis killed half the children in the tenement houses, you know . . . and adults too. Yis couldn't get away from it. T'was the spitting that made the disease spread to others, but I suppose no one knew that in those days.'

'Spitting?' asked Mary.

'Yea, coughing up the nasty stuff and spitting on the streets, in the slop bucket and anywhere they were. But what could they do? Handkerchiefs were for the rich and fortunate, we had to do with old newspapers. Never had much in the way of illnesses me self, mind, thank the Lord.

'You must have been very lonely on your own for all those years.'

'No, I was never lonely, not in the tenements, although it took a long time to get over losing Jimmy. Everyone took time to keep me occupied. We were all family. And of course, I had my own family; me mother, father and me sisters. I worked at the Rotunda hospital from school as a cleaner and had many friends, and Jaysus, there was such laughter. Molly was a very supportive when Jimmy died, I don't know how I would have coped without her in those early days. And fer the love of God, didn't she feel guilty every time she was pregnant?' Mrs O'Conner laughed.'

'You knew Molly a long time then?'

'We were at school together . . . different class, she was older than me, but we were very good friends in school. We were excited to be sharing the same tenement block when we married the same year. I was

269

there through all Molly's pregnancies and helped her out to the day she . . . disappeared.'

Mrs O' Conner did cry then, just for a little while. Mary had nothing but admiration for this lovely woman. She was only small, but very strong by nature.

'Okay, the television is tuned in now Mrs O'Conner.' Jack announced. He had fixed it a while ago but didn't want to break the conversation. Mrs O'Conner was a remarkable lady.

Jack had managed to get a good clear picture and Mrs O'Conner couldn't take her eyes off the screen when she turned around to look. She'd been watching the flickering screen since the day she moved in. She knew no better, not ever having a television in the tenements.

Mary was relieved she had something to take her mind off their discussion. She was overwhelmed with confusion. She found today that she longed to know all about her poor birth mother, and to learn more of the mother who'd first adopted her. The mother she never knew, a mother who'd loved her; but whose life had ended when she was so happy, yet so young. She had much love, empathy and compassion for the woman who'd been her mother for the first three years of her life; and she had immense love for the only mother she ever really knew. Three mothers who had three completely different lives.

*

Mary rang the bell on the big iron gates and looked towards the home. A sense of gloom filled her heart as she tried to picture her mother being torn away from her baby on that fateful day. On the outside, Harry and Helen Mitchell were thrilled at the prospect of adopting a baby. Whilst on the inside, there perhaps stood a mother with a broken heart. She felt Jack squeeze her hand tightly in his. 'Be prepared for the worst Mary. You've heard the stories of how hard it is to get to know anything from these places.'

'I know. Dear God, I can't believe I was born in a place like this. There's so much sorrow behind those gates . . .'

'Good afternoon.' A voice suddenly called out.

'Good afternoon Sister. We have an appointment.'

'Yes, yes, follow me.' The young looking nun said, fiddling with a large bunch of keys, trying to find the right one. Mary stood and watched the nun lock the gates behind them and felt a shiver run through her body.

The young sister escorted Mary and Jack into the office and the Reverend Mother asked her to bring in some tea. There was the usual small talk before the tea was brought in and Mary explained why she was here.

'I'm sorry you came all this way Miss Reiner, but I did explain on the telephone we cannot give you any information regarding your mother. You have given yourselves a wasted journey. I did tell so you when you rang. Of course, I wasn't here in those days, but your mother would have signed the contract of her own accord to allow the baby to be adopted.'

'Yes but, under the circumstances at that time. . .'

'Why bother after all these years.' The Reverent Mother interjected, 'anyway, she's probably forgotten about you now. Most of the mothers want to put those years behind them.'

'Sister, we weren't intending to just turn up on her mother's doorstep.' Jack said firmly.' We understand she may be married with children and she has the right to decline Miss Reiner's offer of meeting. We appreciate that, and if it is the case, then we will accept it. But I doubt very much she has forgotten about the baby she was forced to give up.'

'Who said she was forced to give up the child? These mothers sign of their own free will, and she had the sense to offer the child a good home with a good Catholic family.'

'You sold the baby . . . not you personally, but the baby was sold to an American couple thirty years ago.'

'Thirty years is a long time ago. I think it's time you left the premises now please.'

'I'm very sorry if I sounded a little abrupt. If we could just leave a telephone number that you could perhaps pass on. She might. . .'

'I think you should leave. I've told you; the contract was signed and in the contract it states quite clearly that . . .'

'I know what the piece of paper stated.' Jack said with an out of character bitterness to his voice.

271

'Please sister.' Mary pleaded.

Ignoring her, the Reverend Mother stood up and walked to the door, holding it open.

On their drive home, Mary was quiet, and Jack asked if she was feeling all right.

'How could they sell babies to strangers Jack, just because the couples were Catholic? I was lucky, but how many poor little children ended up in the wrong hands. And how many died in the process. They had no one to turn to, not even the church.'

'I know. It's hard to comprehend. But I haven't finished trying to find your mother yet Mary. I was so angry in there. Perhaps I could break in, I know just the right person who . . .'

'No Jack. You have your business to think about. We tried. And I did get to see where I was born. I don't want you doing anything illegal. It isn't worth it, and anyway, the Sister may be right. My mother could have wanted to put that part of her life behind her. Who am I to want to bring bad memories back into her life?'

'I was proud of you today Mary. You were full of emotions, but you kept your cool. I could have punched the arrogant woman in the face right there and then. They don't half hide behind those clothes they wear. They are so superior and know how to put the fear of God into young people. Can you imagine how far their authority would go if they wore ordinary clothes for Christ's sake.'

Mary laughed. Jack had a funny way of letting off steam.

'I love you Jack. We'll pack tonight and call in and see Mrs O'Conner tomorrow before we go. We'll take her some flowers to say thank you for all her help.'

*

The following day Mary tearfully handed the flowers to Mrs O'Conner who was really grateful and kissed her goodbye. She had grown to like Mrs O'Conner with her 'straight to the point' ways, her humour and her lovely Irish accent.

'Ah Jaysus, yis may as well come in until this bloody rain stops now and have yerselves a cup of tea.'

'No, really, we had best be going.'

'It might be a good idea Mary. The traffic is terrible. There's something I would like to ask you Mrs O'Conner . . . purely for my own . . .'

'Come in, come in. I'll put the pot on.'

'I'm, gonna miss your tea Mrs O'Conner. And you of course.'

'Ha, go way wid yeah.'

'What I was wondering was, were any of the neighbours, besides you, suspicious of the father? He could have murdered the mother for all we know.'

'Molly only had trust in me. She wouldn't want the rest of the street to know her business. Sure to God, we grew up together.'

'True' Mary replied, 'I wonder what happened to those poor kids.'

'They won't be kids now, and as I said, there's a lot of secrecy goes off behind the walls of the Christian Brother institutions, and the Maggie homes.' said Mrs O'Conner, filling the kettle for the second time since their arrival, trying to hold on to her company. 'I've heard a lot of tales about those places from me auld friend Kathleen Naughton. Now her next-door neighbour's daughter was a midwife in one of those places. Oh, Jaysus, the horrors of those poor girls, sure to God, they weren't given the much needed stitches they should have had, or not so much as an aspirin fer the pain.'

'I thought that was all confidentiality stuff,' said Jack, he smiled at Mrs. O'Connor.

'It is, but yis wouldn't be hearing anything from me now. Help yer selves to bread and butter while I pour the tea.'

'Is your friends neighbour's daughter still working there?' asked Jack leaning over to cut a slice of bread?'

'No, she left the home years ago. Kathleen told me, in confidence mind, and according to Kathleen Naughton, she never went back to nursing. Neither did she marry, you know. She didn't want children, so she told her mother, who told Kathleen, who told me. I suppose it's enough to put a woman off, seeing suffering as she did.'

'She must have been working in the late 1940's.'

'I don't know how long ago she was there, but she left, as I said.'

'Mrs O'Conner, I don't mean to go on about this, but do you know where she worked. It's just a hunch and a million to one chance she worked at the home where Mary's mother was, but we have to try everything we can.'

'Jack. We agreed. No more.' Mary protested. She had taken as much as she could on this trip to Ireland and couldn't face any more shocks.

'I know darling, but just this once. We have nothing to lose.' He turned again to Mrs O'Conner, 'did Kathleen ever mention the name of the home where her friend's daughter worked?'

'Now it wouldn't be right to tell you anymore, not that I remember which home it was, but there's the confidentiality to think of.' said Mrs O'Conner, holding her head high.

'I promise I won't say you told me. Where does she live?'

'She lived with her mother, but her mother is dead now, God rest her soul.'

'Is your friend Kathleen still living?'

'Course she's still living. How old de yis think we are, fer God's sake.'

'I wasn't sure if she was much older than you Mrs O'Conner. I didn't mean to upset you. I just . . .'

'Don't be making excuses, it's too late.' She sniffed. 'Kathleen is as fit as a fiddle like me self, but her neighbour died and her daughter, Glenda, took over the house. She worked for the Corporation after she left the home, but now she takes care of a lady over near Dolly Mount.'

'Mrs O'Conner, would you like to help us.'

'Help you in what way.'

'Could you take us to your friend, and somehow introduce us to Glenda. We have to leave soon and get back to our jobs at home in the States. We may not have this opportunity again for a while. It's unlikely Glenda worked for the home Mary was born in, but she may be able to give us information as to where we can learn more about babies who were adopted by Americans.'

'Well, I suppose I was due for a visit there . . . and she would be thrilled to meet two Americans in person. But I will have to look at my diary first.'

'Of course. . .'

'I was joking. Now why would I have a diary?' She laughed. I'll get me coat and hat.'

Mrs O'Conner sat in the back of the car. Her white hair tucked beneath her hat, her coat buttoned to the neck, hoping her new neighbours were outside to see her travelling with the Americans. When they finally came to the street her friend lived on, Jack was sure Mrs O'Conner had followed the bus route. They seemed to have driven from one housing estate to another, and she did seem to know a lot of people, from the amount of waving of her hand to one and all.

*

'Peggy O'Conner, come in, come in, I was only thinking of yis me self this morning. And who might you be.' She queried, looking at her other two visitors in surprise.

Mrs O'Conner introduced them and explained briefly why they were here.

'Well, I can tell you myself where Glenda worked. T'was an institution called the Sisters of St Martha's.'

'That's where I was born in 1946.' Mary gasped.

'Glenda delivered a lot of babies during the time she was there, so it's unlikely she'll remember one individual baby, and anyway, I wouldn't want to be sounding negative, but she left before you were born. I'm sure she left in 1945 and you say you were born in 1946. Now, would yis like a cup of tea and some soda bread?'

'Sure would, Mrs Naughton. Nice place you have here.' agreed Jack, trying hard to get on the right side of Kathleen Naughton, who seemed a little more suspicious than Mrs O'Conner had been when she heard the story.

'Ah to be sure, the furniture is older than me self, and that's saying something.' She laughed, handing a plate to him. 'Now what about you, Mary, would you like some bread?'

'I would. By the time I get home, I'll be so fat, no one will recognise me.'

'Bread is good for the soul. Isn't it now, Peggy O'Conner?'

'Sure to God, tis the very best and I'll be having a slice me self.'

Two hours passed by, during which time questions were asked about life in New York. Jack saying how much he loved Ireland, having been a few times to study Irish history. Finally, Mrs Naughton said Glenda was home. She had heard the front door open and close. 'Give her time to have a cup of tea and I'll go and have a word with her me self first. She may not want to get involved; you understand.'

'Of course, and we do understand if she isn't willing to talk about her life there.' Mary replied. 'It's such a long time ago, like you said.'

The clock ticked slowly. It seemed an age before Mrs Naughton returned to the house with the woman known as Glenda, who quickly said hello before sitting on a chair opposite Mary. There was an awkward silence until Jack said he was sorry to hear her mother had died.

'Ah, sure, she was ill a long time. She did well to hang on as long as she did, God rest her soul.'

Mary shuffled uncomfortably under the gaze of the woman who seemed to be looking her way, until finally Glenda explained. 'I can't remember the names of all the mothers during my time at the home. Most of the time names were changed anyway, and often they were given a number, so I don't know how I can help.'

'I realise it's difficult after all these years Glenda, and I also realise it's a million to one chance you knew my mother, but we've come this far and we have to go back to the States very soon. I suppose you could say it's my last chance. If nothing comes from it, I'll accept it and get on with my life.'

'What was the name you were given at birth?'

'I don't know. My adoptive parents died when I was three years old and there aren't any papers as such. She was called Helen Mitchell but changed her name from Marianne McNamara I believe. My adoptive father was Harry, Harry Mitchell. . .'

'Is that all you have to go on? What year were you born?'

'I was born in 1946.'

276

'I left in 1946 . . . I don't think I can . . .'

'But you would have been there when my mother was pregnant.'

'Perhaps, but do you realise how many girls were pregnant in 1946 in that particular home alone. I'm sorry, but I can't help.'

'Could you ask the Sisters there, they might give you information knowing you worked as a midwife. I know it's a lot to ask . . .'

'No. I'm sorry. I will never set foot in the place again. I have to go now; I'm tired and it's been a stressful day. I wish you all the best. Goodnight.'

Disappointed, Mary and Jack thanked Mrs O'Connor and her friend Mrs. Naughton for all their help, suggesting it was probably time to drive Mrs. O'Connor home.

'I'm sorry I couldn't be of more help to yis all' Mrs. Naughton called out has she waved them off. Mary looked at Jack and smiled as they sped off into the darkness listening to Mrs O'Conner talking about friends who lived in various places.

*

Sleep didn't come easily to Glenda. She tossed and turned for three hours or more. Jesus Christ, she just wanted to put the life of being a midwife behind her. It was 2:00 am when she decided to get up and make a cup of tea. Thank the Lord it was her day off tomorrow. She reached for her reading glasses and pulled out her old paperwork from a box in the wardrobe. Why she had kept the paperwork all this time, she had no idea.

The box was full to the brim of old photos, documents of her mothers and condolences from family and friends. At the very bottom of the box was the admissions book, with brief histories of her patient's health and the records of their pregnancies. A lump came to her throat. She had enjoyed her life as a midwife, and dearly hoped she was replaced with someone who showed compassion. There were girls in the home who were totally innocent, pregnant through incest and rape. Some of the younger girls over the years were pregnant by lodgers who shared their home, and in some cases, their beds. Many tenement homes took in lodgers to help pay the rent. The greedy landlords took no pity on these poor souls. If they couldn't pay, they were evicted.

She read through all the births of 1946; there were so many. To narrow it down, she listed the babies who were adopted, although, she wasn't even allowed to know who they were adopted out to . . . or sold to. She felt so sorry for the girl, Mary. To find out you were adopted once is a shock . . . but twice!

'Oh fer fecks sake, I'll help if I can. I won't bloody rest 'til I do.'

*

Mrs O'Conner went to answer the door, expecting to see Jack and Mary, seeing as they kept coming back. 'Oh, dear God, Glenda, what the hell are you doing here? Did Kathleen become ill, is she dead?'

'No, she's fine. I just wondered if your friends were here.'

'You mean the detectives. No, I think they may be packing to go home, but they'll be dropping off some photos before they go, though what the hell I want them for, I don't know. Haven't seen Marianne since she was thirteen, but then, I don't want to hurt the girl's feelings now, do I'?

'No, Tis sad for the poor girl. Perhaps it might have been best not to know her adoptive mother's past. It wouldn't do any harm for her to think she came from a good family now, would it?' Glenda said without thinking.

'No. I never said much me self, you understand, I only filled them in with little bits. Would yis like a cup of tea and some soda bread?'

'I might stay a while and see them before they go, so yes, I wouldn't mind.'

Chapter 29

Mary and Jack arrived at Mrs O'Conner's flat, surprised to see Glenda sitting there. 'Hi, Glenda, we are on our way back home tomorrow, so it's good to see you again before we go.'

'I just dropped in to say I'm sorry for the way I spoke to you yesterday.' Glenda apologised to Mary. 'I didn't mean to sound so negative. Sure, tis terrible enough without me being rude to yis.'

'I understand Glenda and you don't need to apologise. I'm fine. I've accepted I may never know my mother, and perhaps it isn't such a bad thing. It's just that . . . well, this time last year, I had a mother and now . . . I don't know . . .' Mary broke down in tears and Glenda rushed to her side.

'Tis good to cry Mary. You've been through an awful lot in such a short time. Listen . . . I'm not promising anything, but here is a list of names of my patients during 1946.' She said, passing the book. 'Now you have to understand, it may not be the right home. Your grandfather may have got a little mixed up if they visited more than one home.'

'No, he didn't get mixed up.' Jack jumped to his defence. 'He was there on the day the papers were signed. Unfortunately, we can't find those papers. They must have been destroyed by . . . well, I assume so, and we don't really know anything about Helen, or should I say Marianne, apart from her changing her name.'

'Mary, Jack, and you too Mrs O'Conner; you have to promise to keep me out of this, or I may never work again. This is very confidential stuff. Mary, you're a lawyer, you must understand the consequences of such a thing, although the book was for my own personal use I may add, and not the main records of the home. The books aren't by any means a legal document or proof either.' Glenda said gently, passing over her record book.

Mrs O'Conner made more tea while Mary looked through the list.

'No Glenda, no names come to light, apart from the name McNamara, which is the name of my first adoptive mother, Marianne, but it isn't her. That wouldn't be possible. This one is Lillian McNamara. . .'

There was an almighty crash. Mrs O'Conner dropped the tea pot. 'Just as I suspected' she said, oblivious to the smashed teapot. 'So Lillian didn't go looking fer work in Galway. She was pregnant and sent away.'

'Mrs O'Conner, I'm confused. Who is Lillian?' Mary demanded.

'Lillian is Marianne's younger sister. The time is right . . . Glenda are you all right. Do you want me to get you a glass of water?'

'No, I'm fine, thanks Peggy. I just felt a little dizzy.'

Mary ignored the fact Glenda had suddenly gone very pale and carried on talking. 'So my adoptive . . . for God's sake, let's use first names then we know where we are. You're saying Marianne adopted her sister's baby without knowing.'

'Yes, it is what I'm saying.'

'Not necessarily.' Jack butted in quickly. 'McNamara is a very common name in Ireland. Besides which, even if it was Marianne's sister who gave birth, it doesn't mean she adopted that particular baby. It may not have been you Mary; you were adopted at four weeks. It was only the mothers who'd enough money to pay for their way out of the home so soon after giving birth. From what I gather, the mother, Lillian, wasn't in a position to pay her way out.'

The room was quiet, each with their own thoughts. Mary looked at Glenda and was about to ask if she remembered anything. 'Glenda I . . .'

'That's true Jack' Glenda agreed, they didn't normally let babies go so young, unless the mother died and . . . and she did die. I was there.'

'Who died?'

'The Mother died, Lillian McNamara.'

'Oh, Mother of God. God bless her soul. Dear Lillian. She was such a lovely girl.' Mrs O'Conner cried, clearing the broken tea pot.

'My adopted Mother, or should I now say, my Aunt, took a baby home without knowing it was her sister's baby? Jesus, this gets worse. Both of them died within the space of three years.' Mary said, dabbing her eyes. 'It's not fair. Two of my three Mothers died within my first three years of life.'

Mrs O'Conner was in shock. 'How the hell did she get pregnant fer God's sake, she hardly ever left the house. I never saw her with a boy.'

Mary spent a while in the bathroom; while Mrs O'Conner put the kettle on without realising she had broken the teapot. She swallowed her pride and went out to ask a neighbour for the loan of a teapot for a couple of hours. 'Tea is good fer the soul and helps calm the spirit.' She said to her neighbour, who emptied the pot and asked if everything was all right. 'Sure to God it isn't alright, but I won't be saying anything, Mrs McBride, confidentiality and all that you understand. Thanks now fer the loan of the teapot.'

While Mrs O'Conner was out of the way, Glenda was able to speak to Mary and Jack alone. She was a lovely woman, but she knew only too well Mrs O'Conner liked to gossip, and knew too much already, but if anything were to come of it, and the home found out, she had a few tales to tell herself.

'Mary, there's more, but I need to speak to you in private out of Mrs O'Conner's way.'

'Okay, would you like to meet us in the hotel lounge, and we can go up to our room, say in an hour.'

'Yes, that'll be the best thing.'

Mrs O'Conner came back with the teapot in her hand, and Mary looked in her bag for the photos of Marianne. 'Here you are Mrs O'Conner. These are for you; I thought you may like to hang on to them. We'll have to be moving on now.' Mary said, offering the photographs. 'We owe you so much for what you've done. We will be back again one day, and can we write to each other to stay in touch. I would very much like that.'

'Thanks very much for the photos; it's been nice knowing yis.' She sighed 'I'll be missing yis, and that's fer sure . . . why have you given me these. There isn't one picture of Marianne on these photographs. I don't know this girl.'

Mary took the photos back. 'These are of Helen, sorry, I mean Marianne, on her own when she was younger, taken during in the war. I don't understand.'

'This isn't Marianne. I'd know Marianne all right and this isn't she.'

'Mary, have you still got the photo in your bag of your mother and Helen.' asked Jack.

Mrs O'Conner took the photo from Mary's hand. 'This is Marianne, the tall girl.'

'Mom . . . Mom was Marianne. *She* was my birth mother's sister.'

Mary fell to the floor, her hands over her face. 'Mom was beaten by her father. *She* was the one who was my aunt, not Helen, and Helen was her real name after all. Did my mother know Helen had adopted her sister's baby?'

'No' Mrs O'Conner said definitely. 'She couldn't possibly have known. I know that fer sure. The letters stopped coming from Marianne before Lillian left home. Molly never told me about Lillian being pregnant, she said she was staying with a relative of hers and had got herself a job in Galway.' cried Mrs O'Conner, who was now wiping her eyes on a tea cloth. 'I thought at the time it was funny, her leaving like that. Sure to God I never heard of any aunt in Galway, but I trusted Molly.'

'Plus, it was Helen and not Marianne who adopted a baby.' Jack butted in again. 'Helen didn't choose the baby either. She and Harry were offered a baby they never saw before then.' It was all a coincidence.' Jack said realising perhaps it wasn't the right thing to say.

'And the soldier, Patrick, was my uncle and not Helen's old boyfriend. Oh Jack, how can I live knowing how my mother and her family suffered so.'

'Molly would have wanted Lillian away from Joseph's hand,' cried Mrs O'Conner. 'He would have killed her. Poor Molly, what else could she have done?'

'Why did she change her name to Kate Doyle,' Jack said.

'Doyle, did you say?' Mrs O'Conner asked 'Doyle was the name of her cousin. Katharine . . . Kate Doyle. She must have used her identity. She was two years older than Marianne. Molly had a badly burnt tin box they found on the bomb site in the North Strand. There were all sorts of certificates in there; all damaged, such as birth certificates, weddings, baptism, communion and all sorts of other stuff.'

*

Later, when Glenda walked toward the hotel; she was now unsure what to tell them. If she told the truth, that her mother lost her life because she was denied a doctor, then the information would open a whole new can of worms. *'Oh, why did I have to stick my nose in? Jaysus, any other day, I would have been working.'*

Coffee was ordered and the three of them sat nervously. It was Jack who spoke first. 'Glenda, don't be feeling this was your fault, because I know you do.'

'I know, but I was thinking I shouldn't have interfered.' She said dabbing her eyes with a handkerchief.

'You didn't.' said Mary. 'I was desperate to know my birth mother. I can close a chapter in my life now. Thank you for your help Glenda. Would it be too much to ask how she died and what she was like? Do I look like her? I'm sorry. I'm not giving you time to answer, am I.'

'When I first saw you, I tried to remember where I had seen you before. So yes, you do look like her. It's such a long time ago. She had beautiful hair . . . unfortunately long hair wasn't allowed, and Lillian was very upset when the sisters cut it. She was very pretty. We used to chat when she came to the clinic. I grew fond of your mother, and . . .'

'How did she die? Did she die to save me? Did she suffer?'

'She had a condition called Preeclampsia Toxaemia. She suffered a fit and went into a coma. We did everything we could, but sadly she died. The disease has killed thousands of women over the centuries, and unfortunately, is still a killer today. The only thing that can be done is to deliver the baby as soon as possible.'

She couldn't possibly put Mary through more pain by telling her of the terrible neglect and trauma Lillian went through, but there was something she should know and she didn't know how to tell Mary. Mary interrupted her thoughts.

'What about my father, who was he? Does he know about me?'

'It might be better to forget about him Mary. He was . . . she was raped.'

'Oh no, no, no. was he caught? Did he go to prison?'

'He wasn't caught, and I am the only person she told.'

'Didn't she tell her mother?'

'No, she was protecting her.'

'She was raped by her father, wasn't she? Just like her little sister.' Jack said very quietly, looking down at his coffee.

'Yes, she was. I'm sorry to hear about her younger sister also being raped; I didn't know until Mrs O'Conner told me. I'm so sorry Mary.'

Mary sobbed uncontrollably, and Jack was angry at himself for pursuing this search. He'd had a bad hunch about it at the beginning and he should have listened to his intuition.

'Mary, there is something else.'

'Leave it now Glenda, Mary has had enough.'

'But Jack, this is important.'

'Tell me, sobbed Mary. I might as well know. I can't be anymore shocked or upset.'

'You have, or had, a sister.'

'What?'

'You were a twin. The first twin was having trouble breathing; it was a very long and difficult birth. Usually, a baby born this way hardly stands a chance of surviving, and if they do, it's possible they may have brain damage. Just before Lillian had a fit, she screamed, and I could see another baby. I managed to pull you out, seconds before she died. The poor girl wouldn't have even known she had another baby.'

284

'What happened to my sister? Is she dead? What did you mean, I have, or had a sister?'

'The Reverend Mother told me to leave her be, and not to try and revive her, "for her own sake", she added. We usually put babies in a special room, those who died or were born severely disabled. Your twin sister was put in this room to die, like all babies who were born blue and suffered from lack of oxygen. Usually, windows were opened to allow them to die of hyperthermia very quickly.'

'That is so terrible Glenda, how could they do that to a child.'

'They did this to save the child from a terrible life in an institution. I know it is very sad.'

'So my sister died.'

'Let me finish first. I didn't like doing this without giving the baby a chance, so when the Reverend Mother left the room for a short while, I rubbed her feet and kept tipping her gently upside down. She coughed and then screamed. Remember, this was in the 1940's, times were hard, and no-one wanted a disabled baby to adopt or foster. Though I didn't like the idea of just leaving the babies, in some cases it was kinder to let them die than live a life of hell.'

'Did she live or die?' asked Mary anxiously. 'Tell me.'

'She lived, each day I filled a baby bottle from other mothers who had plenty of milk to spare, or still had milk left over from having their baby adopted. I named her Fiona and put her with the other baby's as soon as I knew she wasn't going to die. I'd heard from one of the Sisters that you were to be adopted almost straight away, but I didn't know who to, or where you were going.'

'What happened to Fiona?' asked Jack.

'I don't know. I was finished 4 years after Lillian died. The Reverend Mother told me my services were no longer required. I didn't have a reference to work as a midwife again. And I wasn't allowed to visit Fiona, who I had taken care of for all that time. I knew the Reverend Mother had a visit from Lillian's mother, demanding to take her and the child home. One of the mothers' told me; she was cleaning the floor outside the room at the time and heard everything.'

285

'Was Fiona all right when you left? She must have been heartbroken.'

'So was I, but the other mothers would have cared for her. They all stuck together. I looked into adopting her, or at the very least, fostering her, but I was single and unfortunately that went against me.'

'Oh my God, Jack. Where do we begin?' Mary cried out.

Jack buried his head in his hands and didn't reply.

'You could start with the orphanages.' enthused Glenda 'probably the Sisters of Mercy . . . from there; they would go to an industrial school and then the Magdalena laundries. There's always the chance she may have been fostered out. I hope not, you may never find her. They sometimes move from one foster family to another.'

'Mary, we can't stay here much longer, we have jobs. This could take months.'

'I understand that Jack, but I have to find my sister. She must have had an awful life and I have been blessed with so much love and happiness. Jack, it could have been the other way around.'

After much discussion, it was finally agreed they head home to catch up on their backlog of work, and in the evenings do as much research as they could by telephone calls and letters. Before heading home, they called in to see Mrs O'Conner to say goodbye and tell her about Mary's twin. She was of course, upset and delighted at the same time that there may be a chance of finding her.

'I can't understand why Marianne didn't try to get in touch with Lillian, or her mother, after she left to go to Liverpool.' Jack said thoughtfully.

'Marianne was a strange child. She was always older than her years, whereas Lillian was young for her years.'

'It takes a brave person to make such a journey at that young age Mrs O'Conner.' Said Jack 'But we'll never know now.'

'I know someone who might know, Jack.' Mary butted in. 'Her friends in Liverpool might be able to tell me. They came to the States for her funeral, although I didn't get the chance to talk to them on their own, they only stayed a week due to work commitments.'

'Well, I suppose we can look into that as well when we get back.'

They called in to see Mrs O'Conner before leaving for the airport to tell her about finding out Mary had a twin. As they left everyone in Ireland behind, goodbyes and tears were shed, but Mary knew she and Jack would be back.

Chapter 30

Hi Brenda, its Mary Reiner here, are you all right to talk or shall I ring another time.'

'Hello Mary, of course it's all right to talk.'

'We're going back to Dublin next week, and I was wondering if we could call and see you first. Dublin isn't that far away from Liverpool.'

'Is everything all right Mary?'

'Yes, it's just there so much I want to tell you and also, so much I want to ask you. Telephoning isn't really good for what I have to say. I won't be offended if you are too busy.'

'Mary, it would be lovely to see you. Let me know the date and I'll arrange to have a day off from the hospital.'

They said their goodbyes and Mary told Jack, who wasn't too keen on dropping off in Liverpool at first but said he would for Mary's sake. He knew she wouldn't rest until she found out why her mother had lied to her and her father for all those years.

*

The weather wasn't too good in Liverpool and reminded her of her first visit to Ireland. They hired a car and followed the map to Brenda's home. After a few heated discussions about the map reading, they finally found the address. Brenda must have been waiting for them; as she was stood at the window. She rushed outside and threw her arms around Mary. 'It's so good to see you again. We didn't get the chance to talk much at the funeral. It was good of your father to let us stay there. We knew you wanted to be alone. Are you all right Mary?'

'I am now, thanks. I went through a pretty bad time, but that's over as well.'

'And you are Jack' Brenda smiled, giving Jack a big hug, 'how lovely to meet you.'

'It's great to meet you too Brenda. I've heard so much about you from Peter.'

'Bless him. It's a pity he didn't come too.'

'I'm sure he will be over soon. He says he would love to see Liverpool again, but it's awkward with three kids. He says he may come on his own one day.'

Brenda had sandwiches already made and a little buffet of hot and cold food, which Jack and Mary really enjoyed. After the meal, Jack asked if they would mind him taking a walk around Liverpool while they talked. 'Just to take a look around the place, I won't be long. I was a student the last time I was here.'

When Jack left the house, Mary told Brenda a little about her life, and asked Brenda about her life too and how she was now. 'Are you happy Brenda?'

'I'm very happy. My kids are grown up, and I have a little granddaughter. Maurice died as you know. He never got over his injuries from the war; he was a very nervous man. There were so many killed, both away on active service and here in Liverpool from the terrible bombings we had. But we have to move on. I'm just grateful for the time we had together. He was a lovely man. He even helped take care of my mother until she died; she also loved him. I have my job at the hospital and I'm a Sister now.'

'That's wonderful Brenda.'

'Now, what was it you wanted to ask me?'

'Brenda, I know I was adopted.'

'Oh dear, that must have come as a shock.'

'Not as much as finding out I was adopted twice.'

'Oh, Mary, I can't imagine how hard it was for you. We told Kate to tell you before you found out yourself, but she wouldn't have it.'

'I'm all right with it now, and I still have Dad. Would you believe even though he isn't my birth father, he's always been a wonderful Father to me.'

'Peter is a lovely man, everyone liked him. Your mum was very lucky. A lot of these so-called GI marriages ended in disaster. Young girls whisked away in what was seen as an escape from Liverpool, to nothing more than filthy out of the way shacks, while some had to share a house with their new in-laws.'

'Yes, I can imagine that. Brenda, could you tell me about Mom's life here in Liverpool and before.'

'Okay, I'll tell you what I know. Your mother, or should I say Aunt, took her cousin's identity from some papers they found in a tin after the Strand bombing. That was where her mother's family were killed. Her real name was Marianne McNamara, as you probably now know.'

'Yes, but how did she manage to get to Liverpool with no money. I know about her being in hospital. But what happened from there.'

'A complete stranger, a woman, found . . . I have to talk about her as Kate, you understand, as that's the name I knew your mother by.'

'Yes, it's all a little confusing with names.'

'Anyway, Kate was found on the side of the road and the woman took off her cashmere coat and wrapped it around Kate to keep her warm. Kate was suffering from shock I believe. The ambulance men lifted her onto a stretcher and apparently, the woman asked them to wait a minute to let her take something out of her coat pocket. The pocket of the coat Kate still had over her shoulders. The woman told the medics she would pick the coat up from the hospital another day.'

Brenda explained to Mary about the money the woman had obviously put in the coat from her handbag before the ambulance set off.

'Kate and her mother, Molly, had sat on a bench deciding what to do. Her mother suggested that Kate should go to Liverpool and start a new life. I get the impression she was frightened of her daughter going back home, more than venturing into the unknown. Anyway, back to where we were.

There was plenty of work in Liverpool compared to Ireland with the war and all.'

'But a complete stranger left that kind of money . . . in those days. I don't get it, Brenda.'

'The money was obviously from someone who had been through something similar and felt sorry for Kate. The only women I know in Dublin who had that amount of cash *and* wore a cashmere coat were Madams from the Monty.'

'What are Madams and the Monty? I don't understand.'

'They're women who run brothels on Montgomery Street in Dublin, Monty for short. Don't get me wrong. The women took care of the girls. They looked after them. Perhaps that was the reason the stranger didn't want identifying. When we were young and went to visit our Irish family, we were told to keep away from that particular area. But of course, we didn't. When you're told not to do something as a child, you just have to do it. And we did. You could see the girls hanging over the windowsills with a red light glowing. If you saw them in the street, they would give you money to run errands. My mother would have thrashed the daylights out of me if she ever found out.'

Mary found this really funny because Brenda had such an infectious laugh. 'But, where did Mom go? She was only thirteen years old.'

'Well, you could say she was fourteen. Her birthday was only weeks away. There were plenty of lodging houses outside the City, and that's where she went. Of course, you were expected to share a room if necessary, and unfortunately Kate didn't get on with her companion. From there she moved to Halewood, where the four of us got together to share the rent on a house. Bloody hell, that house was freezing. The walls were wet from the damp. But we had our share of laughter.'

'Mom was very daring to go to a large city at such a young age, particularly as there was a war on. Living in a stranger's house?'

'Yes, but that was Kate. At that time people lived in stranger's houses all over Liverpool. There was a terrible shortage of houses.'

'I understand her changing her name, but why didn't she go back to her own name?'

'I sort of get the feeling Kate enjoyed her new identity, and we only ever knew her as Kate. We were shocked the night she told us the whole story. We were all very close, and each one of us had a story of our own to tell.'

'Why didn't she let her mother know she was all right?'

'You won't like this, Mary, but when Kate met your father she changed. She was ashamed of living in the house we had shared for so long. Kate didn't want Peter to know about her past either, so she made up a story. Her lies were so real, she could have fooled anyone. There was no way she was going to introduce her boyfriend, who had a millionaire father, to her family. She was from the slums of Dublin, like most of us were. She told Peter her family had all died in the Blitz. Kate wasn't even living in Liverpool during the Blitz! She bloody acted the part so well to people she met, including Peter. She had siblings in Ireland and didn't bother to contact them, apart from writing to Patrick.'

'How did she get in touch with Patrick?'

'I have no idea on that one. Perhaps they'd always kept in touch, from when he was still in touch with his mother. Marianne could have seen the letters at that time as she was at home. Patrick was shot in the head you know. He was a true hero. He used to write to Kate and he once sent her a lovely photo of himself in his uniform. Patrick was so good looking.'

'I feel as if I don't know this woman who took me in at three years old.'

'Kate changed. She became all posh, and even tried to speak like an American. It was just as well she met Peter at the end of the war because she was becoming unbearable to live with to be honest. We were very disappointed in her, having been through so many traumas, laughter and tears.'

'My mother was a snob, you're right there Brenda. It explains why she was so obsessed with the house and materiel things. She spent money all the time on things she didn't need. I would never have guessed she came from such a poor background. She was a good Mother and I loved her with all my heart . . . and still do, but I can't find it in me to forgive her now. She lied all through my life. She was ashamed of her own family, and could have helped Lillian, my birth mother, but she left her mother and siblings in the past. I can imagine Lillian and the rest of the family were worried, wondering what had happened to her, but she didn't care. How could she do that to her own mother, my grandmother, who sounded like a wonderful person?'

'I'm so sorry Mary. I have been honest with you. Perhaps it would have been best to . . .'

'No Brenda, I needed to know, and I thank you for that.'

'I was surprised to hear Peter left her for another woman. I thought they were so much in love with each other.'

'When my father left home for Amy, Mom just carried on as normal and I wonder now if she ever really loved him. . . She married him for his money, didn't she Brenda?'

'I don't know. Perhaps she did. She hated the GIs and swore she would never get serious with one, even though she let them spend money on her. She was jealous of Helen you know. Helen adored Harry, even when he told her he couldn't have children. She was a lovely, kind and sincere woman and she was happy for Kate when she found out she was pregnant. Not in the slightest upset, knowing she would never be able to have children of her own. When Kate lost the baby and had to have a hysterectomy, she tried to persuade Helen not to go ahead with the adoption.'

'That is so terrible. It's true about Mom trying to lose her Irish accent, but it did slip out from time to time. I feel as if my whole life was false and based on lies. Thank you so much Brenda, and by the way; I found the cashmere coat at the back of her wardrobe and couldn't understand why she had such a coat. It must have been far too big for her. She never wore it. I guess she held on to it for sentimental value. From rags to riches, eh, I gave it to a children's charity for them to sell.'

'Jack has just walked up the path. I'll make us another cuppa shall I?'

'No thank you Brenda. We have to be going. It was so good to see you again. How is Anna by the way?'

'She died only a few weeks ago, bless her; Gynaecological problems. She was in hospital a long time. She never had children.'

'Oh, I'm so sorry to hear that. Anna sounded a really nice woman too. I find it strange that Dad used to talk about Mom's friends more than she ever did. Thank you again Brenda, for everything. Please do keep in touch. You're welcome into our home anytime you want to come and visit.'

'Glad I was of help. Try not to feel bitter Mary. The anger inside of you will pass, and you will go back to thinking about the happier times. Everything has hit you all at once. Goodbye and God bless.'

Chapter 31

Dublin

'May we speak to the Reverend Mother please?' Jack asked the nun who came to the gate.

'Do you have an appointment?'

'No, we don't, but I have important papers here if you would like to see them.' Jack answered, with a slightly superior tone to his voice indicating he wasn't going to be put off.

Reluctantly, the nun opened the gate and allowed them in, knowing the Reverend Mother wouldn't be pleased. 'Follow me.' She said, already walking towards the house, the material of her habit making a swishing sound as she walked.

Mary trailed behind the nun, holding Jack's hand nervously. She'd believed, after all the research she and Jack had spent getting things in order, she would be bursting with happiness on this day. Only she didn't feel that way. There was heaviness in her heart. Her sister was brought up in institutions, while she, herself, had everything, including the unconditional love of two sets of parents. Unexpectedly, the tears began to flow. The nun turned to ask if she was all right, and Mary was touched to see genuine concern on her face.

'It might be a good idea not to hold hands when seeing the Reverend Mother. I'm sorry, but she doesn't allow physical contact in the home.'

Mary quickly let go of Jack's hand and walked through the large wooden door. The Reverend Mother looked none too pleased to see them. Shooting a look of annoyance towards the nun who had dared to allow them in without an appointment, she waved her away. The Reverend Mother seemed to ignore her visitors, carrying on writing for what was probably only minutes, but seemed an eternity to Mary.

Jack finally coughed to attract her attention.

'I'm sorry, but we are very busy here. What is it that you want? I can only spare a. . .' The Reverend Mother's face changed when she looked at Mary for the first time. She was clearly shocked by something. However, her attitude continued as before and she repeated the fact that she was busy. 'What is it? I'm very busy, can't you see?'

Mary also noticed she was avoiding eye contact with her and looking directly at Jack. She felt a little uncomfortable by this and wanted to ask the nun what was wrong, but Jack started to speak. 'We're here to take Fiona McNamara home. This is Mary, Fiona's sister . . .'

'I'm sorry; you can't just come and take a girl out of here.'

'She is not a girl, sister, she is a woman of thirty-one years and has been here since leaving the mother and baby institution in 1957 when she was eleven.'

'I'll need to look into . . .'

'Let me introduce ourselves. This is my wife, 'Mary Langley. A *lawyer,* and her birth mother was Lillian McNamara. My name is Jack Langley and I am a private detective. I can assure you; we have spent a long time doing our research. We have all the necessary papers and background of Fiona McNamara you need. We also have a court order to take her with us. Mary is Fiona's twin sister who Lillian McNamara gave birth to in 1946.'

'But she has been in institutions since she was born, and not once did she have a visitor. You just can't take her away. She doesn't know any other life outside of here.'

'Well, it's time she did!' Said Jack in defiance, and then on a more sensitive note, just in case the Reverend Mother made things hard for them, 'you have taken care of Fiona for a number of years now, and we thank you for that, Reverend Mother. Mary had no idea she had a sister until her adoptive mother passed away a few years ago. It's only natural she wants her sister home.'

'May I see her please?' Mary asked in a childlike voice, her nerves starting to show through.

296

'Yes. You can see her for thirty minutes to tell her who you are, but unfortunately, we will have to look through the paperwork with our own legal advisor before she can leave here. After all, we have to ensure she won't be in the wrong hands. You will need to come back in a week.' The Reverend Mother stood up and walked towards the window, 'I have to say, it will come as a shock to Fiona. She's always been a good girl and we will miss her. Sister Collette will show you through to the visitor's room while I collect Fiona.'

Fiona was in the garden pulling out weeds. Her knees were sore and the blades of coarse grass growing among the weeds caused cuts and blisters on her hands. It was a hot day and the sun felt as if it was blinding her. She wore nothing to prevent her head from burning in the mid-day sun, and out in front of her she could see the never ending weeding that was waiting to be done. There were six girls weeding in total, all dripping with sweat and suffering from backache. They could not converse with each other as they were spread so far apart, they couldn't hear what the next girl was saying. She sat back on her knees to wipe her brow. The Reverend Mother was walking quickly towards her, which was unusual as she hardly ever walked over the weeds and nettles.

'I'm sorry sister, I was just stopping to wipe my brow and'

'Forget about that and come inside. Now, don't dawdle.'

Fiona followed her and was worried. This had not happened before. She surely must be in trouble for something. Had they found Angela? Did they find the magazines under her pillow again? Her thoughts were broken. 'Sit down, and don't look so frightened. You're not in trouble. I have a couple in the visitor's room who claim to know you.'

'I don't know anyone. I was . . .'

'Be quiet and listen. The girl claims she is your sister, and there is indeed an uncanny likeness. They want to take you home with them and have papers for your release. But Fiona, you don't know these people and you don't have to go.' The Reverend Mother said more softly. 'This is your home.'

Fiona was only half listening. She had a sister. This could not be, not after all this time. She must also have a Mother. 'Can I go and see her please.' Fiona blurted out.

Fiona walked into the room and almost fainted from shock. The girl who stood to greet her was crying. It was like looking into a mirror, only, a clean mirror. The stranger rushed forward, calling out 'Fiona.' But Fiona stepped back; she wanted to run out of the room. She suddenly felt very ashamed of herself, stood there covered in grime and dirt, her hair short and spiky. While in front of her was another version of herself, dressed in clothes she had only seen in magazines.

Mary sobbed. 'Oh Fiona, what have they done to you.'

'Please stay back. I need to think.'

'Take your time Fiona; I was also shocked when I first learned of you.'

'But, if you are my sister, why has it taken you so long to come for me?' Fiona said angrily. 'Were you put in a home too?'

'No, it's a long story . . .'

'Why was I put in one, and why didn't you come for me sooner?' Fiona sobbed. 'And where are our parents?'

Mary couldn't answer for crying. Jack stood up and introduced himself. 'I think perhaps you should leave me and Fiona alone for a while, Mary. This is far too traumatic for you both. That's if it's all right with you, Fiona.'

'Yes, that's fine. I would like Sister Collette to be with me.'

'I understand Fiona.' Jack turned to Mary, who was dabbing her eyes with a handkerchief and nodded his head. 'Perhaps you could sit on the bench outside for twenty minutes or so.'

Mary left the room and walked around the dreary grounds, watching young girls and women garden without the proper tools; each one staring hard in her direction. Twenty minutes later, Jack opened the door and Fiona rushed into Mary's arms, just as heartbroken as her sister was.

Unfortunately, before Mary had time to speak, the Reverend Mother walked through the door. 'You have to leave now; we have Mass very soon. Leave me your details and I will contact you shortly.'

They said their goodbyes and Fiona was sent back out to work. She didn't care. She was floating on air. 'I have a sister. *I have a sister.*' She decided not to tell the other girls. There was always this fear in her head she was having a weird dream again and would wake up soon, or perhaps, she wouldn't be allowed out of this hell hole for some reason or another. She couldn't believe her sister was an American. 'My sister is an American!' Fiona whispered to herself. She had seen pictures of New York in a magazine and had kept the magazine under her mattress, or pillow, only bringing it out to look at before going to sleep each night. In one of the pictures, it was Christmas time and the entire City had lights everywhere . . . and there was snow.

Unfortunately, one night she fell asleep with the magazine lying on her chest. The sister on night duty dragged her out of bed demanding to know where she had got the magazine from. 'It was outside Sister, lying on the ground when I took the rubbish out. I don't know where it came from; perhaps it blew over the fence.'

'Blew over the fence? There are no buildings around here. Who are you trying to protect this time, Fiona? We do not tolerate disgusting trash like this in our house. Do you understand? You'll be given extra duties tonight and you will repeat the Rosary for one hour.'

'Yes Sister. I'm sorry Sister. It won't happen again Sister.' But Fiona knew it would. She also knew she couldn't tell the truth. She had found the magazine in Sister Theresa's waste basket. The punishment for stealing would have been much worse than lying if she had she told the truth.

Thoughts started to go through Fiona's head. Where would she stay when she was released from here? Mary and Jack would surely have to go home. Would she be let out if she had nowhere to live? You had to have a job and a home to go to before you were allowed to leave the House. Would she be able to adjust to the big wide world after living in institutions all her life? What of her friends. Could she simply walk away from them after all these years of living and sleeping in the same room? Oh, the times she had seen penitents being rescued by some aunt or relative, knowing this would never be her fate. Of course, they all promise to write but only a few ever did and the letters soon stopped coming. She waited and prayed to one day have a letter from Angela, but the one's that got away had a new life now and perhaps didn't want reminding of their past. Fiona was happy for them not to write in a way . . . apart from Angela that is. To read about things she could only ever dream about or see in pictures hurt the most.

While Fiona's thoughts drifted into the future, Mary and Jack made their way back to the centre of Dublin and then out to Summer Hill. Mrs O'Conner almost fell through the door when she saw her American friends.

'Jaysus, Mary and Joseph,' called out Mrs O'Conner. 'Dear God, what a surprise. Come in and I'll make yis some tea.'

'And some soda bread please.' Mary laughed.

'How are yis? I got the photos of your wedding. There, now.' She said, pointing to a photograph of Mary and Jack in a frame over the fireplace. 'Did yis have a good time in the Bahamas? It looked grand from the postcard yis sent me.'

'Oh, Mrs O'Conner we had a lovely holiday. The wedding was wonderful too, but we chose to have just a quiet wedding. To be honest, neither of us have a lot of friends and not much in the way of family either. But it would have been lovelier still if you could have come.'

'Ah bejezus, sure I never stepped on a plane in me life, I was thinking of you, mind, and prayed to God you had a safe journey to the Bahamas. Jaysus, I never heard of the place before. The Bahamas, I said to me friends. They are in the Bahamas. "Where's that place now?" said me auld friend, Myra Morey. "Is it in Birmingham? Sure, I know someone who went there. And the Bahamas is not as grand as one might think. So I heard. Tis a grey place". No, says I, tis the other side of the world where trees grow on the beach, not in bloody Birmingham fer fecks sake.'

Mary and Jack laughed so much; Jack almost choked on his tea.

When they had caught up with all the talk of the wedding and holiday, it was time to give Peggy O'Conner the news. 'Mrs O'Conner, 'we have a surprise for you. We've been to see my sister' Mary beamed, still unable to recognize the fact she had a sister. 'We are identical twins, would you believe. It was like looking in a mirror, although she is extremely thin. I can't wait to take her away from that terrible place.'

'Holy mother of God, how is she? Did yis tell her about me? Did you tell I knew her mother, Lillian?'

'I didn't get to talk to her much, it was too emotional. Jack spoke to her and yes, he told her all about you. I can't wait to see her again; we have so much to catch up on.'

'I would tread very carefully there darling; your lives are worlds apart. Let Fiona ask the questions.' Jack carefully suggested.

'You're right Jack. I will. I hope she doesn't hate me for being the one who was adopted. She will have had time to think about it now.'

'The adoption could easily have been the other way. She was a sickly child from what Glenda told us, so adoption was out of the question anyway for her. Think about this Mary, who's to say you would have had such good parents if Harry and Helen hadn't adopted you. It was pure coincidence they found you. You know what your father and grandfather told us about babies being sold to anyone, as long as they were Catholics.'

'I'm so scared Jack. I was sick this morning with worry. I just want to get her away from there.'

'I see, it's a honeymoon baby, is it?' smiled Mrs O'Conner.

'No' laughed Mary. 'It can't be. I've just not been myself this last couple of weeks.'

'I know a pregnant woman when I see one. In the early months you can see it in the mothers face.'

'Jesus, Mary. Is it true? Are you pregnant?' asked Jack, who was standing now.

'Well I . . . I don't know. We've been so wrapped up in all this I hadn't noticed. I suppose I could be. This morning wasn't the first morning I was sick. I . . . I just put it down to nerves.'

Jack lifted Mary from the chair and hugged her. 'I'm so happy. A baby! We're having a baby. We need to see a doctor and get it confirmed. We'll do that today.'

*

The day came for Fiona to be released. The week had dragged by. There were tears as she said goodbye to the only friends she'd ever had. The few sisters she had come to love came to say goodbye with tears in their eyes, to the dismay of the Reverend Mother, Fiona hugged them for the first time in her life.

'Good luck my child and God bless. We will miss you Fiona' said Mother Theresa fondly. The Reverend Mother simply said goodbye and walked away without any emotion.

When the gates were finally locked behind them, Fiona looked at the building through the car window. A sob caught in her throat.

'Fiona, are you all right.'

'I feel a bit strange really. Sure to God, I will miss my friends, and I feel guilty at the same time for leaving them there, but I . . . I could have been there until I died if you hadn't come for me. I don't ever want to go back. I would rather die.'

'You will never go back Fiona, I promise. You're family and families grow. You're going to be an aunty. I'm pregnant! I got the test result back an hour ago from the Rotunda Maternity Hospital.'

Fiona was overwhelmed. 'I have a sister, a brother in law and now I'm going to be an auntie. Dear God, please don't let this be a dream.'

'This is not a dream Fiona. I've missed you all my life unknowingly.'

'I used to pretend I had a sister when I was a child.' Fiona smiled 'I could see a little girl, who followed me everywhere, even sleeping with me. I named her Lilly Rose. I used to talk to her as if she was really there, you know. We laughed together and when I cried, she cried too. One day she disappeared. I thought I had upset her or something and pleaded for her to come back. I felt so lonely when she left me.'

'They're called imaginary friends,' said Jack. 'Imaginary friends are very common in young children. Lonely children invent their own special friend that no one else can see, to keep as their own. She would have been very real to you, speaking to you in a way that only you could understand. This friend of yours possibly made life easier to cope with in lonely or traumatic times . . . a friend you could trust. At this point however, I have to say it isn't always a lonely child or unhappy children who have imaginary friends.'

'That's so true jack. A few of my friends had imaginary friends and they were from happy homes.' Mary added and then turned to Fiona 'what seems strange to me Fiona is that you never knew our mother, yet you named your friend Lilly which is short for Lillian.'

'I don't know where the name Lilly came from, but there was a nun named Sister Rose who was very kind to me when I was very young. She made me a doll from clothes peg, and I loved my special doll. I named her Lilly Rose too.'

'The name Lilly could have come from your subconscious mind.' Jack surmised. 'Even from birth we store a lot of information in our minds without knowing; in fact, some people have even been known to remember the birthing process. Under hypnosis, they have recounted all the details of a traumatic birth for instance. You may have heard the name Lillian said at some point in your early life, such as in conversations about your history when you moved to a new place for example. Perhaps that's why your friend disappeared; you have so much going off in your life when you reached a certain age, such as schooling.'

'Well yes, that was about the time Lilly Rose disappeared Jack, though I can't say I remember the name, Lillian, being said, unless it was said but I didn't take it to mind.'

'Perhaps she was a spirit friend; possibly, a child who had died at a young age, and latched onto to you to help take away the fears and loneliness she herself had in life.' Mary stressed. 'Perhaps she left you to go onto the next stage in her death. That's what Mom would have said . . . oh, I'm sorry Fiona. I mean the Mom who brought me up.'

'It's okay to keep calling her, Mom, Mary. She was your mother and I'm so happy you found good parents to take care of you. I don't feel any resentment or jealousy. That's the way things turned out and we can't change it. I'm also happy that my mother wasn't a prostitute after all. Not someone who left me in a dirty bag outside the orphanage, as I was meant to believe. The poor woman not only died bringing the two of us into the world, but her name was blackened to me. I hated her for what I thought she had done. And now . . .'

'Fiona, please don't cry. I promise you, I won't rest until I find where she is buried. We can tell her then how much we love her when we have a proper burial. I couldn't get anything from the Reverend Mother about her death. Not even a death certificate. But I will.'

Chapter 32

Back at the hotel, Mary and Jack told Fiona the history of their family, at least all they had found out from Mrs O'Conner. Mary also told her, from the information given by Glenda, how wonderful and brave their mother had been, and how one day Mrs O'Conner would tell them all about their mother's earlier life one day. Jack was the one to bring up the subject of Molly's strange disappearance, and also about the rape of Alice.

Fiona was inconsolable. 'I heard about many rapes while I was in the home, some poor souls as young as poor Alison who were raped at ten years old. To be honest, even they were never comforted. You wouldn't believe a child so young could be chastised for losing her virginity; it was as if they were to blame. The girl's lives were destroyed and it wasn't their fault. Being taken away from their families was "For their own good" they said. Classed as sinners as young as they were, and I'm sure poor Alice would have been the same. Did they ever find our grandmother?'

'No, the Gardaí looked everywhere for months. They questioned neighbours and friends, asking where she was most likely to go, but everyone said the same, that she was fine when they last saw her. She can't have got very far without clothes or money either. Mrs O'Conner told us Molly would never leave her kids. In Mrs O'Conner's words *"Molly had something on her mind the last time I saw her. She went away and came back, only to leave the kids with me while she ran upstairs two steps at a time."* And then there was poor Alice, who Molly had taken the time to give Mrs O'Conner clean clothes, knowing she would put two and two together.'

'But where could she have gone for three hours before.'

'I have a hunch' Jack said, leaning forward. Something he did when he wanted to say something serious. 'What if she went to the Magdalena home to see Lillian, convinced she was raped too? But then, I can imagine

Molly was sent away without seeing Lillian. She may have wanted Lillian to admit her father had raped her too, so she wouldn't have to see Alice dragged through the court. She knew he'd raped Alice, but she wouldn't have had any real proof. The girl was traumatised and couldn't . . . or wouldn't speak.'

Jack went down to the bar to leave the Mary and Fiona to chat on their own, while he did some thinking. His gut feeling was that Joseph had killed Molly. But what did he do with the body? All the local areas had been searched, and he had no form of transport to take her out of the vicinity. How did he get her downstairs without being seen, he would have had to drag the body?

Fiona and Mary were happy to be left on their own for a while and strangely the conversation started to mirror Jack's thoughts.

'What do you think happened to our grandmother, Mary? 'Fiona asked.

'I don't know, but perhaps the trauma of Alice being raped sent her over the edge and she had a breakdown. But on the other hand, she doesn't sound like a weak woman to me. It's obvious she loved her children too.'

'I suppose she could have suffered a breakdown, like you said, Mary, what with the life she had. Some of the nuns had nervous breakdowns, usually the lay nuns, who worked harder. A few of the older women who'd been there all their lives went into the Holy Order as nuns. Can you believe that?'

'Maybe they weren't as harsh, knowing what it was like to be on the other side.'

'I would say, very much the opposite. They were cows.'

'A case of showing their authority I suppose.'

'True. Mary, how could Molly send her daughter away knowing she wouldn't be able to come home again? Our mother would have had an awful time in one of those places. I know she would. I heard tales first-hand of what went off in the labour room. Sometimes they were forced to have the baby on a cold metal bed pan to save blood from spilling all over the bed, sitting there for hours at a time. They weren't given so much as an aspirin for the pain. Sometimes, they were split nearly in two from instruments used to pull out the baby. Most of the girls were just left with open sores. They should have been stitched, but they weren't. As for the adoptions, when the baby was taken away within a few months or sometimes straight away; the mother was left with painful leaking breasts, not to mention the heartache.'

Mary unconsciously covered her stomach with her hands. 'Grandmother wouldn't have known this Fiona, I'm sure. Maybe she had plans to bring her home again after the baby was born.'

'You're right. Sorry. It's just that I feel so much sorrow for our mother. Raped and beaten by her own father, only for me to believe she was a bad mother who dumped me for her own selfish reasons.'

'Let's change the subject Fiona. Tell me about yourself. Your likes and dislikes. Let's see just how much bond there were between us when we didn't know each other.'

'I didn't have much choice in either. I had what I was given and did without what I would have liked. Even something as simple as a book; I liked reading. I used to take magazines from the trash cans in the sister's offices. They said magazines were seen as dirt and filth, but someone read them.' Fiona laughed 'there was nothing dirty or filthy in them. It was just the modern world I wanted to see; the pictures and the real life stories. Sure, we had books in the library, but they were handpicked to make sure we didn't read something, well, you know. But those magazines were my life, until I got caught out, that is. I used to dream a lot and make stories in my head about them. I suppose you could say it was a sort of escapism. But my dreams were so real Mary. I saw things I couldn't possibly have known. My friend, Angela, listened to my dreams . . . she understood. She said I was astral travelling in my sleep.'

'I'm sure Jack would have a logical explanation for that, but I believe you. It's so strange, I used to have dreams of what I now know were nuns, but in my dreams they were people dressed in black, who used to shave my head and lock me in a little room with . . .never mind. Sorry.'

'Mary, you were picking things up from me, I suppose being twins that sort of things happens. I had my head shaved for having head lice quite a few times which really hurt when they cut into my scalp. I would lash out, kick and scream until I was dragged into a room where they locked me in for a full day and night.'

'Shall we change the subject? We'll do some shopping tomorrow and we can look at some books. Maybe . . . but only if you want to, you could perhaps have your hair cut in a more fashionable style and buy some new clothes.'

'Mary, I couldn't possible take advantage of your good nature, and I don't have any money.'

'But Fiona, you don't understand. I so want to be your friend as well as a sister. I want to shop with you, laugh, cry and tell each other secrets, like sisters and friends do. I have money. More money than I will ever need.'

'Will you stay with me when I have my hair cut? I hate the very sight of scissors.'

'Of course I will, Fiona. And the scissors are very small, believe me.'

*

The following day, Mary took Fiona to a quiet salon in a side street, and just as she had hoped, there were only a few people there. She knew from Fiona; the way the girl's hair was cut in the institutions.

The young hairdresser was very chatty, making suggestions of the sort of style she might like. 'You have good thick hair with a natural curl like your sister. But you have a lot of scars on your scalp and a few sores, so we need to keep the volume . . .'

Both Fiona and Mary were amazed how the young girl, only sixteen or seventeen years old, hid her shock at the sight of Fiona's scalp; disfigured by all the years of her hair being literally hacked off. The transformation was unbelievable, and Mary gave the girl quite a good tip before leaving.

'Jaysus Mary, sure, it didn't hurt one bit. Did you see how small the scissors were, and did you notice how she knew we were sisters.'

'You look lovely Fiona. I was thinking. Instead of me paying for everything today, I want to give you some money to buy what you want to buy . . .'

'No Mary, I can't do that.'

'Yes, you can. You have to get used to spending money. You can buy whatever you want without feeling embarrassed. Fiona, please take it.'

Fiona threw her arms around Mary's neck and told her she loved her. This was the first time she had spoken those words and it felt good. 'Shall we go into one of those coffee bars again before we shop?' Fiona giggled.

*

While sitting in the cafe, Mary told Fiona about her father and his wife, Amy. She also told her about their grandparents. 'Grandpa will be so pleased to meet you, and so will everyone else. They are all your family now. I'm sure my father will want you to call him Dad. He can't wait to meet you. And Amy is lovely, she's been a true friend to me and never tried to take Moms place . . . and wait while you meet your nephews and nieces, oh Jesus, they are so sweet.'

'All this still seems like a dream to me.' Fiona confessed.

'It's real Fiona. Hey, you must meet Mrs O'Conner; she is dying to see you . . . and Glenda too. She tried to adopt you . . .'

'Adopt me. But I thought no one wanted me.'

'Glenda was there when we were born. Nurse Carey, her name was. She saved your life. You were meant to die . . . oops, I'm sorry to sound blunt Fiona; I mean the Reverend Mother told her to leave you to die. You were starved of oxygen, or so the Sister said, and thought you would be brain damaged. Not wanting to take that chance, Glenda was told to leave you in a room to die, but she fed and nurtured you and you recovered. When Glenda left the home she immediately put in for adoption but was turned down because she was a single woman. She was very upset Fiona.'

'She wanted to adopt me. She knew our mother. She knows what our mother looked like?'

'Yes. Glenda says we look like her. Our mother was such a lovely person Fiona. 'It's so ironic. Babies and young children were being adopted and fostered out to complete strangers, but not to someone like Glenda who loved you. The problem was, Glenda didn't have a job at the time, which also went against her. But then, the Reverend Mother wouldn't have liked the idea of family and friends asking questions. There's something that doesn't seem to add up.'

'You're right. Oh, I wish I could have told my friend Angela all about you Mary. She was the nicest person I ever knew, up to meeting you.'

'And you have no idea where she is.'

'No, she could be in the asylum where they intended to take her, but, although Sister Theresa didn't actually say Angela had run away, she insinuated she had. Angela always said she would escape one day to her aunt's farm. All I know is the farm is in the middle of nowhere further up North. She did say once, but I can't remember.'

'I'm sure with Mrs. O'Conner's help, Jack will find her.'

'Oh Jaysus, Mary, do you really think he could? That would be grand.'

*

A few days later, they took Fiona to meet Mrs O'Conner, who was the only person who knew of Lillian's past. She could also tell them about their Father, and Lillian's brothers and sisters. Fiona was almost frightened of what she was going to hear.

'Come in, come in. Sit down and I'll make some tea and slice some bread. Jaysus, yis weren't wrong when you said Fiona looks like you Mary. I'm so pleased to meet you Fiona.'

'And you, Mrs O'Conner, I've heard so much about you. I've been told you were very good to our mother's family.'

'Ah yes, lovely family, apart from that poor excuse of a man. Bully he was. He beat your grandmother and the kids. Nearly killed Marianne and Molly, now let me make tea and we'll talk.'

Mrs O'Conner put the soda bread on the table and shared the tea. 'Your grandmother was a lovely person, never complained, never pulled anyone down. I helped Molly out as much as I could. She could always rely on me. I was there the day Alice was raped. Molly carried Alice downstairs and left some clothes, which was strange; she only lived two flights up. *"I won't be long" says she, "I have an errand to do. There are some clothes for Alice here. She may need another change. I will tell you everything later Peggy. Thank you".* And that's all Molly said. She was gone before I had chance to say a word. Three hours later, she pops her head around the door and said she would be back down to take the kids. That was the last I saw of her. It was like she was on some sort of undertaking. I never saw her this way before. She was angry. Very angry and upset.'

'Would she have had somewhere to go?'

'Everyone who knew her was out there looking. No, she had nowhere to go.'

'What about Shaun, James, Alice and Laurence' Asked Fiona. 'Where would they be now?'

'Ah sure, they'd be all grown up . . . if they survived the hell holes. The Christian Brothers Home was where the boys went, which I very much doubt poor James would have survived. Sure, they chose the young pretty ones.'

'Choose the young pretty ones for what?'

'I won't be going there. I can't speak of things they do to boys, but James was the cutest boy I ever saw in all me life. Dear God, if they did live through that place, then they could have families themselves now, except for poor Alice. She would be in a mental institution. I wouldn't give much hope for her, poor child.'

'Where's the most likely place the nuns would have buried our Mother?' Mary asked Fiona, trying to get away from a subject she couldn't bear to think about. 'We could go and say a few prayers, lay flowers and perhaps buy her a nice headstone.'

'I don't know.' Fiona said quietly. 'We often had to clear weeds and rubbish from where there were graves, but most of the headstones were for the Sisters. There was a grave for the babies who were all buried in one spot, but they were buried without names in a large unmarked grave. I know people died in the home, but we never saw their names on a grave, but then, we were just a number to the Sisters.'

Glenda knocked on the door, and Mary fell into her open arms. Fiona walked slowing over to Glenda, her heart beating so fast she thought she would pass out.

'Fiona, oh Dear Lord, how good it is to see you. I've often wondered what became of you. You are just like your mother. You both are. I'm sorry I had to leave you behind but . . .'

'I know what you did, Glenda, and you have nothing to be sorry for. You saved my life, which in many ways wasn't worth living.' Laughed Fiona, 'but I have thirty to forty years in front of me yet, God willing, and now I have a family.'

After much catching up, Jack spoke for the first time. He had sat back and let the women talk and felt great pride in knowing he was a part of this reunion.

'I went looking to see if I could find anything about Joseph McNamara, while you and Fiona were shopping. He seems to have disappeared off the face of the earth; none of his friends know where he is. One of his drinking buddies said no one was home when he went to look for him. His door is never locked so he went in to check to see if he'd done a runner. A neighbour of his saw a young girl going into his flat one afternoon. She said the girl seemed very upset.'

'A young girl, what would a young girl be going there for?'

'I don't know Mrs O'Conner, but the neighbour said he was always bringing young girls back. Listen to this. The neighbour said the girls tried to keep out of sight and only went to his flat during the night usually.

'Well, that doesn't surprise me now. Joseph McNamara was a good looking fellow, despite the drink. Sure, he could charm the arse of a . . .'

'We get the picture Mrs O'Conner. Jack laughed. 'Apparently Joseph was behind with the rent and the neighbours thought he must have been evicted, but his clothes and personal stuff were still there, along with some loose change on the table. Apparently, it was just as if he'd nipped out for something. The van he was driving had vanished too.'

'That is very strange. I wonder if he fell into the River Liffy on his way home from the pub. Now that would be a good thing. Sure, the devil will welcome him with open arms.' Mrs O'Conner said indignantly.

Jack laughed again at Mrs O'Conner, who sat straight backed, her arms folded across her chest and her chin held high in defiance.

'On my way back to the hotel, I started to think of Alice. I don't believe she was mentally retarded. I think she was a young shy girl who had seen such violence in her life, she thought it might be best not to speak, that way she wouldn't be in trouble.'

'She would always speak to me.' Mrs O'Conner said, pouring herself more tea. 'And her mother of course, Molly always understood her. She had the gift you know.'

'Who had a gift, and what sort of gift' Jack replied.

'Alice. She knew things before they happened . . . has done since she was very young. Molly told me so.'

'Are you saying she was psychic?'

'You could say that I suppose, but Molly told me they came to her in dreams. Alice used to tell me of things she couldn't possibly have known. The strange thing was, she spoke loud and clear. Almost like an adult. Joseph never got to hear her talking. She was frightened of him. Knew things about him, she did.'

Mrs O'Conner wasn't sure it was right to bring the subject of Alice seeing her dead husband with her child in front of so many people.

'Perhaps it was just the case of a child's imagination and coincidences.' Jack suggested.

'No Jack. I believe her.' Fiona cut in. 'I too have dreams. I see things, but being stuck in there, I didn't know what was real and what my imagination.'

'Go on Fiona. We're listening.'

'I had a friend in the home, a good friend. Her name was Angela. She was the closest person to me I ever had in my life. She understood. I could tell her about my dreams, and she didn't laugh, in fact, she explained things to me in great detail. She . . . she was taken away.'

'Angela was taken away. Where was she taken?'

'I don't know.' Fiona wiped away a tear with the back of her hand. 'One of the girls reported us to the Reverend Mother. We were talking about dreams and . . . I'll start from the beginning. I had dreams where I'm leaving my body and flying through the sky. I could see all over Dublin, the houses, fields, people and colours. I saw the oceans and could hear people talking. Angela listened to me and didn't mock me. She says the dreams are called Astral Travelling and explained how you're attached by a cord. But I felt more like a 'see through' ghost. I could see people, but they couldn't see me. I guess being dead must be like that, or they could have been just dreams. I know that . . . but.'

'Go on Fiona. I know about astral travelling, or dreams where you are out of your body.' Jack said, leaning forward.

'Quite a few times I saw a man and something in his hand. Blood was dripping from it and . . .'

'Jaysus Fiona.' Glenda gasped. 'Your mammy had the same dream just before she died. She said it was her father.'

They all went quiet for a moment trying to make sense of it all. Mary was the first to speak.' Did you see anyone being killed, Fiona?'

'No, but when I was flying, floating, whatever you want to call it, out of my body, I was over land and near the sea. There were no houses, but the waves were crashing onto the rocks. I could hear it. I saw a man digging. There was thunder and lightning and the sky lit up and I saw his face, and suddenly there was a piercing scream. A woman dressed in a shroud of some sort rushed towards him and he fell. His head was bleeding. I woke up sweating. It was a terrifying dream.'

'Fiona, what did the place look like? Jack asked. 'Was it grassed over?'

'No, it was all very muddy and dark coloured. Not green like grass.'

'This could be worth a shot. What's say we take a look.'

'But, Jack. Where do we start? We have no idea where to look.'

'Mrs O'Conner, where do we start?'

'Sounds more like a peat bog to me.'

'What better place to hide a body than a Peat Bog. A body could be there years if hidden in the right spot'.

*

With Mrs O'Conner and Mary in the back of the car, and Fiona beside him in the front, Jack drove through country lanes for miles, knowing in his heart that Joseph couldn't possibly have travelled this far on foot, at least not with a body over his shoulder. He felt a little deflated. His dream to investigate a murder was not to be. At the bottom of his heart, he'd believed he would solve the case of the missing woman, Molly McNamara. But he had to be careful not to take Fiona's dreams too seriously. She must have a deep psychological hatred for her parents after all those years, and of course her dreams would reflect on them in a damning way. No wonder she had nightmares, poor girl, being locked away and told her mother was a prostitute, who'd dumped her outside the gates of an orphanage. The only image of her father was that of a paying client.

Jack began to wonder if Fiona needed psychiatric help. Yes, he'd read books about Astral Travelling and he did believe it was possible. On the other hand, there is what's known as lucid dreams, where people actually dream of leaving their bodies. These people describe places and scenes they swear they couldn't possibly have known about. This is, in fact, their subconscious mind. The part of the mind that can see and remember things the conscious mind cannot; such as in Hypnosis. Under hypnosis, memories of people and places often come to the surface, which in turn may stir up upsetting incidents that could have been buried deep down in our subconscious mind as a kind of protection. On the other hand, hypnosis has been known to create false memories, which can be extremely disturbing. Our imagination can be a powerful weapon.

Astral travelling is when you are awake before you feel yourself being 'lifted'. A feeling of tingling and sleep paralysis occurs before separation from the body; just as the subconscious mind drifts away. Jack remembered a case history in his studies at College. The case study was of a child who had lost his beloved grandmother to cancer. The boy, who was three years old at the time, was travelling in the car with his parents. Calmly, he told them to turn around as there was a car crash involving a white van and a red car, explaining the road was blocked. His parents laughed and asked how he knew about the crash. The boy said that his Nan sometimes took him from his bed, and they flew through the sky together. He told them that the night before, he and his Nan witnessed a red car being hit by a white van. The little boy's parents took the story with a pinch of salt; after all, he was just a child with an imagination like all children his age. Fifteen minutes later there was a hold up in the traffic. An accident had just happened and there were sirens blaring out from behind them. As they drove a little closer, they could see a white van and red car at the side of the road. There was no way anyone could have seen or heard about this collision. The accident had only happened since leaving their house.

Jack knew there were children who often described flying through the sky, but unlike adults they accept it as being normal and often don't even bother to talk about it. He decided it was time to call it a day and admit defeat. He would have to continue to daydream about solving a murder. The weather was turning cold and it was raining heavily by now. In fact, he wondered if it ever stopped raining in Ireland, and laughed to himself remembering the old saying about 'the girls being pretty due to all the rain on their skin'.

Driving was becoming difficult and it was hard to see where he was going on the narrow road. The wiper blades were battling with the rain, giving him a migraine. Out of nowhere, a heavy truck came whizzing around a corner taking Jack by surprise. He was dazzled by the headlights and skidded across to the other side of the road; just as sheet lightening lit up the sky followed by a clap of thunder. Fiona immediately noticed the tree which looked as if it had two long arms reaching out in front of her.

'It's there. The tree is over there, near to the wall. I recognise the tree where the woman in the shroud was stood.'

Jack suggested the three of them waited in the car while he took a quick look and wondered if perhaps they should all come back for a better look the following day when it was daylight. He wasn't going to get excited about finding anything; he still had doubts whether or not Fiona was just dreaming. But then, the human brain isn't fully understood, and there are too many unexplained phenomenal occurrences to judge people.

Trudging carefully onwards, his shoe stuck to the mud and came off his foot. Cursing, he forced his way through the sludge back towards the car, holding his shoe in his hand. There was a distinct sinister atmosphere to this place, Jack decided. Thunder and lightning added to the eeriness even more so. Trying hard to see where he was walking, and avoiding the shallow pools of water, something . . . a sound or a feeling made him look up. He was frightened of this place. He wanted desperately to get back to

316

the car, but at that moment Jack saw something move and he rubbed his eyes to wipe away the rain. There, in front of him, was a woman dressed in a white robe. The woman wasn't stood on the ground; she was floating. After what seemed an eternity, but was probably just seconds, the girl pointed to the wall behind him.

'Come on now Jack. Don't be a wimp. You didn't see anything. It's all this talk of the lady in white.' But curiosity took over and he walked without his shoes to where she was pointing. 'What the . . . Jesus Christ.' Jack froze on the spot. In front of him was a body of a man with the sharp corner of a spade sticking into his head. Wiping his brow, Jack held onto the wall for support, and the young woman dressed in a white shroud, quickly floated towards him. He covered his face with his hands, frighten to death, peeping through his fingers. The apparition smiled at Jack just as lightening lit up the sky. And she was gone.

*

Two week later, Jack was asked to go to the station to make a statement. He was also told not to leave the City. He had no reason to feel nervous, but it *was* he who found the body, and now they were looking for the murderer. He was dreading going to the station; explaining how he had stumbled on the dead man wasn't going to be easy. The last thing Jack wanted was for Fiona to be carried off to an asylum, or him to be accused of murder.

'Good morning, Mr Langley. I won't keep you too long. There are just a few questions I would like to ask you.' The detective said, offering Jack a chair to sit on. 'Can I get you a coffee? I understand America's prefer coffee to tea.'

'No thanks, I'm fine. I had one when I first arrived over an hour ago.' Replied Jack, indicating how long he had to wait around before starting this interview.

'I see. Sorry for the wait. Right, we'll get down to business. Can you tell me, Mr Reiner, why you were in that particular place Tuesday evening? Sure, it was dark and pouring down with rain. 'Tis a very muddy place for someone such as yer self to be walking . . . and I have to say, the body of a man, big as he was, would not be easily visible from the roadside. The grave was dug there for the purpose of not being found.'

'We were on our way back from Malahide and seeing as it was my sister in law's first time out for a good while, we took a detour rather than coming back the same way we went.' Jack tried hard not to look embarrassed. He was thinking over the excuse he had come up with and hoped to god it worked. 'Well, I . . . I needed a pee and with three women in the car, I had to find somewhere out of the way. The lane was wet from the heavy rain and a truck came around the bend causing me to skid and pull over. Having had to stop and recover from almost being hit, I took a walk, intending to take a leak while I was there. I saw someone or something move near the wall and went to take a look, but it was a piece of fabric. That's when I saw the body of a man on the ground with a spade in his head. I didn't realise it was a grave. I kinda made my way back as fast as I could, minus one shoe, which I dropped in the mud.'

'Yeah, we found the shoe. I think I would have been dubious of walking over to the wall if I thought there was someone there. Sure, they would have been up to something. Your life may have been at risk. Do you agree?'

'I was afraid, yes. But I wasn't thinking straight, the rain was blurring my vision. I was on my way back to the car and decided to turn around and take another look in case someone needed help.'

'I've had some reports that you've been asking a lot of questions about a missing person.' The Detective said firmly.

'No . . . yes' stuttered Jack, who was terrified now of being involved with the murder. 'My wife has been desperate to find her birth mother. Unfortunately, her mother died in childbirth in one of the homes . . . Jesus Christ; I can't remember the name of the home.' Jack mumbled; his head covered by his hands.

'Don't worry. I already know. Mr Langley, we're not accusing you of murder.'

'You're not? Oh Jesus; I was so frightened of how it was looking. Sir, I need to tell you the whole story.'

'That's all right Mr Langley, we already know that too. Margaret O'Conner has a lot of friends . . ., who have friends,' he laughed.

'Who was the dead man? Was it murder or an accident?'

'His name was an alias, Joseph McNamara. His real name was Patrick James McNulty. We're not really certain of how he died. He could have slipped on the mud and fallen backwards. There doesn't appear to be any indication of anyone else being there with him. Besides, he was a big man and would have needed a big push to fall on the spade with such an impact . . . his head was split in two or just about.'

'Jesus Christ. Joseph McNamara is my wife's father . . . sorry, I mean her grandfather.'

'Yes, I know. I'm going to tell you something now, between you and me for the time being, you understand, Mr Langley . . . may I call you Jack.'

Jack nodded his head. To think all this time, he was being checked up on. Some Private Dick he was.

The Detective began again, 'I'm telling you this, as you're a Private Detective in the States, I trust your awareness of confidentiality. We also found two more bodies beneath Patrick McNulty . . . Joseph McNamara. It seems he was in the process of burying a young pregnant girl, Jacqueline Humphries. Her distraught parents identified the body. Sure to God, they will never be the same again. Her mother told me she would have taken care of Jacqueline and the baby. The young girl came from a very good family.'

'I'm so sorry to hear that Sir, but I don't understand. You say a young girl, but I believed his wife had been murdered . . .'

'She *was* murdered. Molly McNamara was the woman beneath the girl. She was strangled by her husband in 1951. We suspected him from the start, but we had no body and no proof.'

'This just gets worse. Could Joseph have been killed?'

'That is the biggest mystery. We have no idea. His head was almost split in two, but a fall backwards would not have caused such an injury, yet there is no evidence of murder. The only footprints are from McNulty and yer self. Besides, he was dead a while before you found him. We believed he also killed his own mother, but that's another matter that doesn't concern you.'

*

Jack didn't go straight back to the hotel. He went to the nearest bar and ordered two whiskies, which he gulped down each one in one go. He was about to leave when he saw a pretty woman with dark hair and blue eyes looking at him. She was wiping down the tables. A shiver went through him and he couldn't understand why. The girl looked vaguely familiar. *'Oh, please don't say this is another fucking ghost.'*

When the barman told her off for being too slow, it appeared not. As he turned to face her once more before closing the door, she smiled at him and *he saw Mary in her smile. She was her double, though about eight, ten years older than Mary.*

*

'Dearly beloved, we are gathered here today . . .' and at that point it started to rain. Mary looked towards the sky, remembering what her mother had told her about the person who has died being happy now. *Would her grandmother, Molly, be looking down on them? Was it her who steered the car off the road, leading them to the discovery of the grave? Oh, the terrible fate of that poor girl and her baby. Her parents must have been heartbroken. I wonder what happened to the rest of the McNamara family. What would Alice look like? She would probably be in her late thirties, or early forties, about twelve years older than me. The boys were older, although there was a baby come to think. Would they want to be found, or would they be like Mom . . . Marianne, who never wanted to be with her family again. Would Jack help to find the rest of her Irish family or had he had enough of the McNamara mysteries.*

'God Bless you, Grandmother.'

Mary linked Fiona's arm on the way back to the car. 'Fiona, we have to go home soon. I would love you to come and live with us. It would be wonderful to have you there for the birth of the baby too.'

'I would love to go with you, but I need my independence. I can't lean on you all my life and that's what I would be doing. To be honest, I need to find my feet here in Dublin first. I'm going to miss you, Mary. I would love

320

to be near you for the rest of my life . . . but not yet. Glenda has offered me a room at her house for as long as I want, and I would like to learn more of our family from Mrs O'Conner. I feel she is more like a relative. To be sure, she knows so much about our history; it would be nice for her to live nearer to Glenda and me. We could perhaps care for her in later years, but . . .'

'Fiona, that's a wonderful idea. Don't worry about trying to find somewhere. I'll sort something out with my . . . our father. He'll find a little bungalow for her. She isn't happy where she is, and from what I gather, she is a very sociable woman who loves company. I'm going to miss you too Fiona and I promise to come to see you again very soon. Perhaps all three of you could come and visit us in New York. You don't have to worry about the cost of the flight. It's my treat to Glenda and Mrs O'Conner for bringing you into my life again.'

'That would be grand Mary. Yes, I would love to come and I'm sure Glenda and Mrs O'Conner will be thrilled.'

Chapter 33

When Mary and Jack had to go back to the States, Fiona, with Glenda's help, set about finding Angela. Finally, they managed to find her address. Fiona wrote to her telling her briefly about her sister and explained she would fill the details in when they could meet each other. Providing Angela wanted to see Fiona again of course. She was thrilled to receive a letter from her dear friend within a few days, inviting her to stay on the farm. Glenda helped Fiona pack a few items of clothing in a small case and wrote down the number of the bus she would need to catch back home again.

'I'll take you to the depot and see you get on the right bus, but when you get to your stop, which I have written down, you will need to go to the farm by taxi. Mrs Morgan, over the road, has kindly let me have her phone number. I don't have a telephone, as there are plenty of phone booths around.'

'Thank you so much Glenda. I need to start finding my way about now. It's with God's blessing I have you in my life.'

Glenda gave Fiona a big hug. 'Sure, I should have had you since you were a baby, but you're here now, and I will treat you as my daughter.'

'Thank you, Glenda; I wouldn't be here at all if not for you. You gave me life.'

*

Fiona settled down on the bus and was amazed by the wonderful scenery before her. Dublin was so beautiful, even more beautiful than all the pictures she had seen in magazines. She hoped and prayed Angela hadn't changed and was happy to see her again. The bus lulled her into relaxation. Whatever happened, she would always have those wonderful memories of the three years she spent with Angela. Their midnight talks and giggles, the mischief they somehow seemed to get away with, trying hard not to laugh when one of the Sisters passed wind. She could hear Angela now. *"Sure to God they have a hole in their arse like everyone else. That means they have shite coming of their arses as well as their gobs."*

*

When Fiona climbed out of the taxi, Angela rushed to greet her. 'Oh Fiona, I am so happy to see you, you look wonderful. Holy Mother of God . . . Just look at the clothes you're wearing.' She held Fiona at arms lengths to get a better look of her in jeans and a white sweatshirt, and hugged her again.

'Mary bought me more clothes than I'll ever need.' Fiona said, looking down at her outfit with pride. 'Glenda said to wear them; sure, I was wearing the same outfit day after day. "You're not in the home now". Glenda kept telling me.'

Fiona stood and stared at Angela with a lump in her throat, 'you look fantastic too, and your cheeks are as rosy as a red rose.'

'Now that's due to all the hours I spend outside.' Angela laughed.

'In your letter you said you own the farm now. I'm so happy for you Angela; everything could have been so different.'

'Come inside and I'll tell you all about it.'

After Angela showed Fiona to the room where she was to spend the night, they settled down to a lunch Angela had prepared earlier. They talked the first hour or so of their short lives they had shared for three years and agreed there were some happy times in the home.

'I helped my aunt work the farm up to her going into a care home. Her mind went all funny, and I couldn't leave her on her own at all. She was a real danger to herself. I tried really hard to look after her and the farm too, but she didn't even know me. A man came to the door when I was out and told her he was her son. She didn't have any children! He took a few things, but she had nothing of real value to be honest, apart from her rings, which the bastard took off her fingers.'

'Oh, dear Lord, that's so terrible. Did they catch him?'

'No. She just kept saying it was nice to see her son again. So, whether he had been before, I don't know, but she was so convinced it was her son.'

'Did your aunt ever lose a child, perhaps her mind went into the past somewhere.'

'Yes. She had two sons who both died from TB when they were children. So perhaps you're right. Anyway, let's lighten up a bit or we'll both be crying again. You tell me first about your sister.'

Fiona told her about how surprised she was to learn she was a twin, and the resentment she first felt when she saw her sister, and how easy it would have been to hate her. 'It wasn't easy for Mary either. She's lovely Angela, and I love her. None of this was her fault . . . and Glenda is like a mother to me. I wouldn't be here talking to you right now if she hadn't saved my life. Like I said in the letter to you, she wanted to adopt me.'

'Fiona I'm thrilled everything has worked out for you. If you need a job, there will always be one here. I did write to let you know you were free to leave Maggie's if you had a job and a home, but when you didn't write back, I knew they hadn't passed my letters on. I was very careful what I wrote too. The last thing I wanted to do was get you into trouble. The authorities couldn't take me back when they did eventually catch up with me. My father died while I was in Maggie's, and Ma was happy for me to live and work with Aunt Martha. I had a job *and* a home so they could stick their laundry up their fecking arses.'

'Tis good to see you haven't changed at all. I have to say I was worried you might have. I thought about you all the time Angela, I missed you so much.'

'And I missed you too Angela. I suppose three years of living, working and sleeping next to one another, was worth more than someone being friends for twenty years. The girls in places such as Maggie's knew how to bond as you and I did.'

'True, but they knew how to fight too, Jaysus, those fights some of the girls had. *We* never fell out though, did we? You were my guardian angel Fiona.'

'And you mine, but, oh, those fights; I'm sure the nuns took pleasures from watching the girls fight. I kept myself to myself when you left the home. I had no interest in new girls. No one could replace you. I'm happy for you Angela. I was upset when you were gone and cried myself to sleep for weeks. God only knows why they sent you away and allowed me to stay.'

'I know why. Because they knew it would hurt you more. They knew how caring you were and how it would haunt you for the rest of your life. That was your fecking punishment. I did come to see you quite a few times, but they told me you had moved to another 'appropriate place'. I thought they were lying and kept turning up at the gate, but then I began to fear the worst. I thought they had sent you to an asylum, Fiona. It was just awful to think that was where you were.'

'Sister Theresa gave me a hint that you had run away' Fiona smiled 'and I knew where you would go if you got the chance, but I still missed you even knowing you were probably safe. But *how did you escape*?'

The bloody men in the van were scaring me to death with tales of hearing screaming in the Looney bin. Thought I was deranged, so they did. Later, I overheard the driver asking the other man if he knew where Ballinasloe was. The man said he did, and not to worry because he had been there before. I didn't know this place, but I did notice signs for Galway. Did I ever tell you about a cousin of mine who suffered from epilepsy?'

'No, I don't remember you saying anything about her. Why?'

'Well, what I did was, I made a funny sound with my throat as if I was choking and started shaking all over, and rolled my eyes upwards, just as I'd seen Wendy do. The driver jumped out of the car and ran to find a phone booth to call an ambulance, and the other man helped me out of the car. I jumped up and ran through the Barley field towards some trees, thinking I could hide behind one, but when I looked up at the branches, I knew I could climb up to the top of the tree. The men were running all over the field, but they never looked up. Tell you what though. They stopped to light a cigarette and were too near for comfort. I nearly shit me self. Can you imagine shite falling on their heads?'

After recovering from laughing, Fiona asked how she managed climb a tree.

'Easy, I told you I was good at sports and won certificates for running and jumping.'

'But how did you get to your aunts farm without money.'

'A lady found me by the side of a stream where I was drinking water with cupped hands. She took me back to her house and I told her everything. I'd no other choice. She listened while I explained about the boy and . . . well, everything, even about being caught talking about ghosts and spirits, which she found funny and interesting. I accepted the fact she was probably going to turn me in, but instead, she asked where I had planned to go. I was shocked. The woman told me her niece had been in one of the Magdalena homes and she found her a hairdressing job by a friend of hers. She let her niece stay with her for a while and heard first-hand what went on there. Her husband drove me here to my Aunts. It took a while to find the farm, but we eventually did. I'm so grateful to that dear woman Fiona. She saved my life. I would have killed myself if I was in a bloody nut house.'

'I'm so glad they didn't get you there, Angela. Once you're in, tis hard to get out. Oh, it's so lovely to see you.'

'I believe those two were Earth Angels. That's what me Nan would have said. The couple were so lovely. It was strange really, they dropped me off and wished me luck, I turned to wave, and they were gone. They must have driven very fast to disappear down the lane so quickly or . . .'

'What are Earth Angels?'

'Now, that is something I will tell you about tonight. And what about you, what are you doing now?'

'Oh, you know, just waiting for you and me to set up a fortune telling business of our own in the City centre.'

Angela was stunned until Fiona laughed. 'I had you then. Oh, by the way, Pauline apologised for having you sent away, she was very upset. She admitted she was jealous of our friendship.'

'Ah to be sure, tis the bloody place that puts the devil himself into a person. I suppose she thought we would only be punished. It would have come as a shock to her, me being taken to a loony bin.'

'Yeah, I told her it wasn't really her fault. I was lost without you Angela; you brought so much laughter into my life.'

'I never forgot you either Fiona, but I felt sure I wouldn't see you again.'

'Did you marry?'

'No, I do date a man now and again. His name is Derek, but we haven't made long term plans. I love my independence and I'm happy as I am; and you, do you have a job? You could always work here with me.'

'Glenda got me a job caring for the elderly in the city, just to put me on. But after being in Maggie's for so long, I would love a job outdoors here with you. I just love the trees; the sky and I'd even get to see the sea every day in real life.' Fiona laughed. 'Thank you for the offer of a job, though it may be a while, I'm off to New York with Glenda and Mrs O'Conner for my niece's christening, would you believe. Another of my dreams has come true. I am so nervous Angela. Imagine me on a plane.'

'To be sure now, tis better than flying on yer own.'

They laughed again like they used to all the time and Fiona remembered something she wanted to ask Angela, 'going back to dreaming? Do you remember dreaming of your father being dead? What did happen to him?'

'That is so strange Fiona, because he did die around the time I had the dream. It was a heart attack, so Mammy didn't kill him.' Angela explained laughing 'I shouldn't laugh, but he put me in an institution for nothing. I'm surprised Mammy didn't die first. She was heartbroken when I was taken away, and from what she told me, she never spoke to him again; unless she had to.'

Fiona had much to tell about her dreams, but decided to wait until later, when it really would be like old times.

327

Chapter 34

New York

Mary and Jack named the baby Lilly Rose. Fiona was delighted with the name they'd chosen and also overjoyed to be her godmother. Peter insisted on Fiona calling him Dad and was just as wonderful as Mary had said he would be; as were Amy and their adorable children. Fiona wondered what she ever did in her life to be treated with so much love, and still hoped it wasn't one of her dreams she might just wake up from.

Fiona, Glenda and Mrs O'Conner, were thoroughly enjoying their two month stay in New York, though Peggy O'Conner was eager to get back home to tell the neighbours about the places she had seen . . . and the fact she was on a long flight aeroplane at seventy four years old.

'Oh Jaysus, wait while I tell them I was in a real detectives office and made tea fer the clients while they waited, and the Twin Towers, Jesus Mary and Joseph, the bloody size of them. Sure to God, it's to be hoped the lift never breaks down, or there's never a fire. And as for Central Park, oh, they'd be so jealous, but I won't be rubbing it in now. No, I won't be boasting. Do I sound like an American? I think my accent is changing already. Jaysus, wait till they hear that now.'

As for Fiona, it was like history repeating itself. She took photographs all over Central park using the camera her 'new' father had bought her.

She had albums full of photos of all the family, including Glenda and Mrs O'Conner, who were now considered family, and of course lots of photos of the christening. Fiona had taken Mary's advice to date and name each one on the back, so she would never forget who was who later in life.

'Mary, I was thinking. I'd like to try and find our uncles and our aunt.'

'I was thinking the same thing myself Fiona while watching you running through the park. You looked so happy and carefree. Yes, it would be wonderful to find them. I'll start on some research while I'm off work. You find out what you can over in Dublin. I just hope they are all alive and safe. Poor Alice, I hope she's all right. I would have loved to have met her. But we'll soon find out.'

The whole family were there once again for the last party before Fiona, Glenda and Mrs O'Conner went back to Ireland, and Karl Reiner had a surprise for Mrs O'Conner. A small bungalow, near to where Glenda and Fiona lived. There were tears all round.

Fiona threw her arms around Karl 'thank you, you are so generous . . . I can't find the words to . . .'

'You don't have to say anything. My lovely wife and I have gone from having one son, to a daughter-in-law, four granddaughters, a grandson and a great granddaughter, plus new friends.' marvelled Karl, holding Mrs O'Conner in his arms while she wiped her eyes with a tea towel.

*

Mrs O'Conner received a small parcel with photographs of the bungalow and two sets of keys when they arrived home. She moved in immediately, that is, after going door to door to show her neighbours the photographs, using an accent that was meant to be American. 'Sure, it isn't far away, only a short bus ride. You can come and see me and have a cup of tea and some soda bread . . . in the garden with me grass. My niece, Fiona, only lives a few streets away with my friend, Glenda. Did I not tell you I had two nieces and one of them has a baby, well now, where do I start . . . ?'

Back in New York, Mary and Jack were looking at the many photo's Fiona had taken. 'Jack look at this, it's a lovely picture of you, me and the baby.'

Taking the photo out of Mary's hand, a big smile came on his face and he looked at Mary. 'What? What is it Jack?'

He held the photo in front of her, showing a couple stood, looking down on their daughter. 'This is where it all began.'

'Oh Jack, thank you for everything.'

Other works by Margaret are

From Pit Boots to Green Wellies

And

Night time Shadows
Patrick's Story

Both available from Amazon in paperback and on Kindle

I hope you enjoyed my book as much as I enjoyed writing it. I almost feel as if I know the characters after all this time, although, Mrs O'Conner was based on my Irish grandmother. The tenement house, her new flat and neighbours, is how I remember it all. We had many happy times in Dublin, the story telling, the laughter, and the closeness of all the tenants. It seemed like one big family, to a point where I was never quite sure who was a relative and who was a neighbour!

Although the book is purely fictional, there are plenty of facts and true events; such as the Magdalena homes, which I'm sure with all the publicity of a few years ago, most people will have heard of. Before 1952, adoptions were illegal in Ireland, yet, over 60,000 babies were sold to rich American families, mostly from these mother and baby institutions.

My father often talked of his life at school, and how the children were hit across the back with a stick if they didn't know the story of Kevin Barry, or other heroes of the 1916 uprising. He hated school, but his knowledge of Irish history was excellent, even as far back as the Viking settlements.

Liverpool was almost obliterated during the Second World War, yet the people stuck together and shared what they had, including their homes if they were lucky to have one! I was really amazed when doing my research on WW2 just how much the women put into the war effort. To read their stories was amazing, they certainly didn't allow Hitler to take away their spirit. I find it ironic how the slave trade built Liverpool over many years, and how the Germans destroyed it in less than a year.

Now, of course, the city is a beautiful again. There are amazing buildings built by the people of Liverpool, who lost so much during the war, yet were determined to restore it to its former glory.

I could put a lot here of the subject of slavery, but for those who are interested it's well worth a visit to the Museum of Slavery, built beside the original docks of Liverpool.

Much of my research came from Irish Newspapers, YouTube, and people's stories of their life during the war, the radio recordings of the attack on Pearl harbour and most of all the museums and libraries, in England and Ireland that we have visited over the years.

I would like to thank my husband Geoff, who being in the Royal Air Force himself, helped me describe life for the American Gis when they were stationed at Burtonwood. He also helped me greatly with the research into the great depression in America.

Printed in Great Britain
by Amazon

83077455R00194